# RedBone

# RedBone

*T. Styles*

Withdrawn

www.urbanbooks.net

Urban Books, LLC
97 N18th Street
Wyandanch, NY 11798

ISBN 13: 978-1-60162-604-2
ISBN 10: 1-60162-604-5

First Mass Market Printing July 2014
First Trade Paperback Printing April 2012
Printed in the United States of America

10 9 8 7 6 5 4 3 2 1

Distributed by Kensington Publishing Corp.
Submit Wholesale Orders to:
Kensington Publishing Corp.
C/O Penguin Group (USA) Inc.
Attention: Order Processing
405 Murray Hill Parkway
East Rutherford, NJ 07073-2316
Phone: 1-800-526-0275
Fax: 1-800-227-9604

# RedBone

*T. Styles*

I dedicate this to
Charisse Washington.
Thanks for holding me down.
Always.

# Acknowledgments

To Charisse, thank you for always keeping me lifted. Writing can be a tough job, but I am blessed to have you on my team. To Carl Weber, thanks for tapping me on my shoulder. I hope you enjoy my contribution to your literary camp. I admire you. To Seven, thanks for always being in my corner! To Angel, thanks for always reading my work first, and giving me your stamp of approval. It means the world to me. To Terese, thanks for being the best friend a writer could have. To my grandbaby JR, my son Kajel and his wife Sonya, take care of one another. To Metha and Kim, you guys are the best. We love having you on the team. To Lakisha, you make me proud for holding Cartel business down. Thank you. To Luh Rod and Michelle Turnipseed, I could never forget you babies either. Your energy is contagious!

Last but not least, thanks to every T. Styles fan who loves a little something different. If you guys weren't in my life, I am afraid to think where my sick mind would have sent me. I hope you enjoy my twist on street fiction. I love you all, and welcome to my crazy-ass world!

T. Styles

www.facebook.com/authortstyles
www.twitter.com/authortstyles
www.thecartelpublications.com

# Prologue

## *Present Day*

Mooney sat in front of her open window, trying to wash the shitty taste of cigarettes and black coffee from her mouth with a glass of cheap bourbon. From sunup until sundown, being a spectator was her daily ritual. Although it was only the beginning of October, the weather outside resembled a cold winter's day. She pulled the belt on her blue robe, as her brown eyes peered outside at the situation brewing with a group of rowdy children from her building. In her opinion, the things she witnessed outside of her small apartment in Washington DC were better than anything available on television, so she didn't own one.

Eyes locked on the group of screaming girls, she zeroed in on the leader of the pack—thirteen-year-old Cutie Tudy. Mooney could hear Cutie's screeching voice loud and clear, as she screamed at the top of her lungs. The tight waist-length pink coat she wore was opened low enough for the boys hanging on the sidelines to see the top of her budding breasts.

"You ain't nothing but a ugly black bitch, Seona! You and your twin!" Cutie Tudy said, screaming in her foster sister's face. Her light-skinned cheeks were flushed red from all of the excitement. "I saw you in my fucking room last night . . . and now my shit missing!" Trying to entertain her six-member crew, she placed her index finger on Seona's warm nose. She wanted her to do something, anything, so that she would have an excuse to push her to the ground and kick her in every available place on her body. But Seona knew the routine, and stood as still as a Macy's store mannequin. The warm tears rolling down her face, and into the corners of her mouth, were the only indicators that Cutie's meanness was getting to her. "What you gonna say, huh? What you gonna do?"

Seona Taylor wanted to run but knew they'd all chase her, push her to the ground, and beat her in places she couldn't imagine. In her opinion it was better to stay where she was and get beat down by Cutie alone than to be jumped by many. Seona's dark walnut-colored skin was loaded with tear streaks.

"Punch that bitch, Cutie! You know she stole your iPod!" one of her screaming friends said, begging to see a fight. Trying to get things started quicker than fire to gasoline, she stepped behind

Seona and pushed her closer to Cutie. "Oh shit! She stepped to you now!" Cutie's crew crowded around them so tightly they couldn't move if they wanted to, and spectators on the far outside stepped closer to catch a view.

"Why you steal my fucking iPod, blackie?" Cutie taunted. "You shouldn't even have been in my room."

Seona had no idea what she was talking about. She stayed as far away from Cutie as possible when they were home, but she knew her answer wouldn't matter. She could still taste the vinegar from the pickle she was eating on her front step before Cutie approached her, as she thought of what to say. "I didn't do it," she whispered. "Please don't hit me."

With tightened lips, Cutie drew back her fist and slammed it into her nose and mouth. Blood splattered on her coat, two of her friends, and all over the grey concrete beneath them. Seona fell to the ground, curled up in a ball, and covered her head. Fashionable shoes kicked and stepped on her, leaving her brown coat covered with dusty footprints.

"Cutie, get up here!" Mooney yelled from the window. "Now!"

Hearing Mooney's voice caused everybody to shudder. Very few people heard her speak, and as far as most knew, she was on the run from something or somebody, and found refuge in the projects. In her five years there, she'd seen everything from a man getting shot, because he didn't want to turn over the keys to his car, to Homeless Henry dying from hypothermia in an abandoned truck due to last year's winter storm. She wouldn't speak to the cops no matter how much they asked, believing silence was the best policy.

With everyone staring at Mooney, the crowd around Seona opened up, and she dodged into the building for shelter. Cutie looked up at the window, put her hands on her hips, and said, "What you want with me? My mother said I can be outside."

"I didn't ask you that. Come up here now. I want to talk to you."

Cutie passed her friends with their quizzical stares. She wondered what the strange woman wanted, and why she would embarrass her in front of her crew. When she knocked on the door, Mooney opened it up and Cutie trudged in and plopped on the sofa. It was the same place she sat whenever her foster mother asked Mooney to watch her for a few hours. During those times, she couldn't wait until she was thirteen so she would be allowed to watch herself. Even back then she believed she had an understanding with Mooney: you don't say shit to me, and I won't say shit to you. So what had changed?

"What you want with me?" Cutie said, her arms folded angrily over her chest. "My mamma say I can watch myself now. I don't have to be sitting up in here looking at you watch little kids."

From her brown leather recliner by the window, Mooney examined the little girl. She could see herself in her and that wasn't a good look. Mooney's light skin was covered in an array of brown freckles, in different sizes and shapes. Although she was a little over forty, these days she resembled a sixty-year-old woman. Placing a cigarette in her mouth, she held the lighter to its tip and flicked it until it glowed with a speck of orange. She could feel Cutie growing agitated, and it was what she wanted.

"Can you tell me what you want with me?" she said, pushing her medium-length hair out of her face. "I wanna go back outside to play with my friends, dang!"

Mooney, on her own time, took two puffs of her cigarette and said, "Hang your coat up." She nodded toward the rack at the door. "Over there."

Cutie turned her head to look at the rack before she faced Mooney and said, "No. I wanna keep it on. I'm not gonna be here long anyway."

Mooney could see right through her. The tough-girl exterior she presented was fake . . . a façade.

"I just wanna go back outside."

"You're not wearing a shirt under your coat, are you?" Mooney asked, removing the cigarette from her lips, placing it in the glass ashtray. "You're outside, being loud and crazy to get attention. All for a bunch of boys who don't give a fuck about you. You look ridiculous." She laughed. "I bet you don't even know who you are, do you?"

With her lips poked out she said, "I'm Cutie Tudy from Southeast! I know who I am." With multiple neck rolls she continued, "All the boys like me because I'm light skinned and I can fight."

"I didn't ask you what you look like. I asked you do you know who you are?" She frowned. "You can't even tell me without talking about your outside appearance. Which can be taken from you in an instant." She snapped her fingers. "Trust me, I know if it doesn't fade first."

Cutie was embarrassed and tried to buck at the woman to ruffle her feathers the way she'd done hers. "Fuck do you want with me? You ain't nothing but a washed-up-ass bitch!"

She giggled. "And everybody around here know it, too." She paused. "Anyway, I done already told you my mamma said I can watch myself now." She got up to walk away.

"Sit the fuck down," Mooney said. "Now." Cutie took a seat. "Why did you hit that little girl?"

Cutie blew out a puff of air, fell back into the seat, and took her iPod out of her pocket, with the white headphones attached, before stuffing them in her ears. She still had the blood of Seona on the front of her secondhand pink Baby Phat coat. Growing irritated, Mooney stood up, pulled the belt harder on her robe, and snatched the iPod and ear set away from her. "I asked you a question! Why would you strike your foster sister?"

"I did it because she stole my shit!" she lied.

"You mean this iPod?" she asked in a monotone voice, completely void of emotion. Mooney threw the device in a box on the floor next to her. "You hit her in the face for something she didn't do? I know Melinda has her shit with her, but where did you learn to be so cruel?"

The troubled teenager, caught in her lie, felt her stomach juices swirling around. "Leave me the fuck alone!" she said, pulling her phone out of her pocket. She was as done as a piece of burnt fried chicken. "You ain't supposed to be taking my stuff." Her fingers moved quickly over her phone as she sent a group text to her friends:

Please tell mi Y this bitch just took my shyt. I'ma tell my motha when she get home from work and she gonna fuck her up 2.

Dee Dee responded:

Well hurry back outside. We talkin bout jumpin that bitch tmo at skool!

Mooney looked at the tight jeans Cutie had on, the small traces of blush on her face, and the cleavage spilling from her coat, and felt sorry for her. Tudy Ranger, aka Cutie Tudy, had stayed in Melinda Sheldon's foster home longer than any other child. Usually the government never allowed children to stay with her long, because of past complaints. Most stayed no more than six months to a year, mainly because she would spend the money allocated for their care, and kick them out when they complained. It was obvious that although Melinda was unfit, she had a soft spot for Cutie. The damage being placed on her young mind bothered Mooney, and for the first time ever, she was going to tell someone the story that had been burdening her for years.

Mashing the cigarette out in the damp ashtray, it sizzled. Rubbing her left elbow she said, "You remind me of somebody."

Cutie looked at her and then focused back on her phone. Small dings rang out every time she received a text. "Let me guess, you gonna tell me I was like you when you were a kid? Right?" she said in a sassy voice.

"You could never be me," Mooney said. "You remind me of somebody who was so focused on outside shit, they became something else . . . just to fit in."

Cutie rolled her eyes and continued to stab at her keypad. "I don't want to hear about it, because whoever you talking about wish they could be as cute as me."

"Well, you gonna hear it anyway, otherwise I'm gonna tell the cops you hit that girl, and they'll take you away. I know how much you love your foster mother."

Her eyes widened. "You can't do that!"

"I can do that and more." Mooney rubbed her left elbow again. "When you were outside, before you hit that child, you called her an ugly black bitch. Why?"

"Because she a ugly black bitch, and not cute and light skinned like me, that's why!"

"What makes you think she's ugly, because she doesn't have the same complexion as you? How are we that different?"

Cutie sighed, looked at the ceiling, and said, "Everybody knows red bones are cuter than dark-skinned girls. That's just life." She shrugged. "Most of the boys at my school are on Team Light Skin . . . that's what they call it anyway." Cutie sounded so ignorant but she didn't know. Her young mind was infiltrated with the opinions of stupid adults, and she didn't have an opinion of her own. When she tried to read Mooney, she said, "I don't know why you mad at me, you light skinned too."

Mooney sat down. "The story I'm gonna tell you is about a girl just like you."

"This ain't no Halloween story is it?" She stabbed at her keypad again. "'Cause I ain't got time for all of that, 'cause nothing about me is gonna change."

Cutie was suddenly inundated with texts but Mooney didn't worry, because she knew when she heard the craziest story never told that she'd have her complete attention.

# Chapter 1

## *Many Years Earlier*

### "Mamma got it wrong about what happened behind the school." —Farah

Twelve-year-old Farah Cotton was stunned silent, as she looked at her classmate being handled so roughly by the people she loved most.

"Hold his arms, babies! Hold 'em tight, too!" Brownie ordered her children Mia and Shadow, as they stood behind a bush in the back of Farah's school. "I want him spread out like he Jesus on the cross!" A maniacal grin covered her chocolate skin, and her pink tongue hung out the side of her mouth. There was nothing more in life she loved than inflicting pain on others and the sight of blood. "That's good. Just like that," she coached. "Get ready, Farah. 'Cause I need you to pull his shorts down."

Without looking into the boy's eyes, she pulled down his shorts.

"Good . . . Now get his drawers, too!" Brownie said.

With her eyes slammed shut, Farah pulled the boy's drawers down, exposing his penis.

"Perfect, now get ready to kick him where it counts."

"But what if he gets loose and hits me?" Farah asked, this time looking at her classmate, a boy she liked very much, a kid who just a few hours ago loaned her a few pieces of paper and a number 2 pencil to do her work in class. Her light skin, riddled with old sore scars, was flushed and she felt like she was five minutes from breaking out in hives. All her life, she along with her mother, sisters, and brother suffered from what they believed were allergies of the worst kind. Although their attacks seemed to be few and far between, Farah's were triggered by anything from stress to the scent of household chemicals. "I don't wanna do it!"

"They not gonna let him get you!" Brownie yelled, growing irritated with her daughter. "Are you, babies?"

"We got him, Mamma!" Shadow said, gripping Theo Cunningham's wrist harder, as his older sister, Mia, grabbed his other wrist and pulled in the opposite direction. Shadow's face, which was deep chocolate like the rest of their family, formed a row of sweat, which he quickly wiped away with his free hand. "He ain't going nowhere!"

When they had a good hold of the twelve-year-old's arms she said, "That's good, Mia and Shadow! Keep him right there."

"Sure thing, Mamma!" Mia said as she struggled to grab a few much-needed breaths due to being overweight. "This nigga gotta pay for the sins of his mother!" she continued, repeating Brownie's deranged words. Brownie smiled in approval.

Farah stood next to her siblings, and looked at how they all seemed to enjoy what they were doing to the boy. Her confusion seemed to bring more attention to the fact that she was not like them. If you were to walk into the DC project they lived in, and pointed out the members of the Cotton family, you would surely pass over Farah a million times. People told her all the time how she was the pretty red one in the family and how she should be grateful she didn't turn out as black as her mother, father, sisters, and brother. Farah never looked at the difference as a blessing. In her eyes, it was quite the contrary. She never wanted anything more than to look like the people she lived with every day.

She felt like an outcast when people would walk up to them, single her out, and say, "You so pretty, even with them scars on your face, and you got good hair, too." What she wouldn't give to sit between her mother's legs in the kitchen and have her hair pressed and then styled with green grease like Chloe. How she prayed she'd wake up with a smooth, dark complexion like Mia, but her wish was never granted.

Her skin was yellow, her hair black, wavy, and shiny, and her heart was nowhere as hollow as the members of her family. It was true: nothing about Farah said she was a Cotton, except her last name. It wasn't like the rest of the family wasn't beautiful. When they weren't fighting, and causing problems in the neighborhood, they were quite stunning to look at with their smooth skin tones reminiscent of the kings and queens of Africa. But because they were so unruly, nobody gave a fuck about outside appearances. They were ugly inside, so that made them ugly outside too.

"Please let me go," Theo begged, as long strands of snot oozed from his nose and fell into his mouth. He quickly lapped up the salty nasal mucus to continue his pleading. "I didn't do nothing!"

"Stop standing over there looking crazy, RedBone!" Brownie yelled, waking Farah out of her trivial thoughts. "Kick him in his dick! And do it hard, too, like we talked about!"

Farah looked at Theo, who was crying harder. "I don't want to do it, Mama," she refused. "He let me use his pencil at school today. He's really nice!"

"You heard what the fuck I said, girl!" Brownie screamed as she pointed her long finger in her face. "That's why I know you're not no real Cotton! You not a fighter! And if Cottons don't do nothing else, we fight and defend our name!"

"I am a Cotton!" Farah said with wide eyes.

Brownie always embraced an opportunity to make Farah feel inferior when she wanted her to do something. "Then do it!"

Farah walked slowly over to Theo, closed her eyes, and with all her might she kicked in Theo's direction.

"Ouch!" Mia screamed, rubbing her knee. "Open your eyes and do it, Farah." Mia knew her sister was scared but she also knew if she didn't do as told she could end up in far worse trouble with Brownie. "So what, he gave you a pencil? We your family! Kick him!"

She didn't move and Brownie was growing impatient.

"Do it, Farah!" Shadow encouraged. "Keep your eyes open and look him in the face, too!" Using Pig Latin, which his mother didn't understand, he said, "*Ihay ontday antway OmMammay otay uckfay ouyay uphay!*" which meant, "I don't want Mamma to fuck you up!"

Hearing her brother's words, this time with her eyes wide open, she kicked him hard between the legs. Theo screamed out in pain and his body fell forward.

"Let him go," Brownie said. They released him, and Mia and Shadow laughed at the child crying out in pain. Brownie walked over to him and stood over his little body. She was a grown woman, orchestrating the beat down of a child, and she was emotionless. "Y'all go on over to the car." She pointed up the hill. "Your father is waiting. Don't spoil the surprise, either. I wanna tell him what happened myself." Before they left Shadow kicked him in the stomach before Mia hog spit on top of his hair.

Farah, on the other hand, didn't budge. She wanted to help Theo out, and tell him how sorry she was. He was the only friend she had at school, and now she was certain that he'd hate her. "Come on, RedBone," Brownie said, putting her hand on Farah's shoulder. "You did good today."

When Farah didn't move quick enough for Brownie's taste she yelled, "Bitch, get your red ass to the car. It ain't like the little nigga dead! He just got his nuts pushed up." She laughed.

Worried her mother would order her beat down next, she followed her family to her father's car. They all jumped inside, and the moment the last door was closed, Ashur Cotton sped away from the scene.

In the car, everyone but Farah seemed to be glued to the news announcer's voice on the radio. A few days ago in Virginia, a pregnant teenage girl was stabbed to death in her stomach and face, along with her father. After a proper investigation, they learned that her boyfriend, who she dumped because he hit her in the stomach, in an attempt to abort the baby, murdered her. When the boy frantically escaped the scene, he left his high school ID and the knife with his fingerprints on her bed. When he told his mother and father about what happened, they were distraught, but decided to help him cover the crime. The plan was to get his ID and knife, after wiping the fingerprints away. But they didn't account for her father being home from work early. Unaware that his daughter was murdered in the room, the boy's parents killed him and went on the run. Somebody recognized the boy and alerted the police. Everybody in their neighborhood was up in arms about the heinous act, accept for the Cottons.

"I hope they don't catch him," Ashur said, turning the radio down. "The little bitch probably deserved it."

"They're probably in Mexico now," Brownie responded, waving at the radio.

"Y'all get him good?" Ashur asked his children, who were in the back seat. He put his Marvin Gaye tape in the deck, and cruised down the road on the way back to the house.

"Yeah, Dad." Shadow smiled. "We did everything Mamma planned."

"Just like we talked about, right?"

"What you think?" Brownie asked. "These my mothafuckin' kids we talkin' about!" She laughed. "They were born for war." She crossed her thick, sexy legs, and wiggled her foot. "We ain't come here for nothing."

He laughed. "You may have pushed 'em out that fat pussy of yours, but it was this nut," he said, gripping his dick, "that made it possible."

"You right about that." She laughed, and lit a cigarette.

Brownie looked back at Mia and Shadow, who were smiling slyly in the back seat. She hated that Farah's head hung low as she looked at her shoe, which was tinged with Theo's blood. *What's wrong with Mamma? And Daddy?* Farah thought, looking at everyone. *I don't wanna be like them. He was my friend.*

"You thirsty, baby girl?" Ashur asked Mia, waking Farah out of her thoughts.

"You know it, Daddy." She rubbed her ashy hands together. The smoke from her mother's cigarette choked the air.

"Y'all thirsty too?"

Shadow nodded and Farah said, "Yes, Daddy." Ashur tossed eighteen-year-old Mia a beer, and threw Shadow and Farah an RC Cola from the small cooler in the front.

"I want a beer too." Shadow pouted, frowning at the drink.

"Not if you want teeth," Ashur countered. "You want your teeth or a beer?"

"I'll drink the soda," Shadow said, defeated.

"That's what the fuck I thought." Focusing back on Brownie he said, "Did he cry? They swear the boy tougher than our son. So if you ain't make him cry, it won't make no difference." Ashur handed Brownie a beer to open for him.

She popped the top and handed it back. "He whined like a bitch." She smiled. "Trust me."

Ashur had already gulped half of his beer as he continued down the street. "I bet you he won't be playing no football now." He laughed, incensed that his own son couldn't even stand outside in the sun for long periods, because his skin would blister. His children's condition was so bad at times that he would often stay out of the house for days at a time just to avoid hearing their cries. "I want him useless at the football game on Saturday, Brownie."

"Trust me, he was crying like a bitch." Brownie laughed. "Mia and Shadow beat his ass and then Mia kicked him in the nuts." She was laughing so hard she couldn't contain herself. "You should've seen him holding his hands between his legs with his mouth all open." She slapped her knee. "I'm telling you that bitch gonna get the message now, and the boy ain't playing no football."

"It's okay, because if that don't work we'll break his arms.

He definitely won't be playing then!" Ashur looked at his half-crazy wife, leaned over, and kissed her passionately, while barely looking at the road ahead of him. He almost hit a car and the driver beeped loudly to avoid a collision.

Farah jumped and held on to her brother's arm, praying they didn't get into an accident. Since her condition could also be exacerbated by feeling panicked, Shadow whispered, "It's okay, Farah. Don't be scared. Daddy got the car." The smallest matters always went from zero to one hundred when she was with her family. Every day she was learning traits that wouldn't suit her well in life.

Ashur broke away from his beautiful wife's kiss and looked at the driver who had just beeped them out. Since both cars arrived at a light, Ashur rolled his window down to taunt the man. He was angry all the time, and loved antagonizing others. "Watch where the fuck you going, nigga!" Ashur yelled, pointing his gun in the car's direction.

"Unless you want me to bury you and that bitch!" Brownie added, aiming her gun also.

The driver was so alarmed that he sped away from the scene with his life in tow. Ashur snickered and could feel his dick growing rock hard because of all the excitement. Every time they got into shit together, he wanted to bend his wife over on the front of his Lincoln and fuck her in her asshole. They were deliriously in love and they could not see life without savagery and pain. The Cotton family, with Ashur as their lead, was a group of fucking troublemakers and everybody in Southeast DC knew it. That didn't stop them from moving about the city as if it were not true. Many said the world would have been better off if Ashur had never stepped to Brownie the first day he saw her face.

Many years back, when Ashur Cotton pulled up on Brownie Johnson in the summer of 1972, it was a match made in hell. Before meeting the woman who would soon be his wife, Ashur was a small-time street thug whose heart was filled with rage and confusion. Although he was violent, women doted on him, not because of his smooth, chocolate-dark skin or fit body, but because he was unpredictable, and that made him dangerous and fascinating. If he wasn't robbing hard-working citizens of their paychecks, he was defrauding insurance companies by purposely getting into car accidents. Ashur had a hustle in mind at all times, never wanting to miss an opportunity to hit his big payday.

*After leaving the bank one Thursday on June 29th from cashing in on one of his get-rich-quick schemes, he spotted the sexiest bowlegged female his eyes had ever seen. She was stacked like an Amazon with fat titties, a shapely derriere, and thick, pretty legs. Although he approached her with lustful ventures in mind, the average man would've kept it moving because nothing about Brownie at the moment was appealing. She was dripping in her own sweat, barefoot, and wearing a pair of dingy blue jean shorts and a white noxious-smelling T-shirt. Her fists were balled up tightly as she fought off three light-skinned females, who were tired of her fucking with their family.*

*Brownie Johnson loved to cause shit. It was her life's work. If you said it was Thursday, she'd purposely say it was Friday just to get a rise out of you. And if fucking with your head didn't evoke the right response by mixing the truth, she'd throw a "fuck your mamma" insult your way, knowing that would always do the trick. On the streets of DC, Brownie slashed more faces of beautiful light-skinned women than the most popular Beverly Hills plastic surgeon.* Her name rang bells and if you were in her presence and your skin was lighter than the color of a paper bag, you'd better split. It wasn't only that she hated lighter women; she derived a sick pleasure out of seeing people cry and the color of blood. She and Ashur were undiagnosed sadists.

*On the day Ashur pulled up on her, the girls she was fighting were tired of being afraid. They decided to approach her when she was off guard, slash up her face and break her fingers so she would be out of the slicing business. They hadn't counted on Ashur getting involved. Seeing her fight for her life, Ashur parked his silver Lincoln and strolled out of the car. At first Brownie thought he was coming to help them, so she pulled out her switchblade and pointed it in his direction. "You's a pretty-ass, nigga," she said, looking at his fly brown suit and crocodile shoes. "And I sho' would hate to stab your ass. But if you come near me I'ma slash you to the white meat, I swear before God."*

*He laughed at the woman he thought was stunning even at her worst. Directing his attention to the three sisters he said, "What can I give you ladies to drop whatever beef you have with this sister?" He reached in his pocket and pulled out the wad of cash he'd just gotten from the bank, envelope included.*

*Brownie looked at Ashur and then her enemies. She knew their beef ran deep. Two generations deep. Their family didn't like her dark family members, thinking they were too ugly because of their skin tone, and Brownie's family couldn't stand their mix-breed members thinking they believed they were better than the world. Society peppered the media with inconsistent images of beauty, and they were all brainwashed.*

*"Nigga, this bitch is gonna get the business today," sister one said. "So why don't you just crawl back in that Lincoln and move to wherever you came from."*

*"I see she's unreasonable." He looked at sister two. "What do you say?" He raised the cash bundle. "You wanna make some paper or not?"*

"Why don't you mind your fucking business?" Brownie interrupted, eager to add their faces to the list of slashes she'd created over the years. "I don't need no fucking help from you or nobody else!"

He laughed and said, "Listen here, bitch, you can talk swiftly to these three sluts over here, but you not gonna speak to me like you fucking crazy. Now I'm trying to save your life, and when I do you owe me, and you better be good at it too. We got an understanding?"

Brownie had never met a man who talked to her so seriously, so she remained silent. Most men knew about her cousins and wouldn't dare break bad, knowing it could be hazardous to their health.

"Like I was saying," he continued, focusing back on the women, "what can I offer you ladies?"

The sisters looked at each other and sister one said, "Unless you plan on killing this bitch, you can't do nothing for me, man."

Then they turned to Brownie and sister two said, "We'll see you again."

"Count on it," Brownie said, wiping the sweat off of her forehead with the back of her hand.

When the sisters walked away, he offered Brownie a ride and she accepted, curious. She wanted to know what kind of man Ashur was, and although she had a boyfriend named Jay, *who she'd been with since high school, he never wanted to be with her in public.*

*Before long, she started spending more time with Ashur, and less time with Jay. It wasn't long before they realized they both shared the same sick personalities and traits. They both loved street boxing because of its gore and violence, and they both wanted children. They drank hard and played harder and, after a while, only the sickest pleasures could entertain them properly. At the end of the day, their happiness meant others would have to suffer and that was the bottom line.*

"You my crazy baby," Ashur said as he tossed the empty beer can in the cooler and went to grab another. He was still thinking about the driver they'd just scared off. He handed the beer to Brownie so she could open it. "You know I would kill you if you left me, don't you?"

"What you think I'll do to you?" Brownie smiled, handing him the beer. Thinking back on Theo, Brownie said, "I bet you that bitch will stay out our business now." She was referring to Theo's mother, Dinette, who used to be her good friend. "Telling mothafuckas we had something to do with that robbery at that convenience store last week. That bitch just jealous we ain't let her and Tommy in on that shit. Everybody knows when it come to busting a gun, he suckers up."

"I hear you, but I told you before that you gotta watch who you hang around. Now you finally seeing what happens when you don't listen to me. Shit goes wrong."

Ashur, Brownie, Dinette, and Tommy were very close, when all of a sudden things changed. Farah wasn't allowed to play with Theo, and Dinette stopped accepting Brownie's calls, and that hurt her because she was her best friend. What she didn't know was that the real reason Dinette isolated Brownie was because last month, Dinette came home early. When she walked down the hallway she heard a lot of panting and moaning. Opening the bathroom door, her heart sank when she saw her husband, Tommy, bent over on the bathroom sink as Ashur put dick to ass. Although Dinette never said a word, for fear of what Ashur might do, she also never forgot.

"Ashur, that shit will never happen again. Trust me, I learned my lesson." She paused, thinking about all the nights she and Dinette talked about life, only for her to cut her off.

"Good, because none of them bitches in that building are our friends." He looked into her eyes before focusing back on the road. "You hear what I'm saying? In this car right here is where it's at. I'm the only friend you need."

As Farah's parents spoke among themselves, she thought about her mother's recollection of the events behind the school. Although Mia and Brownie held his arms, it was she who had kicked him between the legs. To some it may have been irrelevant, but Farah needed all of the credit she could get since she was already an outsider. "Daddy . . ." she said in a low voice. Mia was on her left and Shadow was on her right. "Daddy . . ." she said again. At first Ashur didn't hear her. So she spoke louder. "Daddy!"

Ashur turned the music down and said, "Is that my red baby calling me?" He looked at her face in the rearview mirror.

"Yes, Daddy." She smiled, circling the top of her soda can with her finger.

"What's up, baby?"

"Mamma got it wrong." She swallowed. "About what happened behind the school. I'm the one who kicked Theo in the dick."

Brownie turned around, reached into the back, and slapped her in the face. All five of her fingers immediately showed upon her red skin. "Fuck you lie on me like that for?" She pointed. "That's your problem, you're too fucking grown!"

The moment she drew her hand back, Ashur grabbed Brownie's throat so hard, she thought her windpipe was going to flatten. With one hand on the steering wheel and the other on her neck, he pulled over to the side of the road and parked his old Lincoln.

With her throat still in his grasp, he pointed the finger on his other hand in her face. "Listen here, bitch, you may be tough out there in them streets, and I don't doubt it one bit, but I better never see you hit one of my kids like that again." He squeezed tighter, and a tear rolled down her face. "You hear me, black bitch?" She nodded and he released his hold.

Brownie rubbed her neck and sat angrily in the seat with her arms folded over her breasts. It was bad enough that she was cursed with a child the same complexion of the people she hated most. To make matters worse, her own husband wouldn't allow her to discipline her kids like she saw fit. No worries though, she would simply wait until he was out on one of his drunken binges with his friends. And when that happened, she'd give Farah exactly what she deserved.

# Chapter 2

**"You gotta learn that you are blessed because of your complexion, Farah. And you gotta know some folks might resent you for it, too."** —Grandma Elise

The sun was brighter than ever when Farah woke up to the smells of her grandmother's fried chicken. She knew without asking that they were having some kind of party later on that day and she couldn't wait to entertain company. Today was a better day because she wasn't as sick as she normally was, and the weather wasn't as hot. If her mother wasn't still angry, she hoped she'd allow her outside so that she could scratch a hopscotch board on the ground, in the hopes of luring new playmates. Friendless and lonely, Farah looked for small ways to entertain herself. Her siblings, who were not as sickly, had friends and lives of their own, so Farah was normally confined to the bed at home.

When she tried to move out of the full-sized bed, it angered her that she could barely budge. She was pinned down due to Mia's sweaty, wet thigh being draped over her body. "Move, Mia!" she said, hitting her leg. She knew it would never work, because Mia slept harder than a bear hibernating for the winter. "Get off me!"

Mia didn't budge, so with one hard shove, Mia's leg fell off of her body. Since she was sleeping in the middle, she hopped over her baby sister, Chloe, who was fast asleep on her right. Sharing a bed with her sisters was uncomfortable, but the fact that Mia was getting bigger each family meal made her sleeping arrangement unbearable.

Out of the bed, Farah grabbed her pink robe off of the chair, and stepped over Shadow, who was sleeping on the floor next to the bed. Since they all shared an apartment with their grandmother, Elise Gill, in Southeast Washington DC, they had to get in where they fit in. Elise's tiny projects apartment had three bedrooms that could easily be mistaken for walk-in closets because they were so small. But Elise didn't care. She came from the age where family did what they could for one another, even if it meant putting themselves out. So when her daughter said her family needed help two months back, she accommodated them. Her grandchildren shared one room, Brownie and Ashur shared the other, and she had the master bedroom. The living arrangements worked fine for the kids on the nights they didn't hear Shadow jerking off to the Janet Jackson swimsuit poster on the wall.

With the robe wrapped around her body, Farah eased out of the bedroom so she wouldn't wake up her siblings. She didn't know how much cereal was left and wanted to pour as much as she wanted into her bowl.

Right before Farah cut the corner into the kitchen she heard her grandmother talking to her mother, and she stopped dead in her tracks. "Brownie, you know she don't mean nothing to that man," Elise said. "But you gotta give mens enough rope to wiggle. You can't hold 'em hostage. Otherwise, they'll just leave you."

Brownie smacked her tongue. "So I'm just supposed to let him fuck who he wants to in front of me?" Brownie was so disrespectful, she didn't care about cursing in front of her mother, and Elise was so hood, she was used to it. "I'm his wife, Mamma. That shit ain't gonna fly no more."

"Did you see him fucking Dinette?" Elise asked. "With your own eyes?"

"No, Mamma! But he was always at her house, and whenever I call over there, mysteriously nobody answers the phone. We were best friends and now she's closing me out of her life."

"So that's what this is about. You miss her." She shook her head. "Just go apologize, child."

"I didn't do nothing wrong!"

"Brownie, y'all beat her child where he can't play football no more? You better be careful about the message you showing your children, especially Farah, because she is taking notes. That girl don't wanna do nothing but be like you."

"Mamma, that ain't what I'm talking about! I'm talking about my husband!"

"Listen here, child, don't lose your man on account of something stupid. Now, you got the man. He belongs to you, else he wouldn't have made you his wife. Be happy for that and leave the rest alone."

"It's not that easy!"

"You sure you don't still love that other man? I heard you been running around town with Jay every now and again. You better be careful . . . If your secret gets out, it will destroy your marriage."

Brownie remained silent and Elise knew she struck a nerve. "Mamma, you think Jay left me because I'm dark? It just seemed like we were so good when we were alone."

"Who knows? . . . Anyway, you married now." She shrugged. "Could've been a lot of reasons it didn't work, if you know what I mean. As far as your complexion, I been told you all your life, you black. You that blue black like my mamma, and her mamma before that. Everybody not blessed with pretty skin like Farah. You ugly but you not dumb, Brownie. It ain't nothing to be ashamed of neither." She continued, "You gonna spend your whole life chasing away mens if you get mad they like a little something different from time to time." Farah heard the sound of a spoon stirring in a pot. "Focus on Ashur and leave Jay alone," Elise said sternly. "Most men don't make a woman as black as you they wife. Be glad for that."

"But I wish I was different. Seems like Ashur is into red bitches too!"

"Why are you so obsessed with being something you not? Embrace your blackness, baby. It's the color of our ancestors."

"I don't wanna be like our ancestors!" Brownie yelled. "I wanna be different."

"Brownie—"

"And why would you name me that, Mamma?" Brownie sobbed, interrupting her mother. "Do you know how many bitches I had to fight because of that name? I'm already black; did you have to give me a name that brings attention to it?"

"I named you that because I loves it. And I wanted you to also. But you black, baby. Some people gotta be black and fight harder for what they want, while others don't. Be glad one of your children don't have to be cursed like we are."

"See what I'm saying, Mamma? You think we're cursed."

"I'm just up on the world, Brownie. And I'm gonna always shoot you straight. Life ain't easy for people with skin like ours, but we can learn to make it better."

Somewhere in Brownie's heart of hearts she knew what her mother was saying was wrong. She would look into the mirror and see a cute nose, wide, beautiful eyes, and pink pouty lips. Yet when she'd go out into the world, she'd feel ugly by her own people.

"So, you really think I'm ugly, Mamma?"

"I think you's black. And to some folks, that's one in the same."

Overcome with sorrow, Brownie stormed out of the kitchen and bumped into her daughter, who was on all fours ear hustling on the floor. "Fuck you doing right there? And how long you been listening to my conversation?" Brownie stared down at Farah. When she didn't respond she yelled, "How long, girl?"

"Brownie, is that RedBone?" Elise asked from the kitchen.

"Yes, Mamma." Brownie rolled her eyes. She was trying to think if she should beat her ass, and deal with Ashur later.

"Well, send her in. It's time for her to eat." Brownie didn't say anything. Instead she thought about inflicting all of the pain she had in her heart at the moment on her child. "Brownie Cotton . . .

did you hear what I said? Tell her to come in here and eat, now!"

She swallowed hard. "Okay, Mamma." She frowned and said, "Go see what your grandmother wants." Brownie stormed off toward her room.

Farah stood up, wiped her hands on her robe, and walked into the kitchen. Elise, without saying a word, grabbed a bowl out of the cabinet and the milk out of the fridge. Then she set the box of Cap'n Crunch along with a spoon on the table in front of her. Elise believed in silence and wouldn't speak until someone sparked a conversation. She learned a long time ago that the best advice one could give was dressed in quietude.

"Sit down."

Farah could smell the stench of her grandmother's musty underarms as she tended to the food. Elise didn't use deodorants, hair sprays, or detergents. She washed her clothes and dishes with scalding hot water and they always appeared clean. Her hands had scars because of it, and the tops had lost most of their sensitivity. Since she also had what she believed to be allergies, which were exacerbated by various household products, she avoided them at all costs, soap included.

When Elise pulled a sheet of aluminum foil from the container, she noticed her grandchild was not eating. "Eat up, RedBone," Elise said, taking her fried chicken out of the pan before stirring her gravy. "We got a long day ahead of us."

"We having a party?" Farah poured milk onto her cereal. Her eyes lit up at the prospect of having company. Outside of going to school, Farah felt as if she were living in a bubble.

"*We* not having a party," Elise corrected her. "This one for grown folks. You got to wait until the family celebration to party with the adults."

Farah pouted and Elise walked over to her and placed her fists on to her hips. "Why you frowning, pretty girl?"

"'Cause I wanna go to the party too," Farah whined, knowing she could always get her way with Elise. "I don't never get to do nothing."

"That ain't no reason for you to be pouting," Elise responded. "Hell, they'll be plenty of parties for you to go to." She patted her back softly. "You just don't forget to practice for The Jackson Five performance routine you doing with your brother and sisters. I'm tired of my sister Irma's grand-kids winning the family competition each year."

"She not gonna be in no performance," Brownie said, walking back into the kitchen with her purse over her shoulder. She grabbed a yellow cup and poured water inside of it from the faucet.

"And why is that? This my grandchild."

"'Cause ain't no red bitches in The Jackson Five, that's why." She smirked, looking at Farah. "She ain't brown enough."

"What is wrong with you, Brownie?" Elise asked, angered by her daughter's harsh words. "I know them streets got you beat, but this child belongs to you. And you ain't got to treat her that way!"

"You can't never stand up for me, can you?" Brownie glared at her mother. "Not even when I need you most."

"What do you want me to do?" Elise threw her arms in the air, sending her strong body odor through the small kitchen.

"Love me! For who I am."

"That's what I'm trying to do," Elise pleaded, slapping the back of her hand into her palm. "By showing you how to love your daughter. The way she should be loved. This child is watching everything you do, and all you showing her is pure evil."

"If you love her so much more than me, then let her be your daughter!" Brownie threw the plastic cup into the sink. "'Cause like you said earlier, she sho' is the right color now, ain't she?"

Brownie stormed out of the apartment and Farah cried over her cereal until her grandmother lifted her chin. "She don't mean to be mean, baby." Elise choked back her own tears. She truly didn't understand what she said wrong. Elise came from a family full of women who were made to feel inadequate because of their dark pigmentation. So how could she teach her something different when she didn't know any better? "Don't be sad, baby. When we get these scars off of your skin, you are going to be striking."

"But I wanna look like Mamma. And you."

Elise smiled. "You gotta learn that you are blessed because of your complexion, Farah. And you gotta know some folks might resent you for it, too. In the long run it'll pay off. Mark my words, RedBone. Mark my words."

# Chapter 3

**"I wanna show her that I can make her happy too." —Farah**

Nighttime fell on the projects and everybody in the house was trying to find Farah. They were in the middle of the worst heat wave DC had ever seen, and she was a sickly child who never went out without telling her parents. As everyone hung in the living room waiting for word, they all felt that Farah's disappearance may have been stimulated by the way Brownie had treated her earlier that day.

"If my baby ran away I'm gonna hurt you, Brownie!" Ashur said, sitting on the sofa and drinking his seventh beer, while a cigarette dangled from his other hand. "You hear me, woman!" Brownie was struck with fear, knowing full well what her husband was capable of.

"Don't threaten my fuckin' child, Ashur. Not in my house and not in front of me, anyway," Elise said, setting places at the dining room table for her card party later that night. "Fussing and threatening never helped nobody. Trust me. I know."

"Well, I'm tired of her treating her bad," Ashur continued, giving his wife evil looks. "If my kid don't show up in the next fifteen minutes I don't know what I'm gonna do." He looked at his wife and mother-in-law with a creased brow.

"She gonna be fine. Herbert out there looking for her too," she said, referring to the maintenance man. Mia, Chloe, and Shadow sat quietly in their room, waiting for the verdict. They knew better than to get into their parents' business. In fact, the last time Chloe gave her two cents on a matter, while Brownie was washing her hair, Brownie screamed in her face so long her hair dried.

After fifteen long, antagonizing minutes, Farah walked slowly into the house with the dopehead Herbert, the project's maintenance man. She was wearing nothing but her white cotton panties. A strange odor that resembled burned meat seemed to follow her as she stood in front of her parents for judgment. Her skin was red and blistered, and she could barely put her arms down. The abscesses on her body were filled with puss, and she looked like a monster. Farah had spent the entire time outside, trying to be brown like her family. Trying to look like them, in the hopes that Brownie would love her more. "I found her on the roof," Herbert said. His grey uniform was ashy. "She awfully beaten up but she alive."

"We got it from here, Herbert," Elise said. She was so rattled by the sight of her granddaughter that she dropped the plate of chicken on the floor. "Go on now."

"You got a few bucks?" he asked, scratching his arms. "I'm hurting really bad."

"Nigga, get the fuck out of here!" Brownie screamed, pointing at the door.

When he left, Elise asked, "Did somebody rape you, child?" When Farah didn't answer her quick enough she said, "Did anybody touch you, child?"

Farah shook her head. "No, Grandma. Nobody touched me."

When Ashur saw the terrible condition of his daughter, he smashed his cigarette out on the wooden floor and hopped off the couch. "Then what happened, Reds?" he asked, looking over her scarred body. "Where have you been?" He figured after all the kids he abused, God was ready for payback.

"I been worried about you all day!" he said, pulling her into his embrace.

"Daddy, no!" she screamed due to the sunburns and blisters that covered her skin. "It hurts."

Ashur pulled himself from her body and looked at her. "What did you do to yourself?"

"I went to the top of the roof. And took all my clothes off." Everyone looked at her with wide eyes. They always knew Farah was going to stir up shit in the family, but no one thought it would be like this.

"For what, child?" Elise asked.

"So I could get a tan." She cried softly.

"Why would you do something so stupid?" Brownie laughed, thinking it was funny that she was riddled in pain. "You know you can't be outside like that! You ain't trying to do nothing but hog up all the attention!"

"I wanted to look like you." Tears fell down her red face but she was afraid they would hurt if she wiped them away. "But, Mamma . . . it hurts real badly. So bad I wanna scream but I'm afraid."

Elise stepped up and said, "We gotta take this baby to the hospital. This don't look too good."

Farah was in the hospital for two days as the doctors tried to understand the nature of her illness. They knew she stayed out in the sun for hours trying to get a tan, but what they couldn't understand was the reason for the blisters and hives that covered her skin. Farah was in so much pain that she could barely move. She'd already pulled a few pieces of hair out of her scalp, to eat the follicles before swallowing the strands. She did this when she was miserable and uneasy about life, which was often. Even at the moment, she had a bald spot the size of a golf ball in the middle of her head, and because Brownie left Farah to groom herself, she was able to keep her secret. To conceal her personal abuse, she'd brush her hair into a ponytail and cover it up. She suffered from trichophagia, the compulsive need to eat one's own hair, which could be deadly.

For the first few hours she was hospitalized nobody came to visit, and she was devastated. That was, until the hospital called about her vagina and the possible sexual assault on a family member's part, or so they thought. Because Farah was on the roof with no clothes on, the lips of her vagina were also damaged. So when the Department of Social Services came to investigate, Ashur and Brownie went to the hospital to defend themselves. With the help of the doctors, and several tests, they were able to convince everyone that the marks between her legs were also as a result of the sun's strong rays.

But when the confusion was over nobody stayed, due to the drama in the neighborhood because of what they'd done to Theo. Dinette was threatening to call the authorities until she kissed the barrel of Ashur's gun. And although her grandmother called to check on her frequently, she seemed too busy to give her the face time she so desperately needed. It seemed the more she tried to be like the rest of her family, the more they pushed her away.

Lying in the bed, she grabbed her black diary. Farah didn't journal like most young girls her age. She wrote her life on the pages of her book the way she wanted it to be. She believed it wholeheartedly when Elise told her she could have anything she wanted in life, if her heart was in the right place, and she jotted it down on paper. *Once it's on paper, it becomes life,* Elise would say.

Grabbing her favorite red pencil she wrote:

Farah was on the roof baking in the sun. She was so excited when she saw her skin turning the color of her mother's. When it got late, she went home and all her family could talk about was how beautiful her chocolate skin was.

Later, she went outside to play with the prettiest girl in her school, who was also her best friend, Coconut Elway.

Farah knew it was wishful thinking to think a kid who didn't fuck with her could be her best friend, but this was her book. Continuing her story, she wrote:

Coconut talked about her boyfriend and Farah talked about hers. She said his name was Sam, and his skin was as dark as her mother's, and that he was as handsome as her father. The coolest thing about Sam was that he was as strong as Superman.

Hearing a noise outside, and missing her family deeply, she looked toward the doorway. When she saw a few people who didn't even acknowledge her, she grew angry. Opening her diary back up, she wrote:

And then somebody killed and raped Farah and everybody in the family felt guilty because they didn't come see her!

Pushing her book aside, loneliness kicked her in the gut, and she cried herself to sleep. But on the second day, when Mia and Shadow caught a bus to the hospital to see her, she was elated. The doctors and nurses did their best to make her feel at home, but in her opinion there was nothing on the earth like family.

"You know they were trying to say Daddy fucked you, right?" Mia said. "The house been real fucked up lately, and we owe it all to you."

Farah frowned. "What? Why would they think something like that? Daddy loves me."

"Because you sat in the sun naked with your legs open," Shadow said. "What kind of shit is that?"

"Farah, why you do that?" Mia sat on the edge of the bed. Farah was still wrestling with what people thought of her father, and tuned her siblings out. "Who goes on the roof butt-ass naked trying to get darker? You can't change your complexion by getting a tan."

"Permanently anyway," Shadow added, eating the Jell-O Farah pushed to the side hours ago. "Dad was supposed to be taking us to the movies, but you fucked that up for everybody." Tears poured out of her eyes, and like his father, Shadow wanted to run. He wasn't good with emotions and preferred it if the women in his family refrained from being so sensitive. "Stop that crying shit. It makes my ass itch."

"I don't mean to cry." Farah wiped her tears away. "But I want Mamma to love me like she loves everybody else. Why was I born like this? I wanna look like y'all since it's obvious that's why Mommy hates me!"

"Love is overrated," Shadow said. "You ain't missing nothing."

"I'm serious!" Farah barked. "Maybe I can do something to make her proud, like help y'all out with the routine for the family celebration," she said with wide eyes.

"You know you can't do that," Shadow said. "Mamma don't want you being in that shit. Just leave it alone. It's stupid anyway."

"But maybe if you taught me the routine, she would like it." She looked at her elder siblings. "Please . . . I wanna show her that I can make her happy too. I wanna make her proud."

Reluctantly, Mia said, "We might as well show her. It ain't like we wanna do the shit anyway." She played with the remote on her bed and turned on the TV.

"Okay, but if Ma get mad, you make sure you tell her it was all your idea," Shadow added.

"Done," Mia said, stopping the channel on *The Golden Girls*. "I ain't scared of nobody out this bitch, including Mamma."

"So we'll teach you, but you gotta stop crying and being soft. I mean, why would you wanna look like us?" Shadow asked. "All I fuck with is red bitches anyway. Dark-skinned bitches ain't poppin'."

"You so fuckin' ignorant," Mia said. "And how all you fuck with is red bitches when your mamma black?"

"Well, I ain't fucking my mamma, now am I?" Shadow said.

"I don't know . . . you tell me."

"I just prefer light-skinned chicks. I guess you could say I like what I like. So see, Farah, you ain't gotta look like us to be better. You already are."

# Chapter 4

**"I'm Farah Cotton, and I want so much to be your friend." —Farah**

The gym class was a madhouse at Farah's school. Balls were flying everywhere but in the direction of their intended targets. As always during this sorry excuse for a class, Farah was dressed in her blue and orange gym uniform, and was sitting on the bleachers alone. Her diary rested on top of her dark blue shorts as she looked at her classmates having fun. For her, this class was the pits without Theo, and she hated every fucking thing about it. She wondered if he would ever return to school, because she missed him already. Normally when the weather was nice the gym would be silent, and she and Theo would sit in the bleachers and talk all day. But thanks to her parents and her rare illness, she was a social outcast during the most critical time in her life.

She was about to start writing how she wanted her life to be with her make-believe boyfriend, when Shannon, Nova, and Wendy came running up the bleachers like their lives depended on it. The wooden steps rocked under Farah, and she put both hands to the side for support. When they were seated next to each other Coach Jaffrey said, "What are you ladies doing up there? Unless you have a letter excusing you like Farah, you need to be down here playing dodge ball with the rest of the class." At the mention of her name, everyone looked at Farah and she held her head down. Because she was hospitalized recently for her condition, her light skin looked like she had chickenpox, and parents warned their kids to stay away from her. Farah's classmates hated how Farah always seemed to have favor with the coach. They would've taken their anger out on him if he didn't live in the very neighborhood they did all of his life.

"I'm serious now. You and the girls need to come back down here and participate. The only one allowed to sit out is Farah."

Shannon, the leader of the pack, was a brown-skinned pretty girl with medium-length black hair and a body more developed for her age. She had ass, titties, and hips too early and she knew it. "Mr. Jaffrey, we just got our periods and we can't play." The gym erupted into laughter, knowing if there was one thing Mr. Jaffrey avoided, it was the topic of little girls' menstrual cycles. "If you want to check my pad, I'll go in the bathroom and take it off and show you."

With his face beet red he said, "No . . . please don't . . . Never mind." Then he blew his whistle, and addressed the rest of the class, mainly boys. "Everybody else get back to work!"

After laughing so hard they couldn't contain themselves, Shannon and her crew huddled together to discuss the real business at hand. "That bitch is so fucking nasty. She was over my house spending the night, right?" Shannon started. "When all of a sudden, she gonna ask me if she could borrow a pair of my panties, because she was seeing her boyfriend later that night and wanted to take a bath." She frowned. "She must've forgotten her own."

"So what you say?" Nova asked. The girls were so close together they looked like conjoined triplets.

"I said fuck no!" Farah was ear hustling so hard, her neck was hurting. "What I look like?"

"She is so not clean," Nova said, not liking the subject of their conversation anyway. She was also a cute girl with honey-colored skin and short, curly hair. "Who the fuck uses somebody else's drawers?" She glared, shaking her head.

"Exactly!" Wendy added. A little on the chunky side, she was still considered a cutie because of her silky black hair and dark Indian skin. "Coconut is so trifling!"

"Damn, bitch, why you say her name all loud and shit?" They looked around and Farah pretended to be playing with her kneecaps. "She still my friend," she proceeded with narrowing eyes. "You know how people gossip at this school and shit." She looked at nonessential Farah, and determined she was too spotty faced and quiet to say anything. "Anyway," she said, rolling her neck and poking her lips out, "a few days later, I put on my favorite red panties and the next thing I know, I got a yeast infection."

"Ugh!" Nova said. "That girl is a mess!"

"How you know she gave it to you?" Wendy asked.

"'Cause I never get yeast infections, bitch, that's why!" Wendy felt stupid. "Plus when I looked in my panties it had extra cum in them. I don't make that much cum. Only girls who don't wash get those things, not me!"

"Oh . . . I see."

Farah couldn't believe what she was hearing. She always wanted to be friends with Coconut but so did everybody else, including Rhonda and her crew. She couldn't get over her luck. *Coconut is nasty?* she thought. It didn't make a difference, because she was both pretty and cool, and that's the kind of person she needed to hang around. Farah wondered, if she told her what she'd learned, would she accept her into her fold? Elise warned Farah about keeping up shit, as she quietly took note at the change in her behavior. Farah desired too much to be loved and fit in, and her grandmother knew where that would lead her if she didn't change. *You can make more friends by being nice and being yourself,* Elise would say. Farah would then look at her large, smelly grandmother and make assumptions about her life. In her book she was lonely, and that was not the life Farah wanted. Farah wanted friends so very badly that Grandma could suck a horse dick for all she cared. She was tired of being the quiet, nice, spotty-faced, weird girl, and she was going to do something about it today.

"You ain't still cool with her, are you?" Wendy asked. "I know I wouldn't be."

Shannon was just about to respond when Coconut, Rhonda, and Natasha marched up the bleachers. This was the most excitement Farah had ever had in gym, and she wondered if Shannon would tell her to her face how stank her pussy was. Coconut's light skin was painted lightly with makeup. Since her mother was black, and her father was Caucasian, she was biracial and was often mistaken for white, especially since her hair was littered with gold streaks.

"Hey, Shannon, y'all coming over my house later, right? Everybody else is staying the night, and we gonna watch my mother's dirty movies."

When Farah heard the invitation, she thought, *I want to come over. Can I?* When everybody looked at her, she wondered what was wrong. And then it dawned on her; she'd said what she was thinking out loud. She wanted to take her statement back, but it was too late.

There were about ten more seconds of uncomfortable silence before Coconut gritted on her and said, "Your test-tube, spotty-faced ass can't come nowhere near my house! We don't even know what you got." All the girls scooted a few feet back to get away from her.

Everyone broke out into heavy laughter. "This chick is really crazy," Shannon said. Farah could feel steam rising off of her head. *You don't even like my friend! You talk behind her back!* If she was possessed with the same violent current as the rest of the Cottons, Shannon would probably be dead by now. She didn't hate anybody more than her. "What you need to be doing is minding your own business!"


"I wish I had some perfume on me to spray in her face. Since everybody know she can't be around nothing sweet smelling without melting away," Shannon continued as all the girls laughed harder. "Anyway, I'm coming," she said in her fakest voice. "And Wendy and Nova coming too." Wendy frowned, until Shannon elbowed her in the side on the sly.

"Uh . . . yeah, I'm coming too. I just gotta get my drawers . . . I mean, overnight bag, and ask my mamma," she said, clearing her throat.

Farah sat alone and embarrassed beyond belief, but she didn't blame Coconut. At that moment, something new was occurring inside of her. She felt a sensation she hadn't felt much before, and that was blinding rage. Suddenly she wondered what Shannon would look like if she sliced her nose open wider. She reasoned her mouth wouldn't be so loud then if blood was in it. There was no doubt about it; she was going to tell Coconut everything that was said behind her back, and then they could be best friends.

When Coconut left with Rhonda and her friends, Farah got up, grabbed her diary and pencil, and followed them toward the locker room. For some reason, she looked back at Shannon, and she was surprised to see her staring directly at her. *Yes, I'm gonna tell her everything you said. Coconut is a nice person, and people shouldn't be talking behind her back.*

Turning back around, she continued on her mission. But since she couldn't be around fragrances like perfumes and hair sprays, she whiffed the air by the door before entering. When she smelled the scent of musty, unwashed gym clothes, and putrid toilet bowls, she walked inside. Next to the lockers, Coconut and her friends were getting undressed and putting on their street clothes.

Farah looked at Coconut's half-naked body and tried to envision her own, when she rocked her out of her thoughts. "What the fuck are you looking at, spotty face? I don't do the lesbo shit." She eased into her jeans. "What you need, some bleach for that scarred-up face?" Farah thought about putting anything harsh on her skin and what it would do to her body, and shook her head. "Then what the fuck do you want? You giving me the creeps."

Farah's heart thumped harder than a beat by Dr. Dre. "I wanted to tell you—"

"You can't come to the party," Rhonda interjected. She was a cute dark-skinned girl with a big personality. "So stop begging."

*I wasn't even talking to you, bitch.* "That ain't it," Farah responded, still salty from all the sidebars. "It's something else. Can I tell you in private?"

"No, you can't, now what do you want?" Coconut was tiring of her quickly, plus, she didn't want the plague everyone said she had. "Unlike some people, I got a daddy who loves me and he's buying me a new outfit for my birthday tonight," she continued, assuming Farah was a bastard.

"I do too." She smiled, hoping they'd have something in common.

Coconut looked back at her friends and said, "This girl is crazier than I thought." She put her shirt on. "Please get outta my face."

Defeated, Farah walked away but stopped at the door. Turning back around she said, "Shannon was just talking about you on the bleachers. Real bad, too." She swallowed the bitter spit that formed in her mouth and placed her hand over her stomach to stop it from rumbling with anxiousness. If she didn't calm down, she would force herself into an outbreak of blisters. Taking a deep breath she continued, "She said you wore her panties and got them dirty when you spent a night at her house."

Coconut was chagrinned by what Farah Cotton— a nobody, an outcast—was telling her about one of her best friends. Not wanting Rhonda and the girls to hear anything else, she grabbed her gym bag and shoes and walked to the other side. "Come over here." Farah quickly walked up to her. "What's your name, spotty face?" She cleared her throat. "I mean . . . what's your name?"

"I'm Farah Cotton, and I want so much to be your friend."

Coconut smiled, flustered by her forwardness. "I can be a really good friend, too. I won't talk behind your back, or lie to you. I promise."

"Look, let's keep it light for right now," Coconut said, quoting her favorite phrase. "We'll talk later about all that. For now, can you tell me exactly what she said about me?" She placed her shoes on. "When you were up there."

"Right before you walked up to her, she said you wore her red panties and gave her a yeast infection."

Coconut frowned. "She's lying like shit! My daddy buys me real nice panties. What I need her stuff for?" It was obvious it was true.

"I know . . . I didn't believe her, but I wanted to tell you so you can watch your back. She's real sneaky. The other girls were calling you names, too, so I wouldn't let them come to your house if I were you." Feeling as if it were all or nothing, Farah decided to remind her of the party. "Can I come to your party now? Since I told you about them?"

"Yeah . . . but you gotta say what you telling me in front of Shannon." Farah's heart thumped wilder and she tried to calm down. Her body wasn't fit for all the excitement. "If I believe you, we gonna jump her. If you help, you can come to my party and be in my crew."

Farah wasn't a fighter and she knew it. Just moments ago she experienced rage for the first time, and already she wasn't mad anymore. But if this was what it took to win Coconut over, she was down. Cupping her hands together she said, "You got it!" She was so excited she wanted to run away before she changed her mind.

Coconut snatched Farah's diary and pencil and wrote her number on the page of her last story. When she saw her name in the journal, she read what it said:

Later, she went outside to play with the prettiest girl in her school, who was also her best friend—Coconut Elway.

She looked up at her and wanted to run. Farah Cotton was proving to be stranger by the moment. "Here . . . call me in a few days, and I'll let you know where everything is going down." She paused. "And if I find out you're lying, we gonna jump you instead."

# Chapter 5

### "I'll give you a chance.
### If you can help me." —Farah


After school, Farah, Mia, Chloe, and Shadow walked home. Although they ranged from elementary school to high school, the Cottons didn't walk the streets unless they were all deep. A week had passed since she was hospitalized, and Farah was starting to feel ill again. Living in pain, and in the bed, was a regular part of her life. She'd missed so many days from school. Out of pity her teacher would pass her, believing that, in her condition, it was just a matter of time before she died anyway. When she was well enough to go to school, all she thought about was Theo, and each day she'd pray he would be there so she could explain how she had nothing to do with what her mother did to him. Theo never came back. His parents pulled him out for fear of what Ashur and Brownie might do to him next.

It was especially hard for her to get out of bed today until it dawned on her: today was the day she had to call Coconut, and she wasn't all that excited about their friendship. It wasn't because she didn't want to be cool with her, but Farah wasn't a fighter. She tried desperately to think of a way out of confronting Shannon about what she'd said about Coconut. She couldn't ask her siblings for advice because they breathed danger and would've probably walked her to the altercation personally. After the doctors told Farah to avoid the sun, for fear she'd get blisters again, she walked down the street under a black umbrella. People may have laughed behind her back, but not one of them was bold enough to talk that shit to her face with Mia and Shadow present.

When they were some feet away from the building, Mia saw her archrival, Boo. Boo was older than her by one year and, just like Mia, loved keeping up shit. They'd fought so many times that people got confused on who could give the other more go. In the end, it was said they both were time enough for each other. "What the fuck are them bitches up to?" Shadow asked, not liking the looks on their faces.

"I can't stand Boo's ass," Mia said, looking at Boo and her friends leaning on a fence in front of their building. "I should go spit in that bitch's face."

"If you do you betta be ready to scrap," Shadow continued, wondering what Boo had planned. "'Cause I got a feeling this bitch is up to something."

"You think I'm scared?" Mia frowned. As always her clothing was tinged with remnants of her meal for the day. In this case, dried ketchup was over her right breast. She needed to take better care of her physical appearance, but it never was a priority.

"Don't play me for soft," he said. "I'm just saying be ready. You know I'ma make sure nobody jump in. That's for sure."

"I don't wanna fight," Farah said. "I just wanna go inside.

I'm not feeling good."

Everybody sighed and rolled their eyes. Mia said, "Farah, you better stop being a punk. I'm sick of that shit. You the only one in the family who start shit but don't back it up." Farah wondered what she meant. "Oh, don't think I don't know about the stuff you started at school with Shannon. That's probably why her cousin Boo over here now."

"I'm not scared." Farah swallowed. "I just don't like fighting, unless I have to."

"Seems to me since we got your back, you never have to," Shadow said. "And I can't be banging on no bitches when I got sisters." Farah remained silent. "You better learn to fall in love with blood."

"What we waiting on?" Chloe asked, skipping the subject. She was striking and she knew it. With big eyes and a winning smile, she embraced her chocolate skin unlike her mother, believing it made her special. "Let's beat these bitches' asses. I ain't afraid!"

They all looked at her and laughed. "First of all, girlie, you're only ten years old," Mia said. "You be more likely to get in the way than you would to help."

"I fight all the time at school!" Chloe said. "Bitches know I'm thorough with my hand game." Farah, like her sister and brother, ignored the youngest member of the family as she continued to tell them how she was a beast in them streets.

When they made it to their unit, Mia and Boo rolled eyes at each other as the Cottons disappeared into their building. The moment they hit the first step, Boo opened the building door and threw a stink bomb into the hallway. She and her friends laughed heartily as they closed the door and leaned into it. They knew from earlier experiences at school that whatever affliction the Cottons suffered from, they could not deal with fumes. Their illness was their weakness, and everybody with a vendetta used it against them.

Mia and Shadow tried to push the door open, but Boo and her friends outnumbered them as they pressed their weight against the opposite side of the door. "Run upstairs!" Mia ordered, as the fumes from the toxic bomb crawled up the stairway like fog in a horror movie. "And cover your noses and eyes."

"Oh, no!" Farah yelled under her hand. Since she was extra sensitive to everything, she feared the worst. "I'm gonna have to go back to the hospital again."

"Don't worry about all that! Just go!" Mia continued.

When they made it to their floor, they banged heavily on their grandmother's door. Since she was under the hair dryer in her room, she didn't know that her grandchildren were in danger, and fighting for their lives. "Let us in, Grandma!" Mia said, banging on the door with heavy fists.

"Please!"

The fumes, getting the best of their bodies, caused them to fall to their knees and clench their stomachs. Farah started throwing up while the rest of them experienced migraine-like headaches. Farah tried her best to prevent any more fumes from going into her body, but the vapors effortlessly rolled into her nostrils, and waited for her to release her breath so they could attack her organs. When she did she panicked, and passed out cold on the grungy floor.

For the second time in less than thirty days, Farah was hospitalized and alone. She couldn't imagine what Coconut thought about her and hoped she didn't rescind the offer to be her friend. She was so inconsolable at the moment that she couldn't write in her diary. Life was dark, and not worth living, and she hated being sick. Her desire to be well and have friends choked every moment of her day. She couldn't wait to see her family and leave, so the moment she saw Shadow, Mia, and Chloe, she beamed. At least they always seemed to love her. In a strange way, the disease they shared was a reminder that she was part of the family after all.

"Damn, your face is destroyed!" Mia said. Farah had scars, sores, and blisters on every inch of her body. The rest of her siblings didn't take a beating on their outward appearance.

"I look that bad?" She rubbed her face. "Please say no! I don't wanna go back to school like this!"

"It's not that bad," Mia lied, looking at Shadow. "You ready to get the fuck out of here?" Mia asked Farah. "'Cause I know I am!"

Farah was starting to believe that if she didn't have the illness, her social life would be way better. She was willing to do anything to be normal; she didn't care what it was.

She grabbed her duffle bag that sat on the floor and put it on her bed. "So where's Mamma and Daddy?" Her appearance was still on her mind.

"They on their way up the hallway," Shadow said. "They were fighting again."

"About what?"

"Daddy ain't come home last night again," Chloe said, adding her two cents. "I think he's fucking mommy's friend or something. That's what I heard them talking about anyway."

"Stop being fast, Chloe!" Mia said.

Chloe rolled her eyes and said, "Bitch, you not the boss of me." She folded her arms over her chest but remained silent.

When a pretty black nurse walked into the room, Shadow tried to puff out his chest and appear cool as he leaned up against the wall. She moved right past him like he wasn't in attendance. "Hello, Farah." She smiled. "My name is Erica and I'm here to check your vitals before you leave." As she checked her pulse, she couldn't stop looking at her. "You are so pretty and I'm sorry your skin is so damaged right now. I'm sure the doctor can give you something, so make sure you ask him. As cute as you are, you gotta always make sure your appearance is on point. That's all we got in life."

"Beauty runs in our family," Shadow added.

The nurse looked back at him and laughed. "This not your sister, boy. Stop playing." She turned her attention back to the blood pressure cuff on Farah's arm.

"Fuck that's supposed to mean?" Shadow asked.

"Well . . . it means she doesn't look like she's related to you."

"Well, she is our sister!" Mia said.

"Y'all related for real?" She looked over all of them.

"Yes," Farah said softly. "This is my family." Farah wanted the nurse to leave because she caused enough problems as it was. Every time somebody pointed out their differences, she felt like her family members were given another reason to hate her.

"I didn't mean it like that," the nurse said. "It just looks like you're mixed, and they are so dark skinned that I assumed . . ."

"Are you finished?" Mia asked. "Because I feel like I'm about to unleash on your ass."

"I'm done now." The nurse removed the cuff.

"Then hurry up and get the fuck out of here before you get stomped." Hearing the thunder in Mia's voice, she gathered her things and made a speedy exit.

When they were alone Farah felt bad. "I'm sorry, y'all. I hate when people do that shit." She looked at her scarred hands, which she was sure resembled her face. The nurse was right; she would have to do something to get her appearance in check. But what? Everything she used would only make it worse. She was beginning to feel very discouraged. "The nurse was just being dumb."

"What you gotta be sorry for?" Shadow said. "You know how many times Mamma gets looked over because she so black?"

"Boy, you only listening to what she say," Mia interjected. "Ain't nobody looking over Mamma. If she think people are being rude, they gonna be rude."

"Whatever, Mia. You and me both know that ain't true," he said. "Farah . . . you just need to be grateful you lighter, so start acting like it. I'm tired of having a pity party for you when it ain't deserved."

When Ashur and Brownie walked into the room Farah was relieved. It was the confirmation she needed that, for the moment, she was going home. "How you feel, RedBone?" Brownie asked. It was evident by the tone of her voice that she didn't care. "Still in pain?"

"No. I'm kinda better." Wanting affection she walked over to her and said, "Can I have a hug?"

"Girl, get you worrisome ass outta here. You in the hospital every other day now. Stop trying to get more attention." Brownie walked away and looked out of the window, while Farah sat down and sulked.

Ashur wanted to smack the shit out of Brownie but he left it alone. Instead he looked at all of his children and said, "I don't know why my kids gotta go through this shit!" It was obvious that he'd been drinking. "Them white people who got money would've been had medicine for this. And they keep telling my kids they got fucking allergies! I don't believe nothing they tell me, Brownie!"

"I know, honey." Brownie walked up to him and rubbed his back. They put aside the beef they had earlier for a greater cause—their children. "But a new doctor is coming today. Maybe he can tell us something."

After waiting five more minutes, a white male doctor walked in, and automatically Ashur and Brownie were hopeful. Racist against their own people, they believed at first that they'd get better service because of his race. The badge on his doctor's coat indicated that his name was Dr. Martin. He had a solemn look on his face that no one could read. His black-rimmed glasses seemed to set off his piercing blue eyes and his large nose. For the first time ever, Farah felt hope. "Hello, everyone, I'm Dr. Martin," he said, walking up to Ashur and Brownie to shake their hands, "and if you don't mind I'd like to talk to you about your children."

Ashur didn't know much about medicine, but he'd been in the streets long enough to know a rookie when he saw one. "How long you been practicing medicine?" Ashur asked with disdain in his voice.

"Not long. I'm an intern in my first year of residency." He adjusted the glasses on his face.

Ashur looked at the ceiling, threw his arms in the air, and stomped over to the window. "I shoulda known the moment I saw a white doctor that he was an intern. They don't give the black children no good white doctors. Just the ones that don't know nothing, so they can be lab rats."

"Sir, I am a good doctor."

"I bet," Ashur said sarcastically.

Dr. Martin was insulted but he was used to it by now. "I understand that you're upset. I truly do," he said. "But I might know what is really going on with your family."

Brownie walked closer to him. "You do? Because me and my mamma got this shit too, even though the kids have it worse."

"I think I know, but first I want to run some more tests. Tests I think might sum up everything you all are going through. I've seen the records. Farah in particular has been here one hundred days out of this year alone." Farah knew it was a lot, but she was surprised at the number. "Her body is taking a toll but we need to be sure before we medicate."

Brownie frowned. "Naw, doctor, I don't feel like putting them through no more tests, only for you to come back and tell me they got allergies," Brownie said. "So you can stick your funky test up your white ass and get out of my face." She looked at her kids and grabbed Farah's bag. "Come on, y'all, let's go home."

Everyone marched to the door when Dr. Martin said, "Mrs. Cotton, I haven't been practicing medicine for a long time, but I can assure you of one thing, and that is you and your family do not suffer from allergies. Give me a chance."

Farah walked up to him, grabbed his hand, and said, "I'll give you a chance. If you can help me."

# Chapter 6

**"Chloe . . . what the fuck are
you doing? I'ma tell Ma!" —Farah**

Farah held the lime-lemon juice jug to her lips, stuck her pink tongue through the spout, and guzzled as much as she could in one breath. Stopping for only a moment, she did it three more times before realizing she drank half of her mother's juice. If Brownie didn't play one thing, it was someone fucking with her shit. Whenever she went to the market, and used her food stamps on the first of the month, she would warn her children against eating and drinking everything within the first few days. Her words always fell on deaf ears, and when the fridge was void of snacks, they'd often spend hours begging for hers, despite the answer always being no.

Noticing her white T-shirt was covered with three green drops from the jug, she knew she would have to cover her tracks before Brownie came home. Farah looked at the kitchen's entrance, and when she was sure no one was coming, she turned the cold water on and placed the jug under the faucet. She filled it with water until she felt it was in the right place. A lighter green than it was before she got her paws on it, she put it back in the fridge.

When Farah was about to pass her grandmother, who was sitting on the couch soaking her feet, she was stopped. "What were you doing in that kitchen, child? You got a guilty look on your face, and a few green spots on your shirt. You wasn't drinking your mother's stuff now, were you?"

Farah choked back her guilt, covered the stains, and said, "No, I'm 'bout to see what Chloe doing." She smiled. "I'll be right back, Grandma." Rushing away from her she opened the door to her room knowing she needed to change her shirt. Chloe was sitting on the bed, with her back facing the door. "What you doing, Chloe?" Chloe hopped up, and a tin can once used for cookies fell out of her lap and clanked to the wooden floor. Dried blood was smeared all over her outfit and she looked petrified. "What's that red stuff?"

"Nothing . . . why?" she asked, as if she'd been caught doing the devil's work. "I was just playing with stuff." She looked at the floor. "Leave me alone."

Farah stepped farther into the room. "I sleep in here too."

When she was next to Chloe, she finally saw what was in the can, and she wanted to run. Chloe had severed the heads of two dead rats as if she were performing some type of sick surgery. "Chloe . . . what the fuck are you doing? I'ma tell Ma!"

Chloe rushed up to her and said, "Shh . . . Please don't say nothing! I won't do it again! I promise." Farah looked down at the dead rodents, and felt something strange come over her. The feeling was so awkward that she backed up toward the door just to get away. And when she turned around, she ran into her mother. Chloe had her mind so fucked up that she didn't hear her come inside the house.

Brownie was angry and it appeared to be directed at Farah. "What y'all in here doing now?" She looked at Chloe and then Farah. "I heard you all the way in the living room." She went through the leather purse hanging from her shoulders.

"Nothing," Farah said. "Just playing."

"Well who the fuck drank my juice and put water in it?" Farah's body started trembling. "I told y'all about drinking my shit, didn't I?" Brownie removed a pack of cigarettes from her purse, lit one, and blew the smoke into the air. "Well . . . which one of y'all touched my shit?" she asked, talking to them both but looking directly at Farah.

Farah was overcome with the dead rats and the fact that her mother was asking her if she drank her juice as if she already knew. If she told the truth, since her father wasn't home, she was positive Brownie would do her harm, even though she could count on her hand the number of times she'd done it. Although she was never the subject of her violence, it didn't matter. Brownie's name rang bells in the streets and her crimes caused more stitches then fifty handmade quilts. "Mia did it. She was in here earlier and I saw her."

Brownie didn't believe her, but until she talked to Mia, she didn't have proof. "I better not find out you're lying! If I do, I'ma fuck you up!" Brownie pointed in her face. "Now clean up this room. I'ma take a bath and then prepare dinner."

When she walked out, Farah turned around to face Chloe, who had already cleaned up the carnage on the floor. "Why did you do that? That's so gross," she whispered.

"I don't know. I do it all the time. I guess I like it." Chloe shrugged, walking toward the door with the can. "It's not a big deal though. Relax." She walked around her and out of the room.

Wondering how she could get out of the lie she told on Mia, Farah walked back to the living room. Once again Elise stopped her. "Come over here and sit next to me." Farah walked slowly to her grandmother. Steam rose out of the pot Elise's toes were soaking in, and carried with it a scent similar to corn chips. "Sit down on the couch." Farah sat next to her. "Why did you lie to your mother just now?"

Farah looked at the TV and said, "I didn't lie."

"Farah, I saw the juice on your shirt," she said softly. "Baby, you have to be careful how you act. Lying and hurting people is the wrong way to live. And you gonna have a tough life if you don't recognize that now. I'm talking about total chaos all the time." She touched her softly on the knee. "You're learning a lot of lessons you shouldn't be from your parents and I know it's hard, but I'm still here for you."

"But I didn't do it." Farah said, wishing she'd just shut the fuck up.

"Farah, when you get older, maybe I'll tell you why your mother is so angry with you, and focused on what people think about how she looks. I would tell you now if I didn't think it would be so heavy. For now I just wanna make sure you kids don't go down the same path they are. That road don't lead to nothing but trouble."

When there was a heavy knock at the door, Chloe came running out wearing a change of clothes to answer it. Farah was relieved because her grandmother's words of wisdom were weighing on her more than a sack of potatoes on her head. A few seconds later Chloe said, "Farah, that popular girl is here to see you. She wanna know if you can come outside."

The sun was nowhere to be found and it looked as if it would rain as Farah sat on the steps of her building. It was the perfect type of weather for her. When Chloe told her Coconut was there, she almost didn't believe her. But since Coconut and her crew barely spoke to her, she wondered why they bothered. The way they looked at her scarred face and carried on conversations without her made her uncomfortable. So she preoccupied herself with small pebbles by throwing them toward the wired fence.

She saw a local drug dealer named Randy Gregory standing in the doorway of the building across from hers, holding a bag. He looked around before exiting and approached a white Yukon. Throwing the bag inside the back of his truck, he was approached by an angry man, and Randy walked his way. Whatever was going on, it didn't look nice. Although Randy was six years older than her, she had a crush on him like no other. His smooth dark skin and low haircut reminded her of Ashur, except he never noticed her. Randy would wear all the latest fashions, and kept a fresh pair of tennis shoes on at all times. A gold chain hung from his neck with a medallion that read Randy Ran.

"We gonna have so much fucking fun when we go to Virginia Beach!" Coconut said, louder than before. "You sure your mother won't let you go, Farah? Some cute boys gonna be there too." Farah stopped throwing rocks, and looked at her. This was the first time she'd acknowledged her since she asked if she could come out fifteen minutes earlier.

"I know you missed my sleepover, but this is gonna be even better."

"What's gonna be happening at the beach?"

Coconut looked at her friends and fell out laughing. "We gonna be on the sand . . . getting tans. And stuff like that. Also we gonna get finger fucked by cute boys."

Farah thought about the illness the doctor said she had, which required a lot of medicine that never seemed to work. Since she couldn't pronounce the term he used properly she'd say "Porpia." He explained that she could be stricken with it her entire life. Under no circumstances, he'd explained, was she to be exposed to strong chemicals and the sun. Out of the entire family, her condition was surely the worst. "I gotta ask my mother." She looked at all of them and could see their irritation. "She might say yes."

"If your mother won't let you hang out with us, we can't be friends," Rhonda said. "We only roll with girls who can do what they want."

"Stop coming down on her," Coconut said, walking up to Farah. She sat on the step next to her and pulled a joint out of her pocket. Farah examined the small white roll. "You wanna hit this with us? In your basement?"

Farah didn't want to do drugs, but she'd already disappointed Coconut so she said, "I guess so." She wanted to go to the bathroom first, because she could feel a tingly sensation pulsing between her legs.

"I'ma use the bathroom first."

"Later for all that," Coconut said, putting her arm around her. "You can do that after we're done."

Leading the way, Farah and the girls walked down the steps, and into the dark, musty basement. She could hear rusted pipes dripping water onto the floors. The thought of bugs crawling on her made her nervous. She was about to go to the laundry room when Coconut said, "Don't y'all have a storage room down here?"

Farah knew the place well. It was where she'd seen Mia get fucked by her boyfriend, when she followed her last month. While being nosey, a spider dropped on her upper lip and sent her into a panic, which ended in her being hospitalized for a month. It was her longest stint yet and gave her another phobia. She finally made it to the storage room door, but when she looked behind her, the girls stopped. "We going in?"

"You not going nowhere," somebody said.

Farah turned around and faced the voice. Shannon, Wendy, and Nova walked out of the darkness and into her path. Their hard facial expressions were serious as they slapped their fists into the palms of their hands. "You told Coconut I talked about her at school?" Shannon asked, ready to drop her on the floor. "I'ma fuck your ass up for lying on me!"

When Farah turned around she bumped into Coconut and her friends, who formed a human wall that blocked her escape. She walked right into a setup and she was ill prepared. "Tell her what you said she said at school that day," Coconut said. "If you ain't lying it shouldn't be a problem for you to say it to her face."

This wasn't what she thought would happen when Coconut knocked on her door. Her chest moved up and down and she felt an outbreak coming on. Turning around, she pushed past the girls, and ran upstairs and out of the building. Running aimlessly for a moment, eventually she hid on the side of an adjoining building. From her viewpoint, she could see all the girls, with the exception of Coconut and Rhonda, running around outside looking for her. She reasoned the other two were waiting in her building so she couldn't go home right now.

Farah knew it was a matter of time before they found her, so when she didn't see the girls outside anymore, she ran toward Randy's truck, praying to God it was open. When she tugged at the back door handle, it clicked and she jumped inside, closing the door behind her. Luckily, a large blue moving blanket covered three bags on the back seat. She lifted the cloak, curled her body between the middle of two bags, and covered up. From under the sheet she could hear the girls running back and forth outside, trying to find her. She'd never been more scared in her life.

Fifteen minutes later, when she heard someone open the door, she prayed it wasn't them. *Please don't let them get me. If you don't, God, I promise not to lie anymore,* she lied again. When the engine started, and the car moved, she exhaled. Farah was fine, until she realized she was being driven away from home. Things were getting worse by the second, and she had no doubt her parents were going to flip the fuck out. After she came in the house that day from sitting on the roof, they demanded that she come in before the streetlights turned on, whenever she was allowed out. She had no idea how she was going to get out of the truck, or where Randy was driving. Five minutes into the ride, Farah began to feel hot, as if she'd been running around all day. A few minutes after that, she was full of energy and felt an extreme need to move. She'd inhaled the remnants of bags stored in a drug house.

When the car stopped moving, she waited for his car door to close so she could run away. But when the cover was raised, and the tip of a gun was resting on her nose, she knew it was too late. "What the fuck are you doing under there?"

Farah sat up and tears rolled down her face. "I was hiding. Some girls were going to jump me." Her eyes rolled around and she was sweating profusely. Randy knew immediately she'd caught a contact from the bags. "I just wanna go home." The moment she opened her mouth, he knew she was high.

Randy Gregory, who was a runner for his father, Willie Gregory, was already having a bad week. Recently his girlfriend was kidnapped and murdered by two men looking for him, and today his father had, in no uncertain terms, said he would be nothing but an errand boy. Now, he had to deal with a girl who was high from sniffing his drugs. Normally he would not have been caught slipping by leaving his door unlocked, but when Willie called him back for the bullshit, it threw him off his game. If he had been more careful, he wouldn't have to deal with her. Randy opened the back door, grabbed the bags, and said, "Come inside. I can't take you home until you come down off that shit."

"Come down where?"

"Just get the fuck out."

Farah eased out of the car and followed him to a nice-sized home. She had no idea where she was but she hoped he wasn't a pedophile or a serial murderer. Once inside, she marveled at how bright everything was. The color white dominated, and that included the drapes, leather couch, and plush carpeting.

Randy closed and locked the door, and placed the duffle bags on the kitchen table. "Ma . . . I'm home!" he yelled toward the back.

When Helen Gregory walked into the living room wearing a cream silk pants pajama set, which looked so elegant it could be worn outside, Farah felt inferior. She was extremely beautiful and favored her mother, Brownie. Helen was dipped in diamonds and gold and her long hair brushed against the sides of her ebony face. Holding a glass of cognac in one hand and a cigarette in the other, she looked at the scared child hovering in her living room corner. Placing her drink on the table, and mashing her cigarette in the ashtray, her white feather high-heeled slippers click-clacked in Farah's direction. "Before I forget, honey," she said, looking at Randy, "the nursing home called and said you can volunteer again next week if you want."

"Thanks, Ma. I'll call them tomorrow."

Standing over her she said, "Now . . . what do we have here?" She looked at her son. "You didn't tell me you had company."

From the kitchen Randy said, "Oh, yeah . . . Pops fucked my head up, and I accidently left my shit open. The bitch hid in my truck." He placed the bricks of cocaine on the table. "I think some broads were after her or some shit like that. I'ma take her home in an hour." He looked at her as if she were a pest. "She caught a contact from my coke and got high. I ain't want to take her back to Ashur like that." He focused back on the bricks. "I don't feel like killing that dude."

Farah had to piss so bad now she could barely hold it, but she was scared to ask to use the bathroom. Helen placed her soft hands on her chin and lifted it up. "You know . . . you would be a pretty red thing, if your face wasn't so spotty." She looked at Randy. "You should keep her around. When she gets older, she can give you all kinds of yellow babies." She released her.

"That's a kid, Ma. Why would you even say that?"

"She got to be about twelve or thirteen," Helen continued.

"Five years is gonna fly by and before you know it, she'll be having her period. What's your name, girl?"

"Farah." She swallowed, placing her hand between her legs to pause the urge to piss. "Farah Cotton."

"Well, Farah, get something for that face. You too young to look so hard." On to another thought, Helen turned to Randy and said, "Was that white bitch Eleanor around your father today?" She picked up her drink and lit another cigarette. "All she's trying to do is steal my husband."

"Ma, I don't know about all that. I just need you to cook this shit, so we can make the drop-offs."

Helen rolled her eyes. "Take your father's side if you want to, but I'm sure he'll stab you in the back just like he's doing me before long." She paused. "Let me go freshen up, and then I'll start working on it."

When she disappeared into the house Randy asked, "You hungry? Thirsty?"

Since she'd unconsciously sniffed cocaine in his truck, she'd completely lost her appetite. "No . . . but I gotta go to the bathroom real bad." She started moving around in place, pressing her hands between her legs. "Can I?"

"Yeah . . . it's around the corner." He pointed. "Hurry up back, because I'ma feed you anyway before I drop you off."

Farah rushed toward the bathroom, trying her best not to make any jerky motions, which would cause her to piss in her clothes. A fear of hers. When she opened the door, she was surprised to see Helen standing in the shower, naked from the waist down. She was squatting and holding a pink douche bag between her legs. The bathroom was heavy with the scent of the cigarette resting on the edge of the sink and the vinegar in the bag. "What you looking at, girl?" Helen said. "You never saw a woman douche before?" Farah shook her head. "Well, what you want then? I'm busy."

"I gotta pee."

"Well, come on in." She squeezed the bag a few times. "I'm not gonna be much longer anyway."

Farah walked to the toilet, lifted the lid, and sat sideways on the cold seat to prevent facing Helen. When the urine poured out of her body, she exhaled. For the moment it was the best feeling in the world.

"I don't know why," Helen said, removing the tube connected to the bag from the inside of her pussy, "but I got a feeling you gonna be my son's wife." Farah remained silent, and focused on the lit cigarette on the sink. "Make sure you take care of your body when you do get him," she said, screwing off the tube and rinsing them under the tub's faucet. "Men love a woman with a clean pussy and a pretty face." She stepped out of the tub and eased into her silk pajama pants and slippers. "I don't know why your skin so bad, but if you don't do nothing . . . You better take care of your looks. It's all you got in life."

Helen opened the medicine cabinet, pulled out a pack of razors, and removed one. Without washing her hands, and while Farah was still on the toilet, she said, "Open your mouth." She did. "Keep this in your mouth"—she stuffed it on the inside of her cheek—"but whenever you're about to fight, or you think you may be in trouble, put this between your teeth and your cheek like I just did. Now close your mouth." Farah was nervous as hell that she would get cut. "Whenever somebody fuck with you, slice them fifty times across the neck or the temple and your problems will be over."

# Chapter 7

**"Dear God, please be with that child. I'm begging you."** —Elise

Brownie was helping Elise prepare the project's rec for her annual family celebration. Before bringing in the food, Elise had her friends check for roaches and bugs in case they needed to use any sprays. She wanted to prevent her family from having an outbreak. The theme was black and red and Elise saw to it that everything coordinated, including the plastic plates, forks, spoons, and napkins. With four sisters, their children, and their grandkids, the family celebration would be huge. When the hall was beautifully decorated, the food was brought in and laid upon the table. The moment Elise opened the doors for everyone they crowded into the hall. When all of her sister's children started hovering around the food table Elise looked for Brownie. Spotting her sitting in a chair in the corner, rubbing her feet, she walked over to her.

"Where are my grandbabies?" She scanned the room. "My sisters' kids are about to punish the food if they don't grab something to eat."

"You know they getting ready for the show, Mamma." She'd been up all day and it was taking its toll on her body. She hated the celebration with a passion. "Relax, they coming."

"Don't tell me to relax," Elise rebutted. "Now I know Mia can skip a few meals, but the rest of your kids are almost skin and bones."

"Mamma, they're coming," Brownie said, growing tired of her mother's over-protectiveness. "You wanted them to perform, so all they thinking about is the show right now."

"Well, where is Farah? Since you told her she can't participate, she should at least be here."

"She still *not* participating. After that stunt she pulled by coming in the house late again the other night, she's lucky I don't kill her." She slid back into her shoes. "I told Mia to keep an eye on her right now. I don't feel like dealing with her."

Every year at the celebration, the grandkids would get together and compete in a competition with their cousins. Mia and Shadow hated it because they were damn near adults, but Chloe always got a kick out of throwing her hips from side to side and popping her ass just to see everybody's reaction. Usually they danced to music from The Jackson Five, The Supremes, the Temptations, and the like, since the show was clearly for the amusement of the elders, and not the children.

"Well, set them some plates to the side." Elise looked into her daughter's eyes, which seemed to be getting colder. "Are you and Ashur having problems still?"

Grateful she was asking about her instead of the kids, she said, "I'm sick of his shit. He's driving me insane. We don't have sex and he's barely home. He don't love me no more." She looked as if she wanted to cry. When it came to Ashur, she was vulnerable. "If I can't have him, I don't want nobody else to. I'd rather see him dead or in jail!"

"Stop talking like that!" Elise warned. "God grants wishes when you think He's not listening. Now you gotta be present for your kids." Brownie rolled her eyes. "All men act up, but the good ones come back around. Only you know which one you got. You gotta be careful, though, because Farah is watching you and you're giving her the wrong impression."

When Elise heard the noise rise in the room she knew the family competition was underway. The kids of Elise's oldest sister, Irma, were first up. Irma's grandsons chose to sing the Temptations classic "My Girl" a cappella, as Irma stood proudly on the sidelines with her hands clasped over her chest. She was always amazed at how talented they were. It was just a matter of time before one of her four grandchildren got discovered, the family was sure of it.

"Go find your kids. My babies are going to kill it! I just know it," Elise said.

Unenthused, Brownie said, "You do know they just lip syncing, right?"

"As long as they perform from their hearts, I don't care what they doing."

When everyone clapped, the first performance was over. "You're up, Elise," Irma said with a sly grin on her face. "Where your grandkids?" The moment she asked, Mia, Shadow, and Chloe glided into the room dancing to "Never Can Say Goodbye." Shadow held a boom box on his shoulder and a black Kangol was tilted on his head. Although both Mia and Shadow thought the events were lame, whenever they saw the looks on their great aunts' faces they felt better. Shadow set the box down on the floor behind them.

They lined up and pretended to be The Jackson Five with only three members. But because the routine was so well put together, everyone enjoyed the show. The only awkward part about the evening was that both Shadow and Mia kept looking at the door, as if they were waiting for someone else. "What are they looking for?" Elise whispered to Brownie.

"I don't know, Ma. Maybe that's part of the performance." She shrugged her shoulders. The only thing on her mind was Ashur Cotton and his whereabouts. "Just enjoy what they doing." She looked at her kids. "Whatever it is." The family was cheering and singing with the threesome, until Farah came through the door doing signature Michael Jackson moves. The applause simmered down and everyone leaned in to see her clearly.

Elise, not believing her eyes, took a closer look at her granddaughter. "Oh, my dear God," she said to herself. "What did you do to your face, baby?"

Seeing her face, Brownie was overwhelmed with Farah. She was a fucking curse . . . a way for God to get her back. *How could this bitch do this to me?* she thought. Farah, in an attempt to fit in, used permanent brown Magic Markers to color in her entire face and hands. She took what Shadow said to heart when he said tanning would not be indefinite but she was certain a permanent Magic Marker would. But because she ran out of ink, her yellow neck remained its natural color. "What the fuck are you doing?" Brownie asked, walking up to her. "Why are you trying to ruin my life?"

"Why are you mad, Mamma?" She backed away, and into a table full of food. "I wanted to be brown like you said so I could do The Jackson Five routine. I don't want you mad at me no more. I'm sorry for coming into the house late but these girls tried to jump me. And I'm sorry for staying on the roof that day, trying to get a tan. I know I mess up so much, but I'ma do better. I wanna make you happy." She was beside herself with emotion. "I thought this would work, Mamma. I really did. So you could love me more."

"Bitch, you not answering my question! Are you out of your fucking mind?" she screamed. "You think it's funny that I was born with this skin color and you weren't? Huh?"

"No, Mamma." She shook her head. "I really thought you would like it! I wanna look like you. I wanna be like you." She sobbed. "I didn't stay out in the sun this time so I wouldn't have to go to the hospital. I thought you would be happy." Tears ran down Farah's face and she wiped them away, causing the marker to smear. Now she looked unrecognizable.

"Brownie, let me take her to wash her up," Elise said, wanting to take her daughter and grandkid somewhere more private so that the rest of the family could enjoy the event. Besides, she understood Farah, since it was obvious Brownie did everything in her power to make her feel like an outsider. "It won't take me but a moment." She extended her hand. "Come on, RedBone," Elise continued. "Let me take you to go get cleaned up."

"No!" Brownie slapped her mother's hand away, and looked at her with contempt. "I'm tired of you stepping in my fucking business."

"I'm not stepping in, Brownie," Elise said, trying to maintain her composure. In her younger years, Brownie would've been dead and dumped where they couldn't find her. "But this is my granddaughter and I wanna help."

"I'm gonna give her what she deserves this time," Brownie continued. "And I don't give a fuck what you or Ashur have to say about it."

"Don't hit that child, Brownie," Elise warned, pointing a finger in her face. "Your husband already told you about disciplining them in that way . . . especially while you mad."

Brownie laughed. "Look around, Mamma, the nigga ain't here. Besides, you and me both know he don't need to say shit about Farah!" With that she snatched Farah's arm and stormed out of the party.

"Dear God, please be with that child," Elise said to herself. "I'm begging you."

# Chapter 8

**"Well, you better get a third and a fourth job while you at it, nigga!" —Ashur**

Ashur was speeding down the highway, holding a bottle of Courvoisier in one hand and the steering wheel in the other. Personal demons haunted him on a consistent basis, and he was starting to think that if he died, his family would be better off. It disgusted him that instead of being there for his wife at her family affair, he elected to receive a blowjob from a homeless man he'd known no longer than thirty minutes. The moment the man swallowed his nut, Ashur stole him in the face so hard he passed out on the filthy alley ground beneath him. A closeted bisexual, Ashur chose to deal with his secret by taking his problems out on people who weren't deserving. Hiding his bisexuality from the woman he vowed to spend the rest of his life with killed him inside.

Ashur couldn't tell Brownie that he begged for Tommy's forgiveness after hurting his only son.

How could he, when she didn't even know the real reason for the hit on young Theo? All because Tommy said he could no longer live a lie and sleep with another man. Upon hearing his words, Ashur went mental. It wasn't until Tommy's isolation that he realized he was in love with him, and that losing the friendship would hurt him on the deepest levels of his soul.

When he came to a light, he took a huge gulp of liquor. Some of the alcohol fell down the sides of his mouth and he wiped it away with the back of his hand. *Maybe I should go to that bullshit with my wife,* he thought. He reasoned that although Brownie might be mad now, the fact that he showed up would go a long way later. Ashur was still in his thoughts until he heard a noise on the back of his car. When he adjusted the rearview mirror and looked out of it he saw a teenager, not watching where he was going, bump into his car. "What the fuck?" Ashur said to himself.

Although the light turned green, Ashur hopped out in the middle of the road. People bonked their horns, but eventually went around him to get to their destination. Ashur couldn't give a fuck; he had tunnel vision as he approached the couple sitting at the bus stop with the boy.

"So what . . . you can't control your fucking kid?" Ashur asked the man and woman who pushed the boy behind them. The teenager looked angrily at

Ashur. "I mean . . . look at my shit! He ruined it!" Ashur pointed to the slightly chipped paint job and grew angrier.

"I'm sorry about that, man," the father said. "I didn't see him do it until you parked the car." He looked at his son and saw fire in his eyes. It was obvious he wanted to fight Ashur. "Sit down . . . now!"

"Well, sorry ain't gonna get my car fixed now, is it?"

The man bit his tongue and said, "If you wanna take it in to see how much it'll cost to get repaired, I'll see what I can do. I'm working two jobs right now, but I'll take on a third if I have to. Seeing as how it was my boy's fault."

"Well, you better get a third and a fourth job while you at it, nigga!" Ashur said, stepping closer to his face. He wanted to fight so badly he was being unreasonable. "'Cause I didn't pay for a nice ride to have my shit fucked up by your brat."

The father was just about to step to him until his wife said, "Joseph, come over here! Please!" Joseph didn't budge. "We don't have time for this. He ain't worth it." She looked at Ashur. "Let it go."

Joseph looked back at his wife and then at Ashur and said, "I know you mad about your ride, and I respect that. But if you disrespect me in front of my family again, I swear on everything I love, I will kick your mothafucking ass out here today!"

Ashur heard the seriousness in the man's voice and slowly backed away. For some reason, he felt fighting the man may prove to be more trouble than he felt like dealing with at the moment. After all, he'd been drinking and wouldn't be at his best for a brawl. Not to mention that the nick was small, and blended in with the other one Brownie made when the button of her jeans scratched up against it as he fucked her from behind. Although the car was old, it was the same car he was in when he first met Brownie, drove his first child, Mia, home from the hospital, and fucked Tommy for the first time. Like it or not, the car held memories and it was important to him.

Stepping back in his car, he pulled back into traffic and took a swig of liquor. Always a hothead, the vision of the teenager falling on his car swelled in the spaces of his mind. The liquor wasn't doing anything but making matters worse, so when he was two blocks away from the scene he thought about how the man played him and decided to do something about it. Besides, there was no way he could face his wife, knowing he'd punked out in the worst way. So he bucked a U. Pulling up to the bus stop, he rolled his window down and saw the look in the man's eyes as he raised his .45 in his direction. The sound of three shots rang out as he executed the family in broad daylight, before speeding away from the scene of the crime.

# Chapter 9

**"I don't wanna see them . . .
They tried to jump me." —Farah**

The pillow underneath Farah's head was wet with tears from hours of crying. Her mother did the unthinkable and she would never, ever forgive her. All she wanted to do was make her happy and it seemed as if nothing she did worked.

Earlier that day, when Brownie snatched Farah out of the event and walked her toward the rec's restroom, she had no idea what she had in store. Alone with her horrible mother, Farah watched her turn the water on before smacking her multiple times in the face. Brownie's blows were so heavy that her hand burned, but instead of stopping she alternated from right to left. Farah was stunned at the rage she expressed, and for a while, she didn't feel anything but extreme pressure on her cheeks.

After about thirty blows, Brownie sat on the pissy public toilet, no tissue, and pushed down as hard as she could using her stomach muscles.

Fifteen minutes later, she was able to make a bowel movement, but instead of flushing, she put her hands in the vile bowl and picked up a chunk of her shit. She walked toward Farah and she backed up into the door. "You still wanna be black like me?" Brownie laughed and cried at the same time. "Then here you go." She smeared the soft feces all over her face. Farah moved her head swiftly back and forth, but eventually Brownie was able to hold her head in place. She didn't care where she put it and that included her daughter's eyes, lips, and nose. She snapped a long time ago. "How you like that, bitch? Huh?"

Farah's body temperature rose, and she could feel herself breaking out into hives. The humiliation she endured in the restroom was nothing compared to what Brownie put her through when she made her walk back into the party. Her younger cousins, older aunts, and grandmother looked upon her with pity and she wanted to die. No matter how many years passed, this would be the moment they'd all remember. People covered their mouths and noses as the smell of shit rose from Farah's face and Brownie's hands. Irma, unable to control her bodily functions, ran toward the door so she could throw up outside . . . She couldn't make it. Two feet from the door she lost everything she ate an hour earlier, as it splashed to the floor.

"Now . . . how does she look, everyone?" Brownie grinned, showing her crazed maniac side. "Isn't she still the cutest Cotton of us all?"

Farah's chest rose and fell as she sobbed and looked upon the adults for help. *Someone . . . anyone . . . do something, please.*

"Brownie, what the fuck is wrong with you?" Elise said, rushing toward her with a murderous look in her eyes.

"Don't worry, Mamma. She's all yours." Brownie ran away, leaving Farah alone in the middle of the floor.

"I'm sorry, child. I really am." She watched her daughter scamper away, and hugged Farah tightly before ushering her out of the party. Elise couldn't hate her daughter more at that moment if she tried. Rage, confusion, and sadness filled her heart, and their relationship would never be the same. Brownie would pay for this in life, but Elise didn't know how.

At a phone booth outside the rec, Elise called Cosmo, Farah's cousin on her father's side, to pick her up. She figured the change of location for a few hours would do her good, plus she wanted a few moments alone with Brownie that she doubted would be nice. When Cosmo saw what Brownie did to his kid cousin he flipped. Since Elise didn't give him the heavy on the phone before he came, he had to leave her outside the rec until he could go to the grocery store to buy some trash bags. Laying them all over his seats, he scooped her up, and took her to his mother Angie's house. It took them two hours to clean her up, and Farah enjoyed the time she spent with her aunt and cousin. Angie was into holistic medicine and looked ten years younger than her actual age. She never got so much as a cold and hadn't been sick since she was a kid. When she went to make them dinner, Farah decided to ask Cosmo a question as they sat at the dining table.

"Cosmo, did Grandma tell you what I have? The Porpia?"

He laughed at the way she pronounced it. "Yeah. That's fucked up that it's hereditary, but that's all I know about it. That and that it makes your skin look bad."

"I wish I didn't have it." She looked down at the wooden table. "I can't go out in the sun sometimes, and nobody likes to hang out with me because I can never leave the house. All I want to be is normal."

He felt bad for her because he knew she was given a tough break in life. "Look . . . I don't care how long it's gonna take me, I'll find out more about this shit. And when I do, I'll get you the help that you need." She believed him.

Cosmo had been there for her many times before. Like when she suffered from extreme headaches when she was five, and nothing seemed to work. He felt if she calmed down they would go away, after talking to his mother. He told her how she said she should breathe, but they still wouldn't go away. Thinking on his feet, he suggested she drink orange juice with chocolate syrup and things would be fine, and it worked. The concoction had nothing to do with getting rid of her headache, but Cosmo knew she needed to believe a remedy would do the trick. Farah was so destroyed that it was hard for her to fathom that she alone was able to make things better. To her, he was very close to God.

She enjoyed the rest of her time with them until Elise requested he bring her home. Cosmo respected Elise, but he wasn't bringing her anywhere until he could be sure Brownie was nowhere to be found. Elise told him she wasn't allowed back in her house for at least two days so he said he was on his way.

"Cosmo, how come Mamma hate me because I'm light-skinned?" she asked from the passenger seat of his car. "I don't think she ever really loved me."

Cosmo, a young drug dealer and recreational thug, believed in family so it killed him to keep the secret he knew about Brownie from her for so long. If his little cousin wanted the truth, he would give it to her, ready or not.

"Your mother hates herself . . . She just takes it out on you." He continued to drive.

"I want her to love me, but I don't know how or what to do."

Cosmo frowned and said, "Your mother fucked that white coach at your school. Coach Jaffrey or some shit like that, but niggas call him Jay." Farah looked at him strangely, not sure if she heard him correctly. "They used to be together when they were kids, and from what I heard it was serious. Brownie wanted more from the relationship but I don't think Jay could do the public thing. Your mother's dark skin walking next to his white skin gave him a complex when people looked at them out in the streets. You gotta be real strong to deal with that kind of shit.

"I ain't gonna say if the white boy loved her or not, but I know your mother loved him more, so she couldn't handle the rejection. When she met Ashur, she left Jay alone, and got serious with my uncle. Me and Moms thought she was done with Jay for good but then people started saying they saw her around town with the dude when she was married to Ashur." He took a sip of the bottled water in his car. "This was all before you were born." He looked at her and saw he had her undivided attention. "Anyway, Moms told him to watch out for Brownie, because she was not to be trusted, but Ashur wouldn't listen. We figured he'd done so much shit in the dark that he would forgive the sins she committed in broad daylight."

He shook his head. "That white boy fucked her mind up . . . and she ain't never been the same." He looked over at her. "So no matter what you do, Farah, you'll never be able to get through to her. The only thing Brownie wanted was to marry that white man, and your light skin reminds her that she could never have him. A few years later, I think he married some red sister, so he was definitely into black women."

Cosmo was young and without tact but that was his way. He didn't stop to think what the information he dropped would do to her. Farah's stomach swirled and her mind raced upon hearing the news. It dawned on her then that whatever Dr. Martin gave her must be working; otherwise, she would've passed out today, seeing as though it was the worst one of her life. "What are you saying?" Farah asked.

"You already know, little cousin."

She swallowed. "You saying Coach Jaffrey is my father?"

Silence.

She didn't believe him. She needed to speak to her father . . . the one who held her in his arms, and protected her from harm, so it was a good thing she was going home. The smart part of her said it made sense. Her light skin and coal-black hair was just like his. Still, she loved Ashur with everything she had and she desperately wanted to ignore what her cousin was trying to imply. "Cosmo, do you like dark-skinned girls or light skin?"

"Neither."

"Huh?"

"I love women. *All* women. The light skin versus dark skin shit is dead to me. I be seeing chicks all the time bleach out their faces, forgetting their necks, and a whole bunch of other crazy shit like that. Like something is wrong with black period, no matter what shade you are." He shrugged. "In Africa, before we were shipped over to this bitch, the blacker you were the better. Now, dark chicks hate who they are and wanna be something else." He laughed. "The funny thing is, just like Coach Jaffrey was into your mother, a lot of white niggas be diggin' on black bitches . . . the Italians, the Russians, and Chinese too. They just not as vocal as the black dude who dates a white broad for status." He pulled up to her building and parked. "I love a bitch as dark as Grace Jones or as yellow as you. I just don't give a fuck. Then again, that's just me."

That night, when Farah heard footsteps outside the bedroom door she braced herself for the worst, thinking it was Brownie wanting to finish her off. But when she turned around and faced the door, she saw Mia instead. In Pig Latin Mia said, "You wanna kill that bitch, don't you?"

Silence.

"Stop with the crying," she continued. "She not coming home tonight. Grandma was serious as a mothafucka about that shit. Plus she went to see about Daddy, so you ain't got to worry . . . Relax."

When Cosmo dropped her off earlier that night, the neighborhood was buzzing about the triple homicide Ashur committed. Unknowingly, the family he killed was the same family responsible for the murder of their son's pregnant girlfriend and her father. To some, he was a hero, which Elise was sure he would spin to his advantage. More interested in her father than Brownie, Farah asked, "You think he gonna get out of jail again this time?"

"Yes," Mia said confidently. "Daddy always beats the raps." She leaned against the doorway.

"But they saying he murdered some people in broad daylight."

"It don't make no difference. Shit gonna be cool. Plus you know it's the boy who killed his pregnant girlfriend in Virginia. People in the neighborhood loving him right now." Mia walked into the room and sat down on the edge of the bed. It sank a few inches due to her extreme weight. There was love in her eyes as she softly touched her sister's leg and looked at her. "Farah, Mamma was wrong as shit for what she did to you. But that's her problem . . . don't make it yours. The girl Coconut and some other girls are outside to see you. Go hang out and have some fun."

"I don't wanna see them . . . They tried to jump me." Farah pouted.

"And I put them bitches in they place just now, too." Mia frowned. "And your ass should've stood out there and rumbled every last one of them one by one instead of running.

"Oh . . . don't think I forgot about you lying on me about fucking up Mamma's juice that day, either. You owe me for telling her I really did that shit. Anyway, them bitches out there being fake, I know it, but that's what bitches do. You wanna be popular, so you gotta play along, Farah.

"This disease we got fucked you up way more than us; now you got a chance to make a few friends and have a normal life." When Farah didn't seem to be buying it she said, "Let's not forget that it was your fault anyway. You should've never jumped in the business and told that girl what Shannon said behind her back. They probably gonna ask you what happened with Daddy, and all that other stuff. Play along and be a hood star. You deserve it."

Farah wanted to tell her about what she learned about her real father, but she pushed it down into the pit of her stomach, never to think about it again. "But what if they know?"

Farah wiped tears off her face. "That Mamma put shit on my face in front of everybody?"

"How could they? I didn't tell anybody. And you know Mamma didn't either."

"What about our cousins? You know they talk too much, and they were all there."

Mia was growing frustrated at her sister's tender heart. "Fuck 'em!" Mia scowled. "At least go outside to see what they want. If they do know, you want people to see you with your head held high not low. You a Cotton, bitch! Toughen up and act like it," Mia said seriously. "And the temperature gone down, so you know all the cute little boys gonna be out there. Your face clearing up a little bit thanks to Dr. Martin, and if you stop having panic attacks and calm down, you might find yourself a boyfriend."

Mia was right. Why should she suffer because of who she was? Or because of how she looked? Suddenly Farah had a new goal in mind. If people thought she was pretty because of her light skin, she would learn to use the outside characteristic to her advantage. Looking up at her big sister she said, "Fuck Mamma! I gotta do me."

"Now you talking, RedBone!"

# Chapter 10

## *Two Years Later*

**"But I'm not like y'all. I don't
like hurting people." —Farah**

"Hey, Rhonda . . . it's Farah," she said, playing with the white cord on Coconut's phone in her bedroom.

"Me and Natasha was just about to come over there," Rhonda said. "We getting dressed right now."

Fourteen-year-old Farah looked at Coconut's bedroom door to be sure she wasn't coming. "I'm glad you called first because we not going to the party tonight."

"Why not? We been planning this shit all week."

"She got her period and been in pain all day. Her mother making her some tea right now to settle her stomach."

"Where she at? Let me talk to her right quick," she said, concerned.

"I don't think that's a good idea." Farah smiled so it could be felt through the phone. "She really needs her rest."

"Oh . . . okay . . . Well, I'll call her later."

After placing the phone on the hook, Farah sat on the bed and waited for Coconut to come back into her room. Fifteen minutes later she entered, holding a new porno DVD, and placed it in the player. She wiggled her toes as she watched bits and pieces of the porno Coconut was obsessed with playing. While most people played music in the background, she wasn't satisfied unless the sounds of fucking rang throughout her room. Farah watched Coconut comb her hair as she sat on the bed. Her beauty, and the effortless way she moved her body, mesmerized her. Farah wondered how it must have felt not to be plagued with the same social-killing disease that plagued her all her life. Farah wanted nothing more than to be her, have her home and even her mother, Sherry. Unlike Brownie, she wasn't in her ear telling her that she needed to do unspeakable acts of violence to prove her love. So over the years, Coconut's house became her refuge. Although she wasn't allowed to go over there during the daytime hours, because of what the sun did to her skin, she made up for the time by the wild things she did with Coconut at night.

The girls were talking about boys and their lives in high school when Sherry attempted to walk in without knocking. "Ma, get the fuck outta my room!" Coconut yelled, throwing her shoe at the door. Sherry quickly closed the door to prevent getting hit. "You know I hate when you come in here without asking! Damn, respect my fucking privacy!"

"I'm sorry, honey. I was coming to bring your clean clothes," she said from the outside.

Coconut rolled her eyes and said, "Well, hurry up." Sherry rushed inside, as if time were not on her side and she were not head of household. Farah was amazed at how she spoke to her mother and, more importantly, how Sherry reacted to the verbal abuse. She had no doubt that with Ashur incarcerated, Brownie would not hesitate to snap her neck back if she used the same language.

Sherry wasn't always that way, but after Coconut's father died in a freak accident last year—when the shaft of a dump truck traveling in the opposite direction from him on the highway dislodged and slammed into his windshield—she felt guilty. After all, Milton was on his way to listen to Coconut's recital at her school, when Sherry begged him to pick her up from the bar after having gone over her limit of ten glasses of vodka. If he had been with his daughter he would still be alive today, and Coconut hated Sherry for it. It didn't matter that she hadn't had a drop of liquor since.

After Sherry finished neatly placing Coconut's clothes in the dresser, she rushed out to give the girls privacy. "That bitch gets on my fuckin' nerves sometimes."

"She seems nice to me." Farah shrugged. "Nicer than my mother, anyway."

"Everybody's nicer than your mother," Coconut said, combing her hair more. "Anyway, tell your father I said hi." She smiled. "I still can't believe he killed them people back then. That shit is so fucking sexy."

Mia was right: the main reason Coconut wanted to squash the beef two years ago was to get in her family's business. Farah would spend hours telling her about the violent things Ashur did, including how her parents made her kick Theo in the dick. In love with lying, she even made up a few stories along the way. One time when she spent a night over at her house, and they slept in the same bed, Coconut played with her own pussy and Farah's at the same time after she told her about her father's violent ways. Even then Coconut didn't allow her into the crew, until she participated in their favorite game called Smack Down.

Standing in front of Farah, Coconut smacked her with all her might in the face. When she was done, she was allowed to slap her back. They went back and forth, until Farah raised her hand, wanting the game to stop. Even though she lost, they underestimated Farah's desire to have friends, because it took over an hour for her to concede. It wasn't about the game; everyone who played knew Coconut was the most thorough. They realized then that Farah wasn't the mousy, spotty-faced girl they thought she was.

"He told me to tell you hello," Farah said dryly. She wanted Coconut's attention on her at all times, and not her father.

"Good . . . But look, I wanted to tell you something," Coconut said, leaning in. "You know I been fucking with David on the side, right?" Farah shook her head. "Girl, yes, and he has the biggest dick you ever seen in your life. I sucked it earlier today at school and he gave me fifty bucks."

"Ain't he Jake's best friend?" Farah took the comb from Coconut and said, "You want me to scratch your scalp?"

"You know I do. Anyway . . . so what he's his best friend? He ain't gonna tell him and neither am I."

Farah shook her head. In her opinion her boyfriend, Jake, was perfect. He was attractive, on the football team, had his own car, and he gave her money. What more did she want? "I don't see how you do that."

"What? Suck dick?" She laughed. "Hold up, you never gave a blowjob before?"

"I haven't even fucked nobody yet." Farah scratched her scalp harder, the way she liked it.

Coconut laughed and said, "You use the word 'fuck' so freely . . . I mean, you sure you ain't do it yet?" Farah shook her head again. "Park allow that shit? For you to hold out on him with the pussy?"

"Park ain't got no choice. But I jerk him off, though." Farah wasn't into Park that much because in her dreams, the ones she wrote on paper, he didn't fit the bill.

"I hope you ain't holding out waiting for that dark Superman nigga you be talking about all the time, because he ain't real."

Farah laughed. "I said I want him super strong, not Superman." She sighed. "And Park not real either . . . at least not with me. I mean, I like him, but not enough to have sex with him. Not right now anyway."

"Wow. What a lucky guy." She laughed. "Anyway, don't say anything to Park about me fucking David, because if it gets out, I'll know you the one who said it."

Farah was insulted. "I ain't doing no shit like that to you. You're my cousin."

"Play cousin," she corrected her. "Now where is Rhonda and Natasha? I thought they were coming over. Jake and Park said they have some friends who gonna be at that party tonight, and we need more girls."

Farah lied to Rhonda about the party earlier, because she couldn't go and she didn't want Rhonda and Natasha to be around Coconut alone. She worked so hard to win her friendship that she was afraid if they did real fun stuff together without her, Coconut wouldn't want her around anymore. Brownie's strictness was the main reason Farah couldn't wait to get that apartment with Coconut they always talked about.

Ever since her grandmother told her that if she wrote her desires, hopes, and dreams on paper they would all come true, she was religious with her writing. And there were three things she wrote about every day: to have Coconut as a friend no matter what; to meet the dark-skinned, extra-strong man who would love her for eternity; and to rid herself of the sickness that had plagued her life. She was so close to having her dreams come true that she didn't want to lose them like this, so she had to clean up her mess quick.

"I ain't wanna tell you, but Rhonda and Natasha be hating on us, because we light skinned and they not. I heard them talking about it today at school. They were popping all kinds of shit in the cafeteria, like it's our fault we were born this way," Farah lied, combing her hair. "You should not have even invited them."

Coconut glared. "Rhonda and Natasha never acted like that around me. I been cool with them for years. I'm about to call them right now."

For fear of getting caught in a lie, Farah dropped the comb and broke out in tears. She had practice on how to fake it since she sobbed on a regular basis to get Brownie's attention. "See . . . I knew you wouldn't believe me. That's why I ain't wanna tell you. Now you gonna ask them and everybody gonna be mad at me again. I'ma just go home."

Coconut got up and hugged her. "I'm not gonna say nothing." Farah pouted. "Seriously. Me and you way closer than I am with them now. You here like every day. You family for real."

Farah shook her head. "Naw . . . you don't wanna be my friend. I'ma just go home."

"I do wanna be your friend." She hugged her tighter. "Please don't leave . . . Park and Jake on the way over, and I don't want to be by myself." Farah looked like she was still upset. "You my best friend now, and anything we say between each other is kept here. Let's keep it light, okay?" she said, quoting her favorite phrase as usual.

They separated from the embrace. "Thank you." She smiled. "I just want us to always be close. That's all I ever wanted."

"Then you got it . . . but you gotta calm down. Sometimes you do too much, Farah."

"I'll try."

Before Coconut could respond, Sherry knocked on the door. "Come in, Ma." She sighed.

"Sorry to bother you again, but your company is here." In walked Park and Jake. In this instance Farah was right, because they both wanted to talk to the girls because of their lighter skin. When Sherry left, Park hugged Farah and gripped her ass while Coconut jumped on top of Jake and kissed him passionately on the mouth.

"I'm fucking the shit out of you tonight," Jake said, going under Coconut's dress and sticking his finger in her tight pussy. Coconut cooed and kissed him harder. After Farah's kiss was over, she and her boyfriend stood awkwardly in the room, looking at Coconut and Jake go at it. Farah started tugging on the bottom of the dress she wore due to nervousness. She knew at some point she would have to fuck Park if she wanted to keep him. She saw the way he looked at Coconut's body, and it hurt her feelings. As much as she loved her friend, she wasn't sure if she could trust her around him.

After the longest kiss Farah had ever witnessed, Coconut said, "Me and Jake gonna see if we can get some weed and E pills. Y'all can stay in my room. If y'all fool around do it on top of my sheets. I don't want no cum on my bed." Farah frowned. "When we come back we gonna all roll to the party together."

When she and Jake left, Farah walked to Coconut's mirror and swung her hair back and forth the way she saw her friend do it. Park watched her from the bed, enjoying the view. "I ain't know your ass was that fat," Park said. "You gonna make me come lick that mothafucka in a minute."

Farah turned around, leaned up against the dresser, and raised her skirt. "Is that so?"

"Yep . . . So when you gonna let me hit?"

He stepped up to the dresser and she sauntered away from him. To play off his embarrassment he grabbed one of Coconut's perfume bottles and began sniffing the tops. "If you worrying about me hurting you when we have sex, don't. I'ma be easy."

Farah heard his voice but couldn't make out the words. All she was thinking about was that if he sprayed the perfume, she might end up in the hospital. In order to keep her illness in check, she had to stay away from everything young women loved. From makeup to scented soaps; if it smelled pretty, she avoided it at all costs. "Come over here," Farah ordered. "Put Coconut's stuff down."

"If I come over there, you gonna make it worth my while?" He held on to the perfume bottle, as if he were using it as a weapon. She didn't tell anybody about her condition, for fear they would use it against her. But if he didn't set the bottle down, she had every intention of tackling him. "I ain't coming over there for nothing."

"It'll be worth your while . . ." she said, her heart rate increasing. He still hadn't placed the bottle on the dresser. Finally, after a few more seconds, he set it down and walked in her direction. "Come on, Park."

"You not fucking with my head, are you?"

"No, boy," she said in a honeyed voice.

Standing in front of her, he dropped his jeans and boxers. His forwardness scared her because she hoped her first time would be subtler. "I want you to suck it first." She swallowed her nervousness. "And I want you to stick your finger in my ass. I ain't gay or nothing. I just like it like that." Park went from seduction to instruction, as he told her what he wanted. He pressed his hard dick against her stiff lips but they wouldn't separate. His clear pre-cum oozed from the tip. "Open your mouth, Farah." He looked down at her and wished she stuck her finger in his asshole, and opened her mouth. The moment she did, Sherry walked into the room and Farah pushed Park back so hard he fell to the floor before rustling to pull up his pants. Sherry slammed the door.

Farah wiped her soiled finger on Coconut's bed and said, "Mrs. Sherry . . . I . . . I . . ."

"I'm sorry, Farah. I didn't know you kids were busy," she said from the outside of the room. "Your sister and brother are here to see you. They say it's important."

Overcome with embarrassment, Farah pulled herself together and said, "Park, I'll see you later." Running toward the door, she tripped over one of Coconut's shoes. "I gotta go."

Once out of the room she passed Sherry, who avoided eye contact with her, as she sat on the living room sofa. When she opened the front door, she saw Shadow and Mia standing in the hallway. The looks on their faces scared her and she knew right away something was wrong. Once the door closed Farah asked, "Is Grandma okay?"

"She good, but we gotta go talk in the car," Mia said.

"Yeah . . . This a family matter not to be discussed in the hallway," Shadow added.

When she got to the car, she saw Chloe sitting in the back seat, crying her eyes out. Brownie was in the driver's seat, and since Mia and Shadow got in the back with Chloe, she was forced to sit in the front with her mother. "Farah . . . tonight is gonna be the night you prove yourself to me, and the rest of the family." She pointed a finger in her face. "I heard about you not fighting at school, and letting people jump in your face when they talk about your illness," she said in a spiteful voice. "One time I even heard you cried." Farah looked at Shadow, who held his head down. She knew the incident well. It happened a month earlier and she confided in her brother. Now she was thinking it was a big mistake. "But there comes a time in your life when you gotta step up. And tonight is that night. No more crying, no more hiding, and no more being weak. This is it, Farah.

"Now, your baby sister was raped an hour ago."

Farah gasped and said, "By who?"

"Theo."

Farah couldn't wrap her mind around what she was saying. She knew Theo and Chloe were seeing each other, despite what they did to him behind the school, but she vowed to keep their secret. Chloe always seemed to want the men she had. It bothered her at first because she and Theo were so close at one point, and she wondered why he didn't choose her. But life and new friends got in the way and after a while, she didn't care. Besides, when she wrote her story she saw a dark-skinned, strong man, and Theo was neither. Farah certainly didn't think he would ever hurt her sister.

"Now we gotta finish what we started two years ago with him." Farah's heart rate increased, knowing something terrible was coming. "We don't play that shit when it comes to our family, and you know it." Brownie looked at her kids and continued, "So, I want y'all to go into his house, and stab his ass to death." She reached in a brown paper bag and handed them knives. When Farah didn't take hers, Brownie frowned. "Fuck is wrong with you?"

Farah looked at the knife and said, "I don't wanna do this."

"What you mean you don't wanna do this? I just told you that little fucker raped your baby sister." Farah turned around and looked at Chloe, who looked out of the window. "Even she putting in work and you telling me you afraid?"

Farah took the knife. She had done everything she could to make Brownie love her, and to get attention. From serving her breakfast in bed, which she'd always ungratefully eat without so much as a thank you, to swallowing chemicals, knowing she would end up in the hospital. In the end the only thing Brownie wanted to see was bloodshed. "Farah. I need you to toughen up."

"But I'm not like y'all." She looked at all of them. "I don't like hurting people."

Everyone in the car sighed, right before Brownie grabbed the knife out of Farah's hand and jabbed it into the vinyl seat between her legs. Farah pushed back into the seat as Brownie moved the knife toward her vagina slowly. "You ain't no better than us, RedBone. You better recognize that shit." She huffed. "Now are you with us or not?"

Looking at her siblings, and not wanting to let them down, she said, "Yes, Mamma."

Brownie removed the knife from the vinyl seat, and handed it back to her with the blade in her direction. "Good."

"How we gonna get in?" Shadow asked, eager as always to put in work.

"After he raped her, he wouldn't let her leave. But she convinced him she wouldn't tell anybody. For two hours he begged her not to say nothing.

Eventually the little bastard let her go, after Chloe said she'd be back with some food, so the door should be open." Brownie looked at her watch.

"He'll be expecting her back in the next fifteen minutes. So we gotta move now."

Farah sat in her seat quietly. She belonged to a family of savages, and it bothered her terribly. She knew they often did things in secrecy, in the middle of the night without her. Most times they would creep out, and not so much as nudge her. She'd reasoned that before long the moment would come when she would be forced to participate. Now that the moment arrived, she realized she wasn't ready.

When they made it to Dinette's apartment building, Brownie and the children crept slowly up the stairs. "Y'all go in, and I'll come in about fifteen minutes," Brownie ordered.

Chloe turned the knob knowing it would open and walked into the apartment. Her siblings followed. When Chloe walked up to a door in the hallway she whispered, "It's this one right here."

Mia was the first to open the door. The light from the television illuminated the room, revealing someone sleeping under a thick, dark blanket. Shadow, Chloe, and Mia all walked into the bedroom and surrounded the bed. Looking at one another, smiles dressed their faces as one by one they took turns stabbing at the mound. When a woman's voice yelled out in pain, Farah was shocked to see that it was Dinette instead of Theo under the covers. She knew right away that they lied to get her to participate in the crime. Farah dropped the knife and was preparing to run out of the room when she bumped into her mother. Brownie smiled slyly, and walked into the room to taunt the woman she'd hated for so long.

Years would pass before Farah would learn the real events leading up to that night. Theo was staying at a friend's house, and Tommy had left her last year. If they were going to do anything, it had to be tonight. Herbert, the project's maintenance man, gave Brownie a key to Dinette's apartment for fifty bucks to buy some dope. It was easier than Brownie could've ever imagined. After all those years, Brownie never got over her suspicions that she fucked Ashur. Loving the color of blood, she finally sought revenge.

Farah knew the moment she left that room that life would never be the same for her, and she was right.

# Chapter 11

## *Present Day Mooney's House*

Mooney sat in the window and stared at the empty field. She wondered where everyone was, because there was usually activity in front of the building at all times. When there was a knock at the door she rubbed her elbow, stood up, and opened it wide. Melinda and Cutie Tudy were standing outside with attitudes on their faces. Cutie had her hands crossed over her chest, in typical brat fashion, and her ghetto foster mother was chewing gum like a cow.

"You mind watching her, Mooney?" Melinda asked between a few gum pops. She was a hustler's dream. She had a flat stomach, phat ass, and a mouth wetter than the Nile. She was dipped in diamonds and platinum and her face was massaged a little too heavily with red blush. "She ain't allowed to be by herself for a while, since she don't know how to act." She looked down at Cutie and tugged her ear.

"Ow, Ma!" Cutie responded, hitting her hand. "Stop that shit!"

"Shut the fuck up!" she yelled down at her. "Anyway"— she smiled faker than a Gucci purse spelled with a C—"she fought that little black bitch upstairs and now they can't be together because they social workers involved." Melinda started wrestling through her Louis Vuitton purse as she continued to talk. "These kids trying to get my checks stopped . . . I swear to God." Removing a five dollar bill from her purse she said, "Here, use this if she needs something to eat."

Mooney looked at the short money and said, "Naw . . . you can keep that. I have stuff to make sandwiches, and if she don't want that, I'll order a pizza." Melinda stuffed the bill back in her purse so fast she almost punched a hole in the bottom.

"Ma, you said I could watch myself," Cutie whined. "I wanted to go outside and play with my friends. Plus my boyfriend gonna be outside today."

"Until they take that jealous bitch out of my house, and her twin, I gotta keep y'all separated. You heard them peoples. I know how you are when you go out, Cutie. You be out there running your mouth nonstop, and then you get thirsty and wanna come in the house to drink up my wine coolers." She continued with her hands on her hips, "That girl and her sister are up there now, so I don't need you fucking with them."

"But why I gotta be the one to leave my house?"

"'Cause you told me last night you liked Mooney."

"Ma! I didn't say that shit!" Cutie was so embarrassed she wanted to faint.

"Yes, you did, now go on in there." She pushed her inside. "And when I get some money from my sugar daddy, I'll come back and get you."

Cutie's eyes lit up. "Can you tell sugar daddy to buy me a new phone like he promised?"

"Only if you good." Melinda switched away without another word.

Cutie stomped toward the couch and Mooney closed and locked the door. The moment she sat down she dug in her coat pocket and pulled out her phone. Mooney quietly ambled toward the recliner by the window. Although Mooney was irritated, this was the most excitement she had in a long time. As she looked outside, she could feel Cutie's eyes rolling over her, but she didn't acknowledge her existence. Yesterday she spent two hours telling her part of a story she knew she had to hear the conclusion to . . . even though it was a long ways coming.

After about thirty minutes of silence, Cutie said, "Why you ain't got no TV in here? Dang! It's boring as shit in your house."

Mooney looked at Little Miss Rudeness and said, "Hello to you too."

Cutie rolled her eyes. "I'm serious. You done got me in trouble, and now I gotta come over here. I was fine when I was watching myself."

Mooney corrected her. "You got your own self in trouble by lying on your sister." She looked out the window. "Hopefully one day you'll learn to tell the truth."

Cutie sighed. "That bitch is not my sister!" she said in a sassy tone. "I mean, the least you could do is tell me the rest of the story. Dang!"

"Is that your way of asking me to finish?" Cutie ignored her and played with her phone. "Before I do that, tell me what happened when you went home last night. With your foster sister."

"What you think happened? She stayed out of my fucking way."

"You didn't apologize?"

"For fucking what?" she asked with her jaw hung. "It ain't like she dead. We just performed *Stomp* on that ass."

Mooney lit a cigarette and said, "Let's make a deal: if you like the next part of the story, you have to apologize to her tonight. Cool?"

Cutie smirked and for the sake of boredom said, "Yeah . . . okay." Mooney sat back in her seat and said, "Farah went through many stages before she changed into something so horrible, at first it was unbelievable. She had violent people in her life she looked to for love and acceptance, so it was inevitable the way things turned out."

"What about that boyfriend Farah wanted? The one who was gonna be real strong and love her forever. I think you called him Superman! I mean, I know she had that other boy Park . . . but I ain't like him."

Mooney was secretly pleased the girl knew their names, because it meant she was paying attention. "If you hear nothing else I say, hear this . . . you will always attract a mate who personifies who you are. If you're a gold-digger you gonna get a drug dealer who thinks he can buy you. If you hate yourself, you gonna get a nigga who will kick your ass every day and six times on Monday. And if you violent, you're gonna attract a monster. It will always be true. All the time. No exceptions."

# Chapter 12

## *Seven Years Later*

**"I come from a family
of murderers." —Farah**

"Girl, if I show up dead tomorrow, Raping Randy did that shit!" Farah yelled into her cell phone as she maneuvered down an icy DC street in the silver Benz Randy bought her last year. The snowstorm was unmerciful and the window wipers did little to clear her view. Her eyes moved rapidly between the rearview mirror and the road ahead, as she struggled to get away from her crazed ex-boyfriend. "Oh, my God! He's about to hit me again!"

*Clank. Clank!*

Randy's black Escalade hit the back of her Benz twice, causing the bumper to droop a little. Farah's car fishtailed but she was able to regain control. "I don't wanna die, Coconut!" He showed no signs of letting up anytime soon and it was obvious that he either wanted her dead or at a massive standstill.

When he was close enough, he hit her again and the bumper hung off a little more. "I'm scared." She wiped the snot and tears off of her face with the back of her hand.

"He's gonna finally do it! I shoulda left his ass alone when I had the chance!"

"I thought you did! You know how crazy Randy is! That nigga not all together, Farah!" Coconut screamed into the phone. She wasn't saying the right shit in Farah's opinion.

She needed encouragement and Coconut failed miserably. "And what happened to the restraining order you put on him?"

"I don't know, bitch! Maybe he ate it!" Farah said sarcastically. "I just wish he'd leave me alone! I haven't fucked him in, like, six months," she lied. Although she told her best friend one story, she knew the truth was nowhere near it. When she was with Randy life was good, as long as he wasn't roughing her up in the bedroom. It was because of that reason that she dumped him two years ago.

Before she ever dated Randy, Farah was starting to believe all her dreams were coming true. Coconut was officially her best friend and she was well liked in school. The only things missing in her life were the fact that the disease she hosted was still incapacitating at times, and she didn't have in her life the strong, dark-skinned man who reminded her of Ashur. So when Randy approached her at the club on her eighteenth birthday, while she was celebrating with her friends, she couldn't believe her luck. He was rich, powerful, and dark chocolate, all the things she thought she wanted. Before long Randy took her virginity, gave her everything she wanted in life, and then, when the time was right, showed her his darker side in the bedroom. Farah quickly realized she couldn't handle it.

After she left Randy, she wasn't single for long, because a few months later she ran into Zone Miller. He was a dark-skinned brother who had a passion for red bones with fat pink pussies and round asses. Farah fit the bill perfectly. It didn't take him long to make her wifey and to lace her up in the finest gear. Stuff was going great between Farah and Zone, and she didn't think life could get sweeter. Zone wasn't as demanding as Randy in the bedroom; he didn't need to beat her, choke her, or spit in her face to bust a nut. Instead he spoiled her rotten, flaunted her around the city, and put her up in Platinum Loft apartments: the flyest complex in her old stomping grounds. It was still smack dab in the middle of the hood, the place she lived all her life. DC was on the verge of a rejuvenation project, and if you didn't have the cash to support the move, you would get moved out.

Every now and again, Randy would call when she was with Zone, but she never stepped outside of the relationship. Farah considered Randy a pest until Zone got locked up for being caught with a few ounces of cocaine. Suddenly Randy's calls weren't so worrisome anymore. She was willing to do anything to prevent moving back with Brownie, even if that meant giving Randy a little violent pussy from time to time. For the entire year while Zone was incarcerated, Randy laced her up and paid her rent. He even splurged and bought her a Benz, provided they could get down the way he liked it in the bedroom. Things went smooth until Zone was released from prison on a technicality.

Farah continued to fuck Randy on the low, until Zone started hearing things in the neighborhood. He immediately checked the situation, and demanded she straighten up or bounce. A few days ago, Farah decided to comply, after she got one last payday from Randy. This time the money wasn't for designer shoes or purses. She was awful with money but she had plans to use this cash for a purpose. She needed $1,600 to give to Grand Mike, a holistic practitioner who could help her with her illness. She'd gotten the name from her cousin Cosmo, who was locked up for multiple homicides. However, Grand Mike was strict with his schedule, saying, "You miss the appointment, you miss your chance."

Tears rolled down her face as she tried to reach her destination without him tailing her. Her nails dug into the steering wheel and she feared for her life. *Please don't kill me,* she thought. *I don't wanna die.*

"Where you going anyway, Farah? I mean, maybe you should pull over and call the police." Farah was so delirious that she forgot Coconut was on the phone.

"I can't do that!" she screamed. "I got somewhere to be."

"I sure hope wherever you gotta be is worth dying for," Coconut said. "'Cause if it was me, I'd have that nigga locked up with the quickness."

"Bitch, you making shit worse! I'll call you back!" Farah ended the call and threw her iPhone on the passenger seat.

Their relationship had changed drastically over the years because Farah was different. She was more outspoken and she'd formed a tougher layer inside and out. Her relationship with Brownie—after she smeared shit over her face, and after learning the coach was her biological father—changed her for the worse. She started avoiding Brownie most times, and Mia took over her motherly responsibilities. From the background Elise would do the best she could to instill values in Farah, but as the years rolled by, she was so far gone that her grandmother's words bored her to death. It was Mia who she looked up to, and it was also Mia who toughened her up. Farah was no longer afraid of fighting, although she preferred not to because it brought out emotions. Farah's motto was to keep your game face on, and protect your feelings at all times; that way nobody could hurt you. That one trait made her appealing to people because she was aloof. Although she changed, two things remained the same: she was still obsessed with her looks, and she was still obsessed with Coconut's friendship.

When her phone rang she looked at the passenger seat.

Randy's name flashed on the screen. When she looked in the rearview mirror, he waved his phone, indicating he wanted her to answer. Hoping she could talk some sense into him, she picked up the phone and accepted the call. "Randy, why are you doing this to me?" Snot ran out of her nose and entered her mouth. "You gonna kill me. You gotta keep it light and relax." Farah had stolen Coconut's quote, and virtually ran in into the ground by using it every day. She said it so much that Coconut now hated the phrase.

Real calmly he said, "You think you can take my money and blow me off like I'm some bimbo-ass nigga? Bitch, I will kill you first." His words caused her head to throb and she could feel an outbreak coming on. Farah threw the phone on the seat again, and focused back on the road. Randy was uncompromising.

She looked down in her lap and picked up a small piece of white paper. Holding the note in her hand, she examined the address upon it. It was of the man who could save her life. If only she could get rid of her ex-boyfriend, things would be okay. Spotting a police officer, who was giving a ticket to a man in a green Ford Expedition, she pulled over and parked behind them. Randy, seeing this, crept slowly past her and gave her an evil look. From her frosted window she could see him mouth, "It ain't over, bitch," right before he sped out of sight. He hated cops and she was counting on it. When she felt Randy was far enough away, she took a few moments to catch her breath before pulling back into traffic.

Fifteen minutes later she was in front of a dilapidated brick building. Her temples throbbed terribly and her stomach churned. Gas escaped her body, spraying the scent of rotten eggs throughout the car. This was the moment she'd been waiting for. Parked, she looked at the paper in her hand again before her eyes rolled over the run-down dwelling. She couldn't imagine anything of value being inside, but this was her last hope. Before getting out and battling the winter storm, she zipped her black leather jacket, and adjusted the rearview mirror to look at herself. Although makeup hid most of the marks on her face from a recent outbreak she'd endured, it wasn't good enough. Her light complexion would only get worse if something didn't give.

Taking a deep breath, she grabbed her phone and stuffed it in her jacket pocket. Then she snatched her large brown Gucci purse out of the back seat, and placed her hand on the door handle. Before getting out, she checked her surroundings to be sure Randy wasn't lingering around, because the last thing she needed was him running up on her. When she was sure the coast was clear, she moved toward the building and her black Ugg boots trudged through six inches of recently fallen snow.

Once at the building, she pulled on the door's cold handle, but it wouldn't open. Her brown eyes peered through the wired window, looking for anyone. It was dark inside and she wondered if she was at the right place. She checked the address, stepped back, and looked up at the numbers on the building. They matched. Thinking she didn't use enough force, she pulled the door's handle again, and again it didn't open. She was carrying $1,600 that belonged to him, provided he was able to give her the help she needed. She was so desperate to look normal that she was willing to part with such a large sum of cash without having seen any results. Her beauty was more important to her than air filling her lungs. This illness was inconvenient and extremely painful, and she would give anything to be done with it all together.

*Bang! Bang! Bang!* She knocked heavily at the locked door. *Bang! Bang! Bang!*

"Let me in!" she screamed. "Open this fucking door!" She pulled on the handle again, and although the door rattled loudly, it wouldn't budge.

The temperature was well below twenty degrees, yet the hypoallergenic makeup on her face began to streak from sweat pouring off her forehead. It tickled her skin, causing her to wipe it away along with some of her makeup. He was her last hope. She'd seen what the illness did to her mother, and how it made her look like a monster, forcing her to live miserable and alone. Dr. Martin promised that if she followed his orders her condition would get better, but nothing he did seemed to work. He was a liar and she was tired of hearing his fucking mouth. At the rate her illness was progressing, it would eat at her face so much that after a while she would be able to do nothing but play a role in a horror film.

Crying heavily she turned around, and her back fell against the metal door before the seat of her True Religion jeans slapped against the icy, wet step. When her phone rang it startled her and she pulled it out of her jacket pocket. It was Chloe. Farah reluctantly answered. "Yes, Chloe?"

"When are you coming home? I wanted to come over so I can borrow your pink shoes."

"Girl, I'm busy right now. Plus it's snowing and I'm outside. I don't want my phone to get wet."

"Ugh . . . I hate when you act like a bitch!" Chloe hung up. Farah wiped the wetness off her phone and tucked it back inside her leather jacket. Tears fell from her eyes, and snowflakes fell onto her face before melting against her warm skin. All was lost, and she resigned to the fact that she may end up like her mother, partially confined to bed and lonely. She was just about to stand up and go home when a black man in a wheelchair opened the door, causing her body to fall inside. His face was dark and ashy and he didn't have any teeth in his mouth. The hair on his head was thick and wooly, and pieces of lint were littered throughout it.

"Was that you banging on the door? Like you lost your mind?"

Farah jumped up, brushed the snow off the back of her wet jeans, and smiled. "Yes, I'm . . . sorry. But I'm here to see . . ." She searched for the piece of paper with the address, which she'd slept with for two days in a row. When she spotted it on the wet ground, she picked it up and tried to read the blue ink, which was now smeared. It wasn't like she didn't know his name. She'd remembered it along with the address, although at the moment her memory escaped her. "Grand Mike. That's his name. Do you know him?"

"I know him. The name's Dexter," he responded as if asking, "you got his money?"

She dug in her purse and pulled out a white bank envelope. "It's right here." Her fingers trembled and the cash almost plummeted from her hands.

"Give it to me." He reached out for the envelope.

She snatched it back. "Uh . . . if you don't mind, I'd really like to see him first."

He rolled his eyes. "Well, come in. I ain't got all fucking day!"

She was just about to put one foot over the threshold when she spotted roaches crawling all over the hallway floor and walls. Bugs of any kind repulsed her so much that she would often have panic attacks that would result in an outbreak. Sensing she wasn't behind him, he turned his wheelchair around and faced her. "Are you coming in or not?"

"Huh?" Her eyes looked at his, and then at the bugs moving around as if they ran the place. "What you say?"

Insensitive about the fear in her eyes he gave it to her straight. "Look, you're already late! Don't take up more of my time with your shit! Now what you gonna do?"

"But I . . . I'm scared . . ." She pointed at the walls. "I never seen so many—"

"Leave now!" he interrupted her before he rolled toward the elevator.

"Wait!" She sobbed. "I'm . . . I'm coming." Farah walked in slowly and a bug fell off the ceiling and onto the floor in her pathway. "Ahh!" she screamed, jumping around, shaking her hair and tugging at her clothes. "Did it fall on me?" Dexter shook his head, laughed, and hit the button for the elevator. When it dinged and opened, Farah dodged inside, and waited impatiently for the doors to close.

When the elevator doors shut, he looked up at her and said, "You must not be from DC."

"I am," she said, "and I ain't never see no shit like this before." She looked around the elevator, which seemed less harmful than the hallway.

He laughed. "You do know they more afraid of us than we are of them, don't you?"

When the elevator dinged and opened on the second floor, every muscle in her body tensed as she prayed a bug wouldn't fall on her. So many roaches crawled around the floor that they looked like patterns against the grey tiles. Spiders in their silky webs hung in the corners of the ceilings and chips of brown paint barely clung to the walls. When he rolled out of the elevator, she ran behind him and the bugs crunched under her feet like potato chips. When they approached apartment 216, her heart thumped in her chest, as she hoped Grand Mike would open the door before she panicked and passed out. Instead of knocking, Dexter removed a gold key from his funky brown boot, and opened the door to an apartment so gruesome and squalid that she was starting to believe that the holistic practitioner couldn't possibly live there.

Still, she followed him inside. "Wait over there," Dexter said, pointing at an area not too far from the door. "I'll go get him." The door slammed behind her and she examined it, wondering if she could leave if she desired. Her eyes roamed over a red couch with dirt on the armrests, and a blue rug with so many stains on it that it resembled unorganized leopard spots. Fifteen minutes later a tall, dark-skinned black man exited a room and walked slowly toward her. He was wearing a white T-shirt and his ashy elbows looked like someone had rubbed chalk on them, like the tip of a pool stick.

"Are you Farah Cotton?" he asked.

She noticed that, just like Dexter, he didn't have any teeth, and she figured they must be crack addicts. She doubted his skills seriously at this point, and would've run back out the door if her cousin didn't swear that he had what she needed. "Yes. I'm Farah."

"I see your face is bad. You had an outbreak recently?"

"Yes." She swallowed. "A few days ago."

"So you really need me, don't you?"

She placed her hand softly on her cheek, realizing the makeup must be coming off. "Yes. I do."

"Well, you've come to the right place. Next time be on time because every second of my life is precious and I waste it for no one," he said, examining the authentic silver Rolex watch on his arm. "Not even you."

"I'm sorry." She felt awkward. "But you wouldn't believe what I went through to get here. I came as fast as I could."

"You got my shit?"

"Yes." Farah imbibed the clumpy phlegm that formed in her throat.

He held out his hand. "Give it to me."

She gave him the money and he counted it in front of her. When he reached the last bill he smiled slyly, looked up at her, and said, "It's all here. Make yourself comfortable."

*Yeah, right.*

He pointed at the sofa. "Over there."

Farah slogged toward the dirty couch, and her body sank into the cushion. It was in bad condition and she wanted to stand, but was too scared to move. Roaches crawled around her wet Ugg boots and she cringed. *Please, God. Please don't let them crawl on me.* She stomped her feet a few quick times and they scurried out of her way. The filthiness of his place was killing her. Grand Mike moved toward a room on the opposite end of the door he exited, and Dexter rolled back into the living room and smiled at Farah. His grin was out of place, considering he'd cursed her just minutes earlier.

When Grand Mike knocked on another door within the apartment, a white woman opened it. She had on a pair of Tony the Tiger scrubs and she smiled awkwardly at Farah. Not knowing what else to do, Farah smiled back. When the door opened wider, she saw a young black girl sitting on a hospital bed. She seemed zoned out and high and Farah wondered if she had the same illness. Grand Mike walked inside the room, and closed the door behind him. *What the fuck is going on?* she thought. *Who are these people really?*

Twenty minutes later, Grand Mike reappeared with a white cooler in his hands. "This is enough for a six-month supply." Farah stood up and walked toward him. "Contact me a month before you run out, because I have to prepare what you need in advance."

"What is it?"

One of his eyebrows raised. "What exactly are you asking me?"

"I mean . . . . I'm asking, what you giving me?"

"Something to clear up your complexion and keep your disease at bay. Ain't that what you came for?"

"Yes."

"Okay then." He gave a toothless grin. "And don't bother telling your doctor about this, because he'll tell you it won't work. And if I find out you told him anything about me, I may be liable to come looking for you. You understand what I'm saying?"

He handed her the cooler. "Take it once a day by mouth." He looked at Dexter, who rolled up next to them. "If you come here and I'm not available, Dexter here can help you." She looked down at him. "You'll have to get some dry ice to keep it cold and it has to remain chilled." He handed her a card. "You can buy your dry ice from this place, because it's hard to find. Any questions?"

She tucked the card in her purse. "Does this really work?"

He laughed, revealing his toothless grin once more. "If you believe in it, it will."

She didn't understand why he was being so secretive. If her cousin hadn't told her about his services, she wouldn't be standing in front of him, so somebody had to tell her something. Although her illness was rare, it wasn't illegal. So what, she decided to go through unconventional means to get help? Her doctor's medicine and orders were not working. She had to do what was best for her and she hoped it would work.

Farah rushed through the hallway of the Platinum Loft apartments, her icy-cold hands carrying the cooler tightly, for fear it would fall and break. Finally, after so many years, she had an answer to the rare disease. "Porpia," she said, "I won't have to worry about you for much longer." Her heart was filled with hope and excitement and that alone was worth the money.

Holding the cooler in her left hand, she rustled through her purse for the key to her apartment. Tonight would be special now that she was in a pleasant mood. If Zone wanted, Farah was going to allow him to stick his dick in every hole in her body. When he was done she would prepare baked chicken, cheddar cheese spinach, and buttered rice, just the way he liked it. Locating the key, she placed it in the keyhole and turned the knob. A smile spread across her face as she searched for her man inside their lavish apartment. When she spotted him sitting across the room at the computer, she felt warm and tingly inside. That was, until she was dumbstruck as she witnessed him in a world of his own. His back faced her direction, but she saw the pinkness of a woman's slick vagina in HD on the computer screen. Her fingers went in and out of her pussy as she cooed and moaned. Zone responded to the cyber show he was receiving by beating his stiff penis. She walked into the apartment and the door closed softly behind her as she placed the cooler against the wall.

"Open your legs wider," Zone instructed. "And put all five fingers in your pussy at one time."

"Whatever you want," the voice said, coming from the speakers.

The girl's chocolate legs widened, which exposed more of her fleshy mound. Zone stroked himself harder, and he was on the verge of cumming until he sensed he wasn't alone. Jumping up, he stuffed his penis back in his boxers and pulled his blue jeans up from the floor. Running his hand through his black curly hair, he searched for a reasonable explanation. After all, they'd been together for years and she was helping support them. Sure she cheated on Zone by fucking Randy for some dough, but it wasn't like the dude had concrete proof. Rumors loomed in the hood every day.

"Baby, I'm . . . I'm . . . sorry. I didn't know you were home," he said, moving in her direction.

Farah's eyes were glued to the screen, and she noticed something that caused her heart to ache. There, on the woman's inner thigh, was a diamond ring tattoo that read: a Guy's Best FRiend. The thigh belonged to her nineteen-year-old sister, Chloe. *Was this the reason that bitch wanted to know when I was coming home?*

"Zone, where you at?" Chloe asked. Her pretty, deep chocolate face finally came into view on the screen. "I can't see you. Step back in front of the camera." Chloe squinted until she saw her sister. "Oh, my God! Farah, I'm so—"

Hearing her voice, Farah immediately ran up to the computer and turned off the screen. Tears rolled down her face and she looked at him, hoping he'd give her answers. It was the first time she showed emotion to a man, and as far as she was concerned it would be her last. Although she was devastated, it was mainly because of Chloe's betrayal. They were sisters and she loved her very much. Zone wasn't the first person Chloe went at who belonged to her. In Farah's opinion the treachery started with Theo.

She focused on his beautiful dark skin, low right eye, and lips that were black from years of weed smoking. He wasn't perfect by any means, or the man in her stories, but she was starting to care about him. With a little time and a lot of money, she could even see herself falling for Zone. She always favored the underdog, and any man who made a come up because she was in his life was bound to appreciate her even more.

"I ain't fucking with her no more, baby." He walked up to her and massaged her shoulders. "That shit didn't mean nothing too me. You know how freaky your baby sister is. We had a bet she wouldn't do no shit like that, and she did.

She won, babes." He laughed. "Now I owe her fifty bucks."

"Fifty bucks?" Her tone was flat.

He made an unexpected crinkly grin. "It was just a joke. I promise." He was lying and she knew it. She remembered the day Chloe walked out of their bathroom after taking a shower, with water drops beading all over her chocolate skin. Lust was in his eyes that night, and she knew having her around and in her home was risky for their relationship. Chloe was everything Farah wasn't: dark skin and freaked out.

"Talk to me, Farah," Zone said. His eyes moved over her face, arms, and legs, and it was clear he was trying to read her. The silence poked at his guilt and caused his jaw to flex. "Every time we get into a fight, you space the fuck out." He stepped away from her as he flipped the tables around on her so hard, Farah didn't know what was happening. "Bitch, are you listening to me? Are you even here?" Zone was livid at the cool way in which she handled the matter, partly because he was guilty and also because if she didn't lash out, he felt she didn't love him. Farah always acted like this whenever they got into fights so nothing was new. Often times he'd go outside and punch at the impenetrable walls in the hallway until his hands were sore. The only time he saw Farah emotional was when she was beefing with Coconut.

"The only time you react is when that bitch is involved. You sure you ain't fucking Coconut?" When she heard his words, she clapped her eyelids together a few times, looked at the floor, and then back at him. She didn't want to respond to such a ridiculous accusation. Although she was obsessed with the friendship, she didn't want to be with a woman exclusively. The mere idea repulsed her, and she knew he knew that.

"You want something to eat?" She cupped her palms together. "I can fry you some chicken. Maybe make some of that brown rice you like after I shower."

Farah acted as if nothing happened and already she was on to the next thing. Besides, being without Zone was not an option at the moment. She lived with him and although she'd been footing some of the bills—with the help of the blackmail money she took from her mother to keep the secret she learned about Coach Jaffrey, and the cash Randy gave her to dip into her pussy every now and again—it was still his place and she didn't want to go back home.

"You just walked in on some amazing fucking shit and that's all you got to say?"

"You're hungry, aren't you?" She smiled, ignoring his question. "I can wait to take my shower." She walked around him. "Let me cook your food first."

She kicked her shoes off, grabbed the cooler by the door, and walked into the spacious, upscale kitchen. She placed the cooler on the counter and opened the fridge to grab thawed chicken breasts. Not bothering to wash her dirty hands, she took the meat out of the package, and seasoned them the way Zone liked it, minus the dirt from under her fingernails. He was so shocked by her actions that he stood in her presence motionless. When the image of Chloe's waiting vagina danced around in her mind she said, "Baby, you mind turning on the music?"

"Farah, you not gonna say nothing about the shit you just saw?" He walked toward the kitchen. "Nothing at all?"

"What you want me to say?" she said as her dirty fingernails dug into the meat while she massaged in the seasonings. "You said it was a joke, so it was a joke." She shrugged. "I'm not gonna let that shit take any more of my time than it already has."

"So you don't care that it was Chloe?"

"It's not a big deal."

Thinking she wasn't tripping because she was still fucking Randy he asked, "Where were you?"

Farah was quiet. Zone had been with her all this time and she never told him about the illness she was born with, for fear it might turn him off. "I had to meet a friend." She flipped the chicken on the opposite side and seasoned it some more. "I would've been here sooner but there was an accident on the beltway," she lied as she appraised him with narrow eyes to see if he believed her. "Maybe I'll make you lemon drops, too. You really love that drink the girl Angel makes at the bar." She put the chicken in the pan. "If I go to the store now I can catch them before they close to get some fresh lemons." She remembered her bumper was about to fall off and said, "Or maybe I can ask our neighbors if they have any."

"You don't even fuckin' talk to our neighbors."

"There's a first time for everything." She smiled.

"You *really* don't give a fuck, do you?" Her mind raced as she tried to understand what he wanted from her. Essentially she was excusing his trifling-ass behavior by acting as if nothing happened, yet he was unsatisfied. She learned a long time ago to toughen up, after hearing it over and over from her family. Emotion would be wasted on this situation because what was done was done and at the end of the day she didn't like what she saw, but she wasn't gonna leave him, either. He was her escape now and until she came up with another plan, he would have to do.

"Farah, I'm not fucking around with you! We gotta talk about this shit!"

"You want sex? I can suck your dick. Would you like that?" She walked toward him. "I saw how hard you were when I first walked in. That's what you want, ain't it?"

He stared at her like she was crazy. Because at the moment she was. "You know what, I'm so sick of this weak shit."

"What do you want me to say, Zone? That I walked in on you beating your dick to my sister's wet pussy and my feelings are hurt?"

"That's a start."

"Well it *did* hurt, but I'm not gonna leave you. Anyway, you like red bitches." She giggled. "That was one of the first things you told me when we first met. So my sister's too black anyway. You tell me that all the time." She smirked. "What you wanna do, try something new so you can get it out your system? Is that it?" She walked closer to him. "We been together for a few years. Maybe you want to try dark meat. It's not a big deal. My grandmother told my mom every now and again a man likes something different. If you want, I can call her over so you can fuck her. I know she wants you, so we can get that shit out of the way. Just don't ask me to do it again when it's over."

Zone took a step back and said, "I'm done." He moved toward the computer to grab his keys, and stuffed his wallet in his front pocket. Through the large window she could see the snow coming down heavier. "When I get back, I want you out my crib."

"But my name is on the lease. You can't throw me out."

"Naw." He chuckled. "You signed a lease with me, ma, but you're not on my lease. I just did that shit so you could keep the apartment while I was locked up. Our arrangement expires next month. So instead of wasting my time, I want you to pack your shit and be out tomorrow."

"So you want to be with my sister now? Is that it?"

"Fuck no! It ain't even about that. It's about you and me not vibing." He looked at her seriously. "You been different since I been home from jail, and I'm hearing shit I don't like about you fucking Randy. That's probably the reason I can't get put on, and make no more paper in these streets. The nigga runs half of DC. So, like I said, pack your shit and kick rocks."

"Zone . . . I'm not mad at you . . . It's okay."

"Why don't you wanna fight for me?" She was silent as always and he laughed. "I know what it is: you so used to niggas sweating you because you red. Guess what, I don't give a fuck about none of that shit." He stepped closer. "If you really wanna know the truth, your pussy some trash anyway." She laughed, not believing him. "Naw, I'm being straight up. You can't fuck. If you don't believe me, ask the nigga Randy. I'm sure he'll keep it one hundred with you, since he lacing you up." He moved toward the closet, grabbed his brown leather coat, and eased it on. "Like I said, I want you out. I'm tired of your hair being all over my crib anyway."

"Where am I gonna go?"

"Move back with your mamma. It ain't my problem."

"I don't deserve this shit!" She put her hand over her heart. "The least you can do is tell me how you want me to be!"

"I wanted you to be strong. I wanted you to want this relationship. But you can't do that, can you? Because you don't give a fuck." He walked past her to grab a beer out of the fridge before moving toward the door again. "Who else but a bitch who don't care can walk in on something like that, and not say shit?"

She stood in place and looked at him. Her heart told her he was picking a fight to flip shit on her, but what could she do? If she had another place to stay she might've told him where to go and how to get there, but that was not the case.

Zone twisted the knob to the front door, preparing to walk out, when Farah started talking. "I come from a family of murderers. I never gave you my life story because I knew my last name was enough. Plus I didn't think you would deal with me if you knew the whole truth." He closed the door, turned around, and looked at her. "My father is in jail for killing a family all because their son scratched the paint on his car." Tears rolled out of her eyes heavily, but she was laughing. "My mother had us fight and hurt people just because she liked to see them cry and sometimes"—she looked into the distance—"we even killed."

She focused back on him. "I don't want to be that person anymore, Zone. I don't want to be the person I know I can be. So I let shit slide. That's why I don't argue with you a lot, or pick fights I know I can't win. But it don't mean I don't want to be with you." Her hands dropped to her sides. "And it don't mean you can leave me. Right now, I need you." She walked up to him. "You're all I got." Her lips curled into a semi-smile. "So put your keys down because you're not going anywhere. Okay?"

"*Right now* you need me?" He laughed. "What happens when the next nigga with more money comes along? What . . . you won't need me anymore then?"

She was no longer thinking straight, so the truth flew out of her mouth faster than a bullet. "When the next nigga with more money comes along, then I'm gone," she said flatly.

"But let's cross that block when we get there."

He walked over to the window, activated the automatic start on his BMW, and faced her. "Like I said, I want you out." The snow was coming down so hard it sounded as if sand were being thrown against the large-pane windows. He looked at her face and she didn't appear to be listening. "You heard me, bitch? Get your shit and get the fuck out by tomorrow."

She heard him that time. When she looked at his face, she saw the seriousness in his eyes. It was over and she felt it. The bottoms of her feet were sweaty, and her palms were soaked with perspiration. She was trying to push the anger down deep and let his rejection pass, but she couldn't. Who was he to dump her when he was in the wrong? As if someone threw down a red flag at a car race, her toes dug into the cream carpet fibers, and she charged toward him full speed ahead. Running indoor track throughout high school made her quick and agile. She ran so fast that the baby toe on her right foot cracked and broke. But pain was nonexistent for the moment.

When she reached him, both of her hands forcefully touched his chest. With extreme exertion, she pushed him toward the window and watched it fracture as his body pressed against the glass. Small shards covered his hair and face as he tumbled backward. He tried to reach out and stop his fall by gripping at the air but it wasn't working. His body twirled and whirled thirteen feet to his death. He died instantly.

With the window destroyed, the cold air rushed into the apartment and Farah rubbed her arms rapidly for warmth. Walking up to the window, her feet pressed against the broken glass as she looked around until she saw him. There his body lay, against the snow, with his eyes wide open. Seconds later the snow turned red as blood and life escaped him.

# Chapter 13

## *One Month Later*

**"Dumbness, you would fuck anybody. You don't give a fuck what they look like." —Farah**

Farah drove her car out of the Benz dealership, with the music pumping loudly. She just got it fixed, after the damage Randy had done to the bumper the night he chased her. Coconut, Rhonda, and Natasha were riding along so they could all get something to eat later from Mamma's Kitchen, a soul food spot in Washington DC. Her toe still hurt a little after being broken, but it was the first day she could really move around, so she wanted to have fun.

"Slow down, girl," Rhonda said from the back seat. "These roads slick as shit." She rubbed her pregnant belly.

"This my car. I don't need no back-seat drivers," she said, looking at her in the rearview mirror.

"Whatever. If you get into an accident, I'm suing the fuck out of your ass."

"Damn, I shoulda let that nigga suck my pussy," Coconut said while filing her nails in the passenger seat. "He looked like he knew what he was doing, too."

"First off, what about Jake?" Rhonda asked. "And, secondly, what dude you talking about? The one that was all up in Farah's face?"

"Naw . . . the nigga who stepped to me when we were leaving the dealership." Coconut's light skin was painted expertly with makeup. "And don't worry about Jake. We been together so long, no matter what I do he ain't going nowhere."

"Girl, please," Rhonda said. "That nigga wasn't even cute." She rubbed her belly. "If a nigga would've come up to me and said he wanted to lick my clit, I would've punched him in the mouth." Rhonda was still a pretty, dark-skinned girl, with long eyelashes and doe eyes. Even being five months pregnant she could run rings around her friends in the shape department. Rhonda was a black man's dream because she had just the right sized titties and ass. Too bad for them she was swept up in gangster love.

Coconut looked behind her and said, "Who cares about cute, when a nigga got loot?" She turned back around and fired up a blunt. "You saw the nigga's ride. He probably can buy a new face if he wanted to."

"Bitch, you wild as shit!" Rhonda laughed. "You're old and you still fucking cars and purses. I ain't fucked for purses in years. I'm good."

"Yeah, that's 'cause your nigga got you locked," Farah said, getting off the highway to go to the restaurant a few miles away. "From the moment you got with him you been hopelessly devoted."

"Whatever, bitch." Rhonda laughed. "Even if I wasn't taken, I still wouldn't fuck a nigga just because he got a nice ride. It ain't none of mine."

In a mousy voice from the back Natasha said, "He wasn't even that bad." Everyone looked at her. "The dude in the Maybach. I mean, I woulda fucked him too." Natasha's complexion was middle of the road. She wasn't as dark as Rhonda or as light as Farah and Coconut, and in the crew that made her stand out. The only thing about Natasha that fucked up her game was that she had really large titties and a flat ass. Her face was so cute that you would give her a pass, until her clothes came off and everything drooped. She was known around the hood to some as The Illusion.

From the driver's seat Farah said, "Dumbness, you would fuck anybody. You don't give a fuck what they look like. So don't even try it." Everybody laughed.

Over the years Farah became cool with Rhonda and Natasha, just as long as they didn't come between her and Coconut's friendship. It was her way of keeping an eye on them. If the three of them went somewhere without her, Farah would make Coconut feel so guilty that she'd find herself apologizing for weeks. Before long, Farah was in control of the friendship and she was very overprotective. In the end, despite Rhonda and Natasha knowing Coconut first, they backed off, and always went to Farah before planning any group functions.

"That's not true!" Natasha said angrily. "I don't just fuck with anybody."

"Sure you do, dumbness," Farah continued. "You got bad taste and everybody know it."

"Girl, you wrong as shit," Rhonda said, shaking her head. "One day she gonna rise up on your ass."

"Shut the fuck up, Black and Ike's," Farah retaliated. "That girl know I'm just playing with her. Don't you, dumbness?" Farah loved to antagonize to expose weaknesses. She was acting just like Brownie and she didn't even know it.

"I know you betta stop calling me Black and Ike's before I fuck you up." Rhonda giggled. "One day I'ma slap the shit out of you and catch you off guard."

Skipping the subject Farah said, "Y'all know me and Coconut moving together, right?" She looked at Rhonda and saw the sly look on her face.

"So y'all really gonna do it, huh?" Rhonda said. "Live in holy matrimony."

"Don't be stupid!" Coconut said.

"I'm just playing. But Farah be acting like y'all about to get married or something. It's just an apartment."

Farah was so concerned with having Coconut all to herself that she forgot about the reason she needed a roommate to begin with: that she lost Zone to his death. "Y'all so jealous it's crazy. Don't worry, we gonna let you come over sometimes."

"Why you say y'all'?" Natasha said. "I didn't even say nothing."

Farah laughed at her until her iPhone dinged, indicating she had a text. Her eyes alternated from the road to her phone, as she sped faster to catch the light. Doing two things at once, she picked up the phone and saw it was from Randy. It had been a month since he chased her, and she was hoping he'd moved on with his life. Deciding to read the message the moment she saw it, her heart dropped.

I saw you and your friends leaving the dealership. I started to put my hands on you. But I want you alone. I better see you by the end of the week. If I don't, next time I won't be so nice.

"Farah . . . slow the fuck down!" Rhonda yelled. "You can't text and drive at the same time!"

Farah was caught so off guard by the message that she snapped, thinking she was trying to tell her how to drive again. "Rhonda, if you don't like my driving you can get the fuck out my car."

"Bitch, you about to hit a . . . " When Farah looked up, she saw a man walking across the street. She pressed on her brakes, causing her tires to make a screeching noise, and hurting her toe even more. Because it had snowed and the ground was wet the car didn't stop. The man turned around only to see a car coming at him at a rapid speed. He tried to run but the front of her Benz knocked him off his feet and sent him flying into the air. His body bounced on the hood of the car and slid to the ground. The phone, which had distracted her, dropped out of Farah's hand and hit the floor of the car. The girls were stunned silent and nobody made a move. Farah was waiting for him to get up and walk away, hoping he'd be okay. Or maybe he would call for help, indicating he was still alive. "Everybody okay?" she asked, glancing over her friends.

Everyone looked at Rhonda. She rubbed her pregnant belly and said, "We good."

Farah spent another five seconds looking ahead of her.

"You gonna go check on him?" Coconut said. When she didn't answer, she spoke louder. "Farah! Go see if he's okay."

Silence.

"You just hit somebody, bitch," Rhonda said. "Either check on his ass, or pull the fuck off."

Farah slowly exited her car and limped toward the front. Her door remained open, and it was so silent outside that you could hear the clacking of her Christian Louboutin boots walking on the wet ground. Standing in the front, she noticed that the

Benz emblem on the hood of her car was splattered with red blood. When she looked at the man lying in front of her right wheel, she saw that his eyes were closed and he was not moving. Realizing that she just struck a man, she looked around for spectators. She didn't see anyone. When she believed the coast was clear, she bent down and checked his pulse. A few moments later she hopped to the car, jumped in, and said, "I didn't feel a pulse." She looked at all of her friends. "He's fuckin' dead."

"I don't know about you, but I ain't trying to see no police," Rhonda said. "Let me see what this Benz can do, bitch."

Farah backed her car up and maneuvered around the man she just hit. When he was out of her way, she sped off and looked at him through her rearview mirror. Nobody said a word, and it was understood that going out to the restaurant was dead. Since Rhonda was the only one with a house in the hood, they decided to stop past her place first. Rhonda gave Farah a bucket, and she filled it with soapy water to rinse the blood off. When she was done washing away her crime, they all met in Rhonda's bedroom. Natasha was sitting on the floor, Rhonda on the bed, and Coconut and Farah were standing. "I don't wanna really say what doesn't need to be said," Coconut started, looking at the girls, "but we ain't see shit and we don't know shit. Right?"

Natasha remained silent as she bit her nails, which were already nubs. "You hear me, bitch?" Coconut said, looking down at her. "You good?"

"What?" she asked, looking at Farah and Coconut. "I ain't saying nothing. Relax!"

Farah looked at Rhonda. "You cool too, right?"

"Girl, everybody in my family graduates to crime. Don't insult my gangsta."

Farah was partially relieved. She didn't stop to think that everything her grandmother told her about her life—falling out of order if her heart wasn't in the right place—was coming to pass.

# Chapter 14

## *A Week Later*

**"You can do whatever you want, but I think you'll be playing yourself." —Farah**

Farah sat on the toilet with her legs spread. She rubbed her belly because she was in extreme pain and was in need of some relief. With one hand on her knee, the other held the cell phone as she took a shit. Coconut was on the phone oblivious to what she was doing. Farah would've never answered the call if she hadn't been trying to reach Coconut since the hit and run. She hated to admit it, but she thought she was dodging her. "How come you just getting back with me now?" Farah asked. "I been calling you all week."

"I'm not gonna lie, I been out of it since that shit happened."

Farah was on edge wondering if Coconut turned on her, and told somebody about the accident. "Why you been out of it? I killed his ass, not you, and nothing wrong with me. Look . . . nobody saw shit. Ain't no need in worrying. They didn't even bring it up in the news yet."

"Okay. You're right. Look . . . I don't want to talk about it no more. How you been holding up without Zone?"

"I'm better. I can't wait until you move in. It would be so hard to pay the rent by myself. My mother gives me a little bit of money from her social security but it ain't enough."

Coconut seemed really silent. "Hold up . . . you still moving in, right?"

"Farah, I can't move in with you, I'm sorry. I talked about it with Jake and he said we were gonna get our own place soon. I think he gonna ask me to marry him or something."

Farah was so angry that she felt like throwing the phone into the wall. This was why she never approved of Jake, even when they were in high school. He was always groping and pulling on Coconut, and now he was ruining their friendship. "You told me you would move with me. You can't change your mind now. You know Zone died and I need you."

"I know, and I'm so sorry. I really am . . . but I can't."

Farah snapped and said, "You know what, I'ma call you back, since you putting him before me."

"Okay. . . ."

"Wait!" Farah yelled before she hung up. "Don't go." Coconut would normally stop her from hanging up, but this time she didn't. "What am I supposed to do now? You leaving me stranded."

"You should still get a roommate. So you won't have to worry about paying rent by yourself. It ain't like you don't have four rooms in that mothafucka. And you said it yourself, Natasha is looking to move too. Ask her."

"Naw, I need my own space," Farah said, dismissing the idea. "I'm good." It was obvious she had an attitude but Coconut refused to bite.

"Okay." She sighed. "Anyway, what's up with Chloe? I was over Shannon house the other day and people were saying she let five dudes gang fuck her at the same time."

If there was one bitch Farah hated it was Shannon, so she didn't want to hear anything she had to say. After all these years, it angered her that they were still cool. "Don't ask me about that bitch right now."

"Did I miss something?"

"Chloe did some unnatural-ass shit I don't want to talk about. Let's leave the box right there and not open it."

"I don't know what the fuck that means but I'ma drop it." She paused. "Oh, my God, I wish you could see all the things I bought for Rhonda's baby." The sound of plastic bags rattled in the background. "She gonna be so psyched." She giggled. "I found these real cute unisex baby sleepers and bibs. I done bought all this shit and now I want a baby of my own."

The baby shower was taking place in a few months at Farah's house. Everybody who was anybody was going to be there and Coconut wanted to come out looking like God when it was all said and done. "Don't be stupid, bitch. You and Jake ain't having no baby."

"I'm serious! If you saw all these tiny little clothes you'd change your mind too." Still shitting, Farah gripped her stomach and used her abdominal muscles to push out the last few pieces. Moaning, she said, "I can't believe you doing all that shopping anyway." She flushed the toilet. "On her registry she said she wanted gift cards. You could've saved yourself the time and aggravation simply by following the fucking instructions. I bought her a fifty dollar gift certificate."

Coconut giggled. "Girl, I love to shop! I'ma let y'all tacky-ass mothafuckas buy the baby gift cards." More bags rustled in the background. "The baby is gonna be so cute. You know Rhonda and Knight got them sleepy-ass eyes."

All the talk about the baby, and the fact that she was no longer going to be her roommate, was starting to get on her nerves. "Whatever. For all we know the baby won't make it and die."

"Why would you say some dumb shit like that?"

"I'm telling the truth! You know Rhonda's ass be getting high while she's pregnant."

Coconut laughed. "Did you really buy her a fifty dollar gift card?"

"Look, since Zone fell out of that window and you telling me you won't room with me, I'm on my own. I ain't got no money to give Rhonda or her fucking embryo-ass baby." Farah felt a little better since her bowels were clear, and spread her legs to wipe the shit stains from her asshole. Throwing the soiled tissue in the toilet, she flushed again.

"Hold up; was you just talking to me while you were using the bathroom?"

"Coconut, don't act like you don't shit too."

"Yeah, whatever, girl." Coconut paused. "Can you just call Natasha for me on three way?"

Over the years, Farah managed to be the only one in the group who had everyone's number. From erasing contact information to stealing phones, she successfully kept everybody apart. Farah rolled her eyeballs around in her head like they were loose. "Call her for what?"

"Because I wanna make sure we ain't get the same shit from Rhonda's list. If I know her ass, she may try to upstage me."

"I'll do it tomorrow."

"Can you do it now?" she persisted. "If we got the same stuff I'd rather take it back instead of waiting later."

"Damn! You pressed. Hold on!" Farah put the phone on the bathroom floor and washed her hands. Then she looked at herself in the mirror. Since she got the medicine from Grand Mike she was feeling better than she ever had in her entire life. The only thing on her mind now was how she was going to keep her apartment at Platinum Lofts with no money or job. She could kill Coconut's ass for changing up. Farah had a plan that was ironclad before she changed her mind. She knew that if she moved in, Jake's drug-dealing ass would be paying for everything.

Going back home was out of the question. She almost lost the apartment since her name was not on the lease. Vivian James, the property manager, was on a mission. But after taking the matter to court, Vivian learned the agreement she had with Zone was valid, and Farah had a right to be there. On one condition: that she could pay the rent. If Farah failed, Vivian wouldn't hesitate to throw her out on the streets, knowing she could double the rent and secure herself a bonus.

After Farah washed and dried her hands, she put unscented lotion on so that her disease wouldn't flare up. When she was done she picked up the phone. "You still there?" She brushed her medium-length brown hair to cover the bald spot in the middle of her head, due to years of hair pulling, and a few strands floated into the sink. Lately she stopped the hair chewing, and she loved it.

"Damn, bitch! It took you long enough to come back to the phone. Did you bring her to your house or what?"

Farah ignored her and frantically wiped the hair off the sink and floor using a wet piece of toilet tissue. Zone hated hair lying around because it always ended up in his ass or under his nut sack. She was in no mood to hear his mouth, and then she remembered he was dead. She'd seen to it. She threw the toilet tissue in the trash. "Girl, you know that bitch put me on hold and never came back to the phone," she lied. "I told you she sometimey. You keep thinking she your good friend, when she not." Farah walked into her bedroom and looked at the bed. It felt weird being there without Zone, but she was sure she'd get used to it. "Just get a gift receipt and call it a day. That way if she do get the same stuff, you can take it back."

"Naw, I gotta know. Just tell her to call me. I don't know how we keep losing each other's numbers. It's fucked up that we all friends but I still gotta go through you to give Natasha and Rhonda messages."

Farah went to her dresser and grabbed the blunt Zone rolled before he died. It was old, hard, and dry. Feeling in need of a buzz, she decided now was the time to burn them flames, a habit she picked up from Coconut. "Don't worry, if there's an urgent message I can relay it." She blew out smoke. "I'm the only friend you need."

Coconut sighed. "We not kids no more so stop saying that stupid shit."

Already feeling the effects of the weed, Farah's mind went into left field. "Girl, how 'bout that baby gonna be black as shit." Farah laughed. "You know Knight already blacker than the inside of an eyeball and Rhonda ass so dark she look burnt." Farah laughed harder. "That kid gonna be some kind of ugly."

"First of all, you talking about a baby. Secondly, you of all people shouldn't be talking about nobody dark. That's all you keep talking about, having a black strong nigga."

"So the fuck what? Ugly is ugly I don't give a fuck how old it is."

"I'm about to go. Just give Natasha my message."

"Wait! Before you go can you do me a favor?"

"How big?"

"Why not ask how small?"

"Farah, what do you need?"

"I'm trying to go see Tank again this weekend. You know I need money for rent since you not moving with me no more. So he gonna give it to me."

"Bitch, get the fuck out of here. You and me both know Tank's broke ass ain't giving you shit but troubles."

"Well, I think he's gonna give me cash this time."

"Whenever you ready to tell the truth I'm gonna be here to listen." Farah sat on the edge of her bed.

"I gotta go." Coconut was starting to tire of Farah because she was too emotional, and petty.

"A'ight!" Farah said before inhaling the blunt again. "It's like this, I wanna run the ménage à trois scheme again. I asked him for the money when I was at his house and he ain't give it to me like he said he would. Even though I let him fuck me while I was on my period."

Coconut was beyond irritated. "I don't know if I'm with all that."

"Please, Coconut! I'd do it for you."

"But what if that big mothafucka wakes up and wants some pussy for real? I ain't sign up for all of that."

"If he wake up, we gonna do what we gotta do."

"Farah, I'm not down with that shit no more. I got a man, plus the nigga grosses me out. And what's in it for me?" she asked. "The last time we did that shit, you gave me fifty bucks and kept the rest of the money when I was the one who did all the work."

"You'll be helping a friend who's about to be put out. And a friend you didn't tell you wasn't moving in with until the last minute."

Not wanting her friend out on the street, Coconut battled with whether to help her. Truthfully she thought the scheme was dumb because Farah never got more than a couple of hundred dollars from Tank, although she swore he stashed more.

"If I do this shit, when you trying to go?"

Farah was excited. "Tomorrow!" She had her right where she wanted her.

"Oops! Can't do it, boo-boo," Coconut said sarcastically. "I'm taking my boyfriend to get his bunion taken off. If you don't believe me you can call his doctor." Farah frowned. "Sorry, but you gotta get somebody else."

"But nobody else know how to run game like we do together."

"Can't help you, baby. I really wish I could though. Ask Natasha."

"She too fucking dumb."

"Well, unless you don't want your rent paid, I don't believe you have a choice. And why do you keep fucking with that little-ass boy anyway?"

"Because Tank gonna be big time one day. Niggas already saying if he keep it going like he is, it's just a matter of time."

"So? I mean, don't that nigga got a baby by old-ass Boo? His money already divided in too many pieces. The only future he got is in jail . . . and soon, too!"

"Like I care about that ugly bitch! I fuck with him because when he blows up he gonna remember how I was with him when he ain't have shit."

"You love molding niggas."

"Getting an up-and-coming drug dealer's nose wide open is a smart investment. Trust me."

"Whatever. I just hope your little foundation doesn't crumble," Coconut responded. "If I were you, I'd just get a roommate and stop doing all that other dumb shit. You too cute for all that. I'm out."

After she got off the phone with Coconut she called Rhonda. Rhonda never answered the phone like a regular person. When most sane people answered the phone, they were essentially saying that they were prepared to start a conversation . . . not Rhonda.

Looking at the caller ID, Rhonda said, "Hold on, Farah. Knight, please get your fucking blunt off my baby's dresser! Damn, ain't nobody make this room all nice for you to be getting high in here and shit! That's so fucking trifling!" Farah shook her head.

"Bitch, I'm the one who fixed the mothafucka up!" Knight growled in the background. "I can suck smoke out of the baby's bottle if I want to!"

"Nigga, suck my clit!"

In a seductive voice he said, "Bring it here."

Rhonda started giggling. "Move, boy!"

"I love your crazy ass," Knight said.

"I love you back, fucka!"

"Are you done?" Farah asked, irritated by the display of their demented love over the phone.

"Girl, that man is a mess. He done went into the baby's bedroom and got high. The baby liable to catch a contact the moment it comes home." Farah laughed. "Anyway, missy, what's good?"

"Ain't shit, Black and Ike's."

Rhonda laughed. "You call me that one more time and I'ma fuck you up."

Farah giggled and went into the kitchen to get a beer. "I ain't want nothing. For real I'm just calling to check on you."

"I'm fine. But speaking of Black and Ike's, you know Chloe just left from over here, right? She said she was bringing her gift, since you probably won't invite her to the shower. What y'all beefing about now?"

"A long story," she said, too embarrassed to tell her about the computer sex she had with Zone before he died.

"Well, she sounded like she misses you. Kept asking me if you asked about her, and shit like that. You should call her, Farah. I mean, she is your baby sister."

"Fuck Chloe."

"Whatever, that's your sis not mine."

"Right, but look, I'm calling to let you know that I'm giving you a fifty dollar gift card, but I also went in on the gifts with Coconut. She may not want you to know, but she been kinda broke lately. Her and Jake having problems, so he might not be lacing her up all the time anymore."

"Damn . . . that nigga's paid so that's fucked up. It's cool though. I won't say nothing. For real she don't have to do shit. And I appreciate you doing anything too because I know shit hard without Zone. You need all your paper."

*Exactly.* "It's not a problem, girl. I just can't wait to see my godbaby. I know she gonna be so pretty with her chocolate self." She giggled. "But look, let me go. I'll connect with you later, Black and Ike's."

"Your ass is mine!"

Farah laughed. "Bye, bitch."

After she hung up with Rhonda, she called Natasha. She didn't answer, so Farah decided to watch old episodes of *Big Brother* on the living room sofa. Hungry, she made a ham sandwich with grape jelly. The moment she bit into her food, Natasha called back. She put her sandwich down and answered. "What's up, Natasha?"

"Hey, girl. Sorry I couldn't come to the phone. This nigga I fucked with up and got married on me. I just feel like me and him were going to always be." She sounded like she was crying. "We had that kind of bond and he didn't even tell me about that bitch."

Farah rolled her eyes. "Anyway, I'm gonna shoot it straight with you about something, Coconut don't fuck with you like that, because she thinks you gonna say something about the accident."

"I would never say nothing about what happened that day," she said seriously. "Maybe I should talk to her and see what the problem is."

"She don't want you calling. She specifically told me not to give you her number, so just leave it alone, Natasha. And make sure you don't say shit about the hit and run to nobody. Or that I told you she don't fuck with you. If you do I'm not gonna tell you nothing else."

"Trust me, I wouldn't say nothing about the accident. I really feel like I should say something when I see her about everything else, though. I been knowing her for years. She going to Rhonda's shower, right?"

"Yeah, but I'm not sure that's appropriate shit. You feel me?"

"Well, I'll find the right time to talk to her. I know y'all are cool, but I'm not gonna be right unless I tell her how I feel.

I love Coconut. She was the first person who looked out for me in school. I hope you understand that I can't keep a secret like that. If she don't fuck with me, I wanna know why."

Farah was trying to think of ways to keep them apart. This was the biggest lie yet and could possibly backfire in her face. "You can do whatever you want, but I think you'll be playing yourself. So when she carries the fuck out of you, don't come running to me."

"It's fine. But like I said, I love her and I don't want her thinking I'm no snitch or not her friend."

Farah rolled her eyes and smacked her tongue. Natasha wasn't as naive as she thought. "Anyway,

I'm thinking about letting you live here with me. Since you wanna move out your folks' house too."

"For real?" she said excitedly. "What about Coconut? I thought she was moving with you."

"That's what I'm trying to say . . . I don't like how she treats you and Rhonda. You think I'm playing because I'm with her all the time, but I'm dead serious. When I heard her talking sideways, I said if she talks bad about you, she'd do it to me too. You gotta be able to pay your rent, though."

"I got it. Don't worry about that."

"First you gotta help me with something else. If shit work out, me and you both could earn a little paper."

"I'm down! When?"

"Meet me over my house in an hour."

"I'm on my way!"

# Chapter 15

**"You were the best we ever had, baby. All we trying to do is have a little more fun before we part ways." —Farah**

Farah was lying in bed with Tank, praying he wouldn't open his eyes. She was anxious and uncomfortable because his room was extremely hot. So hot that her nose felt dry on the inside, causing her to rub it back and forth.

Lying face to face with him, she held her nose when she smelled the stank of his morning breath, due to all the weed smoking he indulged in the night before. Sweat poured off his husky body and fell onto the cream sheet under him. Perspiration surrounded his body as if he were chalked out at a crime scene. Farah was trying to see her partner in crime on the floor from where she lay, but the room was mostly dark, with the exception of sunlight peeking from the corner of his dirty white vinyl blind. *Don't fuck this up, girl!* she thought. Blinking several times, Farah was finally able to see

Natasha's silhouette on the floor. Directly under his window, Natasha, completely naked, crawled on all fours as she looked for the money Farah assured her was in the house. If Tank woke up and saw her there, he would murder both of them and not miss a day's sleep. *Please don't get caught. Move slowly.*

Tank was a certified hood soldier. He had enough weapons in his apartment to stage a war. There were two .45s, his weapon of choice, a nine, and about ten shotguns. When Farah originally hatched her plan to steal from him, she swore she thought things through. Now she understood that the knife she had tucked in the pillowcase under her head would not be enough to defend herself if things got out of hand. When Natasha bumped against the bed, Farah bit down on her lip and closed her eyes. Because she wasn't really asleep, her eyeballs moved rapidly under her lids. She just knew he was about to wake up and ask what the fuck was going on. A minute later, she opened her eyes and saw he was still asleep. She exhaled.

When the heat came back on, the stench of weed and sex roamed around the room. But his snores got louder, which indicated that he was fast asleep. In the event he woke up, the plan was to tell him how he fucked both of them the night before and how much fun they had. The good thing about the plan was that Tank was twenty-two: young and unable to handle his liquor. Farah was banking on this character flaw if they were caught red-handed.

Natasha moved around quickly, looking for the bag of gold Farah said was at the end of the hellhole. She would've looked for it herself but whenever she stayed over, he had to hold her. So at the moment his heavy hand rested on her yellow thigh, and whenever she moved, he would toss or turn. When Natasha located a bulging Doritos bag under his bed, she sat up against the wall and picked it up. Her large brown breasts drooped freely and her legs were wide open. Shaking the bag, she noticed it was too heavy to be holding chips. She smiled slyly at Farah, opened the bag, and her eyes widened when she saw a wad of money inside. "Bitch, it's right here," she whispered too loudly.

When she felt Tank move, Farah slammed her eyelids shut. She couldn't believe Natasha could be so careless. To make matters worse, Tank's snores stopped, which meant he wasn't in a deep sleep anymore. Her eyes remained shut for a minute but when she opened them, he was staring in her direction. "What you looking all crazy for?" He stretched his arms and legs. "What . . . I ain't dick you down hard enough last night?" He yawned and his breath smelled like a pot of hot shit. "I'd think you'd be knocked out." He removed his hand from her thigh and rolled back on his side. "If you ain't answering me, you must be 'sleep with your eyes open."

"Boy, ain't nobody sleep with their eyes open." She giggled. She was nervous and it showed.

"Then why you not answering my question?"

"What you say again?"

He frowned. "I said, 'did I dick you down right last night?'"

Farah could hear Natasha's soft whimpering in the background, and she was on the verge of paranoia. *Why the fuck is this bitch crying?* "Yeah, the dick was official, baby. Why else would I come see your ass as often as I do? It ain't like you cashing me out."

"You right about that," Tank said, rubbing his stomach. "I don't pay a bitch shit but dick."

"So there we have it," Farah said. When she looked over his shoulder, she was angry that instead of ducking, Natasha was stuck in position with both hands over her mouth. "But you better get some sleep because later"—she pushed his fat finger into her pussy—"I might be up for round two."

"Damn," he said, stirring his finger like a spoon in a pot. "Why you wet all of a sudden?" Farah's pussy was always dry, but because it was so hot in the room it was now drenched with sweat. He would normally have to eat her out just to get it wet enough to stick his dick in. "You make me wanna get some of that right now."

Farah didn't want his large pokers in her box, but at the moment she didn't have a choice. At least he was preoccupied with what she had between her legs, instead of the .45 under his pillow. "My pussy is always wet when I'm with you." She moaned. He knew that wasn't the case but he let her live anyway. "So go back to sleep and we'll start all over in a couple of hours." She closed her eyes, hoping he'd do the same.

"Naw, Reds," he said, pulling his finger out of her pussy. Then he hauled her on top of his body. "I'm trying to bust. You done got me started now." The moment he was on his back and she was on top of him, Natasha softly hit the floor. If the room were lit a little better, he would be able to see her long brown legs on the left side of the bed. But the light was minimal at the moment and Farah was grateful. "Get it hard, Reds," he said, grabbing her hand, and putting it on his clammy penis. "Jerk it so you can get me ready."

"But my arm hurts."

"Well, make it wet then." He looked at her. "With your mouth."

"I'll jack you off," she said, reconsidering.

Farah grabbed his long pole and softly stroked it until he was stiff and ready to perform. Tank's pink tongue moved around in his mouth and his hairy chest moved up and down with each exhale. The tip of his dick oozed pre-cum and dripped on her fingertips. He was in ecstasy already. "Come on, ma, it's ready now. Suck that shit for me."

"I thought you wanted me to jack you off."

"Now I want something different."

Farah didn't care about doing what was necessary, but she was concerned he'd look to his left and see Natasha, who was doing an awful job of hiding. From where she sat on top of his body, she could see her clearly. Now she wished she hadn't suggested she'd get naked because if she created a diversion, Natasha could've crawled her ass all the way home. But without her clothes she could do nothing. "Come on, Tank, let me ride that shit," she said, jerking him harder. "You done let me get you all ready and now you not gonna give me no dick?" She shook her head as if it were unacceptable. "Naw, babes, I'ma have to hop on top of this big black mothafucka first."

He laughed, thinking she was really in to him. "Don't worry, Farah, I'ma save some for you," he said, breathing more into her space. "But I'ma need them lips wrapped around this shit first." He snatched his dick greedily from her paws. "All that other shit you talking can wait."

"Come on, Tank. Please," she whined. "I want you to fuck me."

"Bitch, stop playing with me!" he yelled. "Your mouth way wetter than your pussy, in case you didn't know." He wasn't smiling anymore and it was obvious he reached the end of his patience. He wanted to cum and he wanted her to use her mouth to make him do it. Plus Farah could never move her body right and her fuck game was off. If it weren't for her face, and the fact that a rack of dudes in the hood wanted to fuck her, he would not have given her the time of day. "Now suck my joint. And if you want me to pipe you down later, you got that."

From the corner of her eye she looked in Natasha's direction again and was enraged. She could still see her legs. *Damn, this bitch stupid. Why she ain't ball up instead of stretching out? Fuck! Now this nigga gonna kill both of us!*

Realizing she needed her knife, she said, "You mind if I suck it from the floor, baby? On the side of the bed? I always work better on my knees."

He wanted a blowjob and he didn't give a fuck how it was going to go down. "A'ight." He frowned. "But you making me mad now. I need you to hurry up and break me off."

When he swung his legs toward the side of the bed closest to Natasha, Farah felt faint. His feet were so close to her body, if he moved an inch he would feel her warm skin. "No!" Farah screamed. Then she got on her knees on the opposite side of the bed, away from her stupid friend. "Let's do it over here!"

Tank followed and looked down at her suspiciously. She was acting out of character and he wasn't comfortable with the situation anymore. Looking into her brown eyes he said, "Fuck is up with you? And before you lie to me, you better know I ain't no sucka-ass nigga."

"I know you not, baby," she said, giving him a half smile. "Why you fucking around?"

"Bitch, don't make me break your neck. Now what the fuck is up?"

"I just wanna do it over here, that's all." She was shaking so hard her hair was trembling. "Let's keep it light, Tank."

"I know one thing, you ain't acting right." He looked at her harder. "Something is up."

"Tank, come on." She was working harder than ever. "Ain't shit wrong. I'm just trying to have a little fun and wanted you on my side of the bed, that's all." Then she grabbed the pillow with the knife tucked inside of it, and placed it under her knees in case she needed it. "I'ma do whatever you want. I just needed you over here, that's all."

Tank was young, but he was street smart and far from stupid. The drug game made him hard and he heard about bitches running game and setting niggas up all the time. He just hoped it would never happen to him. He was a foot soldier, with no more on him than a couple thousand at a time, but for a hood rat like Farah, looking to pay her rent, that was a good look. With both feet firmly on the floor, he stood up and looked down at her as she cowered on her knees. His stare was serious and he meant business. "Fuck is up, Farah?" She rose up until he said, "Did I tell you to stand?" She shook her head and dropped back to the floor. "Now, are you gonna tell me what you up to, or do I have to find out for myself?"

"Tank, please!" Tears came down her eyes and gave her away, but he didn't give a fuck. "I'm just trying to make you feel good. That's all. Why you getting all different all of a sudden?"

"I don't believe you," he said as he was about to walk away from her.

"Where you going?" she asked, pulling his hand.

"Bitch, get the fuck off of me!" He walked away from her and his neck swiveled to the opposite side of his room. From where he stood, he saw something out of the ordinary. Squinting, he grabbed his gun from under the pillow, and moved toward the left side of the bed. Farah wanted to run but her legs wouldn't even allow her to stand. This was her fear and she knew it was impossible that they all would make it out of the situation alive.

Naked, with his gun aimed, Tank moved closer to the object on the floor. Then he opened the blinds and the entire room lit up as sunshine burst through the grimy windows. He couldn't believe his eyes when he saw Natasha, balled up, with her hands over her face. She was so scared that she actually thought by hiding her eyes, he wouldn't be able to see her because she couldn't see him. Grabbing a fistful of her hair, he made her rise to her feet. "Open your mouth," he said. She did. He pushed the barrel between her teeth, like it was supposed to be there, and cocked his gun. "Now . . . who are you, and what the fuck are you doing in my house?"

"Uh . . . I was . . . remember . . . we all . . . uh . . ." She was scared and lost the plan within the walls of her mind because of the gun in her mouth. How could she forget? Farah had gone over it with her twenty times just to make sure it was ironclad.

Farah had told her, "If this nigga wakes up and catches us in his house, tell him the three of us fucked the night before. He drinks so much, girl, he won't remember." And now that it was time to show and prove, Natasha was coming up short.

"Bitch, I asked you a mothafuckin' question! Fuck is you doing in my house?"

Her pretty face produced a fake smile, even though a gun rested between her teeth. "You don't remember, Tank? We . . . we all had a little fun last night." She looked at Farah but Farah looked away. She was on her own. Focusing back on the man who was gripping her hair so hard she could hear her hair tearing from the roots, she said, "Don't you remember?"

"Naw." He frowned. "I don't remember none of that shit."

She simpered. "Come on, Tank. I sucked your dick for an hour, then Farah was riding you. We had a ball last night. That's why I'm naked. Look at me, baby." He eyed her naked flesh. She was working it now and Farah was hopeful that everyone would make it out alive.

"The three of us did all that last night?" He laughed, looking into her eyes.

"Yeah. We had a real good time, too."

"Well if that's the case, and we all were together, then why the fuck you hiding?"

"Uh . . . because I thought you would forget and be mad. And I ain't want that. I heard how hard you are in these streets," she lied, and he blushed. "But can you please let my hair go, Tank?" she could hear the soft cracking of her hair follicles being torn away. "You're hurting me really bad."

Before letting her go, he looked at her face, droopy titties, and long, pretty legs. If he didn't remember he sure was in the mood for a refresher. As much as he hated to admit it, he knew she could be right because he drank a lot and could never hold his liquor. With the gun still pointed at Natasha he looked back at Farah and smiled. "We had fun, huh?" he asked, his youth taking over his mind.

"You were the best we ever had, baby," Farah lied. "All we trying to do is have a little more fun before we part ways."

"So you liked sucking my dick?" he asked Natasha, ready to have her do it again.

"Yeah, and Farah was dropping it real good on that dick. You kept talking about how wet her pussy was and everything."

She went too far and he no longer believed shit she said. "Is that right?" He frowned.

"Yep." He looked down and saw the Doritos bag, which held his stash, hanging open. A wave of anger washed over him and instead of releasing her hair, he gripped it tighter. With all his might, he took the butt of the gun and slammed it into her face. Natasha was part delirious as she unwillingly accepted the severe facial blow. Farah couldn't believe what was happening and knew she needed to get the fuck out of dodge, or else she was next.

"Please stop!" Natasha cried as he unmercifully hit her in the face with his weapon, crushing blow after blow.

Natasha wept with all her heart, but Tank couldn't be stopped. There was one thing he hated more than a snitch, and that was a thief. He already had to worry about his mother sneaking into his room when she visited. She was addicted to meth for ten years and he couldn't trust her, even if his eyes remained on her the entire time. His mother's betrayal he would deal with, but he certainly wouldn't accept shit from a bitch he didn't know.

After all this drama, Tank felt fucked up for cheating on his baby mother, Boo. She was a little wild at times and quick with the tongue but at least she never tried to steal from him. He made a mental note that after he took care of Natasha and Farah he would leave all hood bitches alone.

Instead of helping her friend, Farah stood in amazement as the white sheets turned red before her eyes. First he broke her jaw, then her nose, followed by the large, gaping wound on her forehead. Tank beat her repeatedly until her body was limp and her muscles could no longer support her weight. For a moment, Farah saw her fingers twitch back and forth, because they were the only things she could move. But after a few more seconds, there was no movement whatsoever. When that happened, Farah couldn't be sure, but she swore she saw the life leave her body.

While Tank was preoccupied with Natasha's corpse, Farah grabbed the pillow on the floor with the knife, and hit it in the direction of the bedroom door. She tried to take something to cover her body, but didn't see anything along her path toward the exit. She decided it was better to be caught naked and alive, than clothed and dead. When Tank saw her run in his peripheral vision he yelled, "Where the fuck do you think you're going?" She heard Natasha's body thump to the floor, followed by quick, heavy footsteps in her direction.

Relying on her track skills from high school, she ran full speed ahead toward the door. Making her first goal, she flung it open and flew down the stairs. She could hear his heavy breaths but she didn't look back. Besides, there was no need to see the lunatic she knew was coming her way. At the end of the day, if she wanted to survive, she had to catch wheels and that's exactly what she did. Her feet slapped against each step in the hallway as she maintained hold of the pillow in her hand. When she didn't hear heavy breathing anymore, she looked behind her and saw he was no longer there. *Oh, my God, please don't let him get me.*

When she pushed the door to the building open, the cold air smacked against her naked body as she screamed at the top of her lungs. Her feet dug into the snow-covered ground, and the air pushed her hair out of her face as she ran into the wind. She was feeling hopeful that he would be too afraid to kill her in broad daylight and in front of so many people. But when she turned around briefly, she saw he was now coming speedily in her direction.

The brief pause he took was only to grab his black North Face coat and a pair of sweatpants. Unlike Farah, he wasn't willing to be caught completely naked on the cold DC streets. His bare, hairy chest was exposed and he had a look on his face that would murder his own mother.

With each sprint she made, she pled with the angels on high to spare her life. She was able to get enough distance between them until her legs gave out. When she fell on the icy ground, she hit her elbow. Pain rushed up her left arm as she struggled to help herself up. That's when she noticed three hustlers a few feet away from her. Not believing their eyes, they walked over and helped her to her feet. When she was standing, she collapsed into their arms.

"Fuck is up with you, shawty? You on that shit?" hustler number one asked as he allowed her to fall into his arms. It wasn't every day that he ran into a naked, sexy girl, so he was intrigued.

"No . . . Somebody's trying to kill me." She pled, looking for Tank, "Please don't let him."

The moment she said that Tank rushed up to the scene, out of breath but on a mission. "This bitch just stole from me, man," Tank said, leaning on his knees. "I gotta have her back." He wanted her more than ever for causing so much trouble.

"Damn, Tank, you got this bitch out here naked?" hustler number two asked. "You wilding out now, young'un. You gotta keep your bitches in check." They knew Tank well enough to know he had a temper, but his hustle game was surefire so they respected him.

"I'm telling you this bitch stole my money," Tank persisted. "It ain't even like that. I just want her to give me my shit back, and then she can get the fuck out."

They all looked at the naked girl. "Unless she tucked it in her pussy," hustler number one said, "then I'm sure she ain't got it on her now." They all laughed and Tank realized his mistake. He now felt he should've kept shit one hundred.

"You stealing, pretty lady?" hustler number one asked. "If it's one thing I can't stand, a thief is it."

"I didn't take shit from him!" she yelled. "He just killed my friend and he's trying to kill me too." She sobbed heavily. She held on to the pillow but was unable to get it in the right position to grab the knife. The snow was stabbing the bottoms of her feet and it felt like knives cutting into her skin. "She in his house if you don't believe me! We gotta call the police."

The word "police" made them frown and the hustlers looked at Tank and waited for his response. Although they respected him, they weren't about to get caught up in no murder shit, either. "Is this true?" hustler number one asked.

Tank decided not to play games anymore. Time was of the essence and he needed her dead. She was a phone call away from snitching. "Let me have her." Tank looked at all of them directly in the eyes. "I gotta finish what I started and too much time is being wasted right now."

"Please don't," she wept, looking at the men. "I don't wanna die."

"Respect the code," Tank said. "Let me have her."

In silence they made an agreement and hustler number one pushed her into Tank's arms. "No!" she screamed, doing her best to fight back. The pillow holding the knife dropped to the ground, and she was unable to grab it. Tank maintained his hold on her and had no intention of letting go. Onlookers hung from the doorways in the surrounding buildings but none of them bothered to call the police. Everyone assumed someone else would and because of it her life was in danger. With wild legs and hands, Farah kicked and screamed as he carried her under one arm like a football. The low temperature caused her skin to redden, and the soles of her feet were frostbitten. She could hear her heart thump loudly in her ears, and she knew death was eminent.

Tank was almost to his building when rookie Police Officer Phillips, who was patrolling the neighborhood, saw the horror scene from his car. At first he thought they were on some kind of drug like boat, which terrorized the city for many years. But after watching the systematic tread of Tank, he knew something else was going on. He parked poorly at the sidewalk and moved toward the building. Taking his gun out of its holster, he grabbed the door handle to the building Tank had entered.

Farah's screams bounced off the walls and closed apartment doors but Tank wasn't concerned. So many people were murdered in that building that to some, screams were as normal as birds chirping in the early morning hours.

The officer crept up the first floor until he saw Tank and Farah on the second. He already called for backup and hoped they arrived soon, because in his inexperienced opinion, Tank looked like a handful. When he was a few feet away from Tank, he was frozen with fear. *Do something, Phillips!* he said to himself. *This girl is about to be murdered.* "Freeze!" he yelled, as he shakily aimed the gun in Tank's direction. Tank turned around and looked at him. "Put your hands in the air!" Tank didn't move. "Now! Do it now!"

"Please help me," Farah sobbed. "I don't wanna die."

"Sir, I don't want to hurt you." The gun shook harder in his grasp. "But if you don't . . . put your hands up . . . I'll be forced to fire." Tank dropped Farah on the floor and she cowered in a nearby corner.

"Officer, this is not as bad as it looks," Tank said, taking a step in his direction. A crazy grin rested on his face, like the Joker from *Batman*. "I can only imagine what you're thinking right now."

"I'm not gonna tell you again!" Officer Phillips yelled as he took a few steps back. "Don't move or else I'll shoot you."

Tank laughed. "You got this all wrong. This my girl. She fucking with that shit and I was trying to bring her in the house." He looked at Farah and smiled. "Now see what you did, baby? You got this nice officer thinking we beefing. Tell him how we got into a fight and everything is good." He turned around and gave her a devilish look, out of the officer's view. "You know this all your fault anyway, don't you?"

"Please save me," Farah wept, looking at the officer. "If you let him go he's gonna kill me."

"Baby, this cop gonna think I'm crazy." He walked closer to the officer. "You gotta tell him how you got high and started tripping. Or else he's gonna lock me up." Tank's gaze remained on the officer. "You wouldn't want that to happen now, would you?"

"I'm not your fucking girl!" she screamed, her knees pressed against the cold, hard floor. "You tried to kill me and my friend . . . my friend . . ." She pointed upstairs. "She's . . . she's . . ." She couldn't finish her thought and Tank was grateful. Officer Phillips said, "Move any closer and I'll fire. I'm not gonna warn you again, son."

The moment he said that Tank rushed the rookie officer and knocked him to the floor. Dashing out the building's door he was gone in under a minute flat. The officer tried to follow him but Farah screamed for his attention. "Don't leave me!" she sobbed, reaching out for him with both hands. "Please don't go! He might come back!"

Against his better judgment, the officer put his arms around her naked body. The gun in his hand grazed her back. She felt safe. "Everything's gonna be okay now." He rocked her in his arms and she gripped him tightly. Police sirens could be heard in the distance and he released her for a minute to tuck his weapon back in his holster. "I'm not going anywhere," he assured her. "Don't worry about a thing."

# Chapter 16

**"You point out twenty niggas and I guarantee fifteen of them prefer the red bone. It's just their way." —Farah**

Grey weed smoke choked the air inside of Farah's Benz as she, Coconut, and Mia watched Rhonda smack Knight in the face outside of their house. "I can't believe this shit!" Farah said, pulling on the blunt. When she passed it to Coconut in her passenger seat, she opened a bag of chips and ate a few. "She just smacked the dog shit out of his ass in public."

"I swear I hope this nigga don't kill that girl. I'd hate to jump out of here and beat his fine-ass," Mia said. "Give me them chips, Farah."

"Damn . . . what happened to please?" She tossed her the bag.

Mia's overweight body filled a little more than her portion of seat in the back of Farah's car, and the red lipstick she wore rested on the top of her shirt instead of her mouth. "Because I'm tired of seeing them mothafuckas fighting all the time. They should just break the fuck up."

"Shh." Farah paused, seeing Rhonda stomping toward her car. "Here she come right now." Rhonda got inside and slammed the car door so hard the window rattled. Then she threw her folded arms across her chest. "Bitch, don't bring your black ass in my ride with all that shit."

"I'm sorry, RedBone," Rhonda said, breathing heavily. She rubbed her pregnant belly over her baby blue North Face coat. "But you wouldn't believe what that nigga just said to me. He makes me so fucking sick. One day I'm gonna straight leave his ass."

"Black and Ike's, you gonna tell us what he said or not?" Farah asked. "Because we can't read your mind."

"I'm so sick of you calling me that shit." Rhonda was serious. "I told you before I don't like it."

"It is dumb," Mia said. "Sometimes you just say shit without thinking."

"Girl, leave all that sensitive shit outside my car," Farah said, looking at Knight, who was outside with his friends looking at the car. She wished she had a man who loved her so much that people around her could feel it too. She never gave up hope that one day she would meet her Superman, because it damn sure wasn't Randy. "You already know how we roll, we tough in here." She sounded like Mia's protégé. "Now what the fuck did he do?"

"Bitch, why this nigga gonna tell me he staying out tonight 'cause they going to Atlantic City to gamble? Fuck that! How he gonna go anywhere when I'm pregnant with his fucking baby? What if I have this bitch early?"

"The man should be able to go out sometimes," Coconut said. "It ain't like y'all not up under each other's asses every five minutes anyway. Don't make shit so deep."

"Bitch, unless he can take my fat ass with him, he ain't going nowhere. I ain't fuck myself and get pregnant. I had some help, if you know what I'm saying." She looked at Knight again and he started walking over in the direction of Farah's Benz. "Look at him about to try to kiss my ass and shit." He knocked on her window and at first she didn't roll it down, until he knocked again. "Yes, Knight." The cold air rushed inside and Farah turned the heat up.

"Give me a kiss," he said, easing his head into the car. "Before I fuck you up."

"Nigga, please," Rhonda said, waving him off. "Why don't you get one of them bitches in Atlantic City to kiss you? Since you so fucking pressed."

He took his head out of the car and looked down at her. "I'm not gonna go to Atlantic City, Rhonda. I let these niggas get in my head, and for a minute I forgot I got a kid on the way . . . my first one at that. But you reminded me and put me in my place.

Now stop acting like a bitch before I fuck you up out here in front of your friends." He said it so sexy that everybody got turned on. He eased his head into the car again. "Now give me a kiss." She leaned in and they kissed sloppily. When the show was over Knight said, "What you making for dinner tonight?"

"Black-eyed peas, rice, fried chicken, and spinach."

He rubbed his stomach. "That sound good as shit. Now hurry up with your friends. 'Cause I'm over here waiting to walk you in the house." When he left everyone was quiet and she rolled up the window. Farah turned the heat to a comfortable level.

"Girl, you need to stop all that faking. You ain't got no intentions on leaving that nigga," Farah said. "You eat his shit for breakfast."

Rhonda frowned. "Who the fuck said anything about leaving him?" She laughed. "We got our problems, but I ain't going nowhere." Everybody shook their heads.

"So what happened that night?" Coconut asked, skipping the subject. "When Tank killed Natasha. I'm confused."

"I told you already. Shit got crazy. He started beating her when he found out she was stealing his money and I started fighting his ass back," she lied. "We jumped him at first, but he was so focused on her that nothing I did seemed to bother him. It was like he didn't want to hit me for real. I think it got something to do with me being red and Natasha being darker than me."

From the back seat Mia and Rhonda sighed heavily. "You know I hate when you talk like that, right?" Rhonda said. "You sound so fucking stupid."

"Exactly . . . because it's ridiculous and don't make no sense," Mia added. "Both of y'all bitches were about to rob his ass and both of y'all were going to get killed. That's why you on the run."

"I'm just shooting it to you straight," Farah continued.

"You point out twenty niggas and I guarantee fifteen of them prefer the red bone. It's just their way."

"She's telling the truth," Coconut said, having gotten a few perks because of her yellow skin. "If I hang out with any of my cousins on my mamma side, they bound to get the shaft if I walk into the room because if you rich, you want a red bitch on your arm. Bottom line."

"Y'all betta stop smokin' that shit!" Mia laughed. "All niggas don't be on that red shit. Most niggas be on that pussy shit. The problem is most dark-skinned chicks automatically feel inferior because of their complexion due to the media. And it shows in their attitude. They have zero confidence when they shouldn't."

"Exactly," Rhonda concurred. "Dark-skinned Farah from Southwest is fat *and* black yet niggas be on her hard because she think she sexy."

"Easy on the fat shit," Mia joked.

"Sorry." She laughed. "It's just that I know for a fact that I pulled many a nigga over a red bitch in my day."

"You can't really believe that," Farah said.

"I believe it," Mia added. "She telling the truth."

Farah laughed. "Big sis, you delusional."

Mia squinted her eyes. "Well, how do you explain all of the niggas you ever had wanting to fuck Chloe? I mean . . . ain't she darker than you?"

Silence.

"That's 'cause Chloe's a freak and niggas can read into that shit." *Did Chloe tell her about Zone?* Farah thought. *I bet I won't ever have her around another one of my niggas. Believe that shit.*

"I hear you, but if what you saying is true, because you're red, your pussy should be golden and who wants to lose gold?" She smirked. "If anything, a nigga need to give Chloe the boot. But we all know when her little ass walks into a room, niggas' mouths drop and she's as black as night. Just like me, Mamma, and Daddy."

"Whatever, Mia. You just mad because Chloe be pulling your niggas too."

Mia laughed. "You sound like a fool. I just fuck the dudes I hook up with. I don't personally own none of them nor do I want to. That's why I only *deal* with the young boys. If you over nineteen, you can't even get my attention and definitely not my time."

"How you only like young boys when you twenty-seven?" Farah asked. "You gonna fuck around and get locked up."

"Because they don't speak unless spoken to and can fuck me long and hard." She slapped fives with Rhonda. "Them old bastards can't even eat my pussy right half the time."

"Maybe because they can't find your pussy," Farah added. She was really showing off and pushing her luck. Ever since she stepped out of her shell, she was starting to become heartless. "From that muffin top you got hanging over your panties, and the food and makeup that be on your clothes, you lucky any nigga step to you at all."

Mia rolled her eyes.

"I hope you don't be tricking on them, Mia," Coconut responded. "You big, but you too pretty for all that."

"Bitch, fuck pretty. I'm beautiful and don't get slapped." Mia pointed at her. "I don't give niggas shit but pussy." She sat back in the seat and allowed the effects of the weed to take over. "What I look like spending the hard-earned coins I get from the bank on a nigga? I'm not their mamma."

"I heard that." Rhonda laughed as she texted Knight, who drove to the store with one of his friends a moment ago.

"You mean the hard-earned coins you steal from the bank," Farah added.

"The ones I steal *and* earn, smart ass. I'm just being for real. Niggas who stomp on bitches because they dark are dumb. It don't make no mothafuckin' sense."

"So you saying there's something wrong with a preference?" Coconut asked. "I think a man has a right to choose what he want."

"Naw . . . ain't nothing wrong with preference; like I said, I prefer young dick." Mia laughed. "So picture me hating on anybody who prefers anything. I'm just saying niggas is lame who slam bitches because of their complexion. *Especially* when the bitch who gave birth to them is black."

"Right! Move on what you want but don't be downing other mothafuckas in the process," Rhonda added. "I know some girls who wanna kill themselves because of that shit."

"Whatever," Farah said, rubbing her dry eyes. "I get mad play because of my skin tone and that's the bottom line. I'm tired of being stressed because I'm blessed."

Mia started giggling. "What you laughing about?" Rhonda asked.

"Something from when we were little."

"What?" Coconut asked, turning around to look at her.

"Farah, if you love your tone so much, how come when you were a kid you stayed out in the sun until it went down just to get dark?" Mia continued. She was getting higher by the minute and no longer considered her sister's feelings. "She had puss bumps from her head to her pissy pussy."

"I heard about that shit too." Rhonda laughed. "I ain't think that was for real though."

Farah never got over how Brownie treated her after that. She was in pain for weeks after the sun ate at her skin, yet there was no worse humiliation than when her mother pressed feces in her face.

"So where were you staying? Because you haven't been home since Natasha got murdered," Rhonda said, skipping the subject. "You had everybody thinking something happened to you too."

After Tank murdered Natasha, Farah ran away to stay with a drug dealer named Jonsey from Virginia Beach, who she dealt with from time to time. Jonsey was twenty years older than her, generous, and had a nice home. She would have still been with him if it weren't for one thing: he insisted on having his dick sucked twenty-two hours out of a twenty-four-hour period. Farah sucked him off so much that as she spoke her jaw hurt. In the end she stole $5,000 from him and bounced. He'd been threatening her, but since he couldn't find her he had to be reduced to cell phone gangsta status. "Where haven't I been?" Farah said, pulling on the blunt again. "I got too much going on to be caught slipping, so I had to leave town. This nigga Tank is trying to kill me for real! I keep telling y'all that. It's not a game."

"Tank ain't gonna kill nobody," Mia said. "If anything he's as far away from DC as possible. Five-O after his ass; he not hardly worrying about you."

"Natasha's funeral was sad, Farah. You really should've been there. It wasn't a good look, especially since people knew you were there when she was killed," Rhonda said.

"Well, what y'all want me to do, get smoked too because I went to the funeral?" Farah responded. "They say the killers always show up anyway."

"The way that girl died was fucking dumb!" Mia said. "I should smack the fuck out of you for being so stupid, Farah. If you gonna pull some shit like that, the least you could do is have somebody with you who was 'bout it." She shook her head. "What if that nigga killed you too?"

"Then I'd be dead."

"Bitch, I'm serious!"

"Mia, I'm not trying to hear that shit right now. And if you must know I did ask Coconut to roll with me and she declined my offer."

Coconut pouted. "After all that shit, I'm glad I did."

Farah rolled her eyes. "Anyway, what's done is done. I do know this, though, I'm not gonna let this nigga get me on no stupid shit." She continued passing the blunt back and forth, never bypassing Rhonda once. "I ain't even been to my house because I got a feeling he waiting to clap my ass."

"You know his baby mamma Boo looking for you, right?"

Rhonda added. "She said if she finds you, she gonna bust you in the mouth and you better hope she don't bust her gun, too."

Farah looked in the back seat. "You call yourself my friend and you let her say that shit to your face?"

Rhonda gave her a look like "Bitch, please." "Farah, picture her telling me some shit like that to my face. Or even in my presence. Pregnant or not I'd stomp that bitch for blood. Naw, she ain't tell me no shit like that. She told Shannon and them and they got word back to me since they know I fuck with you like that."

"You still fucking with that dumbass bitch?"

"Yeah. They coming to my shower, too," Rhonda continued. "Why? You still don't like them?"

"If the shower gonna be at my house they not coming."

"That's fucked up, Farah!" Rhonda protested. "I'm trying to get as much shit as I can for my baby." She rubbed her stomach for sympathy points. "If anything that'll be a time for you to floss your new crib. Why not let them come?"

"I guess." Farah liked the idea of making them jealous. "If you stopped worrying about shit that happened on the bleachers in school during gym, you'd find out that they are really nice girls," Coconut said.

Farah waved them off. There was nothing they could say to her. She didn't fuck with Shannon in middle school and she didn't fuck with her now.

"I don't care about Shannon but I know one thing, the world would have to flatten itself out before I let Boo put her hands on my sister." Mia laughed. "She shouldn't have had a baby by Tank's ass anyway," she continued, still brewing about the stink bomb she threw in the hallway when they were younger.

"I can fight my own battles, Mia. I'm a Cotton too."

"I know that I taught you everything you know, but I used to beat the brakes off of Boo's ass for exercise." Everyone looked at her large body. "So she can put her hand on my little sister if she want to." Mia pulled on the blunt and coughed smoke out of her lungs. "Just tell her come see me." She hit her chest a few times.

As they were getting high, Eleanor McClendon, aka The Clapper, walked past the car. "Oh, shit! I hope this bitch don't ask for no money," Mia said, watching The Clapper strut to the car wearing a brown worn-out fur coat and a short red dress.

"Right . . . 'cause we ain't one of them niggas trying to see her wrinkled-ass cheeks clap together," Coconut said. "She gonna have to do more than pop that thing to get my money." Everyone laughed.

"I can't believe she can do that shit so good, though,"

Rhonda said, remembering when she first met her. "I would swear her ass was light-skinned and not white, if I hadn't seen the pictures of her mother and father on the wall by her door when she opened it one day."

"Wait . . . you went inside her house?" Farah asked.

"Yeah, right. I was trying to get to my friend's house. And Eleanor lives in her building. So many niggas crowded the hallway to see her that day that I could hardly move past them. Hustlers were throwing ones in the air and everything." She shook her head. "To be fifty-eight, that bitch could put the baddest stripper Atlanta has to offer to shame. Niggas call her the eighth wonder of the world." Everybody giggled. "I wish she didn't fuck with that heroin, because I fucks with her. She kinda cool."

"She right. I get my weed from her," Coconut said. "She gets it from Willie Gregory, the old pimp man who just got out of jail. I think they fucking or something."

"Ain't that Randy's father?" Rhonda asked.

"Yep," Coconut said, looking at Farah.

"I heard he not all that bad." Rhonda shrugged. "He volunteers a lot at that nursing home in South-west. He just not good enough to date," Rhonda said. "And he got money, too." Farah remained silent, keeping her comments to herself.

The Clapper walked up to the passenger window and lightly tapped. Coconut rolled hers down and said, "Yes."

"I was wondering if you girls need anything?" The Clapper said, walking up to the window. "I could give you a show if you want to,"She contin-ued, preparing to raise the bottom of her coat.

"Fuck you mean do we need anything?" Farah frowned. "Bitch, ain't nobody in this car paying you to do shit but get the fuck outta they face!" she yelled across Coconut.

"Unless you got some weed on you," Coconut said.

"I'm out now. If you wanna stop by later I got you." She bowed three times before looking at Farah strangely. "I'll talk to y'all later."

"What y'all about to do right now?" Rhonda asked, seeing her boyfriend pull back up. She missed him already. "Knight about to walk me in the house. I wanna take a nap."

"Nothing, girl," Farah said. "Go 'head and do you."

When Rhonda left, Coconut decided to break the silence. "You went too hard to prove your point earlier, Mia. With the sunburn thing."

"Bitch, shut your young ass up!" Mia said. Coconut knew that when it came to wrecking, Mia could win a championship fight with Tyson in his heyday if she wanted, so she closed her mouth. "My sister knows I'm just playing with her. Right?"

Farah looked back at Mia and said, "Coconut, mind your business. You know my sister just fucking around with me." Coconut rolled her eyes.

"So, Farah, when you moving back home?" Mia asked.

Farah looked back at her and frowned. "Never."

"What you talking about? You know you can't afford that apartment by yourself. Ain't that the reason you got caught up with Tank? Trying to get rent money? Not to mention your roommates keep on dying on your ass."

"First off, Natasha never made it to roommate status and Zone was my man. Secondly, I can't live with Ma, you know that. We'd probably kill each other."

"Mamma ain't strong like she use to be, Farah. She ain't about all that fighting no more."

When Farah's phone rang she saw it was Randy and tried to hide the screen from Coconut before she saw his name. When she looked over at her, she was staring in her face. "What?" Farah frowned.

"If you fucking with that nigga again, you stupid."

"What nigga she stupid for messing with, Coconut?" Mia asked.

"Mind your own, Coco," Farah said.

"Fuck it, y'all ain't gotta tell me shit," Mia said. "I got problems of my own."

Farah was supposed to meet Randy fifteen minutes ago but time flew by. She was starting to realize that as much as she hated him, when it came to a bind, he could easily get her out. She was reckless with money, spending it on everything but its intended purpose. Many times she tried to see him in the stories she wrote every day about the way she wanted her life to be, but his face never seemed to fit the picture quite right. "Look, I gotta be somewhere. I'ma get up with y'all later."

"Ugh!" Coconut said, shaking her head. "I knew you were gonna be stupid. Watch that nigga finish what Tank started."

Now Mia was really interested. "What she talking about? You in trouble outside of the Tank situation?"

"It's nothing, Mia. I keep telling y'all I'm grown," Farah snapped. "I'm not mousy Farah Cotton anymore."

"Whatever," Coconut said. "You just make sure you call me later. I wanna go to that new club in DC I was telling you about. It's called E.A.T."

"If we can get in. I hate when they don't just take our fake IDs and keep it moving."

"Well, I know somebody at the door this time. We gonna be good. I'll call you when I'm ready." Coconut eased out of the car.

"A'ight, li'l sis." Mia leaned forward and kissed her on the cheek because she still felt guilty about what she said earlier. "I'ma get up with you later. I love you."

"Love you too. If Shadow calls from prison, tell him I'll write him soon. Daddy too."

"Cool . . . but you need to call Grandma. She's fucked up that you and Chloe not talking to each other, for whatever reason. And she says you've been avoiding her too."

"I'm tired of her preaching."

"At least you got somebody who cares about you. You'll appreciate that when the time is right. Later."

When she left, Farah drove as fast as she could to Randy's house out in Maryland. It did bother her that she didn't have a bond with her grandmother the way she used to, but she was grown and no longer wanted to be told how to live her life. If Elise wanted to see or talk to her, it would be on Farah's terms and times. She pushed the gas pedal harder because for every minute she was late, he would spend fifteen minutes complaining and asking her to give him a reason why he shouldn't leave her alone. But at the end of every fight, he would give her enough cash to make her problems go away and she would do anything sexual he asked.

Randy had obsessed over Farah ever since he found her in the back of his truck when she was a kid. He never made a move because her body hadn't matured enough for his taste. Really he preferred much-older women who would be obedient to his every command. Although she was young, she did listen when he put the pressure on her, so he felt he could mold her mind. Out of all of his girlfriends, Farah was the only one who could take dick and allowed him to do everything he wanted to her body, whether it hurt or not. Plus the fact that before his mother died, three years ago today, she wanted him to marry her, and that made him want to be with her even more, because he trusted his mother's judgment. Losing his mother hurt and without her guidance he was lonely and unstable. He was trying to build a home, but he needed her.

His place was on a curving tree-lined street and all the homes in the neighborhood, including Randy's, had ample lawn space. When she got to his house, she saw another car out front, which was rarely the case. So instead of exiting her warm car and knocking on the door, she decided to call first. "You got company?" she asked the moment she heard his voice. She checked her makeup in the mirror and then brushed her hair. "Because I thought you wanted to be alone with me."

"First of all, I called your mothafuckin' ass ten times and you just getting back at me now? Why the fuck you ain't answer the phone? You gonna make me not fuck with you no more, Farah."

*Then do it then, nigga!*

"Then what the fuck you gonna do? Who gonna keep paper in your pockets?" He was so arrogant it was gross.

"Randy, I was busy with—"

"Get the fuck in here before I cut you off. You gotta learn to respect me."

"I'm parking now." Farah parked her Benz on the street to prevent blocking the other visitor. Then she grabbed her purse and moved through the snowy sidewalk to get to his house. When she got to the door she knocked twice.

"It's open," a man said. The moment she turned the knob, she wanted to run back outside. To her left was a dude she never saw before and when he saw the distressed look on her face, he slammed and locked the door to prevent her from leaving. But it was the person sitting on the sofa with the North Face coat that had her shaken the most.

There Tank was, glaring in her direction. Things were rolling around in her mind and she was feeling sick. Walking toward the sofa, she stopped in place when she heard scratching noises coming from the bathroom by the front door. "What's going on, Randy?" she asked, breathing heavily. To the left of him sat a table with a bouquet of fresh red roses, which she felt were out of place. Her eyes alternated from the stranger to Randy and Tank. "I come at a bad time?"

"Get over here and sit down," Randy said. She didn't move and the man at the door pushed her toward the chair.

"Tank, I'm not gonna say nothing about what happened at your house! You see I ain't tell the cops nothing even though they pressured me. Your secret is safe with me."

"Farah, sit the fuck down," Randy said. "You wasting everybody's time." Farah walked over to a chair within the room across from Tank. He was ice grilling her.

Farah couldn't read Randy's expression because each look he gave meant different things at different times. Although Randy was a dangerous man, to look at him you'd never know. At the moment his smooth dark-chocolate face was emotionless as he ran his hand over his low haircut, which was riddled with waves. A pair of dark Versace shades hung on his nose and he pushed them back repeatedly out of habit.

"Can you tell me what's going on?" She sat in the seat. When the scratching noise at the bottom of the bathroom door got louder she looked at it. When it stopped she faced Randy again. "I'm confused."

"I'm settling your debt, Farah. That's what's going on."

"Settling my debt?" She pointed at herself. "But I don't owe anybody."

"Sure you do, RedBone," Randy said. "Whenever you 'cause problems, you owe the people it impacts. And we're here to discuss what it would take to clean up your mess. When things are settled tonight, you owe me. Don't worry, I got a payment plan for you."

"But I never took anything from him."

"That's because you didn't get a chance to. This nigga is on the run because he murdered somebody you brought in his house without him knowing. So yes, you owe him."

Randy disappeared into the back of the house, leaving Farah alone with the men. While he was gone she turned around and examined the front door. If she used her track skills she could be outside in less than thirty seconds. Deciding to go for it, when she focused back on Tank, the nose of the .45 that killed her friend was staring in her direction. "You not gonna get away from me this time, RedBone." Tank was sweating, even though the air was on. Needless to say Farah didn't move.

Five minutes later, Randy returned with a book bag full of money. When he saw Tank's gun he said, "Put that shit away." Tank pulled up his coat and tucked the gun in his waistband. When he was done, his eyes found their way back on Farah. He hated her and it showed in the way his nostrils flared with every breath he took. Interrupting his gaze, he handed Tank the bag of money and Tank was about to look through it before Randy said, "Don't insult my fucking intelligence. That's one hundred grand. It's all there."

Finally speaking, Tank said, "It may be all there but it ain't enough to start over." He raised the bag. "I might not get farther than North Carolina with this shit."

"But that's what the fuck you asked for, and we both know that's more money than you've ever seen in your life. You couldn't have been making more than a thousand a week working for me on the blocks, if that." Randy looked at his goon on the door who handled paydays. "What you think, Tornado?"

"Less than that for sure," the goon said, speaking for the first time.

"See . . . So for real you're making out."

"But now I'm on the run, boss," Tank persisted. "Because of your fiancée. She fucked up my entire life. I can't even enjoy this shit and be around my kid now." Farah heard the word "fiancée" and thought he was confused.

"I ain't giving you shit else, nigga," Randy said evenly. "Now you can either take the money, or get your fat ass off my couch and get the fuck out my house."

Tank scowled, stood up, and gripped the bag. Then he walked toward Farah. Just being in his presence intimidated her. Had she not been the gold-digging bitch that she was, none of this would've happened. To make matters worse, she wasn't even good in the bedroom. Tank stood over her.

"Stand up, Farah," Randy ordered.

She glared at him. "Huh? Why?"

Randy tilted his head and said, "Really? You gonna make me tell you again?"

She rose slowly and the moment she was eye level with Tank, he slammed his fist into her stomach. The potato chips she shared with her friends earlier came flying out like chunky balls and clung to his black North Face coat. She dropped to her knees and held on to her stomach. Tank dusted the mess off of his coat with the back of his hand and was about to hit her again when Randy said, "That's it. Get the fuck out my house."

Tank looked back at him and said, "I sure hope this bitch worth it."

Randy laughed. "Don't make me take back my good gestures. And, most of all, don't make me lose patience. Now get the fuck out before you're lying on the floor next to her with your eyes shut . . .

permanently." Tank went out the door with Randy's goon, whose mission was to see to it that he got lost for good.

Farah had a headache so strong it felt like someone was plucking her temples. Everything about what just happened confused her. She didn't know Tank worked for Randy, and most of all she couldn't believe she'd run from this dude all this time, only to be handed over to him by her ex-boyfriend. She felt betrayed in the worst way.

Randy grabbed a red rose from the bouquet and walked over to where she kneeled. Then he got on his knees and rubbed her back, as she balled up on the floor. "I can't believe you would even fuck that dude. The nigga's dirty."

"It wasn't even like that," Farah said, looking at him through teary eyes.

"It couldn't be." Randy scowled. Then he put the rose to her nose. "I got something that will make you feel better. Smell this."

"What?" She frowned, not wanting any part of the rose or Randy. "I don't want to."

"I said smell the fucking rose."

Slowly she inhaled the buds and in her opinion it smelled ordinary. "It's a rose, Randy."

"Smell it again," he ordered. "This time sniff harder."

Farah closed her eyes, and sniffed the rose harder. This time a diamond ring scratched the surface of her nose. When she opened her eyes a five-carat ring sparkled in her direction. "Take it out." Randy grinned. "It's yours." Farah slowly took the five-carat ring out of the rose, and knew immediately what it was. "You're going to marry me in February of next year. This is what you owe me for putting out the hundred grand to save your life. That nigga was gonna kill you, Farah. I saved you, so you officially belong to me." He put the ring on her finger. The scratching at the bottom of the bathroom door grew louder and Randy smiled. "Oh . . . I almost forgot." He got up and opened it. Out ran two tiny chocolate teacup yorkies. Since Farah was on the floor, they leaped on top of her and licked all over her face. They were far more excited about life than she was at the moment. "I got these for you as an engagement gift."

"Why are you doing this to me, Randy? I don't love you."

"I'm sorry you see this as a punishment. But before my mother died, she wanted me to be happy and to have kids. She said it would be you . . . Don't you remember that?" She didn't speak. "I been running the streets and could never find a chick more obedient than you. You're young and you do what I ask." He rubbed her hair. "The only problem I have is that I can't keep my eyes on you at all times. That's about to change too."

Farah knew he wasn't the one, she felt it in her heart. If she moved in with him, she'd never be free and he would dominate her life. Lying was the only way she saw out of this situation, even though she could hear her grandmother in the background warning her against it.

"Where have you been living since Zone died?" She could barely speak because she was in so much pain that she felt as if her bowels were pushed to the back because of Tank's thunderous blow. "You gonna make me ask you again?" he said, holding one puppy while the other jumped all over her lap.

"I'm not trying to ignore you," she said, "it's just that my stomach hurts. That nigga just hit me hard as shit."

Randy chuckled. "That blow wasn't hard enough to do damage." He grinned. "I mean . . . it ain't like we ain't did *way* freakier shit than that before. Now where are you living?"

Realizing there was no way she could tell this fool she was trying to keep the apartment in Platinum Lofts she said, "I'm back home. I'm staying with my mother for now."

"Why you didn't keep that spot in the Lofts? I was hoping we could live there together." Secretly he wanted to move dope out of her apartment, since it was in one of his best drug areas. "I thought it would be nice to have that place and our house here."

"They rented it out because I couldn't afford to stay there. It's already gone."

"You should've said something." He shook his head. "Well, since you're my fiancée, you can live with me."

"Randy, you gotta give me time to tell my family. And my mother. I mean, she's sick right now and needs my help."

"You don't even fuck with your mother like that."

"We been working on our relationship." She smiled weakly, now holding a happy puppy to make her lie more believable. "I can't move with you right now because I don't want to leave her alone, and my sisters are doing their own thing."

"I'm gonna let you stay at your mom's house for now, but when she's better, or not, you're moving in with me. That ring on your finger means you are mine. I'm serious about that. You have to handle yourself in the streets like a lady at all times because I'm watching. You're my queen. Do you understand what I'm saying?"

"Yes, Randy." She bawled, wiping tears off her face.

"You know it disappoints me that you're crying. You used to tell me you dreamed about a dark-chocolate nigga to sweep you off your feet. I never forgot about that . . . so here I am." Awkwardly skipping the subject Randy asked, "So what you gonna name them?" He looked at the dogs.

"Not sure. Guess I gotta think about it." The dogs were the last things on her mind.

"Well, think of something tonight." He grabbed the puppy from her lap and it yapped loudly because he gripped it too hard. He put both dogs' faces up to his and kissed them both in the mouths. His tongue touched theirs and Farah was grossed out. "Now go get cleaned up and then go to my room. I want you face down ass up."

# Chapter 17

**"Welcome to my
crazy-ass world." —Farah**

After Coconut declined Farah's roommate offer, she placed an ad in the *Washington Post*. She was looking for a chick she could hang with who was also her roommate, especially since she found out Coconut was spending more time with Shannon. Her jealously was off the meter. If she wanted to end their friendship she would play that game too. At first she wondered if her neglect had something to do with the hit and run, but after a while it became clear that she was just bored with her all together. Farah's ad was specific and straight to the point because she knew what she was looking for. A red bone. Just like her. Someone who was cute to hang out with but had enough money to pay $900 a month in rent. Yet there the dark-skinned girl sat, applying for a room she could never get. "Your engagement ring is beautiful," prospect number eighteen said. "When are you getting married?"

"Never," Farah said with an attitude.

"Oh . . . well . . . I really like the apartment." Her eyes widened as she looked around the large, luxurious pad. And Farah's expensive puppies, which she named Diamond and Pearl, ran around the apartment as if they owned the place. "I knew the moment I stepped into this building, it would probably be fly in here." She nodded. "I was right."

When she left Randy's house the other day, although he didn't know it, he gave her enough paper to pay rent for two months and buy new furniture. Now she was already broke. She had to be careful because he could be anywhere at any time. But her desire to live alone gave her the reason to try him even though she shouldn't have. Years of being stuck at home and unable to have a life made her live for the moment. Feeling like she needed more things done to her apartment, she also had the maintenance man, who had a crush on her, install new carpet. Since she was in charge and living on her own, she wanted things to be perfect.

"I think we would do good together," prospect number eighteen said, looking intently into her eyes. "You seem like you laid back and I'm wild as a two-year-old." She laughed. "They say opposites attract, so we should get along fine."

"Well, I'm not looking for an opposite. I'm looking for someone just like me." Farah lit the blunt she'd wanted to fire up since noon. Now it was five o'clock and she still hadn't found a roommate worthy of splitting it with. One thing was for sure: she damn sure wasn't giving none to the bitch in front of her. "Now I'm glad you like my place and all, but you can't stay here." Farah inhaled smoke and allowed it to exit her lungs in a pillow-like cloud. "Sorry, but it would never work because I'm moody and you probably would take it the wrong way."

Prospect number eighteen frowned. "I deal with moody people all day. I'm a bartender."

"Well, you wouldn't be able to deal with me." She paused. "Besides, the room is taken."

"I been here for fifteen minutes answering all your bullshit-ass questions and you tell me this now?" She was pissed the fuck off and it showed in the way the lines formed on her forehead. "Why didn't you say that shit before? Instead of wasting a bitch's time?"

"I didn't want to be rude at first, but now I don't care. Because at the end of the day, you read what I was looking for, yet you came anyway. Now . . . is there anything else?"

Prospect number eighteen rolled her eyes and grabbed her cell phone from her purse. "Naw, I'ma call my cousin to come pick me up. Since you seem so occupied with your blunt and all." She shook her head. "You didn't even offer a bitch a hit."

"Can you do that out in the hallway?"

"No . . . I can't." She dialed a number and put the phone to her ear. "And if you keep talking shit, I'ma have my cousin come up in here and stomp you out in your own apartment, bitch!" She stood up and looked down at Farah, who remained seated in her brown recliner. Farah wasn't scared of this chick at all. She just wanted things to go smoothly so she could leave. After all, why should she be mad? She already lived in Platinum Lofts. "Hey, GiGi, I'm ready." She looked at Farah again. "Girl, this bitch was serious about that red bone shit she put in the paper. So hurry up and come get me before I hurt her." She paused. "Thanks girl." She put her phone back in her purse. "Is it because I'm not light skinned?" she said out of nowhere. "That you won't let me live here?"

"Yes."

"You know . . . I started not to even come because of your ad, but I was hoping I could change your mind."

"How could you change my mind? You don't even know me." She glowered. "I was specific about what I was looking for. If anything you wasted your own time."

"I figured anybody requesting a roommate who is a red bone is shallow. I guess I was right. What you have against dark-skinned people anyway?"

"What difference does it make? The room is taken and I don't want you to live with me. Damn!" Prospect number eighteen was heated and Farah thought it was funny. Had she not applied for a room that didn't meet her qualifications, none of this would be happening. "Is your cousin on the way? 'Cause I'm expecting more candidates in a minute."

"I thought you said it was taken."

She caught Farah in a lie. "It is."

"But you said more candidates are coming."

"Oh, my God! You're fucking blowing me!" Farah got up and moved toward the door and prospect number eighteen was right on her heels. When she turned around she looked like she was about to hit her. Farah opened the door wide and was shocked to see the cousin on the other side.

The cousin rolled her eyes at Farah and looked at prospect number eighteen and said, "You ready? 'Cause I double parked outside."

"Hey, cousin!" Prospect number eighteen grinned. "Yeah, I'm ready. I just feel like stomping this bitch out before I leave, though."

"What we waiting on?" the cousin said, trying to step into her apartment.

"I don't know who y'all think I am, but I can't be moved." She went into her pocket and flicked a switchblade. When prospect number eighteen saw it next to her pussy her heart jumped. Then

Farah opened her mouth to show the small razor sitting on her wet pink tongue. It was the one thing she took from her dead future mother-in-law that she never stopped using, except once. The one time she didn't have it in her mouth she almost lost her life with Tank, a fuckup she continued to pay for. "I guarantee you I could slice both of y'all quicker than a honey-glazed ham. Now get the fuck out of my face and house." Farah was starting to have second thoughts about staying with another female. Maybe she would do good to move in with Randy after all.

They both looked at Farah and the knife and ran down the hallway. On their way out they bumped into another girl coming toward Farah's door. She tucked in the knife, and readjusted her tongue blade before prospect number nineteen could see anything. "I take it neither one of them got the room." Prospect number nineteen giggled.

"Not even close," Farah said. "Anyway, come in. My name is Farah Cotton."

"Pleased to meet you."

Farah's nineteenth candidate looked the part. She was light skinned with long hair and was very attractive to look at. Farah was sure that if Coconut saw her she'd be jealous because she and Farah looked so much alike they could be sisters. Prospect number nineteen walked inside slowly, examining the fly apartment. Farah saw a smile spread over her face as she looked at the high ceilings, large windows, and expensive leather furniture. When she eyed the floor, Farah caught her examining the new plush cream carpeting before she took a seat on the sofa. "Wow . . . I had no idea it would be so nice in here." She looked at the ceiling again. "Especially since it's still in the—"

"Hood." Farah laughed, finishing her sentence. "You know they doing a lot to DC now, girl. They renovated so many apartment buildings that in a little while, black people won't be able to afford to live anywhere on earth. I know I don't give a fuck though. Half of them don't know how to take care of nice shit anyway."

Prospect number nineteen frowned. "What you mean? You think all black people are ghetto?"

"No, just most of them."

Prospect number nineteen decided to keep her comments to herself. "Anyway, you have a really nice place. I feel like I walked into an episode of *Cribs*." As she adjusted on the leather sofa, it softly groaned.

Farah giggled at her comment. "Thank you." She grabbed the blunt in the ashtray. "You smoke?"

"Naw." She shook her head. "Not anymore."

"You sure? It's some good shit. My friend Coconut got a line to the best loud DC has to offer. Between me and you, I think she's growing the shit in her house. You sure you don't want a hit?" She shook her head again. Farah put the blunt out and picked up the applications on the table. She was blowing her already because if a bitch didn't like to get high, she couldn't trust her. "So what's your name?"

"Nadia Gibson."

She located her application and scanned over it. "Okay, Nadia, why do you wanna live here?"

"Because it's fly for one." She looked around again. "And for two it's close to my job."

"I noticed you left what you do for a living blank." She scanned the document briefly. "Any reason why?"

"I used to work as a customer service rep for Verizon. But I left them mothafuckas a long time ago. People like to keep up too much shit in call centers."

"Oh . . . I used to work for Verizon too. Well . . . for two days anyway. It was a summer position."

"Wow . . . not even here for five minutes and already we have shit in common." She paused. "Where do you work now?"

"I'm unemployed."

"Unemployed?" Nadia frowned. "Well, if I stay here, how you gonna help with your part of the rent? And bills?"

"My mother helps me out a lot. And there's always a nigga lurking in the background, willing to help a bitch out too." Farah cackled. Nadia didn't so much as grin. "Anyway." She cleared her throat.

"I'll always have my portion so if I choose you to live here with me, that won't be a problem." *This bitch got me fucked up. This my mothafuckin' apartment. Not the other way around.*

"Your mamma gonna help you out forever?" She frowned.

"As long as I keep her secret."

Silence.

"You sure that's gonna work?" she continued. "I mean, I had a roommate awhile back and things didn't end well because she couldn't pay her part of the bills. I'm not willing to get into that situation again."

She seemed uncomfortable and suddenly Farah felt like she was interviewing for the room. "It has been working so far. Me and my mother have an understanding." Farah put the papers on the table and wiped her sweaty hands on her velour pants. "I mean, is that a problem for you? It is my apartment and you are looking for a place to stay. Right?"

Nadia thought about it for a while and said, "No. . . ." She shook her head rapidly. "It should be fine if you reassure me you won't be late on your rent each month. That's the only way I'll stay here."

*Bitch, you don't even got the room yet.*

"It's just that I'm looking for stability, especially with having the type of job I do now. The last thing I wanna do is pack up everything and have to move again in a few months."

"What do you do for a living now?"

"I'm a homicide detective for the DC police department.

I've been there for five years." The meeting was officially over.

Farah looked at the blunt on the table, which she'd offered the officer a few moments earlier. No wonder she didn't accept. She was a cop. She could never live there, especially after what happened to Zone. What was to stop her from telling DC's finest if she ever learned how he really died? "It's taken!" Farah blurted.

The officer frowned. "What's taken?"

"The room."

She leaned in to be sure she heard her correctly. "But why didn't you say that before? When I first got here?"

"I'm telling you now. You can't live here. There ain't even enough room."

She stood like the last girl and looked down at Farah. "It's the cop thing, isn't it? And the fact that you smoke weed. Most people I know smoke, so it's not even a problem. Trust me. You can do whatever you want, just as long as you don't kill anybody."

"I need you to get out of my house." Farah was nervous. "Please."

"You seem fucked up." She smirked. "Did I just pull your card or something?"

"Can you please go?" Farah never looked into the officer's eyes. She was starting to feel panicky.

Although Grand told her to take the medicine once a day by mouth, Farah discovered that she needed it at least four times a day. Something about going into the cooler and putting the liquid to her lips put her at immediate ease.

"Look, I really need this room. If you're worried about me being a cop, like I said, you don't have to. I just need to stay in a place I can afford, that's close to work and safe. This may be in the hood but the building is secure. Plus I have a gun. I have a lot of student loans and the rent is right up my alley. I think this can work."

"It will never work. Trust me."

"You know it's better to have me on your side than it is to have me off?" Every time she opened her mouth all Farah heard was "cop, cop, cop, cop." She could plead with her until she grew hair on her face. Her family was crazy and deranged and she couldn't risk Nadia snooping around and finding out about who the Cottons truly were. "I should've known something was up when you specified that you wanted to live with another red bone." She looked at the applications in Farah's lap. "I bet you don't even have any friends. Or a man, do you?" She laughed harder. "Your neighbors probably don't even fuck with you!"

"Whoever is in my life is my fucking business. Bitches kill me getting mad because I didn't choose them to stay. We ain't fucking! Now bounce before I call the police."

She looked at her and shook her head. "I am the police. Or have you forgotten already?" Nadia looked at her with a penetrating glare. There was something up with this Farah Cotton, she was sure of it. "I don't know why, but for some reason, I'm sure I'll see you again."

Farah moved toward the door. "Good-bye, Detective."

Nadia smirked and walked out. Farah closed the door quickly and leaned up against it to regain her composure. That shit was too close for comfort.

At the end of the day Farah was tired of interviewing a rack of bitches who were all wrong. She realized she needed a roommate but everything she had to go through, in her opinion, was for the birds. Nadia was right about one thing: she never got along with her neighbors. Zone told her all the time that if someone broke in his apartment not one of them would care enough to tell him what they saw. Suddenly meeting the people in her building seemed like a good idea. First she decided to take her medicine. She knew if she did nothing else, she had better take care of her health. It did wonders for her complexion, body, and mood. Often times she would feel better just thinking about it before she even got to the cooler. Prior to meeting Grand Mike she spent $200 a week on makeup, and now she was down to about forty.

Farah walked into the bathroom and sat on the toilet. Grabbing a magazine she thumbed through the pages and saw a girl who looked like her baby sister. She missed Chloe. A lot. As wrong as she was, she was still her sister and they'd never gone so long without talking to one another. Chloe had been calling nonstop saying she had to talk to her about what happened, but for the moment, Farah seen enough of her face and pussy to last a lifetime. After Farah finished using the bathroom, she grabbed her pink Mikasa cup and proceeded on her mission to borrow sugar, which she really didn't need.

Ever since Zone died, she isolated herself even more from those who lived in her building. She would go so far as to ignore people who spoke to her in passing in the hallways. At first, before she met Grand, Farah was too afraid they'd look at the sores on her face and judge her. She didn't have that problem anymore. But it was because of the drama in her apartment that construction workers had to go into her neighbors' homes to redo all of their windows. After Zone's death, the fire department determined the windows couldn't stand up to the safety code and in their professional opinion, had the windows been properly installed, Zone would still be alive today. Of course, they'd be wrong.

On a mission, she grabbed her key and walked out the door. Her naked toes burrowed into the plush burgundy carpet as she walked to the far end of the hallway. Spotting the door she wanted to knock on first, she took two quick breaths because she was nervous when meeting new people. Then she looked down at her neat True Religion jeans and clean white T-shirt. Feeling that she looked fine enough to bum, she knocked softly on the first door.

*What am I doing? Maybe I should just go home.* She was about to abandon the entire idea when a fourteen-year-old pudgy black kid opened the door and said, "What you want?" She'd never seen him before; then again, she didn't see many of her neighbors. When she looked farther into the apartment and saw a picture of him and a large older woman on the wall she realized exactly where she was . . . Vivian James's apartment, who was her property manager and who also couldn't stand her.

"What do you want?" he repeated.

"I wanted to borrow some sugar." Farah raised the cup and smiled. "You got any?"

"Do you even live in this building?"

Farah was tired of looking at his extra round face so she sarcastically said, "No. I just appeared from nowhere with no shoes on, stupid." The pudgy kid looked at her feet and slammed the door in her face. Farah didn't move right away because she contemplated knocking on the door again and smacking him down. Instead, she mustered up enough courage to proceed to the next location.

This time she ran her fingers through her natural brown hair and took two deep breaths. When she was ready, she hit the door twice with her knuckles and stepped back. A smile spread across her face in the hopes that whoever answered would be welcoming.

"Yes?" a girl asked, throwing the door open. She was pretty with large brown eyes and freckled light skin. The only thing missing was her sweet disposition. "What the fuck do you want?" The girl's eyes moved over Farah as she made a judgment.

She took a deep breath and said, "Uh . . . do you have . . . I was wondering . . ."

"You here to see Kirk?" The girl glared.

Hoping Kirk was nicer, she said, "Yes, is he home?"

Air seemed to fill the girl's chest as she balled up her fists and looked sternly at Farah. "I'm tired of you bitches trying to ruin my fucking marriage! When you gonna realize Kirk is married? Huh?" she screamed, stepping into the hallway. If she swung Farah had all intentions of dropping her at her doorstep.

Seconds later, an attractive man with an extra-long beard walked out. "Who is this?" he asked her.

"You tell me!" screaming girl yelled. "I know one thing, I'm sick of these bitches coming over here with this bullshit, Kirk! I thought you said you wanted to make this work! I thought you said you wanted me!"

"I do, baby. I don't know this bitch." He pointed at Farah.

"Well, what the fuck is she doing here?"

"Don't ask me!" He looked at Farah. "Who the fuck are you anyway?"

"I'm . . . your neighbor. I . . . I live down the hall." Farah tried to create a smile but it didn't move upward. Truth was, she was growing weary of the foolishness already. "I was just trying to see if you had some sugar. But if I caused too much drama, I can roll, it's not that deep."

"You wanted to see if we had some fucking sugar?" screaming girl said. "Bitch, don't play games. You came for him so here he is."

"Look, I'm not gonna be too many more of your bitches."

"You gonna be as many bitches as I call you."

"Baby, I don't know who this chick is," he interrupted, "but I swear to God I'm not fucking around on you this time!"

"How come I don't believe you?" screaming girl said, resting her hands on her hips. "She came over here asking for you! Called you by your name and everything," she lied. "Here I am making dinner and sucking your dick in between checking on the meal and you still not satisfied. What a bitch gotta do to keep you?"

"You told my girl you know me?" Kirk asked.

"Like I said, I was just coming to get some sugar." *This bitch is doing too much now.* The moment Farah said that the pudgy kid entered the hallway. Instead of minding his own fucking business he straight leaned against the wall and watched the entire scene unfold while chewing popcorn.

Farah was preparing to walk away when Kirk grabbed her forcefully by the wrist. His long bitch-like nails dug into her skin and she was sure if he didn't let go, he'd break her arm. "You ain't going nowhere until you tell my girl you fucking lied on me! If you don't she gonna be at my throat all night and I don't feel like that shit."

"I don't know him," Farah said to the girl. "I live in apartment 1316. If I knew all of this was gonna pop off, I never would've came over here. You can keep him because I damn sure don't want him." She flashed the engagement ring she didn't even respect. "I have a man."

"You told me you don't live here," the pudgy kid interjected. "When you knocked on my door. Maybe you were coming to see him." He shrugged. "I don't know."

*Fat fuckin' bastard! Why don't he mind his fat-ass business!* "I was just playing with you!" Farah yelled. "I do live in the building and have been here for years. That's why I don't have no shoes on. What I'm gonna do, get out of my car and walk through the snow and hallways with bare feet?" Farah paused. "My boyfriend was the one who died a month ago."

"You getting married already?"

"Yes." She rolled her eyes. "Anyway my ex fell out the window. It was because of that everybody in this building had to get new windows." screaming girl's expression changed and Farah felt she believed her. If she didn't, she had all intentions of reaching into her mouth, removing her blade, and slicing both of them quickly if he let her go. Suddenly, for some reason, all she wanted to do was talk to her grandmother. It was as if she foresaw everything that was happening to her in advance.

"So you fucking a bitch in our building?" Screaming girl frowned. "Right under my nose?" Either she was petty or she was just ready to rumble. Either way Farah wanted no part of it.

Farah was about to walk away when Kirk forcefully grabbed her wrist again. "You ain't going no-fuckingwhere!"

"You're hurting me! Let go!" She dropped to the floor and her pink cup rolled a few inches out into the hallway.

Kirk was preparing to hit Farah when a six-foot-five-inch man came out of the apartment next door. His presence was huge and filled up the entire hallway. His dark skin was so perfect it almost didn't look real. The man's bald head was clean, and with the exception of a scar that ran across the right side of his neck, he was exactly like she imagined. Under the light the mark glistened like liquid platinum under the sun. Farah never, in her entire life, wanted a man more than she did him, from first sight. This was the man of her dreams . . . the one she wrote about since she was a child . . . she was sure of it.

The man looked at Farah and then at the dude who was holding her against her will. He had a younger boy with him, whose skin was also chocolate. "Slade, what you doing?" the boy asked. "We gotta go meet our brothers. Fuck that bitch, man!"

"Give me a second, Audio," Slade said, examining the scene from where he stood. He was trying to figure out if he should get involved.

Kirk grabbed Farah's arm tighter and didn't seem to be phased by the dudes, who stepped into the hallway. "Bitch, you better tell my girl who the fuck you are before I fuck you up!"

Now Slade was involved. He walked up to him and said, "I don't know what's going on and I'm not trying to step into your business—"

"Then don't," Kirk interrupted. "This between me and her."

Slade looked down and, for some reason, his eyes averted toward Kirk's butter-colored Timberlands. There was a large stain on the left boot that looked as if it was dried blood. He fought enough niggas and seen enough blood to know the difference. He wondered why this dude would wear shoes like that. "I hear what you saying, but I know you not about to hit no female. In front of your woman and a kid?"

"Man, I don't know who the fuck you are, but you better mind your fucking business," Kirk rallied. "Anyway, this bitch just lied on me, and I'm not letting her go until she tells the truth."

Farah's eyes focused on Slade. She could smell the scent of his fresh leather black coat. Now she wished she had done more to make herself cute before walking into the hallway. "You not about to hit her in front of me."

"Slade, we gotta bounce," Audio said. Although he didn't want his brother involved with Farah, his eyes moved toward her toes and he wondered what they'd taste like in his mouth. His fetish for feet was heavy. Slade gave him one look which silenced him immediately.

"I think you better listen to your little bro," Kirk added.

"Nigga, fuck you!" Audio yelled. "You don't know shit about me or my brother!"

Slade seemed irritated with Kirk so he slammed his fist into the wall next to their door. It folded under his knuckles as if it were wet paper. Kirk released the hold he had on Farah and she fell to the floor. The pudgy kid rushed into his apartment for fear that Slade would flatten him next. *Oh, my God! And he's strong!* She'd seen Zone punch at that wall a thousand times, never denting it once.

"If you want to hit somebody . . ." Slade said, removing his fist from the hole he just formed with his bare hand. White powdered plaster covered his chocolate knuckles. He stepped so close to Kirk his bitch got scared and rushed into the apartment to save herself, leaving him alone. "Then how 'bout you hit me." Slade looked into his eyes and challenged his manhood. "I guarantee you I won't be as vulnerable as the chick on the floor."

Kirk looked at Slade and then at Farah. He backed up to get out of Slade's way and said, "Don't fucking come to my house again with no more bullshit."

When the door slammed, Slade reached over to help Farah up. She was about to take his hand when he quickly removed it as if she spit in his palm. Farah was confused as she plopped back to the floor. He tucked his hand in his pocket and looked at her. "I'm . . . I'm sorry. But I gotta go."

Farah watched him and Audio walk away before disappearing into the stairwell. *Was it something I did wrong? Maybe it's this fucking ring.* She decided from then on to only wear it when Randy was in the room. Standing on her own, she picked her cup up and brushed off the back of her jeans. When she made it to her apartment, there was a beautiful girl standing at her door and the moment Farah saw her she knew she was the one. Her hair was the same length as Farah's. The only difference was the girl's was black and curly. Her lashes were long and she wore a short black leather jacket and tight jeans with a pair of high black boots.

She was fly and she was the twentieth candidate of the day.

*Maybe twenty is my lucky number.*

"Hi." The girl smiled. "Are you okay? I saw what happened over there. That shit was crazy!" Farah wondered why she didn't help her out, but she ignored that sign.

"I'm cool," Farah said. "I didn't know we had so many wild-ass people in this building."

She laughed. "You sure? You seem out of it."

Farah turned around to see if Slade for whatever reason came back. He hadn't. "I'm sure. It's just that it's been a long day." She paused. "You here to see the room?"

"Yes . . . if it's still available."

Putting Slade behind her she said, "After everything I been through today, you could be the worst roommate ever and I'd still let you live here."

The girl giggled. "Well, you won't have no problems with me. I'm all fun and games, minus the drama and the bullshit."

"That's what's up. So what's your name?"

"Lesa Carmine."

"Well, Lesa, welcome to my crazy-ass world."

# Chapter 18

**"I know we need money and we gonna move on that when we can. But that ain't the priority now." —Slade**

It had been two years since Slade Baker touched his mother, for fear he might hurt her. It had been even longer since he touched a woman. So when he saw the baddest bitch he'd ever seen in his life in need of help, he almost forgot the "no touch" vow he pledged many years ago.

"There go a gas station right there." Audio pointed. "Why don't you stop so I can get something to drink? Plus I gotta use the bathroom." Nineteen-year-old Audio Baker, despite his wild disposition, was easy to look at with his dark-chocolate skin and wide eyes. All throughout high school Audio was popular because he said what was on his mind and let people sort it out. In an age of everybody biting their tongues, to some, he was appealing.

"I saw it, Audio. I ain't blind." Slade couldn't get the chick off his mind and he was vexed. The last thing he needed was to be thinking about anything other than the trouble over his head.

"I'm just letting you know 'cause I thought that bitch still had you wrapped up."

Slade shook his head and pulled into the station. When he found an available pump, he parked his green Ford Expedition. Slade's ride was on its last leg and it was a wonder how they made it all the way from Natchez, Mississippi, to Washington DC without breaking down on the highway. He knew that somewhere his mother, Della Baker, was praying for the safe arrival of her sons.

"Go inside and pay for the gas," Slade told Audio, handing him a twenty dollar bill. His eyes lit up, as they always did whenever he saw money, no matter the denomination. "Audio, don't make me hurt you. Put this on gas only. I got a lot of shit on my mind and ain't got time to be fucking with you. The gas." He pointed. "Go."

Audio walked into the station while Slade sat back and watched everyone around him make moves. He didn't like DC any more than DC liked him, but for now it would have to do. He knew the moment niggas heard his heavy accent that they'd count him off as slow. He would make a fool out of anyone who ever got in his way. Leaving a town that didn't want him or his brothers anymore didn't make him slow, it made him stronger.

Firing up a blunt, flashes of the woman he met earlier ran back through his mind. She reminded him of his girl back in Mississippi, who died in a car accident some years back. When he first saw her in his cousin Markee's building, he thought God was fucking with his mind, because of all the bad things he'd done in his life. But she was real and he felt the connection.

"What the fuck you doing, Audio?" Slade said to himself as he looked at the clock on the console of his car. He smashed out the blunt in the ashtray and was preparing to get out, when through the store's window he could see his little brother being pummeled by two niggas like he was an open quarterback on a football field. Slade's heart kicked up speed and his fingers covered the door handle, which was held in place by duct tape. But it didn't open because he broke it by accident awhile back. Every other gadget in his ride was destroyed because he could never gauge his own strength.

Finally making it out of his truck, he rushed toward the store in a sincere hurry. People who were hanging in the doorway quickly moved as Slade barreled inside. His presence seemed to fill up the entire store and everybody took notice. His fists were clenched tightly and his jaw flexed when he saw strangers lay hands on his kid brother. Ideas of mass homicide were on his mind if one follicle was harmed on his brother's head.

When Slade spotted Audio, a grin rested on his face when he saw him handling his own with blow after blow. But when Slade made it to the brawl, he lifted one of the dudes off of his brother by the back of his coat, and tossed him across the counter. Then he grabbed another and threw him into the store window, which shattered against his body weight. The third man he tossed into the air and he flew into a rack of potato chips. When a fourth tried to help out, who had nothing to do with the shit, Slade grabbed his arm, broke it, and he screamed out in pain. When it came to wrecking with the hands, not too many dudes had shit on him. If they wanted to put him out of commission, it was best to use a bullet because he'd been hit with the best, from bats to knives, and he always came out on top. His body reflected injuries from battles won . . . never lost. He enjoyed inflicting pain on people who did him wrong.

When the fight was over Slade yelled, "Let's go, Audio!" He helped him off the floor.

Audio grinned at one of the men lying by his feet and spit in his face. "Fuck you, nigga!"

"It's time to bounce!" Slade said. "Later for all that other shit." Slade looked at the men who stirred on the floor due to the damage he caused to their bodies, and stepped over them on his way out the door. "I knew some shit was gonna happen."

"But what about the gas?" Audio asked.

Slade didn't feel like talking because his brother disobeyed him. So Audio, without another word, ran behind him as they jumped into the truck and sped out of the parking lot. The sound of sirens indicated somebody called the police and that was the last thing they needed. Wanted already in Mississippi, they weren't trying to add Washington DC to the list. After getting far enough away, he looked for another station.

Slade drove in silence for five more minutes before finally looking at Audio. His breaths were heavy and he felt like checking his chin. He didn't have to ask to know that whatever happened in that store was Audio's fault. Slade took his coat off and threw it in the back seat because he was so mad he was dripping in sweat. Rolling the arms up on his black thermal shirt, the tattoo that read slade on the back of his left forearm was scratched lightly. He didn't even feel it when it happened. The tattoo was in capital black letters except the letter "A" which was red, with the end of it forming a sword. It was one of many he had on his body. When Slade thought he was calm enough, he decided to check Audio for the fight back at the station. Audio was looking out the window, trying to avoid his brother, when Slade asked calmly, "Where my money?"

Never looking at him he said, "What money?"

"You want me to pull this truck over? Or do you wanna stop playing games?"

Audio looked at him, reached in his pocket, peeled a twenty dollar bill from a small stack of cash he somehow inherited, and placed it in Slade's hand. He had more money on him now than before he stepped out of his truck. "What happened back there?" Slade's eyes moved over him slowly before focusing on the road. "And don't hold shit back. You never were good at lying."

Audio turned the radio on and Kanye West's voice sounded in the background. "The nigga bumped into me." He shrugged. "So I stole his ass."

"Fuck is wrong with you? We ain't come out here for this shit! We came out here to keep low." Slade looked at Audio and then back at the road. "You gonna get us hemmed up." He huffed. "I gave you an order, nigga. A direct order at that and you didn't follow it. Tell me why I shouldn't crash your chest?"

Audio was trying to bite his tongue but he was growing up and didn't like being the baby anymore. "So what I'm supposed to do? Let some DC nigga fuckin' disrespect me?"

"You always talking about respect but you never give none." He turned the radio off and looked at his brother. "Matta fact, I don't wanna even hear you use the word respect until you know what the fuck it means. If I do, I'ma crack your jaw." He paused. "We on the run. Our brothers are out there looking for us. We don't need no extra shit on the board right now."

"I'm not a baby no more, man."

"Then act like it!" Slade roared. "Tonight is big. We ain't seen our bros in two weeks. You wanna fuck that up 'cause you think you not getting respect from a nigga you don't even know?" He was going hard because he loved him and needed him to think more carefully. Audio was country to the core and whatever he wanted, even if somebody had it, he took. The brothers were trying to temporarily mold him while in DC, knowing it was a trait that could get him killed. But Audio didn't understand because in Mississippi they ran their small town.

"You know I wanna see my fam, Slade. But I ain't steal his money off the counter. Them niggas lied on me! Honest!" Whenever Audio said "honest," he was anything but.

Slade shook his head and pulled over to the side of the road. "I spoke to Ma earlier. She said Devon's gonna come up and help us out. He got us some fake IDs and a little paper to tie us over. So we gonna be all right. I ain't trying to get locked in with no DC fucking police. We can't do nothing that's gonna jeopardize bringing our family back together. You gotta remember the plan, Audio. To find Knox, link up with Devon, and get outta Markee's crib. When shit die down, we back to Mississippi. I'm about family . . . Don't make me commit homicide because you made a wrong move."

Della Baker, who gave birth to four of her five sons alone in her home, did her best to bring them up the right way, even though trouble followed them so much that they could never seem to do the right thing. They were caught up in so much shit back home that eventually she decided that if they were going to commit crime, she would at least teach them the proper way. None of her sons knew how Della was able to break the law so easily. For real, they didn't want to know. Under her leadership they did everything from stealing cars to moving small amounts of drugs in the city they called home.

And when shit went wrong, and somebody needed bail, Della would throw fish parties to get her sons out. After a while if any crime was committed in their town Della's sons would be accused, even if they weren't anywhere near the scene of the crime. It wasn't long before law enforcement nicknamed Della's sons the Baker Boys. Although they mainly profited from the illegal alcohol operation she ran out of the house, each of her sons favored a different crime. Slade stole cars, Audio stole anything not bolted down, Killa, unlike his nickname, gambled heavily and loved weapons, Major sold weed, and Knox robbed houses. Although the police knew the Baker Boys were usually up to something, prior to what happened a few weeks back, they liked her sons. But that was before the Baker Boys signed a deal with the devil.

Things were in motion for Slade and his brothers
and there was no time to stop. First they had to find
their middle brother, Knox, who fled earlier with
the evidence to keep them alive and out of prison.
They all waited for his call, which up until this point
hadn't come. Not only were his whereabouts crucial
to their freedom, but it was also necessary for the
sanity of their family.

"Audio, if you didn't steal from them niggas,
where did you get the money from?"

"What money?"

"The money in your fucking pocket!" Slade
shook his head.

"I ain't got no . . ." Audio was preparing to lie
when Slade reached into his jeans and pulled out
the dough. Then he hit him in his chest as lightly as
he could, but hard enough to knock a few breaths
out of his body.

Balling the cash up and putting it in his face he
said, "This money."

"I been had that," he lied, rubbing his chest. His
lightest punch was murder.

"Where did you get this shit? When we left
Natchez you were dead broke. Now you got paper?
When I paid for your food and shit all the way up
here?"

Audio held his head down. "I'm tired of never
having enough." A few tears escaped him. He hated
crying in front of his oldest brother. "How come

we can't never have nothing? How come we always gotta take stuff from other people?"

"Shit gonna get better. I know we need money and we gonna move on that when we can. But that ain't the priority now." Slade peeled a fifty back from the stack and handed it to him.

"Hold up! Why you get to keep most of the cash?" he asked, examining the fifty dollar bill in his hand. "I'm the one who took the shit."

"'Cause I know what to do with this and you don't. That's why." Slade pulled back into traffic when his phone rang. "And that's fifty more dollars than you had awhile ago, too."

Slade answered the phone. It was his mother. "Hey, Ma . . . any word?"

"Slade, the boys not gonna be able to meet you today. They'll call you when it's time because they haven't made it to DC yet. They can't call me from this number anymore, because I'm about to move again . . . I think them people found me." His heart dropped but he was happy that, for now, she was safe. "But I got more news I'ma have to push on you that ain't too good."

His heart skipped, thinking his brother might be dead. "What's up?"

"Son, it ain't good."

Slade frowned and drove slower. "You got word on Knox?"

"It ain't about my boy." Slade exhaled in relief. "They found your cousin Devon's body roped to a car. He was dragged a few miles out on a dirt road before they finally killed him. We barely recognized him, Slade, 'cause his face had been rubbed off on the gravel. No nose or lips. Your aunt Betsy is beside herself. These mothafuckas done took shit to the next level."

Slade swallowed the hurt and held it in his gut. He needed to be strong for his family. "How you doing, Ma? I mean, how you really holding up?"

"I'm Della Baker. I guess I gotta be all right, don't I? My sons are still alive and they need me to keep it together. I don't want y'all worrying about me. Just find Knox and your brothers. I'm counting on you, son." He could hear that her voice was different and knew she'd been crying. "Let me go see about my sister. I'll talk to you later."

Slade ended the call and drove in silence, while Audio waited for the word. "What happened?" Audio asked. "Big bro, what's wrong? Ma okay?"

"Somebody killed Devon."

Audio dropped his head, looked back at Slade, and said, "Now what?"

# Chapter 19

### "You mad at me over a stupid-ass game?" —Farah

The bass from the loud music playing in the living room rattled the bathroom door. Farah sat on the toilet with her legs cocked opened as Coconut licked her pussy clean, on her knees. They were drunk and horny and this was the only time they played the licky-licky game. "I'm about to cum," Farah said, grabbing her head. "Keep flicking that tongue." She was overwhelmed by the sensation that Coconut's long, hard, warm tongue was putting on her clit.

Coconut removed her wet lips from her pussy and said, "Shh. . . ." She looked at the closed bathroom door. "I don't want nobody to come in here."

"The door locked. Stop worrying about it," Farah whispered. "Now keep doing it." She continued to eat her out until Farah felt her body tingle all over. Her legs tensed up and she came in her mouth. Since she was on the toilet, her body automatically released a drop of urine and Coconut frowned.

"Ugh," she said, wiping her mouth. "I hate when you do that shit." She stood up, wobbled to the sink, and washed her face. Then she grabbed Lesa's toothbrush, instead of Farah's, and scrubbed her teeth. "You gotta tell me if you gonna pee before you do it."

Farah spun the toilet roll around and grabbed a few pieces to wipe her pussy. "When I did you and you pissed in my mouth, I ain't say all that shit. Let's hurry up and go back to the party before people come looking for us."

Knock. Knock. Knock. The rapping on the door caused both girls to quiver in shame. "What y'all doing in there?" Rhonda asked on the other side of the door. "It don't take all that time to put on no makeup. Mothafuckas gotta use the bathroom."

Farah and Coconut weren't acting like themselves, because of the liquor in their blood. Randy had been stressing Farah out so much about the marriage that all she wanted to do was have a little fun. "We coming out now, Rhonda."

"Well, hurry up. You got a whole rack of niggas we don't know in your house. Some of them fine as shit, too." She screamed, as the music suddenly grew louder, "And if somebody steal something in this bitch I don't wanna hear your mouth."

Since they were being freaky, they cleaned up and walked out of the bathroom. On the way out, Farah could hear her dogs barking in the guest bedroom so she played with them for a few minutes to put space between her and Coconut. At first the dogs were getting on her nerves but now she loved them a lot because they were always happy to see her. After entertaining her dogs, she joined the party and was immediately overwhelmed by so many people. Most of them were friends of Coconut, Rhonda, and Lesa. They were celebrating everything from Farah's new roommate, who was a hit with her friends, to Knight asking Rhonda to be his wife. When she saw everyone, she couldn't believe how many people were in her house. She and Coconut was fucking around so long in the bathroom that she didn't monitor who was coming in or out. The smell of weed and the scent of an apple pie baking in the oven were dominant.

When Lesa saw Farah through the crowd she waved from the sofa. She looked real cute in her tight blue jeans and smooth ponytail. She was sitting next to Diamond D from Southwest DC, who was known for robbing niggas, and she was sure he knew Randy. She wanted to keep the apartment a secret from him but by having the party, she was going about it in the worst way. When Mia walked in Farah felt better, because at least someone was there who had her back.

"Hey, Farah . . . where you been?" Lesa yelled over the music. "I been looking for you all night."

"Me and Coconut was in the bathroom putting on makeup." She smiled weakly. "I didn't know you knew Diamond D." She pointed at him. "You gotta watch that nigga."

"Yeah . . . we go way back. He cool though," she said. "I'm surprised Rhonda knew him . . . She the one who invited him over. Anyway, you got any tampons? I came on my period."

"Yeah . . . they under the sink in my bathroom."

"Cool." She turned around to Diamond D and said, "I'll be right back." He raised his beer and bopped his head to the music.

"Farah, come over here right quick!" Coconut yelled. She was in the middle of a crowd and had a drink in her hand. "We 'bout to play smack down." People were already preparing for the show so whether Farah wanted to or not, she couldn't back down. Normally Coconut was good at this game, but since she was drunk, Farah couldn't be sure. The object was simple: you had to smack your opponent as hard as you could until someone raised their hand and gave up.

"You know you don't need to be playing that shit, Coconut," Rhonda said. "Your ass twisted." She pulled her arm. "Come on over here and sit by me."

She shook her off. "I got this." She pushed her drink into Rhonda's hand. "Come on Farah . . . you first." The crowd around them grew tighter.

Without waiting, Farah smacked her so hard her neck snapped to the left.

"Damn!" Diamond D said. "She nailed that shit."

While the game was in session, somebody knocked on the door and Mia opened it. Farah couldn't see who it was because the house was so jam-packed. In every available place there was a body. When Coconut refocused after her smack, she hit Farah with all she could. Farah laughed and said, "You gotta do better than that shit." Then she smacked her back and she stumbled backward. She was now enjoying the game.

"That's enough!" Rhonda said, looking at Farah. "The girl can hardly stand up."

"Well, she needs to raise her hand if she wants it to stop. She know the rules." Mia refereed from the sidelines. "You want her to stop, Coconut?" Coconut looked at Farah and stepped to her. They'd played this game many times before, yet at the moment she couldn't hold her own. As hard as she could she hit Farah again, but it was weak. Farah slapped her again and the right side of her mouth bled.

"This too much for me to watch," Lesa said, grabbing Diamond D's hand and taking him back to her room.

The party was supposed to show Coconut what she was missing out on by not moving in with her and now it had turned into something else. Coconut, feeling slightly unbalanced, got her bearings and smacked Farah back, but her face didn't move one inch. "Farah handling that shit!" someone said.

Mia laughed and yelled, "Make this one count, RedBone! It's your turn."

When Farah looked at Coconut, she saw that she was pleading with her eyes to stop. Farah looked around and saw all of the people waiting for the show to continue. She didn't want to look like a punk, so using all of the force she could manage she smacked Coconut so hard that she stumbled to the floor. "Damn!" people yelled.

"You handled that bitch!" another said.

"You give up?" Farah asked, looking down at her. Coconut looked up and slowly raised her hand. She'd given up and everybody went wild.

An hour later, when people were dancing and getting high, Farah was in the kitchen making sandwiches. When she looked toward her sofa, she was confused at why everybody seemed to be consoling Coconut, as if she hadn't initiated the game. Rhonda was rubbing her back and Lesa was sitting on the other side, talking to her and stroking her leg. Farah didn't even know she had come back to the party after fucking Diamond D on her period. They were giving her unnecessary attention and she wanted it to stop. This was her party and her house yet the feeling of being an outsider, as a kid, was looming in the air. She needed her medicine. *That bitch started it with me first. I was minding my own business when she asked me to play that stupid-ass game. Now they trying to turn my roommate against me, too.*

"Lesa, you mind getting some ice?" Farah said loudly, trying to break up the group. "We ran out and I'm making sandwiches for everybody."

"I ain't got no gas!" Lesa yelled, trying to be heard over the music. "I'm broke."

"We got an ice machine on every floor in this building. Ours is on the other end of the hallway."

Lesa said something else to Rhonda before walking into the kitchen. She seemed angry.

"You mad at me over a stupid-ass game? Because I didn't even wanna play, and Coconut been playing that shit since we were kids."

Lesa grabbed a bowl for the ice and said, "No . . . but you know that girl was drunk, and you should not have hit her that hard. She supposed to be your friend."

"I was drinking too. So what, I'm supposed to go apologize? What about my sympathy credits?"

"What?" she asked. "Never mind. It's whatever you want, Farah. If that was my friend I would never have treated her that way." Lesa took the bucket and walked toward the door. A few dudes in the party tried to get her attention on the way out but she ignored them all.

Farah thought about what she said because she didn't want them angry with her and now her mind was all over the place. She needed a smoke and decided to get her secret stash from her closet to roll a jay. Going to her room and into the closet, she was caught off guard when someone walked in, turned off the light, and pushed her into the closet. Her forehead slammed into the back of the wall. She fell on top of the shoes on the floor when he grabbed her and turned her around. She just knew it was Randy. "Get the fuck off of me!" she screamed, trying to be heard over the music. He didn't seem fazed as he managed to pull her pants down.

Farah was fighting hard until he stole her in the face and bent her over. Her panties were down and she could smell the funk of his feet rising from his wet Timberland boots. His penis was out and he was about to ram it inside of her when the lights came on. Mia opened the closet door and pulled him off of her sister, by way of a chokehold, as if she were a grown-ass man. Enraged, Mia kicked and hit him all over his body.

Farah crawled out of the closet to join her sister in the beat down. It wasn't until he turned over, and she looked at his bloodstained shoe, that she realized who he was: Kirk, the man who was about to hit her the day she knocked on his door for sugar. "You dirty mothafucka! What the fuck you doing in my house?"

Lesa went to the ice machine on their floor but it was out of order. Deciding to go to another machine, she took the stairs when the elevator wouldn't open. When she made it to the fourth floor, someone was at that one too so she took the stairwell to the fifteenth floor. Filling her bucket with ice, she walked to the elevator, hit the button, and waited. But five minutes later, it still hadn't come. "I hate fucking elevators," she said to herself. "You can never use them when you need them!"

She went into the stairwell and walked down the steps toward her floor. All of a sudden, she heard someone above her say, "There Farah go, right there! Get that bitch before she get away."

When she looked up, she saw two men moving speedily in her direction. Her heart kicked into overdrive and she felt adrenaline course through her body. She dropped the bowl filled with ice on the floor when a bullet smashed into the wall next to her head. They were shooting at her and she was so scared she was weak. "What did I do?" she cried. "Leave me alone!"

One of the men slid on the ice she dropped and she hoped it would buy her some time. Her hopes were in vain when, seconds later, she could hear two sets of footsteps moving toward her again. It seemed like it took forever to reach the 13th floor and to make matters worse, she fell and injured her elbow. One of the men grabbed her leg but she was able to kick him off, forcing him backward into his partner.

Both of them rolled down a few steps and she got up and ran again. Finally she was able to gain space and made it to her floor in one piece. Yanking the door open, she sprinted through the hallway, screaming at the top of her lungs. She could see the door to her apartment at the far end of the hallway and prayed she'd reach it before they got a hold of her. When she turned around she was disappointed to see the men were hot on her trail. She didn't know what they wanted, but they clearly had the wrong person.

"Help me!" she screamed. "They trying to kill me!"

When the elevator opened and two cops got off and walked into the hallway, she fell to the floor, unable to believe her good fortune. But the men ran back through the stairwell and out of sight before the officers could see or apprehend them. They were actually responding to a rape call from Farah's apartment. The officers rushed to her aid and she sobbed heavily in their arms.

# Chapter 20

**"I spent most of my childhood in
bed . . . All I wanna do is have fun
with my friends." —Farah**


Farah was on her way to the gym with Lesa, who
was driving. After what Kirk did to her, she was
thinking heavily about life, and wanted to talk to
her grandmother. "Grandma," she said from her
cell, "remember when you were talking to me about
keeping my heart in check, when I was a kid? What
did you mean by that?"

"Are you okay?" Her voice was heavy with concern. "Sometimes I wish I could lay eyes on you
every now and again, to make sure life is treating
you fine. It would really be nice." She laughed a
little. "I see your sisters all the time. Sometimes I
can't keep them out of here."

Farah loved Elise, but because she did everything
in her power to prevent the illness from controlling
her life, she still didn't use soap or deodorants and
her skin permeated a mean body odor. "I'll try to
come over this week."

"Okay." She sighed. "Well, I meant that if you don't work on being a good person, good can't come to you. Just confusion all the time, baby. Friends will turn on you and if you ever find love, it will be quickly lost. I told your mamma that when she was young but she never listened to me. Now her husband is locked up and her children are trying to find their way around in the dark. The thing is, it's not over for her yet. I wonder if she believes me now."

Farah and Lesa were finishing up their workout at Gold's Gym. They were both on treadmills, jogging and dripping with sweat. Even though they were wearing their gym clothes men could not help but stare at them and Farah loved every minute of it. Since she'd been taking her medicine, she was feeling better each day. "You really gonna have that surgery?" Farah asked as she stole stares at her breasts. "I'm afraid to go under the knife."

"Yep, I'm still going. February twenty-fifth and it's all I can think about, too."

"If I had money, I'd probably do the same thing." Farah looked at her again. "I don't think you need a tummy tuck or lipo though. Your body is perfect."

"That's because I get maintenance." She laughed. "Anyway, I can't believe all that shit happened the other night at your party." Lesa was running so fast, her small breasts moved up and down. "I wanted to have a good time. I ain't expect all that."

"I know. That dude was actually gonna rape me. With all those people in the house and shit. He wasn't even supposed to be there."

Lesa tried to catch her breath. "But you and your sister beat the brakes off of his ass. On the way out, he said you bit him."

"Yeah, to get him off of me. I really didn't need to because my sister loves to fight," Farah said, remembering how Kirk hemmed her in, in the closet. "I'm just glad she was there."

"Right . . . You sure you don't know who that was trying to kill me? Because they kept saying your name. My mother, who I haven't spoken to in a long time, said I should move when I told her about all the things that happened at your apartment already."

Farah hit the button to slow down. "Why you tell your mother all that stuff?" She smiled awkwardly. "It wasn't even that bad."

"I'm not paying that woman any attention." She laughed. "And it was that bad, but normally I carry my gun with me. I'm mad I didn't have it that time. Guess I thought I didn't need it."

"You got a gun?"

"Don't all girls?" Lesa laughed. "I just hope that shit don't happen again because the next time somebody try to touch me there's gonna be trouble."

"It shouldn't happen again." Farah didn't tell her about Tank and that she had so many enemies; it could've been anybody's guess. The conversation she just had with Elise was fresh in her mind so she was trying not to lie.

"Well, they really thought I was you." Lesa ran faster during her last minute. "I mean, you cute, girlie, but I ain't trying to die in your honor."

"Trust me, I just think it was a robbery gone wrong." Farah patted her face with a towel. "People think because I deal with Randy I got money. I'm sure that's what it was. Don't worry . . . you're safe at my house."

"You talk to Coconut?" she asked, looking over at her. "Because she didn't seem too happy when she left the party the other night." Farah shook her head. "You should call her. She seems nice. I was going to invite them over some day this week for dinner."

"I did call and she never answers the phone. You gotta watch my friends, though. They real some-timey. You saw everybody together and thought shit was cool. But they talk behind each other's backs all the time. We not tight like that anymore. Stay away from them, trust me."

"You said they were your best friends." Farah remained silent. Lesa looked at her and laughed. "Farah, I hope you not one of them girls that get jealous when they friends meet each other," she said as her cool-down period kicked in, allowing her to walk instead of run. She leaned on the bar for support. "That kind of cruddy shit is for kids. We grown-ass women now and gotta act like it."

"It's not even like that. It's just that Coconut can be real fake. Plus she be so far up her friend Shannon's ass that she could kiss the inside of her mouth. She know I don't like that bitch. What kind of shit is that? Friends supposed to have each other's backs." Lesa felt she was being immature. "I'm serious. Rhonda is my friend and I bought her all this shit for her baby shower, and Coconut said she bought it." She was lying so much, she had no idea what she was talking about anymore. "She tried to turn her against me. I went ahead and told Rhonda last night, when I finally got her on the phone, that Coconut don't fuck with her like that. You don't know them; they troublemakers. Now I know why her own mother pushed shit in her face when she was a kid."

Lesa frowned. "What? Why would she do that?"

"Maybe she was an outsider. And a liar." Farah dropped her head. Her web of lies brought up bad memories. "Coconut's family is a bunch of murderers. Her father killed this boy and his family just because he bumped into his car and scratched the paint. And they even killed my friend Theo's mother."

"Do the police know about all of this?"

"No. I'm too afraid to tell." She swallowed. "And the only reason I'm letting you know is because you're my roommate and Coconut can be sneaky." Farah lied so much in forty seconds that her head hurt. She would have to drink orange juice and chocolate syrup later. She mixed the truth and twisted it around all to hide who she was. She was digging holes deep enough to get lost in forever. Everything Elise said on the phone went out the window.

"Wow . . . First off, if Coconut's mother did that shit to her, she needs to be destroyed. That's some heartless shit that should never be done to anybody." Lesa words scratched up feelings in Farah, since it was actually her reality. "And if they murdered anybody, they'll get what's coming to them sooner or later. People like that always do.

It just seems like they were all very nice girls but I guess you never really know anybody."

They both got off of the treadmills and moved toward the locker room. "You're right about that. You never really know anybody," Farah repeated. Even though she should've stopped a long time ago, she couldn't stop making up stories as she went along. It was as if she were in a marathon of lies. "Rhonda did say she better never see her because she gonna step to her, pregnant or not."

They walked into the locker room. "Based on you, your friends seem a little feistier than they look. For real they remind me of me and my crew." Lesa moved to her locker and began spinning the dial on her combination lock.

"Trust me, it's serious. Plus, Rhonda holding a secret over Coconut's head."

"What? Heavier than her family being murderers?" Lesa stopped what she was doing and moved toward Farah.

She giggled. "Kinda. Coconut killed this man during a hit and run some time back. We were in the car at the time and saw it. We don't talk about it but we all remember. She can be real dangerous."

"You going overboard to convince me how Coconut is." Point taken; I'm leaving her alone.

Farah opened her locker and grabbed her bag, leaving Lesa to her own thoughts. The moment she opened the door, she heard her phone ringing. When she removed it and saw an unknown number appear across the screen, she knew immediately it was her father. "Hold on, Lesa. I gotta take this."

"I'm jumping in the shower."

Farah looked at her feet. "With no shower shoes?" Lesa kept walking and Farah shook her head. "Nasty bitch," she said to herself before answering the call. "Hi, Daddy. How you holding up?"

"I'm better now that I hear your voice." He chuckled. "I'd be doing even better if you came and saw me, Redbone. I miss you."

"I'm sorry, Daddy. So much has been happening around here that I haven't had the time. But I'll try to come see you next week. You need money or books? Magazines? I can order them today so they'll send them tomorrow."

"You know I've always taken care of myself in here. I would never ask my family to fund my crime . . . I told you that before. The question is, do you need anything?"

"Daddy, I'm fine. And I don't look at it that way. You can't do stuff like order books and things like that. It's the least I can do, Daddy, and I don't mind."

"I'm fine for now. Really. Now, what's this I'm hearing from Dr. Martin that you aren't seeing him anymore? You can't play with your illness, Farah. One wrong move and you could push yourself into the acute stage."

"Daddy, I'm fine." She sighed. "What I'm doing now is working real good. I haven't had a real issue in a minute. Don't worry." While she was on the phone, a white girl got out of the shower completely naked. She used the towel that should have been covering her body to dry her hair instead. Farah hated when people walked around nude in the locker room. When the girl saw Farah staring she rolled her eyes and Farah rolled hers back. The girl grabbed a can of hair-spray from her locker, went to the mirror, and wrapped the damp towel around her body.

"Happy now?" the girl asked. "Since you staring so hard."

"You still there?" Ashur asked.

"Yeah, I'm just tired of dumbass bitches doing dumbass shit." She rolled her eyes at the woman.

"I see you've gotten spicier. You use to be the nice one. Don't change on me, baby."

"You sound like Grandma now." She pulled her gym bag out the locker.

"How's the old lady doing?"

"Good . . . Talked to her earlier today."

"Great. How are you and your mother?"

"We fine."

"So you lying to me now?"

"Daddy, we'll be okay. But if you're asking do I see her, the answer is no."

"We gotta work on getting this family healthy." The girl in the locker room started spraying her hair. "And I wanted to talk to you about a few things that I can't say over the phone. That's why I want you to come visit me. I heard some disturbing news about Theo's mother that I didn't know about until now. The night I was locked up."

"Daddy . . ." The smell of the hairspray drifted into Farah's nose and she started itching and coughing. She was doing so well that she forgot she had to continue to be careful. "Daddy . . . I gotta . . . I gotta . . ." Farah felt dizzy and suddenly was unable to stand.

"Farah! Are you okay? Talk to me, baby!" Ashur screamed into the phone.

When Farah woke up from the nightmare, she realized she was in her bed and not in the locker room. The last thing she remembered was talking to her father in the gym, and now Lesa, Mia, Coconut, and Rhonda surrounded her bed. "How you feeling?" Mia asked. She stood up and walked to the head of the bed, while Coconut and Rhonda stood at the end. "You in pain? Because you fell really hard on the floor. "

Farah rubbed her temples. "What happened? I don't remember nothing after the gym. How did I get here?"

"You had an outbreak," Mia said. "Where is the medicine you said you had? I thought you were taking it."

"I think I missed a day." Farah looked at her friends, who seemed like they had an attitude. She never talked to them about her illness, and wanted to keep it that way. "Can I talk to Mia alone?" Coconut and Rhonda looked at each other and marched out without speaking.

"I'm glad you're up, Farah. You scared the hell out of me in the gym," Lesa said. "I'll be in my room if you need me. Bye, Mia. It was nice seeing you again."

When she walked out Farah said, "What's wrong with Coconut and Rhonda? They didn't even say bye."

"The three of them was talking about something. When I walked in they stopped so who knows what they said." Mia shrugged. "I went to the bathroom to hit a jay and they started talking again." She picked up a yellow cup filled with juice. "Why . . . what you do now?"

"Nothing," she lied. "Mia, I don't want anybody knowing about my disease. So I'd appreciate if you wouldn't talk about it in front of them. You know how people try to use your weakness against you. Like Boo in the hallway that day."

"Don't try that shit. You still lying about who you are?" Mia shook her head. "It ain't like they can catch that shit and it's not your fault you were born with it."

"Well, people act like it is sometimes. They treat you different when you sick." She looked as if she wanted to cry. "I spent most of my childhood in bed . . . All I wanna do is have fun with my friends. And I appreciate if you don't let them in on my business. My roommate either."

Mia raised her hands in the air and said, "Not a problem. They're your friends, not mine."

"Good. Do they know anything now?"

"As far as they know you were allergic to something and had a reaction."

Farah felt dumb for not leaving the locker room when she saw the spray can. "Is my face fucked up?" She touched her cheeks. "Do I have sores on me and stuff?"

"No. Just your arms. You broke out in hives as usual." Farah looked at her arms and was happy it wasn't too bad. "The doctor said you had a panic attack like you always do when you think you're about to have an outbreak. He says that's why you passed out. He doesn't think it was related to the illness. "

"Which doctor?" Farah frowned.

"Dr. Martin was at the hospital when he found out you were there."

She sighed. "Why did you tell him, Mia? Damn! You know I don't like his ass."

"Bitch, I was worried about you! Plus he really does want to help. You just gotta do what he says."

"I'm not playing the fake games anymore with his white ass. The shit he gives me works for y'all but it makes me worse. Just keep him away from me."

Mia shook her head. "Your funeral." She stood up. "Anyway, I know it's too early to tell, but I don't like that roommate of yours. So you better watch your back."

"Why you say that?"

"Something's up with her." She moved toward the door. "And I know you don't like to listen to me. But remember you've been warned."

# Chapter 21

**"But I felt better and looked better. Didn't I?" —Farah**

Surprisingly the building door was open when Farah rushed through, headed for Grand Mike's apartment. Just as infested as before, she hoped bugs wouldn't fall on her body and that he'd give her what she needed even though she didn't have a dollar to her name. She knocked heavily on Grand's door, stepped back, and waited for it to open. When Grand Mike answered and motioned for her to come inside, Farah rushed in and stood in the middle of the floor. "I see you're on time." He closed and locked the door. "You got my money?"

She looked at him and thought about exchanging sexual favors for what she needed. But when her eyes roamed over his dirty nails, matted hair, and filthy apartment, she thought otherwise. "Look . . . I don't exactly have your money but—"

"What do you mean you don't *exactly* have my money?" Grand asked, looking at Farah harshly.

"When you called earlier I thought I made myself clear. Bring my cash and I'll give you what you asked for."

"I'm sorry. I wouldn't even be here if it wasn't important, but I found that in order for me to be good, I have to double or triple my dosage." He didn't respond. "I'm out of medicine now." She pleaded with her eyes. "But I had an outbreak and everything. Even fell out in the gym." She paused.

"I really need your help and I'll be willing to do whatever I can to get it."

"You're not understanding me. I need my money prior to any services rendered. This isn't a charity foundation."

"I know, but—"

"Get out, Farah." He turned to walk away.

She balled her fists up and said, "No."

He stopped and faced her again. Then he slowly approached. "What did you just say?"

She swallowed and moved away from him. "I said I'm not going anywhere until you give me what I need." Tears ran down her face. "All my life this shit has been eating at me, and that's the only thing that works. It's not like I'm not going to pay you back, Grand. When I get some money. Give me a few days."

"You're not hearing me. I want my cash straight up and if you don't have it, there's not a whole lot I can do for you. Are we clear?"

He saw she was desperate and wanted to fuck with her mind, since it was obvious she didn't have his funds, and their relationship would end today. "You are pathetic." He walked around her as she stood in the middle of the floor. "You have no idea that what I gave you only worked because you believed it would."

"What are you talking about?"

"The placebo effect." He winked. "When your cousin asked around trying to find some information about your condition, I got word back to him after looking up your ailment. I knew you would believe whatever I told you, because you didn't want to die. Or worse"—he rubbed her cheek—"lose your looks."

"I don't believe you! It does work for me! I'm better!"

He laughed in her face and said, "Get the fuck out. I'm telling you the truth and you're not even listening. If it wasn't for Cosmo you'd be hurt right now."

Grand was staring at her until he was no longer able to use his eyesight, due to the bullet that penetrated his face. His body dropped on the floor and blood poured out of him and dampened the dirty carpet. Lesa's gun, which Farah borrowed earlier from her room, shook in Farah's hand as she stuffed it in her purse. Looking down at him she said, "It does work. I wasn't gonna hurt you if you just gave me what I needed." She stooped down where his body lay.

She ran through his apartment looking for the cooler he was supposed to give her when he got his money. In the first two rooms she found nothing and she wondered if he had plans to rob her all along. Going into the final room, she noticed a bed, which had rope and a roll of duct tape on top of it. She knew then that he had plans to rob her if she didn't pull the trigger and killed him herself. Now she felt totally justified. Nervous, she wiped her fingerprints off of everything she touched and bolted out the door.

"Cosmo, I need you to keep it real with me," Farah said as she sat in her car in a dark parking lot. Night had fallen on DC, and she was glad because she needed privacy. It was a good thing he called from jail when he did, because she really needed to speak to him. "This is serious."

"Why you gotta come at me like that? You know I always keep it real with you."

She took a deep breath and said, "Good, because I'm not going to be able to use Grand anymore."

"Good. You don't need him."

"No . . . I really need you to understand what I'm trying to tell you. I'm not going to be able to use him but I still need help. Will you help?"

Silence.

"You hear me, Cosmo?"

"Yeah. I . . . I hear you."

"I need you to tell me what he gave me. That made me feel better. He charged me sixteen hundred dollars and it was worth it."

"Sixteen hundred dollars! What the fuck! It was supposed to be fifty bucks! Just enough so you would believe it was real!" Farah was startled and Cosmo was angry that he played his cousin. "Farah . . . I don't know how to say this. You were fucked up all them years and I made you that promise, so I got somebody who said they knew what you needed."

"What was it?" she cried. "Please."

He sighed. "What did it taste like?"

Silence.

Farah rubbed her forehead and said, "Don't make me say it."

"Farah . . . you don't need what he gave you. You probably never did. Grand is in the business of selling dreams and you bought one, and if you asked me, you paid a little too much. If it worked, don't worry about nothing else."

"It was real for me," she cried. "But I felt better and looked better. Didn't I?"

He sighed and said, "I'm gonna kick it to you. You remember the language you used back in the day with your sisters and Shadow?"

"Yes."

"I know it too and you're about to use it again. Starting now."

# Chapter 22

**"I heard our pussy better than theirs, too. It ain't our fault." —Farah**

Farah was sitting on the edge of the sink in her bathroom talking to her mother on the phone. For some reason, she was sure it would be the last time. After all these years she could never earn her love, so she learned to hate. "What happened the other day?" Brownie asked. "They telling me you passed out at the gym. Don't overexert yourself just to keep your body together. When you get older you gonna spread cheek to cheek anyway."

"What I do and how I do it is my business."

"If you passing out in public it's everybody's business. Anyway, I thought you didn't have outbreaks anymore. Everybody been yelling about how pretty Farah is since she did her own thing. What's the problem now?"

Farah sighed. "Let me worry about me. Now what do you want?"

"Whatever," she said with an attitude. "The reason I'm calling is because your sisters might have to live with you. And your brother too, when he comes home. Your father can't help me like he used to because he's not getting it the same in prison anymore. The little money he has he's trying to save for his appeal."

"Ma, I got a roommate now. It's not enough room for her to live here, let alone three more people. If it was it wouldn't be a problem."

"You got four bedrooms in that apartment and two of the bedrooms got bathrooms. I know all about the apartment, Farah, and I know you got enough room. You mean to tell me you can't help your sisters and brother out?"

"Why they gotta leave your place? Can't they stay with Grandma?"

"When your grandmother moved out, she took her social security money with her." Her voice appeared to fade away. "And they don't wanna stay with her, because Mamma doesn't wash up at all anymore. That's why she isn't as bad as us. I'd rather die than not wash my clothes or my ass but that's on her."

Her voice was irritating. "What am I supposed to tell my roommate?

"You know, if it was your father asking for your help, it wouldn't be a problem."

"Do you mean *my* father or theirs? Because we both know we all don't have the same dad."

"You think just because you live a few buildings down from me you better, RedBone?" She laughed. "Bitch, you still in the hood and don't need to be looking down on nobody. I regret passing this disease to your sisters and Shadow. But I'm glad you got every last bit of it."

That was the meanest thing she'd ever said to her, but Farah was determined not to let her know. "I'm tired of you trying to make me feel bad . . . or guilty. That was done the day you put shit in my face. Maybe I should let Ashur know that his wife never got over her little white boyfriend."

"Cosmo was wrong for telling you that. And I tell him every time I see him around."

Farah smirked. "Yeah . . . I'm sure he gives a fuck."

"If Ashur ever found out about you, it would break his heart. And you know it!"

"Mamma, you broke his heart a long time ago. He may even know already I'm not his kid. Just one look at me and everybody could tell I don't belong. I can't believe you fucked Coach Jaffrey." She laughed again. "You must've been one horny bitch."

"You don't know shit about my life! Nothing! That man was the first person who ever truly loved me. And if Ashur knew you weren't his child you think he'd be calling you every week? Or asking about you when I speak to him? As far as that man's concerned, you're his child, and unless you wanna break his heart, you better keep your mouth closed."

"Mamma, I love him. The one thing you'll never have to worry about is me telling him about you. I'll let you take that secret to hell."

"Good! Because if you don't I still have a certain knife with fingerprints matching yours that was involved in the murder of Dinette."

"I didn't have anything to do with that. And I was a kid!"

"We'll let the courts say if that's irrelevant or not."

Knock. Knock. Knock. Farah hopped off the sink, still thinking about what her mother said. She placed her hand over the receiver and said, "Yes? I'm using the bathroom."

"You been in there forever," Lesa said. "Your puppies are going crazy and I thought we were gonna hit this jay. Fucking with me this shit gonna be gone! Plus—"

"Give me a second, Lesa." Farah tried to cover the receiver harder. "My sister Chloe just called me about some problems she having with her boyfriend. I'll be out in a second." Farah didn't know where that lie came from, but if it would get Lesa away from the door, it served its purpose.

"Your sister Chloe?" Lesa repeated. She sounded suspicious. "Okay. Well, hurry up. We got company."

When Farah heard her footsteps walk away, she focused back on the call.

"Still lying, huh?" Brownie laughed. "After all this time you still can't tell the truth. And you got the nerve to be talking about me." She paused. "Remember what I said. You gotta make room for your siblings because, like it or not, they coming with you. Unless you want me to start making a few calls. Oh . . . and the blackmail money for Jaffrey I used to give you stops today."

"Fuck you!"

"Fuck you back!"

After the call, Farah brushed her hair and made sure every strand was in place. Then she applied a little hypoallergenic makeup on her arms since she was wearing a wifebeater and the sores were showing. The sores from the last outbreak were the only marks she had and she wanted to keep it that way. No longer would she have to worry about Grand Mike. Thanks to her cousin Cosmo she now knew what it took to be healthy, so she was fully in charge of her own life and she already put her plan into motion.

When she was presentable, she placed her hand on the white porcelain doorknob and strutted into the living room. The moment she turned the corner, she saw a pair of long legs she hadn't seen in a while. *What the fuck is this bitch doing in my house?* She was wearing tight jeans and a brown pair of Uggs, and Farah wanted her gone.

"Hey, sis!" Chloe stood up and walked toward Farah. Her hair was pulled back neatly. She wrapped her arms around her, but Farah stood in place. "I missed you so much. How come you don't answer my calls?" Farah pushed her off and watched her drop to the floor.

"Hold up, what's going on?" Lesa asked. "She said she was your sister."

"This bitch ain't my sister!" Farah said. "What the fuck are you doing here, Chloe?"

Diamond and Pearl started yapping crazily, sensing Farah's unpleasant disposition. "I'm sorry, Farah. I should've known she wasn't your sister when you told me you were talking to her on the phone," Lesa said. "Especially since she was out here with me the whole time."

Farah was embarrassed for being caught in her lie. "Lesa, it's a long story. I'll explain later."

Chloe stood up, smirked, and walked back toward Farah. "I know you better not put your fucking hands on me again. Unless you forgot how sweet I am with any weapon of my choosing," she said, referring to Dinette's stabbing.

"What are you doing here?" Farah frowned, preparing to gut punch her.

Chloe wiped the stupid smile off of her face and said, "Well, you ain't been answering my calls, so I decided to come over to see you." She raised her arms in the air. "So here I am. It's funny though, you don't seem like you're happy to see me. Why is that, big sis?"

"How come I gotta keep asking what the fuck you doing in my house? The next thing that's gonna happen if I don't get an answer is you being thrown out on your ass. You are not welcome here. Anymore . . . ever."

She grabbed her Louis Vuitton purse and looked at Lesa. "Why don't you hang out in the bathroom again, Farah. That way me and Lesa can talk about how your boyfriend took a fall for the worse awhile back."

Farah's eyes widened. "Fuck are you talking about?" Farah stepped closer to her. "That's your problem. You stay keeping up shit."

"You don't remember, sis?" Chloe continued. "You put your hands right here." She touched Farah's chest. "And pushed."

"Lesa, I gotta talk to my sister," Farah said, interrupting her. "Alone."

"Is everything cool?" Lesa asked.

"Yeah . . . just give me a few minutes." Then Farah looked back at Chloe's large grin. "Come to my room."

When they opened the door Diamond and Pearl rushed into Farah's bedroom, but she grabbed them, kissed them on the mouth, and put them outside the door.

"Pew," Chloe said, pinching her nose as she walked into the room. "They smell like they been shitting and pissing in here at the same time. You gotta potty train them. They too cute to smell like that." Chloe walked deeper into the room and threw her purse on the floor. She was sloppy as always and Farah didn't want her anywhere in her space. Everything about her was nasty with the exception of her outward appearance. Watching her phat ass and tiny waist move toward her bed enraged Farah. She could see why Zone wanted to fuck her and it made her sick to her stomach. Sitting on the bed she said, "You know Ma says I can live here right?" She looked around. "And if I do, I decided to take your room."

Farah giggled. "And what makes you think that's even possible, Chloe? You betta hope I let you live here and sleep on the floor with my dogs. But that's to be determined. You fucking stepped to my boyfriend and that's fucked up."

"I apologize all the time on your voice mail, but you never answer the phone, Farah. It was stupid and I know you miss me too."

"I don't." She looked into her eyes. "And I'm tired of being pushed over by people. You don't have no respect for me at all." Farah walked to her dresser, grabbed her brush, and started brushing her hair. "So how's college?" She skipped topics. "Things working out okay, or are you about to drop out again?"

"College is fine, Farah."

"Your mother called me. How is she for real?"

"If you really wanna know the real reason Mamma wants us to move with you, it's because she doesn't want us to see her anymore. Her skin is so bad she's not even recognizable. She wears a full body cover-up and people think she's Muslim. She don't say nothing to correct them, either. She's dying." Farah felt as if a rock formed in the pit of her stomach, but she remained stone faced. "You don't really care, do you?" Farah brushed her hair harder. "Well, maybe you'll care about this. You didn't turn the computer off that day. You turned off the screen." Farah was nervous. "I saw what you did."

She faced her. "So what did you come here to do, Chloe? Blackmail me? Because I don't have any money to give you. I caught him jerking off to my sister. I let him carry the relationship for years as if I didn't matter. I was tired of his shit, Chloe!"

She stood up, and looked as if she were a kid who held a secret that she was on the verge of telling. "Outside of me wanting this room," she said, smiling, "I don't want nothing else but to be your sister again." She looked into Farah's eyes. "And I want you to forgive me because I'm sorry. I never thought you were even that serious about him."

"He was my boyfriend and I do not forgive you. Now please leave."

Chloe lowered her head, picked her purse up off the floor, and walked to the door. "You can't stay mad at me forever. You know why? Because we're Cottons and Cottons stick together whether they like it or not. We know secrets about each other that would get us locked up for life if somebody said a word. Stop acting like you are that much different than me. The camera was on and I know the truth."

When she left the apartment Farah slowly walked into the living room and lay on the extra-large comforter she had on the floor. Lesa was already on it, smoking a bob. Next to her was a plate of Oreos and a glass of milk: Lesa's favorite.

"Don't tell me," Lesa started. "The next time somebody comes over, you want me to tell you *before* I open the door." She smiled.

"Please ask me first." Farah's puppies jumped all over her and she played with them before throwing their favorite red toy in the corner. While they were preoccupied she said, "Me and her don't see eye to eye no more. Chloe got a lot of growing up to do. So I'ma deal with her shit on my time."

"Understood." She pulled on the bob and passed it to Farah. "Before y'all had that fight and you came out here, I thought your sister seemed nice. She don't look like you though. Y'all got the same father?"

"Yes," Farah lied. "But you'd never know it."

"You know what's funny, even though you were mad at her, it looked like you missed her, too. Maybe it was just me." Farah rolled her eyes. "So what was she talking about?" She leaned her back against the couch. "When she pushed you."

"Remember I told you my boyfriend fell to his death?" Lesa nodded. "Well, she keeps throwing it up in my face. Trying to make me think it was my fault and shit." Farah pulled on the weed and let the smoke fill her lungs. "Platinum Lofts had to replace all the windows in this building. Zone's mother ended up getting a large-ass insurance policy check and everything." Farah didn't like talking about the murder, so she decided to skip the subject. "Let's talk about something else."

"Cool." She paused. "I just got off the phone with the coordinator for the designs I did for the fashion show. I think I'm going to win next week."

"What fashion show? You didn't tell me about it."

"Oh . . . I forgot. I told Coconut and Rhonda." She laughed. "It was at the party and I think you were making sandwiches or some shit like that." Farah tried not be petty, but she realized they got closer at that party than she realized. "I'm so excited about this fashion show, girl. It should be hot," Lesa said. "I bought this beautiful black Gucci dress and I have a red Hermès bag in my closet that I'm going to wear and everything."

"You not wearing your own fashions?" she asked, although she was still thinking about Coconut and Rhonda knowing more about her roommate than she did.

"Bitch, please!" Lesa said. "I want to respect the greats as I"—she pointed to herself—"accept my award. That way I'll feel like their spirits are with me."

"How do you have time to design with you working at the cable company?"

"You make time for what you wanna do."

When Farah's phone rang she saw Randy's name flash across the screen. She was supposed to meet him earlier that day, but with recently killing Grand, and then Chloe coming over and the conversation with her mother, she wasn't in the mood. Hitting the button to answer the call, she crawled away from Lesa. "Hello."

"Farah, why you playing games with me? I told you how it was gonna be."

"Randy, I can't talk right now."

"Well, you better make time to talk later. Or have you forgotten what kind of nigga I am? I wanna see you tomorrow. You hear me? No more fucking excuses."

"Okay, Randy."

"Tomorrow, Farah. I'm not fucking around. Bye!"

When she hung up with him she grabbed the red polish off the glass table. She wanted to do something to get her mind off of him and to prevent Lesa from asking about the call. "Let me polish your toes."

"I was just about to do them myself, but you can knock yourself out if you want to!" She placed her feet in her lap, and Farah started with the big toe on her right foot.

"I bet niggas love to suck your feet, don't they? They so pretty and cute." Farah wiggled the little toe and Lesa felt uncomfortable. Farah caught her gaze and said, "Oh . . . my gawd . . . it's not like that if that's what you're thinking. I'm not into women." She temporarily forgot all about her drunk games with Coconut. "You mind if I don't do this? I forgot I'm allergic to the smell." Lesa took the bottle and twisted the top back on. "So tell me about your friends. And when do I get to meet them? Since you met both of mine already, and even told them about your fashion show before you told me."

Silence.

"Are you always this petty?"

That was the second time she said the word "petty" when she was talking to her. Farah raised her brows and said, "Petty?" She pointed to herself. "Me?"

"Yeah . . . I mean . . . did you not have friends when you grew up or something?"

"I had lots of friends."

"Oh . . . because you seem real overprotective. I don't want things to be so heavy between us." She nudged her. "Anyway . . . I've been beefing with my friends for a minute. That's why they weren't at the party the other night. We got into a fight over some bullshit and things got out of control."

"How long have you known them?" Farah continued, trying to hide the fact that she was still brewing about her comment. Her crazy had been slipping out an awful lot lately.

"Most of my life." She seemed sad. "It's hard to find good friends so when you have them you should hold on tight. If you can."

"Do you got any pictures of them?"

"Yeah." She put the polish on the table and went for her phone. "Here are some pictures we took at a party we were together at last month." Farah looked at a picture of two light-skinned girls and their designer bags. They looked cool, and Farah hoped things worked out so they could all be friends. Especially since she hadn't heard from Coconut or Rhonda since they left her apartment the day she was sick.

"What are their names?"

"The one right here with the short black hair is Lady and the one right here with the long hair is Courtney."

"You should call them! We can make drinks and stuff."

"I'd never call them. I don't care how much I missed them. I told you I'm beefing with them right now, Farah."

Lesa seemed irritated with her anxiousness. "This last shit seemed serious."

"What made it so serious this time?"

"It was two things. For starters they didn't want me getting plastic surgery in February. But do or die, I'm gonna be at that appointment because this is my fucking life not theirs. Second, we all used to mess with dudes who knew each other. Like the dude I fucked with was friends with their boyfriends and vice versa. Anyway, one day I saw Lady's boyfriend at the Wendy's kissing this bitch and I told Courtney."

"Why didn't you tell Lady?"

"I was gonna tell Lady myself, but the shit happened so quick and Courtney was the first person I saw. Anyway, before I could say anything, Courtney told Lady and she got mad with me for not coming to her first. We ended up getting into a fistfight and everything. I'm like, why you mad at me because *your* nigga cheating? It's been over a month and I haven't talked to them since. It's the longest I've ever gone without talking to them two." She looked at her toes. "And since I'm stubborn as hell, and they are too, that's it. I could be dead wrong but if my mind is made up, there's nothing you can get me to do. Including call you." She paused. "It's cool though. I got enough dirt on them to last a lifetime."

"Do tell!"

"I can't do that." She shook her head. "What if we start being cool again?"

"So you *are* going to talk to them again."

"Fuck it! That bitch hit me, so I know I'm done." Lesa laughed. "Here it is . . . Lady robbed this soul food restaurant she worked at five different times during the first of the month with her boyfriend. That's when they get the most cash. Them people still got an award leading to the arrest. If I wanted to be evil, I could've called them a long time ago." Farah raised her eyebrows as she ran down everything Lady did, while they made martinis in the kitchen.

"Damn! What about Courtney? What dirt you got on her?" Farah moved in closer, loving to hear gossip.

"This is heavy."

"I'm not gonna say nothing!" Farah grew anxious. "I don't even know them. Plus you got dirt on my friends. If anything this will make us tighter."

"I guess you right," Lesa said, getting more buzzed by the sip. "Well, she got a son by her boyfriend's brother."

Farah covered her mouth. "Are you fucking serious?"

"Yeah, her boyfriend wanted a son but he couldn't produce. I don't know what was going on with his nut. Anyway . . . his brother Rod got like eight kids he don't take care of." She sipped her martini. "So one day Courtney got his brother drunk and fucked him raw. She knew she was ovulating because she was tracking her cycle, so it was nothing for her to get pregnant. Nine months later, she had a baby and passed it off as her man's. And since the father is his brother her son looks just like him."

Out of the blue Farah said, "Let's tell people we cousins." She was excited.

Lesa looked at her over the rim of her martini glass. She wondered where that comment came from. "What? Why?" She giggled.

"Because I feel you like family to me. And since you're beefing with your friends, and I'm beefing with mine, we might as well live life. Plus we both light skinned, we both cute, and we both fly."

Lesa put her glass down and said, "I never asked you but I'm gonna now. How come you always talk about light skin this and that? You even put it in your ad for a roommate and that kind of fucked me up."

"Because niggas love red bones." She smiled. "I know you get it all the time when you out in the streets because I do too."

"I know, but I've seen some of my darker friends pull badder niggas than me."

"I bet you more times than not you get the nigga." She poured another martini. "I heard our pussy better than theirs, too. It ain't our fault."

She paused. "So we cousins or not?" Farah raised her martini glass, and Lesa thought for one second before clinking her glass with hers.

"Cousins it is." Lesa took a few sips before saying, "Oh . . . I almost forgot to tell you. Vivian James came by when you were in the room with Chloe. She said to tell you to be careful; somebody killed the dude Kirk, who tried to rape you, in the building. Sliced the big vein on his dick and everything."

# Chapter 23

**"I don't wanna shoot you, but I can't make no promises either." —Slade**

Finally Slade would be able to see his brothers after what seemed like forever. He pulled up to Public Storage and drove toward his unit. Entering his code, he waited for it to automatically open, revealing all of his brothers, with the exception of Knox, inside. The Baker Boys were beautiful, each of them standing over six feet tall, and in Mississippi, it was said that they were built to last. Their bodies were chiseled as if they were just released from prison.

Slade and Audio walked into the unit and embraced their family. To be separated from each other was hard because they were together all the time. The moment Brian Baker, aka Killa, and Major Baker saw Slade's and Audio's faces, they knew something was wrong. Slade was the leader in the family and if he was rocked, they knew the foundation was in trouble.

"Where y'all been?" Slade asked. "We were supposed to hook up days ago."

"I know, man. Shit was crazy," Major said, with his hands stuffed in his pockets. His manner was "easy does it" and he didn't get rattled about too many things. "We spoke to Knox some days back and he said not to use cell phones from here on out. He don't trust nobody . . . not even the phone company. He said he gonna hit us at Markee's when he can link up with us. For now that's the only number he feels safe enough to call."

"He also said hold out on going to Markee's crib, but we couldn't call and tell you. That's why we called Ma. He said he might still be followed," Killa responded, leaning up against Slade's truck. Killa was the violent type, who was sometimes arrogant. "We been sleeping in this bitch." He pointed to some pillows and a few sheets in the corner. "We were good though."

"But what's up, bro?" Major asked. "You look out of it."

"You heard from Devon?" Killa asked.

"Naw," Slade said.

"What's going on then?" Killa asked, following his eyes, which moved everywhere but on him. "Everything cool?"

"Is Ma okay?" Major interrupted. "Please don't tell me that white mothafucka got Ma. I knew we should've brought her with us. But she wouldn't listen, saying she could handle herself back home . . ."

"It's Devon," Slade said in a low voice as his brother continued to rant and rave.

"Now something happened to her and its all our fault. What we gonna . . ."

"It's Devon," Slade said again in a low voice, which still couldn't be heard over Major's.

"I'm on the first thing smoking back home. I don't even give a fuck—"

"It's Devon!" Slade yelled. Now he heard him. "It's not Ma." Both Killa and Major breathed a sigh of relief.

His words stung. Killa felt off balance and moved toward the wall for support as Major battled with the space around him by throwing wild punches into the air. Their cousin was like a brother to them, and it fucked them up that he got caught up in the middle of their war. If they were to tell the average person their story it would be unbelievable. Life was normal before the police came to them for help some months back. They'd take one look at their police records, which were thicker than a bestselling book, and draw an immediate conclusion, but they'd be wrong.

They did regular shit they were known for in their neighborhood but nobody expected more from them than minor crimes, with the occasional fist fights due to stealing someone's girl. When a motorcycle club called Killer Bees came into town, whose ten members were convicted of crimes rang-ing from rape to murder, everyone knew they would be trouble. Houses were vandalized, women were raped, and people were brutally beaten and robbed. It wasn't until people started showing up dead that the police realized the crimes were serial and systematic. When the crime spree first happened, the Baker Boys were being brought in one by one to answer for the sudden crime wave. When each of them were able to provide solid alibis, the city officials realized what they knew all along: that the murders were not their MOs.

Eventually crime was so bad that it was hard for the police department to handle without getting the FBI involved. Sheriff Kramer was arrogant and didn't want outside help because of past issues that occurred in his town that he was unable to handle. He feared his job was on the line. So when the sheriff came to Della Baker's house to speak to her five sons and nephew Devon, she knew something was up. The sheriff was essentially deputizing her sons, saying that if they helped him get rid of the biker club, he would forever be in their debt, and so would the city's officials. Della said she appreciated his debt, but she wanted the charges on the auto theft against Audio dropped, which he accepted. All the brothers, except Knox, thought about how much they'd be able to get away with in Natchez if they looked out for the sheriff. Knox didn't trust him one bit. He saw troubles miles away but when they shook his hand it couldn't be stopped.

One by one the Baker Boys, under Della's leadership, assisted the sheriff and deputies in getting rid of the bike club. Things were going great until an official police officer shot and killed another officer while taking down the last member. The officer's murder changed the rules of engagement. Instead of accepting responsibility, he convinced Sheriff Kramer to say Knox and his brothers were to blame. He didn't want to be under investigation only to lose his benefits, since his seven-month-old baby was in a hospital dying of cancer.

So behind the Baker Boys' backs the police changed the script saying that they, in conjunction with the biker club, caused all the murders, including that of the officer. Before long everyone was looking for the brothers, wanting them brought to justice immediately. In neighboring counties, any officer with a badge was looking to get his hands on the men responsible for killing one of their own. The underground message was clear . . . shoot to kill. Sheriff Kramer wanted them dead, and not alive to stand trial. But there was one problem. During the original conversation Sheriff Kramer had with Della, Knox was smart enough to record the entire meeting on his cell phone. When he learned of the recording, he offered $100,000 to whoever turned them over dead or alive. Della Baker would die before she saw her boys harmed in anyway.

When Della learned of the hit, she went into hiding in Mississippi, and ordered her sons to DC to stay with her nephew Markee until they could be reunited. Before they left, Slade made an executive decision and ordered the brothers to split up, since everyone was looking for five black men. Slade and Audio went together and Killa and Major went their separate ways. Knox decided to go solo and Devon stayed behind to protect Della. Everything was working out until Devon came out of hiding to buy groceries. Sheriff Kramer couldn't believe his luck when he spotted him, and hours later he was dragged behind the back of his car. With the news of Devon's murder everyone was wondering if Knox received the same fate.

"Devon's dead?" Killa repeated. "How?"

"They got to him and strapped him to the back of a car. He was dragged to death and they said they couldn't even recognize him if he didn't have his ID."

"We gotta watch our fuckin' backs!" Audio spoke out. "Them crooked-ass cops not playing and why should we? I'm telling you if a cop step to me, DC or not, I'm blowing his mothafuckin' head off!"

"Calm down," Slade said, looking at his brothers. They pushed their feelings down deep and listened to him speak. Besides, if he snapped, everyone would be in danger and it would take days to calm him down. "For now we gonna stay past Markee's and wait for Knox's word, since the only number he can reach us on is at his crib. We need to lay low. No getting into shit with niggas out in the streets." He looked at Audio.

"Not for nothing, Slade, but I hope you taking your own advice too. Because once you lose it, you lose it."

Silence.

"I'm talking about you" Slade said. "Not me."

"I'm not feeling staying at Markee's. You know how that nigga be tripping about his place and shit," Major said. "With Devon dead, I might be liable to snap on that fool if he come at me sideways."

"Yeah, we not gonna be able to stay there long, Slade. We gotta find another place to rest, man," Killa said. "I'd rather stay here."

"Fuck that! It's cold'an a mothafucka in this bitch," Major said. "I can't do another night."

"We ain't got no choice. It's Markee's place or nothing. We gotta keep our heads on and get our family back."

"We not gonna be able to let Ma stay down there too long by herself. It's just a matter of time 'fore they hurt her," Killa said.

"Fuck you saying that shit out loud for?" Slade said as he jammed his finger in his chest. "You speaking that shit into existence? That something gonna happen to Ma? Y'all so busy barking . . . you better think before you talk."

"That shit is real!" Killa said. He was trying to hold his tears back. His own words made him sick to his stomach. "They bound to get at her if we don't get her out of there."

"She can hold her own," Slade said, looking at them. "Plus they want us, not her."

"What about money? We not gonna be able to do shit without paper," Major said.

"That's what I been saying. We can't even bring Ma out here if we wanted to. Right now we broke as shit," Audio said. "I feel like a fuckin' faggy."

Slade rubbed his callous hands over his bald head. His brothers were right and he knew it, but he was in an unknown city, and didn't know the ways of the land. How could he make moves when he wasn't able to see clearly? "I gotta think," Slade said, jumping into his truck. He didn't know if he was gonna scream or cry, but he didn't want to do it in front of them.

"Where you going?" Audio asked.

"To clear my head." Slade put his black knit hat on in the back seat, and then drove down the road, observing his surroundings. For a thirty-two-year-old man, who'd never before left the state of Mississippi, he might as well have been a ten-year-old kid roaming around DC without a parent. He was alone and responsible for his entire family and that was a lot of mothafuckin' pressure.

His mouth was dry, so he decided to grab something to drink. Parking at a convenience store, he walked in and moved toward the cooler. A few girls in the corner looked at him and smiled while on their groupie shit, but he didn't smile back. Slade was so fucking fine that wherever he went, women couldn't help but notice. His looks were both his gift and curse because men were intimidated and women made him weak so he took them in doses.

Walking up to the counter, he pulled the hat over his face and the weapon out of his pocket. His eyes were covered, but through the fabric he could see clearly. Aiming at the clerk he said, "I'ma need all the money in that register, ma'am." At first the woman thought it was a joke until he cocked the weapon. "Please don't shoot me." She threw her hands up in the air. "I don't wanna die. I got kids and a family."

"I don't wanna shoot you, but I can't make no promises either. Now put the paper in the bag and cash me out for the night."

The sixty-four-year-old woman nervously opened the register and placed a total of $1,200 in a plastic bag before handing it back to him. He took the cash and backed out of the door, aiming in her direction. His heart broke momentarily because the woman reminded him of his mother, who he was sure was her same age. He jumped in his truck and peeled out before anybody could spot him. Robbing innocent people was not his thing, but he knew at that moment that he'd do it again if it meant providing for his family. Slade saw the look in his brothers' eyes and knew they were desperate and capable of anything. He would rather take charge of the situation, and do the crime, than have to worry about the three of them.

Six miles up the street, he could no longer control his stomach contents as he thought about what happened. So he parked the truck, opened his door, and vomited. His stomach muscles pulled as he released everything he ate that morning. What fucked him up was not that he robbed the lady, but that everything in him wanted to murder her for no reason.

# Chapter 24

**"Bitch, if you knew me you wouldn't be nowhere near my face." —Farah**

Farah was sitting across from Coconut at Mamma's Kitchen. Although she invited Farah out, she seemed uninterested in anything she was saying at the moment. "What's wrong with you?" Farah finally asked, stirring her Sprite with a straw. "You had an attitude all day. Plus you haven't talked to me since you came over when I was sick."

"Why should anything be wrong?" Coconut said in a conniving tone. "I mean, you haven't been talking behind my back, have you?"

"Coconut, it's obvious you still mad at me about that smack down thing at my party. Which is fucked up because I didn't want to play that game anyway. As a matter of fact, you made me play that game before you would even be cool with me in school."

"I'm not even thinking about that shit. I want to talk about loyalty and lies."

"So you gonna tell me what's bothering you or what?" Farah tore a piece of bread off her roll before chewing with an open mouth.

Coconut sipped her Coke and said, "I talked to Rhonda when you were sick. At your house."

"And?" she said, craning her neck outward. "I wish you'd stop beating around the bush."

"*And* she told me you said you bought all of the gifts I got for her shower." Her nose flared wildly. "Why would you lie on me like that? You supposed to be my best friend!"

"And you're supposed to ask me instead of assuming!" She was caught red-handed and she loathed confrontation. "Just because you talked to Rhonda don't mean it's the truth! You were never a real friend if you think I would lie like that. Just keep it light!"

"She also told me you said that Jake was broke." She rolled her neck. "My nigga ain't never broke."

"Oh, my God! That bitch is *really* lying now! She the one who said that shit!" Farah yelled, trying to be believable by putting on a performance. "Not me! What I look like saying that when I asked you to move with me? You ain't got no job so he was gonna be the one to pay the rent." She tried to touch Coconut's hand. "Why would you let her break us up?"

Coconut snatched away and said, "You're so fucking weird, and I can't believe I let you come in between two girls I knew my whole life! The moment you stepped to me you were trouble!"

"I can't believe you're doing all of this."

"It's true! The first thing you did was invite yourself to a party you weren't invited to on the bleachers. And now that I think about it, I believe you been erasing numbers out of our phones to keep us apart. Natasha would probably be alive today if you hadn't come in our lives!"

Farah had gone too far and she saw it in her eyes. She would do anything to undo some of the lies she told, but fear of abandonment made it hard. "Coconut, please, let's not do this."

"It's too late, and I don't think I can be your friend anymore."

"Why?"

"I just told you the reason." She paused. "Unless you come clean. Did you or did you not lie on me?"

"Everything I told you was true. You gotta believe me, Coconut. Please." In the middle of the conversation Farah was suddenly preoccupied with something in her food. What she was really doing was a poor job of faking it, to get Coconut's mind off the subject while she attempted to come up with a better lie. When she looked up, Coconut was still waiting for a response. "What?"

"Call her." Coconut held her phone out. "Now. And put her on speaker."

"I'm not doing no young shit like that. We been out of high school for years, Coconut. Be a little more mature, especially since you always saying that shit to me."

"Either you call her or I will."

Farah sighed. "You call her if you got her number. Because I'm not."

"Actually I do have her number now." Coconut grinned. "She gave it to me the day you fell out. Now you wanna call or what?"

Farah was just about to call Rhonda when Shannon and her friends walked into the restaurant. The expression on Coconut's face turned from anger to giddiness and Farah wanted to throw up. "Shannon!" Coconut waved and Shannon and her crew walked over to give her a hug. "What y'all doing here?"

"About to get something to eat." Shannon was still a pretty, brown-skinned girl with a wide smile and long natural hair. The members of her crew, including Wendy and Nova, were just as cute and Farah hated that the most. "What's up, Farah?" Shannon asked, although she really didn't care. "I heard you fell down and bumped your head the other day at the gym." She smirked. "I hope you didn't lose your mind." Everyone laughed at her joke.

Farah looked at Coconut, who obviously told her personal business. "Shannon, don't say shit to me and I won't say shit to you."

Shannon cackled. "Coconut, if I were you, I'd smack the shit out of this bitch right here." She pointed down at Farah. "You know a video of you is going around on YouTube with her smacking you at the party, right?"

Coconut's cheeks were flushed. "Are you serious?"

"Dead serious. I wouldn't be fucking with this snake bitch at all if I were you. People saying she uploaded that shit."

"I'ma keep it light right now but, bitch, if you knew me you wouldn't be nowhere near my face," Farah said. Then she looked at Coconut. "Hit me when you leave your little riffraff alone." She grabbed her purse. "I gotta go take care of my health."

The Isley Brothers played in the background as Randy widened Farah's legs while she sat on the toilet. She was completely naked and he turned the water to help her process. "Is it working yet?" He was naked as he stood over her. "You feel like you gotta pee now?"

"Yeah . . . I think this is it." Farah hopped off the toilet, and held her hand between her legs. Drops of yellow liquid escaped her body and she said, "It's coming, Randy. You gotta go lie down."

"Hold it, baby," he said excitedly. "We almost there." When they were back in his room, he lay on a section of his floor covered in plastic. Farah walked over him, removed her hands, and allowed piss to fall all over his stomach, legs, and neck. Randy's dick got rock hard as he looked up at her body releasing urine. "Damn, that shit felt so good," he said, licking his lips, tasting a few drops. "And warm."

Farah had disconnected a long time ago. She wasn't into sick, demented sex but with Randy she had no choice. Lately every time she was with him, she thought about Slade. When she heard her cell phone go off, indicating she had a text message, she tried to see who it was from where she stood.

"What you doing? Stand over my face and focus on me," he ordered. "Now spread your pussy lips apart." He had the best view to see her tiny clit. His mouth watered as he thought about what to do with her body. When her phone went off again, he said, "Next time we fucking, turn your shit on silent. You be with your friends all the time. I need some attention too. After all, you are my fiancée."

"Sorry, baby, you know my mother is sick." The more she hated to admit it, the more it was true. Lying had put her into more situations than she knew how to get out of.

When her bladder was empty Randy said, "Grab the Vaseline on the dresser." Farah's pussy never got wet enough for him, so he had to help her out.

When she picked up the jar off the dresser, she was able to see she had two text messages from Lesa and Rhonda. Since she talked to Coconut at the restaurant, she could only imagine what Rhonda had to say about the matter.

Walking back over to him, she crouched over his face and said, "What you want me to do now?"

"Rub the Vaseline over your pussy and asshole." He jerked his dick so he could stay hard. "Put a lot of it on, too." She slathered as much as she thought he wanted, and globs of Vaseline stuck to her pussy, and ran down the insides of her legs. "That's good, baby." He wanted her so bad he could feel it. "Now sit on this shit." Farah slowly eased on top of his thickness. Whenever she fucked him she was able to detach, never getting off. Randy, on the other hand, was having the time of his life because he loved how sexy a light-skinned female looked with his black dick deep into her body.

When he was inside her body, Randy took control of her hips because Farah couldn't fuck to save her life. "That's it!" he said, bouncing her harder on his dick. "Keep that pink pussy right there, red bitch! Hmmmm! Bounce it!" Farah tried to move like she thought he wanted but she was off beat. "On second thought, just stay right there. Don't move. Just ride that shit like that." Randy mummy fucked her for an hour in every hole on her body, and when he was done, he had her clean up the pissy plastic and they jumped into the shower.

Fresh out of the tub, Randy put his Gucci shades on and eased into the bed. When she walked out of the bathroom he said, "Come over here with me. I wanna rap to you about a few things." Sensing something was wrong, she eased under the covers. "I went by your house a few times last week and didn't see your car. Why not?"

Farah knew he was going to catch her in a lie sooner or later but she was trying to hold him off for a little bit longer. The pressure was starting to really bring her down. "Randy, you know I wouldn't do you like that." She played with the curly hairs on his chest. "When you came by, I must not have been home. Sometimes I have to take my mother to doctors appointments. She's really bad, Randy. All jokes aside."

"If you are lying, you know what I would do to you, right?"

"Yes, and that's why I wouldn't do it. That's also why when this dude name Slade tried to talk to me awhile back, I showed him my ring. He didn't give a fuck and called you out your name." She flashed it for him. "See . . . I love you."

"So now you love me, when at first you didn't wanna even be my wife."

"I was tripping, Randy. But I'm not anymore."

When she said that his phone rang. "Let me get that right quick," he said as she examined his hairy black ass. Although he was violent, he was so attractive that to some girls it was worth the beat down. Farah only wanted to keep him handy to keep her purse on full.

He hopped out of the bed and said, "It's the nursing home. Give me a second."

She used the time to check text messages, starting with Lesa's:

Somebody name Slade came over looking for you. He said he live in the building. Damn he was fine. Hit me back when you can.

After reading the text, the only thing she wanted to do, was rush over there to see what he wanted. And then she remembered, after she left Grand's and took care of business he saw her in the basement. She'd committed a much-needed murder. What if he was going to blackmail her, and ruin her life?

The second text was from Rhonda and it read:

Farah I gotta talk to you about Coconut. Hit me back ASAP.

# Chapter 25

**"I may be lame, but I would've taken up for you. . ." —Farah**

The wind whipped around Farah's and Lesa's bodies as they walked to Lucky 7 convenience store a few blocks from their apartment. Although Farah lived in the flyest development in her area, she was still in the hood, and a few females who hated her eyed them as they moved down the block. Farah had enemies. Many. And although she acted as if she didn't, she knew any normal act could lead into an unprepared battle if she was caught slipping. She could've driven her car but one of Lesa's male friends dug them both parking spaces out of the snow, and they knew if they moved their cars, they would be taken by the time they got back. They were only five minutes into their walk when a white BMW slowly pulled up. "Red bone," the driver called out in their direction.

Farah and Lesa looked at the late-model BMW and were pleasantly surprised. The way they looked,

Farah could keep time with either one of them. As the days passed, she was starting to get lonelier because Randy didn't give her love. What she wanted was somebody to laugh and enjoy time with. The only questions now were who was going to get the driver, and if the passenger had a nice ride too.

"You gotta be more specific," Lesa said to the men. "We both red bones."

"My bad." The driver laughed. "It's not often you see two fine-ass friends together."

"We cousins," Farah lied. "So that's even better."

"Damn, they family," he said, giving the passenger dap.

Farah wanted the driver so she jumped in front of Lesa, preparing to spark up a conversation, so the driver could see her fat ass. "Girl, they are so fucking cute!" She was geeking. "If I knew it was gonna be like this, I would've suggested we walk to the store a long time ago. Which one you want?"

Lesa tried to look around Farah and into the car. "I'm not sure because you're blocking my view. I hope it's not on purpose."

Farah detected a little tension in her voice. This wasn't the first time Lesa started acting differently. It seemed like everything changed between them after she was sick, and Lesa was alone with her friends. "Oh sorry, girl." She moved out her view. "I was just trying to tell you something. Not block your game."

"I'm used to bagging niggas like that all the time. So it's not that big of a deal," Lesa said. "But I like to take my time with shit. If you act too thirsty they gonna try to fuck over you."

Before Farah could make it known who she wanted, the passenger said, "Damn, shawty fat as shit!" He was eyeing Farah. He wasn't her original pick, but he would have to do. Her only issue was Randy and running into someone who knew him.

"I'm trying to holla at you, sexy," the driver said to Lesa. "And my man wanna meet your cousin. How 'bout the four of us get together and have a good time."

Farah was already walking toward the car before Lesa snatched her arm. "What the fuck you doing?"

She snatched away from her. "They called us over. What we waiting on?" *What the fuck is her problem? She heard the niggas call me just like I did.*

"Girl, don't play yourself." Lesa shook her head. "If them niggas wanna holla, let them come to us." She couldn't believe Farah was being so lame. "I wish I would walk up to a fuckin' car to get some rap." She cackled. "And you not either. Not while you're with me, anyway. It's bad enough we talking to them while we standing outside."

Farah was embarrassed that Lesa thought she was playing herself. Instead of walking to the car she maintained her position, even though she hoped they didn't pull off and say fuck it. Being bedridden and sick for so long as a kid made her desperate to meet new people, which resulted in hot-ass moves.

"What y'all about to get into?" the driver said, looking at Lesa, who appeared uninterested. "Trying to take a ride with us or what?"

"Not for nothing, cutie, but I can't hear shit you spitting from this distance," Lesa said. "If you trying to holla at me and my friend, you gotta get out of the car."

The driver laughed. "Ain't no disrespect, Miss Lady. It's just cold out there and we thought you'd be better off talking to us inside here. And I thought y'all were cousins. Why she just say friend?"

"We are cousins!" Farah interjected, while Lesa shook her head in disgust. The cousin shit was ridiculous.

"Well, if your game right, you won't be standing out here with us too long," Lesa said.

Lesa reminded Farah of Coconut and she took notes to be smoother with her game for future references. Now that she thought about it, walking up to them may have been too much.

They made a decision to leave the warmth of the car to holla at Farah and Lesa. They just hoped they got some pussy some time that evening when it was all said and done. The driver approached Lesa and his friend approached Farah, who was so excited about his height and the natural smell of his body that she was moving around in place. Before even talking to him, she felt she hit the lottery. He looked rich just like Randy. There wasn't a connection like when she was with Slade, but it would do.

"You got a man?" he asked Farah. "Because if you do, you don't anymore."

*Glad I didn't wear that ring.* "Naw . . . I'm single." She grinned. "I use to deal with Randy from Southeast. You know him?"

"Naw. His name don't sound familiar."

"Good . . . Well, I been single for a while and could use some company. You got a girl?"

Lesa shook her head at the thirsty way Farah was acting. Now she wished she never agreed to allow her to tell people they were related.

"Let's just say I don't have any attachments." Whatever that meant was good enough for Farah. She could see him hanging over at her house and cooking for him. And judging by the Rolex on his arm, she could tell he had a little change in his pocket, too. "What's your name, pretty lady?"

"Farah Cotton."

"Cool-ass name. Why do I think I've heard that somewhere before?"

"You probably have. My family grew up around these blocks. We got a rep, if you know what I'm saying." She was smiling so hard both rows of teeth and her pink gums were showing. "People know not to fuck with us around Southeast."

"Well, my name is Gary." He smiled as he put his arms around her waist and pulled her into his body, as if they'd been together for years. He was so close to her lips that it looked like he was going in for a kiss. If he did, Farah would have let him. "What you doing tonight, Reds? Being with me or what?"

Farah was cheesing up in his face until she saw the man who infiltrated her dreams every night roll past in his truck.

Slade wasn't driving a designer ride, but he sure made the one he had look official. Slade looked her way, and something about his expression told her he wasn't feeling what he was seeing with his eyes. Suddenly she was blown thinking he wouldn't reach out again, whether it was to approach her about the murder or to talk to her. She was still in Slade World when Gary turned her chin so that she was looking into his eyes. "You a'ight? You know that nigga or something?"

Shaking Slade out of her mind she said, "Uh . . . no. I thought that was my cousin at first but it was someone else."

"So what you doing tonight?" he asked, uninterested in innocent matters.

"I ain't doing nothing. We were about to go to the store to buy some stuff to cook dinner."

"You gonna cook for me?" Gary asked, licking his lips.

Lesa was eavesdropping so heavily she couldn't hear shit Roth was spitting. The driver was mad he chose her, since it was apparent that she wasn't as easy as Farah. "I can cook for you, baby. What you like to eat?"

"Before I tell you what I want for dinner, I want you to tell me what you gonna give me for dessert."

Farah grinned, knowing what he meant. "You can't handle my sweets," she replied as if she could fuck. "You better stick to dinner, boy, before you get yourself into trouble."

"You that good?" Gary smirked. Farah was hot and horny and within the hour, she was positive that she would give him the access granted to bang her back out. "You talking a lot of shit, Farah Cotton." He groped his dick. "I hope you can handle it."

"I can." She rubbed his thickness, all while outside in the open. "So when you coming over?" If Randy rolled past, he would snatch her face off.

"Shit, we ain't doing nothing now. We can come chill with y'all while you cook. I would love to see that sexy ass in the—"

Before he could finish his sentence, Lesa yanked Farah up so quickly her neck snapped. Moving her out of earshot of the fellas Lesa said, "You wanna go to 7-Eleven instead of Lucky 7?"

Farah frowned, not understanding her question. "Naw . . . why you say that?"

"I figured you'd want a Big Gulp since you being so thirsty."

Farah frowned and snatched her arm away. "I'm not thirsty, but I know what I want." She looked at Gary. "I figured we could have some fun, since I been in a bad mood for the past couple of days. I mean, didn't you tell me earlier you wanted to meet some new niggas? Here we go."

"You don't see nothing wrong with picking a nigga off the streets and taking him home?"

"And you don't see nothing wrong with taking Diamond D to your room at my party and fucking him? While you were on your period?" Farah wanted to fuck Gary so badly she was making herself look terrible.

Lesa threw her hands in the air. "Whatever you want, cousin. Do you."

"Good! And just so you know, I'm not gonna take a lot of you grabbing my arm out in public anymore. Be careful, Lesa. You don't really know who I am or who I can be. I can snap if pushed." Farah dismissed everything Lesa was spitting back and walked over to her new friend to discuss their plans for the evening.

Farah was trying to breathe as Gary dug in and out of her pussy raw. She hoped he'd like her enough to stick around, but the way he was acting, she couldn't be sure.

Sweat poured off of his face and entered her eyes, and all she thought about was how cute he looked panting heavily in her face. The bed rattled as if she were Celie from *The Color Purple* and he were Mr. She focused on the light above her head and would sporadically try to move her body to please him. But the only things that moved were her shoulder blades and if he were fucking them, he'd be straight.

"Bitch, is you dead?" he said out of nowhere, looking into her face. He wiped the sweat off of his brow. "What happened to all that shit you was talking outside?"

"Huh? What happened?" His comment came out of left field, and she felt a piercing jolt of unease in her stomach.

"For starters, you not moving right. It's like I'm fucking a corpse or something." He was straight giving her the business. "And your pussy dry. What, you a dude or something?"

She didn't know how he wanted her to operate her hips, but she could certainly get her own pussy wet. "Move for a second. I know what to do." He lifted up and she took a glob of spit, put it in her hand, and slapped it over her pussy, the way Randy would ask her to do sometimes. Then she lay on the bed with her legs open. "Come on, you should be able to get into it now." She smiled.

After seeing that mess, Gary rose up and sat on the edge of the bed. He wasn't about to fuck Miss

Spitty Puss, he didn't care how bad her body was. "Can you at least suck dick? Since it's obvious you can't fuck?" She was too afraid to say the wrong thing, so she nodded instead. "Good . . . Get on your knees and open your mouth."

Farah dropped, and he stuffed his dick into her mouth. She moved her neck the way she thought he wanted, and pretended to be enjoying it as she bobbed awkwardly from left to right. When she looked up at him, his brows were creased and he looked madder than before. It was as if he was growing more irritated with each lick. Grabbing her cheeks he said, "Open your mouth wide." He demonstrated. "Like this."

When he released her, she bobbed her head so ridiculously again that he was about to hit her on top of the head, like the Hungry Hungry Hippo in the children's board game. She thought things were cool until her teeth bit down on him and he pushed her off. Farah was overcome with embarrassment, and immediately felt lightheaded. Standing up, holding his dick he said, "You did that shit on purpose."

She shook her head. "No . . . I didn't! I promise."

"Yes, you did." Gary grabbed his clothes and quickly got dressed. It was as if a bomb were about to detonate and he only had fifty seconds to get out alive.

"Is everything cool?" Farah sat on the bed and looked at him move about the room in a hurry. "Did I do something wrong? I tried to do it the best I could. Maybe I can try it again."

"You bit down on my dick! Of course you did something wrong!" He paused. "Put your shit on and go in the kitchen and cook," he told her as if he were an abusive husband. "Because after what you just did to me, the least you could do is make me something to eat. After this shit, I gotta grab a drink from Riley's." He put his hat on and left.

Farah got dressed and walked to the mirror. She couldn't find her panties and from where she stood, she looked around for them. This was the most mortifying thing she'd ever experienced in her life. Second only to the day Brownie put shit in her face. In the beginning, when she first got with Zone, he asked her if she'd ever had sex. He told her that something was wrong with the way she moved her body and she never knew what he meant until that night. Standing in front of the mirror, with a closed fist, she hit herself in the face once. And a second time. And a third time, until tears poured out her eyes. She could only imagine what Gary was saying to his friend, or Lesa in the living room. Finding her panties on the floor, next to her mirror, she noticed his dirty footprint in the seat of them. Mad at herself for even being bothered with him in the first place, she put them on as a form of punishment against herself.

Picking up her cell, she decided to call her grand-mother. "Farah." Elise had just woken up and was trying to get herself together. "Is everything okay?" Farah started weeping. "What's wrong? Talk to me!" Her voice was heavy with concern. "Are you hurt?"

"Grandma, I know you're not a priest, but if I confess my sins to you, and try to be a better person"—she sobbed harder—"do you think God will forgive me? So that people will like me more?"

"God will always make things better when you trust in Him, but you shouldn't worry about other people."

"But that's what I want. For people to like me," she said seriously.

"Okay, Farah . . . I do believe when your soul is in order, all things will fall into place. Including the people in your life. And no matter what you say to me tonight, your secret is safe with me."

Farah bared her entire soul in the hopes she could be friends again with Coconut, Rhonda, and even Lesa. The call lasted for thirty minutes, as Farah told her about everything vile that she kept hidden.

After dropping her murderous life on her grand-mother, she pulled herself together and walked into the hallway. The moment she turned the corner, she heard two extra female voices in the living room. She saw Lesa and two girls sitting on the sofa and loveseat. Gary and Roth were also in the audience. They all seemed to be having a good conversation until she came into the room.

"Farah, come over here. I want you to meet my bitches!" Lesa said, holding a martini. Farah walked over to them and picked up one of her puppies that was clawing at her ankle. "This is Lady and this is Courtney."

"Hi, Farah." Lady smiled.

Farah was confused. She just confessed her sins to her grandmother, all of them, and this was how God repaid her?

"What's up?" Courtney said flatly.

Lady and Courtney gave each other sly looks before eyeing Gary who, judging by his body language, was obviously feeling Lady. They were so close together that their knees were touching. How could he be in her pussy and mouth a minute ago, only to entertain another bitch a second later? She was growing angrier by the minute.

Thinking of Elise, and still trying to be a better person, Farah's face produced a slight smile as she walked up to them and extended her hand. Lady accepted her gesture first, followed by Courtney, whose handshake was weak. She only hoped that Gary didn't give them the wrong impression by saying they fucked.

"I thought you weren't talking to them anymore." Farah smiled at Lesa. "So what are they doing here?"

"She called us," Courtney said. Farah looked at Lesa. All that shit about being too stubborn to call them was a lie and Farah felt played. She didn't know that her behavior outside inspired Lesa to call her friends. She wanted to be around real bitches. "Why . . . what's wrong?"

"I guess nothing."

"Well, did you have fun, Farah?" Lady asked, looking at Gary and back at her. Gary sipped a beer on the table and avoided eye contact with Farah. "Y'all was in there for a minute."

"Yeah, we were about to cook dinner," Courtney said. "Did you want a *bite* to eat?" she said louder. Everybody burst into laughter and she knew then that he told them they fucked and how poorly she performed.

"Well, come sit down, girl," Courtney said. "I was just telling Lesa that I love your place. She lucky as shit to be living here because a girlfriend of mine was trying to get in here for two years now."

"Thank you." Farah wasn't feeling her vibe. "You're welcome over here anytime you want."

"How did you get a place in this building?" Lady asked.

"Yeah . . . who you have to *fuck*?" Courtney looked at Gary. "Or *suck* . . . to move here?"

Farah was no longer feeling her energy and hoped Lesa would put them in check, but she didn't. "What are y'all doing here for real?" Farah blurted. "It's obvious you don't like me."

"And we're not here for you. We're here for Lesa." Courtney made the correction.

"But why the attitude? It ain't my fault Lesa told me about the reasons y'all stopped hanging together." She paused. "Me and Lesa are like family now, and I'm not gonna let y'all come in the way of that because you are jealous." They all looked at each other.

"Farah, what's wrong with you?" Lesa questioned. "They're just fucking with your head. Why you tripping so hard?"

"I knew that bitch was crazy," Gary said.

"Nigga, shut up," Roth interjected, not wanting to be thrown out before getting some pussy. "You already got put on."

"Yeah, right," he responded.

She looked at everyone and said, "I'm sorry. Maybe I don't feel so good so I'm being snappy. I was just wondering why they here. I mean, I thought y'all were beefing and the next thing I know, they in my house."

"We always fighting with this bitch, but we can't stay away from each other forever. That's real friendship," Lady said.

"Everybody don't beef with their friends over who bought whose baby shower gifts. Or who did hit and runs," Courtney joked.

Farah looked at Lesa. She couldn't believe she betrayed her this way. "Why would you do that, Courtney?" Lesa asked.

"Sorry, Farah." She raised a glass. "I been drinking."

"I hope y'all know that me and Lesa are cousins, so if you gonna be in her life, I am too," Farah said.

Courtney looked at Lesa, who held her head down in shame. The cousin shit was cool when they were alone with a drink in hand, but in front of her friends it was embarrassing. And she couldn't understand why Farah didn't recognize it. She had zero swag.

"This your cousin now?" Lady laughed, holding her stomach. "Damn, y'all ain't been in here that long, have you?"

"Yeah, Lesa . . . what y'all gonna be doing next? Eating each other's pussies out?" Courtney added.

"Picture that shit, bitch!" Lesa remarked. "You always talking sideways."

Everyone was laughing at Farah's expense and she felt the room spin. Everything in her wanted to beat both of their asses, and she realized Elise was a liar. She didn't know anything about life because if she did, why would she be going through this? Things were even worse since she confessed. "We not real cousins," Farah interrupted. "We just call each other that because we have so much in common."

"Whatever," Courtney said, waving her hand at the foolery. "Anyway, Lesa, what you doing tonight? You coming with us to the party or what?

A friend of mine owns a catering company in DC called E.A.T. with his partners." Farah remembered Coconut inviting her to that spot. "At night they rent it out for parties and shit like that. It's real fly, Lesa. You gotta see this shit. Anyway, Juice and his boys celebrating some business venture and they want us to come."

"Yeah, it's supposed to be like that," Lady added.

"Y'all not gonna hang out with us here?" Roth said, looking at Lady. "I was trying to get to know you better."

"How you gonna get to know me more, when you here with Lesa?"

"He wasn't with me," Lesa said. "Farah brought them in here."

"It don't matter if he didn't try to holla at you or not, I got a man." Lady told him. "Plus you can't afford me, daddy. I will admit, you kinda cute though."

Gary, irritated with all of the shit, stood up and patted Roth on the shoulder. "Let's roll, man. Ain't shit jumping off in this joint."

"I ain't ready to go," Roth said.

"You must be trying to get left," Gary sounded off. Farah thought his comment was funny being that he was the passenger. "Since we did ride in my car." *So it was his car?* Farah thought. It didn't matter. Right now all she wanted was both of them gone, because they were constant reminders that she made a character judgment mistake by inviting them over.

"A'ight, ma. I'ma get up with you later, cool?" Roth said to Lesa.

"Whatever." She brushed him off.

When they left, Farah sat down on the recliner and said, "So what time is the party? I got some real fly shit I want to wear, that still got the tags on it. My boyfriend Zone bought it for me before he died, when he fell out the window." Lady and Courtney gave her a puzzled look. "We never went nowhere so I didn't have a chance to wear it. Maybe I should put it on tonight."

"Uh . . . Who said you were invited?" Lady asked.

"Yeah . . . I don't remember giving you an invitation either," Courtney said seriously.

Farah looked at both of them and then at Lesa. The room was silent for forty seconds, as she waited for them to say they were joking. This reminded her of how she felt when she invited herself to Coconut's slumber party. "Are you serious?" she asked. "I really can't go?"

"You're lame, Farah," Courtney continued. "Plus, we don't know you like that. So why would you think you could just invite yourself to our shit?"

Farah put her puppy down and ran into her bedroom. With her bedroom door closed, she looked at herself in the mirror. *You a dumb ugly bitch. Look at you. Your lips are big. Your eyes*

*are far apart. Nobody wants you around them.*
*Look at you. You can't even talk in front of people.*
*You're stupid. You're dumb! Spotty-faced Farah!*
*You gonna always be ugly!*

Picking up the brush off her dresser, she brushed it over her lips repeatedly until they were inflamed. When the tissue was broken, she set the brush down and hit herself in the mouth over and over until blood splattered on the wooden dresser and floor. Her mouth was so red she looked as if she drank blood. She was about to hit herself again when Lesa entered the room without asking.

"Farah, they just playing . . ." She stopped herself midsentence when she saw blood everywhere. She rushed up to her and said, "What happened?"

Farah covered her mouth. "Nothing. I . . . I hit myself in the mouth with my brush by accident." She smiled, exposing her bloody teeth. "I'm fine. Really."

"How did you do that with a brush? You should go to the hospital."

After being in the hospital for most of her life, going tonight was totally out of the question. "I said I'm fine. Now what do you want, Lesa?" Farah grabbed a few tissues from the box and wiped her mouth. "Go be with your friends since you don't wanna be around me anymore. I may be lame, but I would've taken up for you if my friends talked to you like that."

"Farah, sometimes you act like a kid, and I don't like it. I thought you would be cooler when I moved in here. That's why I said you could call me your cousin. But you said that shit twenty times in front of other people and it's embarrassing. Especially when people know we not related." She paused. "But don't be so serious. Now . . . get dressed, you going to E.A.T. too."

Farah's eyes widened and a smile spread across her face. Just like that, all was forgiven. "For real?"

"Yeah . . . I told them you my roommate and to not do you like that." She rubbed her hair. "So I did take up for you. Just make sure you look fly because the niggas they hang with got money and they don't fuck with busted bitches."

"Naw . . . I'm gonna look real cute. Trust me." When Lesa left, Farah looked through her closet. She already made a bad impression and didn't want to make another one by choosing the wrong gear. After moving hangers back and forth, she settled on a black cat suit by Chanel, along with her leopard Christian Louboutin heels, to showcase her toned calves. After taking a shower and fixing her makeup properly, she realized she didn't have her medicine, so she decided to drive her own car so she could make a stop and meet them at E.A.T. later. When she walked into the living room to let them know, Mia and Chloe were sitting on the couch with their luggage by their feet.

"Farah, we home!" Chloe sang.

# Chapter 26

**"How much longer though?
I got somewhere to be!" —Chloe**

Chloe was alone in the apartment for five minutes and already she was going through Lesa's shit. Her closet doors were wide open as she pushed hangers back and forth. Lesa had all the labels a girl could ask for, from Chanel to large, beautiful Hermès bags in assorted colors. She was a hustler's bitch and she had the threads to prove it. When Chloe found a black dress by Gucci, she wiggled out of her clothes right where she stood. Naked in the middle of the floor, she eyed the beautiful gown. Chloe had a tattoo of an eyeball on each ass cheek, complete with the lashes. So when Mia looked in her sister's direction, the eyes appeared to be staring at her.

"I swear that fucking tattoo is creepy!" Mia said, sitting on Lesa's bed. "I don't know why you got that shit anyway. It's ghetto to the hundredth degree."

Chloe turned around. "Girl, bye! Men love to see pretty lashes staring at them when they hitting this from the back." She focused on the dress and pressed it against her titties to judge the fit. "I get mad praise when I push this thing on they dick."

"They?" Mia was disgusted. "You better slow your roll before you come up missing. Anyway . . . couldn't you have just turned around and showed them your eyes? Did you have to get a tat?"

Chloe was silent for a moment because she never considered the possibilities. "No, that's dumb. I love my tattoo and like I said, I get compliments on it all the time."

"Whatever, young bitch."

A hot, sweaty mess from running around DC all day, Chloe eased into Lesa's new dress, which was supposed to be worn at the fashion show. Since the tag dug into her skin, she pulled it off and it floated to the floor like a leaf off a tree. As she pulled the straps over her shoulders she was amazed to see it fit like a glove. Chloe walked toward the mirror on the door and looked at her reflection. "Damn, me and this bitch gonna be the best of friends." She turned from side to side and saw her ass was perfectly round. "My time in the gym is finally paying off!" "Farah gonna be mad as shit when she find out you going through her roommate's closet! You know she don't want you here anyway."

Chloe fanned the air. "Like I give a fuck."

"You can fake with your friends if you want to, but I know it hurt you that y'all haven't been talking," Mia continued. "When you gonna tell me what it's about? You and Farah act like its top secret."

"Never. So stop asking."

"Did you have to pull the tag off? Ain't nobody trying to fight this bitch because you done left evidence that we been in here."

"Damn, I hate when you act all long in the tooth. It's gonna be cool. She might not even know this joint missing with all the shit she got in here."

"Chloe, you worrying about bullshit," Mia said, lifting Lesa's mattress to see if she had anything stashed. When she located a small Baggie of weed she smiled. "This is what I'm talking about right here." She shook the bag knowing it would change Chloe's focus. "Leave all that other shit where you found it and come put some smoke in the air with me."

"So I can't steal the dress, but you can steal a bag of *smoke?* And she won't know that's missing?" Chloe laughed.

"What do we care? We Cottons!"

"You right about that! Fire that shit up!" Mia and Chloe lay face up on Lesa's bed, smoking the best shit they'd ever had in their lives. "So when you think Shadow getting out?" Chloe asked, running her fingers through her toes as she held the blunt in the other hand. "I fucking miss him."

"Can't you stop doing that nasty-ass shit?" Mia said, looking at the way her sister's toes spread as she played with them. "And as far as Shadow is concerned, if you miss him so much, how come you don't go see him?"

"Because I'm not seeing him in no fucking cage," Chloe responded, dropping a little fire on Lesa's expensive down comforter. "I told you that already." She passed the blunt to Mia.

"Listen, Chloe, I know you the baby of the family and all." She took a pull and hit her chest twice. "But you gotta do better when it comes to him. We all we got and Shadow needs you."

"You wanna know the real reason I don't go? They give you a hard time about how you dress and it don't matter if you follow their rules or not. For real it's based on whoever is running the visitation desk at that time. It's fucked up. It seems like all them COs do is hate on bitches who be trying to see the people they love."

"Not all of them, Chloe."

"Enough of them to get on my fuckin' nerves."

"Well, I get in all the time," Mia added. "Ain't nobody ever turn me around and say I can't see him." Chloe shook her head. "What?"

"Look at yourself." Mia looked down at her body. She was overweight and she didn't take care of her personal appearance. "Look at your shirt." She pointed. "How the fuck you keep getting lipstick on the middle of your shirt? I mean, damn, the food go in your mouth, the makeup on your face, what part of it don't you understand?"

"Everybody don't have a gym membership. Some people work twelve hours a day and don't got time for all that."

"Why the fuck not? Every bitch fucking should have a gym membership. And that doesn't have anything to do about you looking dirty. I'm just saying."

Mia was irritated her sister was pulling her card. "Fuck you know about fucking? You ain't nothing but nineteen."

"I been fucking since I been fourteen, Mia. Don't play with me. You and me both know it's true."

"It don't matter how I dress and look, it's my fucking business." It bothered her that both Farah and Chloe could run rings around her in the looks department but she never felt like a glamour girl. Give her a beer, a young boy, and a blunt, and you could leave her the fuck alone. "Back to Shadow, hopefully it won't be too much longer. He was supposed to come home last week but he got into a fight with some dumbass nigga, and they held him up." She shook her head. "I wish he just calm down sometimes."

"Why? Whoever got in his face should've left him the fuck alone. I'm sick of feeling bad when people get us wrong and we step to 'em hard." When the phone rang, Chloe hopped off the bed and answered. "Farah's residence," she sang.

"Yes, is Farah Cotton available?"

"Hold up, is this Dr. Martin?" Chloe smiled. "What you doing, calling here this late at night?"

"I figured it's the only time I can get Farah on the phone. May I ask who this is?"

"Chloe!" She giggled. "You should know my voice by now. As much as I call you."

"Sorry . . . How are you and Mia? With your meds?"

"We fine I guess. Still gotta watch certain stuff."

"I know. It's a life process. Is Farah there?"

"No . . . but can I take a message?"

"Yes. Give her this number—"

"Hold up," Chloe interrupted. "I got to find a piece of paper." She opened one of Lesa's dresser drawers and pulled out a pink stationary pad with green flowers throughout. Using the matching pen she said, "I'm ready."

"Have her call 202-555-8999." He paused. "How does she look?"

Chloe folded the paper and left it on the dresser. "She looks good. I don't know what she's doing but whatever it is, it's working."

"Oh . . . well . . . that's good to hear but I'm still very concerned. I just spoke to Elise and she told me some disturbing news. It sounds as if Farah is using very unconventional means, based on an urban legend. She's gonna end up in jail or worse off . . . dead."

"I don't understand. Like what?"

Dr. Martin cleared his throat. "Can you please have her call me? I really want to talk to her. Maybe even visit her at home. I really would appreciate it." He hung up. Chloe shrugged and put the phone down. "I'ma go get something to drink. You want anything?"

"Yeah . . . bring me a beer. What'd Dr. Martin say?"

"He talking crazy. Saying Farah doing unconventional something or another. Anyway, you know how weird he is sometimes." Still wearing Lesa's Gucci dress, she walked barefoot into the kitchen and grabbed a beer for Mia. Then she opened the icebox and was pissed when she didn't see any ice for her drink. "Damn! They don't even have no ice up in here!"

"Girl, this Platinum Lofts! They got an ice cooler on every floor."

"That's right!" she said, snapping her fingers. "I can't believe they got all that shit in this mothafucka. Platinum Lofts or not, it's still in the ghetto."

"Girl, take your young ass out there and get some ice. But make sure you leave the door unlocked. I'm about to take a shit."

Chloe grabbed a large bowl, left the door unlocked, and tiptoed into the hallway. She was looking for a sign that read ice until she saw the pudgy kid come out of his apartment. He said, "You better be careful. People keep dying in this building."

"Shut your fat ass up and mind your business." He slammed the door.

When she found the machine, she was irritated when she saw someone had made it there before her. He had a bucket of ice on the floor and was working on filling a second one. She forgot all about the ice for a moment, when she noticed the way his muscular back filled his white T-shirt. Before she even saw his face she knew there was something about him that was for her. It could've been the gun in his waistband, or his stylish jeans; whatever it was, she needed to see his face. Instead of saying something nice to get his attention, Chloe got real ignorant-like and said, "I'm saying, can you leave some ice for somebody else please? Damn!"

He turned around, and her heart melted. He looked better than she could've imagined. He gave her a sly smile and immediately her pussy got wet. "I'm almost done." He continued to fill his bucket.

"How much longer though? I got somewhere to be!"

He placed his second bucket down, and looked at her cute toes and dark brown eyes. "If you wanted to get to know me, ma"—he pinched her nipple hard—"all you had to say was hi." He picked the buckets up and Chloe's jaw dropped.

"I can't believe you just did that shit!"

"Yes, you can. I gave you exactly what you wanted." He walked away. "I'm sure I'll check you later."

# Chapter 27

**"Me touching you will depend on how good you gonna make me feel." —Slade**

Slade turned on Markee's stereo so that the sounds of Usher could flow through the speakers and get the women ready to fuck. Markee's apartment was more crowded than it usually was and Slade was to blame. He wanted to put his brothers at ease so, after he robbed the store, he picked up a few women to keep them company. The five bitches wanted nothing more than food, drinks, and smoke, and the moment they saw Slade's handsome face, they packed themselves in his truck headed to Platinum Loft apartments, without caring for their safety or security.

The women were huddled together on the couch and floor, looking at the Baker Boys until Audio walked into the apartment with two buckets of ice. Setting them down in the kitchen, he walked over to Slade and said, "So this how you gonna do us right?" he asked, looking at the women as he rubbed his hands together. He was eye fucking the whorish outfits they wore. "You go out, and come back with some dough, and some fat-ass bitches. That's how you do it, big bro!" "Just a little something to hold you over." Slade patted him on the back. "Now go enjoy yourself." Audio blushed and Slade wiped his hand through his hair. "Don't smile now, li'l nigga. It's time to show and prove."

"You already know what it is. I got this." He winked at him.

Audio walked away and Slade looked at the women and his brothers. If the Baker Boys had one thing in common it was that they all loved pussy . . . often. Alike in a lot of ways, they also had characteristics that set them apart. For instance, nineteen-year-old Audio had a foot fetish that was so bad, when Slade caught him looking at his cousin's toes he busted him in the mouth, resulting in $5,000 worth of dental surgery. Then there was twenty-five-year-old Killa, who enjoyed playing violent video games. He ordered them from Japan, because in the United States the restrictions were too heavy. Outside of women and games, his third passion was guns, and he never moved anywhere without at least two. His favorite? A classic .45, which he swore originally belonged to a serial killer currently on death row.

Twenty-nine-year-old Major was different because he always had dreams of making it big the legit way. He envisioned opening a chain of funeral homes that would take care of all burial needs. His ex-girlfriend back home came from a long line of money, and her family owed it all to funeral homes. Major was certain about three things in life and they were that his dick got hard, people got sick, and everybody died. Thinking in advance, Major had A-1 credit and didn't fuck it up for nobody. Then there was Knox, who at twenty-eight was the quietest and most perceptive of the clan. He thought about things in advance, where others would never see certain scenarios coming. And because of it, he kept his brothers safe on many occasions. It was because of Knox that they had the proof necessary to fight Sheriff Kramer; the only problem now was he was missing in action.

When Audio walked back into the kitchen, he poured one bucket of ice into a large silver cooler, and filled it with beers. As the Baker Boys walked around getting themselves situated, the women were in awe. They could easily be mistaken for a boy band or some famous group, if they possessed a unified talent. Every muscle in their bodies was sculpted to perfection, and their skin tone, although varying in complexion, was flawless. Still, out of all of them not one was finer than Slade Baker. Although he didn't smile much, and often appeared aloof, every woman upon first sight had to have a taste.

"Y'all can get some beer," Audio offered the ladies. "It's in the kitchen." He rubbed his waves with his hand. "And we got food over by the counter too. Eat up." He gripped his dick. "You gonna need all the energy you can get." Audio wasn't normally hospitable, but for the sake of pussy he was a perfect gentleman.

"What else y'all got?" Red Dress asked, looking at the spread. Red Dress was extremely sexy and walked seductively to the counter to get Slade's attention. "Y'all got wine too?"

"Naw, baby." Audio looked at her round ass. "Just beer and soda."

"What about food?"

"We got what the fuck y'all asked for . . . chicken," Killa said, his gun resting in his waistband. He wanted some pussy and wasn't into entertaining. As far as he was concerned they were freaks and should be treated as such. "Now hurry up so we can do what y'all came to do."

"Killa," Slade roared, "show respect."

"To these bitches?" He pointed at them.

"To those women."

The ladies frowned but they were also mesmerized by Killa's bad-boy behavior. They had never hooked up with a group of dudes where every last one of them was sexy. Usually somebody would have to take one for the team. This time was different. After Killa snapped, the girls ate and drank to their hearts' content. When they were heavy with a buzz, Audio dimmed the lights so that they'd know what time it was. Relaxed and in the mood, the girls all made a move for Slade.

"You know, I never did get your name," Red Dress said, as her friends huddled in the background like birds tripping to get a piece of bread. "How 'bout you tell me now."

"That's because I didn't give it to you," he said as Red Dress and her friends moved closer. "As fine as you ladies are, I only need one," he said, sipping his beer. "The only question is which one of you is it going to be."

"Why you only want one?" the girl with the shoe boots asked. "A man as strong as you should be able to handle two."

Slade grinned. "I could but tonight I'm looking for a little one on one."

"My big brother might not be up for it, but I'll take two," Audio said, practically morphing into the conversation.

After forcing the women with him by way of wrist snatching, the other brothers made their selection and disappeared into various parts of Markee's apartment. Slade knew he was wrong for having the women in his cousin's home because Markee specifically asked them not to, but his brothers were in a bad mood. Luckily for the Baker Boys, Markee was out of town on business.

Audio didn't waste any time undressing the two women he selected. In the kitchen, the sound of balls slapping against an ass rang out. He seemed like he was in a world of his own as he bent Shoe Boots over the edge of the counter, while Hoop Earrings rubbed his back and whispered how she wanted next in his ear.

Red Dress, who stayed with Slade, looked in the kitchen and smiled. "Sounds like your brother is having fun already," she said, standing over him. "You think we can outdo him?"

Slade eyed the dress she was wearing, along with her sexy black boots. "You wanna talk about them, or worry about what we do over here?"

"What's your name?" she asked as she slinked down to her knees. "Because I like you already."

"I told you, ma. My name doesn't matter."

"So you the cool one . . . The big brother who likes mystery. Am I right?"

"I'm being me. That's all I can say."

She frowned but the harder time he gave her, the more she had to have him. Slade wasn't the type of dude to talk a bitch to death, but he was a gentleman, although an angry one at times. He just wanted the conversation to cease because the purpose of their union was purely sexual.

When she eased out of her dress, Slade witnessed the prettiest titties he'd seen in his life. Her waist . . . small. Her legs . . . thick. Her body . . . outrageous.

She unbuckled his pants as he sipped beer and watched her do her thing. At first she thought he was playing hard to get, but when she saw he didn't fall all over how sexy she was, she realized she was dealing with a different type of dude all together.

With his jeans at his ankles, she released his dark-chocolate dick from his boxers. Her touch. So soft. So warm. Red Dress eyed his thickness and thought about how great it would be for him to be inside of her. She could feel icing coating her panties, and wasn't sure how much more she could take. She continued to stroke his dick back and forth until he was so hard, she could feel him pulsating under her fingertips. "Seems like he likes me." She looked down at his dick. "But I wonder how you feel."

Slade wished she'd go mute by stuffing his dick in her mouth. If he knew she was going to be so talkative, he would've taken Shoe Boots instead. Her seductive words were good for Act One, but now he was ready for Act Two. "Can I feel your hands on me?" she asked, looking up at him, her mouth inches away from his penis. "Please."

*Why I gotta touch you?* he thought. *Just do the shit!* "Come on, baby," he said, "I'm just trying to have a little fun. Nothing more, nothing less."

She pouted. "Aww . . . come on, rub my shoulders, pull my hair," she suggested, "do something to show me you're participating instead of just sitting there." She wanted from him what he couldn't give: an emotional connection. "I'm not cute enough for you? Is that it?" The sound of Major banging Yellow Dress's back out in Meek's room temporarily interrupted their thoughts.

"What's your name, beautiful?"

"Shannon." She smiled, loving the sound of his accent.

"You know what I want?" She shook her head. "I want to feel your pretty lips wrapped around my dick. I wanna slide up in that pussy, and put a smile on your face. And then I wanna see you safely home. Is that gonna work for you? Because that's all I got."

She frowned. "So you not gonna touch me for real?"

"Why you want me to touch you so bad?"

"I don't know." She shrugged. "I guess because it makes me feel good."

Trying to get her to shut the fuck up he said, "Let's do this . . . me touching you will depend on how good you gonna make me feel."

That was all she needed to hear. She lowered her neck and her entire mouth covered his dick. Although he wasn't anywhere near a small brother, the hairs on his crotch tickled her nose. Slade's head fell back into the recliner as he enjoyed her warm, wet performance. He wanted to feel her badly, but he made a vow never to touch a woman again, and he would stick to it. His female family members all thought it was weird that he wouldn't hug them during family get-togethers, but he didn't care.

His unmanaged strength harmed many, even though it was never on purpose. It started when he was a child; he ruined everything from expensive furniture to antique dishes simply by handling them. At first Della would scold and warn him to be more careful, but as he got older, she realized the strength he possessed was really a gift. Although Della researched her son's abilities, the closest answer she could find was a condition called myostatin-related muscle hypertrophy. The condition causes people who are born with the rare mutation to have increased muscle mass, with virtually zero body fat.

On many occasions he helped rescue his family, like when he was ten years old and an unstable tree fell on Knox's legs after a rainstorm. Slade was able to move the tree enough so his brother could free himself. Although his wrist broke, even the doctors said it was amazing what he was able to accomplish. But Slade never considered the condition a blessing and because of it, he focused on the negatives.

Like when he accidently broke his baby cousin's hand while helping her out of the car on Thanksgiving. Slade was beside himself for two months afterward and visited her every day to wait on her hand and foot. It didn't matter that his family told him it was a mistake, and to be easy on himself. He was overwhelmed with guilt. Then there was the time he saw an elderly woman crossing the street while a car moved speedily in her direction. Trying to save her life, he rushed toward her to push her out of the way. The woman's head slammed against the concrete, and her blood spilled onto the pavement. Although she was alive, the once-independent lady was confined to a wheelchair for the rest of her life.

Finally there was the day he'd never forget, when he moved to hug his mother, to tell her how much he loved her, only to crack her rib cage, resulting in the signature limp she possessed to that day. After that, he vowed never to touch another woman, even in pleasure, and he hadn't broken it since.

Shannon moved her tongue like a snake along his dick, as she gave him the best head game known to man. Her pink tongue seemed to glisten as she ran it around the tip and sides at least fifty times. Repositioning herself, she devoured him whole and his eyes popped open. Slade didn't imagine that he'd be in for such a treat. She was a pro, who seemed to love what she was doing. Moving her neck up and down like a crane, she was on a mission to make Slade think of her long after she was gone. As he looked down at her pretty face, he wondered what life served her that she would be so great at pleasing a man that way. She was young, but her fuck game was old and long, like she did it for a living.

"Right there, ma." Slade's heart rate sped up as he battled with whether to touch her to keep her in place. Sex was the only time it was hard to keep his vow. Having to explain to women why he couldn't touch them had become a work of art. He knew the right things to say and how to say them. For most women he came into contact with, this quirk gave them a challenge and, as if it were even possible, made him more desirable.

He was almost there and imagined how her long hair would feel wrapped around his fingers as he pushed her head down farther on his dick. "You not gonna touch me yet?" she cooed, as her mouth made sloppy noises. "Even"— slurp—"while"— slurp—"I'm handling my business?"

He didn't respond and that seemed to do the trick, because Shannon immediately refocused. "Keep it like that, baby. That shit feels so good."

When Shannon made her mouth hotter and wetter, Slade could feel a strong nut coming his way. Out of respect, he was about to warn her, but she was looking directly into his eyes and virtually begging him to bring it on. "It's okay," she mumbled. "I want to taste you. *All* of you."

Without another word, he released his cream into her mouth, as his fingers dug into the fabric of the recliner. Cum oozed along the sides of her large pink lips and she slurped it back in before swallowing every drop. "How you like that?" Shannon said, licking her lips. "Was I good enough for you to touch me now?"

Slade smiled, knowing full well she already knew the answer. He was just about to congratulate her on the performance when the front door to the apartment flew open. Slade reached for his weapon preparing to fire, until he saw it was his cousin Markee.

"I thought I told you niggas not to bring nobody in my house!"

# Chapter 28

**"Whenever you ready, bitch.**
**Whenever you ready." —Farah**

It was Farah's first time hanging out with Lesa and her crew and already things were not going as planned. Her car wouldn't start after making a stop, so she had to catch a cab. After spending fifteen minutes in a cab so funky she held her nose the entire way, she was surprised to see the line to E.A.T. wrapped around the corner. As Lesa promised, when Farah called she came outside to greet her. Once inside, she didn't understand why it wasn't filled to capacity.

"Why they not letting people in?" Farah asked, yelling over the music. "It's a nice crowd in here, but it's not packed."

"That's a promotion move," Lesa said. "To make people passing by want to get inside." Then she looked at her face. "What's that red stuff on your lips?" she asked, preparing to wipe the mark away.

Farah slapped her hand and glared. "Don't do that." Then she spit on her finger and wiped the corner of her mouth.

"Sorry . . . I just don't like people touching my face. I break out easily."

Lesa leaned back and said, "You know what, I'm not even doing this with you tonight. If you want shit all over your face, so be it. I was just trying to help. Anyway . . . come on." She turned around. "We over here."

As Farah followed Lesa to their seats, she was pleasantly surprised to see hand-blown chandeliers hanging from the ceiling, and large plush sofas with cherry-wood tables in front of each private section. In the middle of the floor were large beautiful tables with hand-carved wooden chairs. Toward the back was a dance floor where the DJ was set up, playing the old-school classics. "This is nice as shit!" Farah said, observing her surroundings. "I shoulda worn my other dress if I knew it was gonna be like this."

"You fine, girl," Lesa said. "I'm sure niggas gonna try to holla left and right. Good thing you single because you gonna meet some moneymakers tonight. Instead of that bamma-ass nigga Gary you bought to the house." Farah was starting not to like Lesa, but she was gonna let her live, because she had a feeling her attitude was because her sisters moved in. Farah only wished she had more time to ease her into it.

She knew Lesa could be territorial over her things and her sisters respected anything but people's possessions. She already got into an argument with her when Farah borrowed her shoes one day without asking, even though Lesa said she could help herself to anything she owned.

Farah's phone dinged with a text message from Randy:

Farah I haven't talked to you. Where the fuck you at?

She hated having to answer to anybody, especially a person she didn't want to be with, so she didn't respond. All he wanted her to do was come over and get dick beat . . . she just knew it.

When Farah and Lesa were seated in VIP, Courtney walked up to them and said, "Juice said our spot is over there. We in the wrong place." She pointed to a section with two couches and a table marked ReseRved. The girls swaggered over to the table and took their seats, and Farah bopped her head to the music.

Everyone looked so sexy that she wanted to have a picture, in case she got up with Coconut again. When a beautiful white waitress with long red hair came over to serve them Farah said, "Ooh . . . can you take our picture please?" Farah waved her cell phone and handed it to her. "Thank you!"

"Not a problem." She smiled.

Farah awkwardly moved in the available space between Courtney and Lesa. "Can you see all of us?

If you can't let me know now so we can move closer together."

"Yep, I see everybody." She smiled. "Say cheese."

Lesa looked at Courtney and Lady, who were visibly blown by the way Farah was acting. She tried to calm down, but this was the first time she hung out with girls who appeared to be upscale. "Cheese!" Farah sang, while the other girls remained silent and stone faced, not a cute picture at all.

Handing back Farah's phone, the waitress asked, "What can I get for you ladies?" A sincere smile dressed her face. "Juice said anything you want is on the house, and I'm here to see that you have a great time tonight."

"That's what I'm talking about!" Farah said, trying to give Lesa a high five, who left her hanging. She put her hand down in her lap, and tried to play it cool like the other girls. "That was real nice of him."

"Why was it nice?" Courtney pronounced with an attitude. "He supposed to treat us like this." Farah had never been in VIP so to them, she was acting inappropriately for the crowd. Lesa and her friends were used to this sort of treatment and wished she just slowed her roll.

"Bring a bottle of Ketel One and some Red Bulls. That's what we usually have," Courtney said to the waitress. She looked at her friends with a nod of approval. "That'll be all . . . Thank you."

"Actually," Farah said, stopping her. "I'd like something different. Can you bring a bottle of Patrón, too? Since he said we can get whatever we want!" She yelled to be heard over the music. "Thank you." The waitress, seeing nothing wrong with Farah's request, walked away to fetch their orders.

"Farah, we usually drink Ketel One," Courtney said, her brow creasing. "I mean you think you that thirsty, where you gotta drink a whole bottle of Patrón? All you doing is wasting liquor and shit. That's so stupid."

Farah looked at Lesa, Courtney, and Lady. She hadn't been there for fifteen minutes, and already she was getting on everybody's nerves. No matter how hard she tried, tonight she was doing all the wrong things. "I can go tell her never mind," Farah said, not wanting to leave a bad taste in their mouths. "It's just that I don't normally drink Ketel One. It always makes me sick in the morning. I can just get a soda."

"It's not that big of a deal," Lesa said, looking at Courtney and Lady. "Juice said we can get what we want, so I say we get what we want." Lesa taking up for her finally made her feel at ease. "You cool, Farah."

Sitting back in her seat Courtney said, "So what's up with your new roommates, Lesa? I thought it was gonna be just you and Farah. It looks like y'all have a full house now. What y'all about to do, film some reality TV show or something?"

"At first it was gonna be just us." Lesa's eyes rolled over Farah. "But they staying with us for a little while until they find another place to live. Right, Farah?"

"Yeah. They just staying for a month. And when my brother gets home they probably gonna leave sooner than that." Farah crossed her legs, and wiggled her shoe. "I think the three of them are getting a place together but I'm not sure."

"Where your brother at now?" Courtney persisted.

She stiffened up. "He in college."

Courtney didn't believe her because of her body language. "The college of life or education?"

"What's the college of life?" The girls laughed. "Did I miss something?" She was sick of their sidebars. "What's so funny?"

"Is he in jail or in college, Farah?" Lady interrogated. "Do you understand now?"

"He's in college," she lied. "He's graduating soon . . . with a master's degree and everything."

"Really?" Courtney leaned in. "I know you're happy and your mother too."

*I hate this bitch. She gonna make me hurt her if she keeps pushing me.* "Everybody's proud of him."

"So what's he taking up?" Courtney continued, nudging Lesa's leg.

Farah could tell she didn't believe her, so she decided to shut her down. "Law. He's gonna be an attorney."

Courtney and Lesa doubled over in laughter, as if she were Kevin Hart. "Let me stop fucking with this girl," Courtney said. "Because it's obvious she's a fucking liar."

Farah uncrossed her legs, leaned over, and said, "What the fuck is up with you? All night you been tripping for no reason."

"It's nothing wrong with me." She grinned. "So what school is he in?"

"Harvard," she said flatly.

Courtney looked at Lesa and back at Farah. "You a bigger liar than I thought, if you think somebody gonna believe that shit. What happened to you as a kid? Were you too weird to have friends or something? You was stuck in the house all day? What?"

"Courtney, please shut up!" Lesa said.

"Answer the question, Farah. What made you such a liar?"

"Can I talk to you in the bathroom alone?" Farah said, running her tongue alongside the blade inside of her mouth. She was going to deliver her. "Please."

"Let's go."

She was about to get up when Lesa said, "Just drop it, Courtney, damn."

"There Juice and them go right there!" Courtney said, waving her hand wildly to get their attention. The waitress brought the drinks to the table and everything seemed to move in slow motion. Courtney's antics didn't work, because every time the men took a step, someone else would pull them.

"Damn, bitches on them hard as shit!" Lady said.

"Right," Courtney added, feeling dumb. "Give 'em room to breathe, damn! They ain't going nowhere."

When the men finally moved toward the table, they were with someone who took Farah's breath away. Although they were all dressed in designer jeans and shirts, one of them stood out in the pack. Wearing a pair of black-rimmed Gucci shades, his button-down shirt was rolled up at the elbows, exposing his slightly hairy forearms and tattoos. For a moment Farah forgot how crazy Randy could be, because he looked like money.

"Damn, the nigga Juice gets finer by the day." Courtney licked her lips. "All of them for that matter! I wish he didn't look at me like a little sister."

"Bitch, you betta slow your roll before Don breaks your back in." Lesa laughed. "He know every last one of them."

"I said he looked good, I didn't say I wanted to fuck him, Lesa."

After the men said their hellos, they finally approached the VIP table. Randy was so caught up in sexy Lesa, Courtney, and Lady that, at first, he didn't see his fiancée sitting next to them. When he saw her, the sly grin was removed from his face as he approached. "I just texted you and I didn't get a response. Why you in here being a whore?"

Farah readjusted in her seat. "It's not like that." She looked at Lesa. "I was just hanging out with my friends."

"Well, how come I haven't been able to reach you?" He walked up to her, and the girls moved out of the way so he could sit next to her. "I just hit you."

Farah tried to choose her words carefully, knowing he would snap if he didn't get the answer he wanted. "Randy, I been kinda busy with my—"

"You don't live with your mother, do you?"

Farah looked at Lesa, Courtney, and Lady, who were all looking in the opposite direction. This was the worst time for this to be happening.

"I stopped past your mom's house a few times and you weren't there. I'm gonna have somebody in front of your building every night to make sure you go in and don't come out until the morning."

"Randy, you gotta trust me, baby. If you do shit like that, we not gonna work." She smiled. "I do live there, but I might be gone when you come by." She looked at everybody and felt relieved that they were heavy in conversation. She touched his hand. "Stop trying to catch me in something. I belong to you since the day I eased into the back seat of your car and you got me away safely."

He looked at her fingers. "Where is the ring?"

She snatched her hand away. "Somebody robbed me. I was too afraid to tell you because I know how you can get." At this time Lesa and her crew were waiting for Randy to get out of Farah's face, so that they could meet him. "I was going to call you so I could come over tonight. So I could tell you. Plus I miss you . . . a whole lot too."

"You coming with me tonight. We'll talk about it then." Turning his attention away from Farah, he looked at the other women. "What's up, ladies?" He extended his hand to all of them and they shook it softly. "I'm Randy and I see you all came out looking very luscious tonight."

While he was talking, Farah saw Coconut and Nova, and she wondered where Shannon was. Ignoring her, she placed a fake smile on her face and looked at Lesa and her friends, to pretend she was having the best time. Every so often, she would glance in their direction, but they were having too much fun to pay her any attention.

"Hello," Courtney said, showing too much teeth. "It's nice to meet you, Randy."

"Calm down 'fore my nigga Don beat that ass, Courtney," Juice added, stealing a few looks at Farah between his mild talk. For some reason he wanted her bad. "You already know how he go."

"I know ain't no nigga putting they hands on her sexy ass," Randy said, as if he didn't smack Farah around in the bedroom for fun.

"Look at this old chivalrous-ass mothafucka," Juice said, digging into the bottle of Patrón. Farah smiled, because he'd chosen to sip the drink she ordered. "Always trying to steal all the bitches. You ain't no playa, nigga!"

"Why would you say some bamma shit like that in front of my girl? I'm taken so it ain't even like that." He rubbed Farah's thigh.

"Boy, shut up!" Courtney said, hitting Juice on the arm. "I'm out here by myself tonight, and it ain't like you don't have a bitch at home too. Randy can be nice to me if he want to." She made it known that her legs could open for business if Randy chose to enter. "Anyway it's a pleasure to meet you. I'm Courtney Love."

"Get the fuck out of here!" Randy laughed. "Your name Courtney Love for real?"

"Yes, and she loves every bit of it too!" Lady said. "I'm Lady, and it's a pleasure to meet you."

"Lady, huh?" Randy loved being in the spotlight and stealing shine from other niggas. The look on Juice's face showed he was tired of his game show antics. "Well, you certainly are a woman." He turned his attention to Lesa, who didn't seem as wild as the other girls, even though she was just as beautiful. "And you are . . . ?" Farah would not have minded his performance, if he didn't make it known that they were supposed to be together. Now he was playing her in front of everybody and making the situation worse.

"My name is Lesa." She grinned. "And I've heard a few things about you."

"All good I hope."

"Nigga, sit the fuck down," Juice said, unable to take anymore of his antics. "I'm sick of looking at your ass on stage. It's time to drink and celebrate getting money." He waved the waitress back over to the table. "Bring two more bottles of Patrón." He looked at the women. "Since I see you ladies are already drinking, did you want something to eat?"

"I can eat," Farah said.

"Yeah . . . get her some of them garlic baked wings," Randy interjected. "And bring out them scallops wrapped in bacon, too." He took a sip of his drink. "She don't need nothing else."

"Damn, nigga! You ain't even give her a chance to open her mouth," DeWayne, their other friend, said. He was just as fine as Randy and didn't fuck with him like that for real, but hung with him for the love of money. "Ma, is that what you want . . . or can we get you something else?"

"I'll eat that. I wasn't that hungry anyway."

"See, nigga . . . I know my bitch." He put his arm around her shoulder, and pulled her to him. "We good over here." He joked, "Get your own." Juice laid his eyes on Farah a little too long again and Randy caught him. "You need to get some oil for your eyes? 'Cause they keep getting stuck over here."

Juice raised his glass and didn't dispute. "My bad." He wanted Farah to know he was watching. "Your girl like that." Farah blushed.

She picked her cup up off the table and stirred her drink with her straw. "So where you know Farah from, Randy?" Courtney asked.

"Why didn't you ask me?" Farah said.

"'Cause I'm asking him. Why . . . your name Randy too?"

"I've known her for a minute. We met in the neighborhood," Randy said, checking his Rolex. Although he was part owner of E.A.T., his true passion was the dope game and he had a meeting with Tornado and Markee in fifteen minutes about their trip to New York.

"Why you ask, beautiful?" His boys shook their heads because he was laying the compliments on too thick. "You know me or something?"

"Nope." She crossed her legs. "Just asking, because I thought Farah was feeling the nigga Gary we met earlier at her house tonight." She shrugged. "She was in the room with him so long, I could've sworn they were fucking." Not being able to take anymore, Farah grabbed the bucket off the table, complete with bottles of liquor, and threw it toward Courtney. One of the bottles hit her in the nose, and the other crashed at her feet. "Bitch, I will murder you!" Courtney yelled, jumping up and moving in Farah's direction.

Farah grabbed one of the bottles on the table, held it upside down, and said, "Move one inch closer, and I will punish your ass in here!" She rocked back and forth, waiting for a chance to react. "Go 'head, Courtney! Jump! You been wanting to do it all night anyway." The men rushed to separate the women and Randy held on to Farah tightly. From the corner of her eyes, she could see Coconut laughing at the situation brewing. It was evident now that she wasn't having as good of a time as she faked when she first saw her ex-best friend.

"You gonna see me again, bitch!" Courtney said, trying to get back at her, knocking ice cubes out of her hair. "That much I promise."

"Why put off later what we can do tonight?"

"It's time to go," Randy said, gripping Farah tightly. He took the bottle from her hands and put it on the table. He had to admit, the performance turned him on. "You know you can't be fighting in here and shit. You too classy for all that."

"She lying on me, Randy. Ain't no nigga hardly been in my house. I wouldn't cheat on you like that! That bitch don't know shit about me."

"I know, baby. You know better than to cross me." He positioned her chin so that he could stare into her eyes. "Don't you?"

"Can y'all drop me off at home?" Lesa interrupted. She was fucked up with Courtney for going too far. Ordinarily she would've taken her friend's side, but tonight she was just plain messy, and all of her shit was in Farah's house. "I'm tired anyway."

"We can't!" Farah shrieked. "I mean, you gotta get a ride from them. I'm going straight to Randy's." She couldn't risk him dropping her off at Platinum and finding out that she lived there too.

"A'ight . . . you okay?" Lesa asked her.

"I'm good."

"You gonna see me again," Courtney mouthed so that only she could read her lips moving.

"Whenever you ready, bitch. Whenever you ready."

# Chapter 29

**"It's cool, the girls
about to be out." —Slade**

When Markee walked into his crib, and saw his
four country cousins fucking the dog shit out of
five bitches, he was heated. His large body covered
the doorway, and he eyed them in disgust. Markee
Baker had been jealous of them his entire life. When
he was younger, family members could never stop
talking about how attractive Della Baker's sons
were, and how any girl able to land herself a Baker
should consider herself lucky, because they hardly
ever settled down. If he was the subject of conversation, the dialogue would be quite different. Instead
of praises they'd talk about how Markee needed to
lose weight, and get his body in order. Tired of living
in their shadows, he left Mississippi and moved to
DC for a better life. Six months after his arrival, he
was able to save up enough money to make his way
into the drug industry, hoping to prove his family
wrong. No matter how much money he stacked, he

could never measure up. So when his mother, Irma, called and asked him to make room for his cousins temporarily, he was furious. Not only would he have to hook them up with a key, which he left at the rental office, but he would also have to grant them access while he was out of town.

"I know y'all didn't disrespect and bring bitches in my crib while I was in New York?" Markee wolfed. He was showing off in front of everybody.

"Sorry about this, man. We were just having a little fun in the new city," Audio said.

Markee closed the front door, and the four men put their hands on their weapons. A white towel hung over the edge of Markee's brown leather coat and he wiped away his sweat.

"So I guess you know these niggas?" Tornado, Markee's main goon, asked.

"Yeah, they my mothafuckin' cousins." Hearing the commotion, Major walked out of his room with his dick exposed, while Killa stepped out of the bathroom with Markee's monogrammed towel wrapped around his lower body. Markee couldn't help but steal a look at what God blessed his cousins with, and it pissed him off all over again.

"Sorry, man." Major smiled. "We didn't think you were coming home tonight. We done, though. The girls about to leave."

"You didn't think I was coming home?" He tilted his head.

"Nigga, I live here!" He stabbed his finger into his chest.

"This my mothafuckin' crib!"

"It's cool, the girls about to be out," Slade said. He handed Shannon his coat to cover her body. "Can you fellas turn around so they can get dressed?"

"You don't run shit in here, Slade!" Markee said, eager to get out on the king of the clan. "I make the rules here. We ain't in Mississippi now! This DC!"

"You got that," he said with his hands raised. "I'm just trying to get them out so you can have your spot back." Slade knew his cousin was weak and he didn't want to embarrass him in front of his men. Right or wrong, he was out of order for bringing people in the house. And if he told his mother, she'd let him have it. "We good?"

"Fuck no!" Markee said, shaking his head from left to right. "We not good!"

"Well, what you want us to do then, nigga?" Audio yelled from the kitchen. Neither one of his bitches had bothered to get dressed. "Let you fuck one of 'em or something?"

"Ugh . . . no!" one of his girls yelled. "He too fat and nasty." Audio laughed and this infuriated Markee even more.

"You niggas think it's a joke! I might be the funnyman down South, but out here, mothafuckas respect me! I'm boss," Markee continued, getting everything off his chest he wanted to since he was a kid. "Y'all ain't got the family telling y'all that you better than me out here." Slade shook his head, knowing he was hurt about the past, but it wasn't his fault. On many occasions he came to the rescue for him, when the family ragged on him. So he tried to hold his tongue, because if Slade flipped, it would be a wrap and someone would have to pay.

"We know this your crib, nigga," Killa said. "How many times you gonna say that shit?"

"Killa, stop," Slade said, raising his hand. He looked at Shannon and her crew. "Ladies, go in the other room and put your clothes on. Let us talk to our cousin for a minute."

"I don't want them bitches in my room! I don't want them in my house!" Markee continued. "If they gotta get dressed, make 'em do it out here." Then he looked at Major. "Tell that bitch to get dressed out here too." He pointed at the girl behind him in his bedroom's doorway. "Y'all been in there long enough anyway. My sheets probably got all kind of butt juice on them now. And y'all washing my shit, too!"

"Markee, we fam," Slade said, using his body to cover Shannon. "So you ain't got to be doing all of this in front of your crew. Because you already know what it is if I go off, and not one of them punks would be able to hold me back."

"Nigga, you don't know me," Corey, one of Markee's goons, said. "You don't know shit about me."

Slade looked at him and said, "You right, nigga, that's why I'm not talking to you."

"Just tell them bitches to get the fuck out!" Markee continued, clapping his hands. It was so important that he get them to follow his order for the first time in life that he wasn't thinking straight.

Slade's jaw flexed because he couldn't reason with him while he was grandstanding. There he was . . . fat and sweaty in his leather coat . . . he was a hot-ass mess. And there the Baker Boys were: fit, handsome, and surrounded by naked women . . . so it was easy to relate to his envy. "Ladies, get dressed in the kitchen." Slade pointed. He was tired of talking to him.

"You think it's a joke?" He looked at his men. "Toss them bitches out!"

When Corey decided to be the first to step up to bat, Slade hit him with a sleeper that neither his face nor body could handle. Lying face up on the floor, with his eyes closed, it was apparent that he wouldn't be waking up anytime soon. Seeing the chaos, the girls huddled up in a corner in the living room, and scrambled to put their clothes on where they stood.

The rest of the Baker Boys rushed the other two goons, while Slade handled the third. Markee stepped out of the way, finally realizing the trouble he started, all because his ego was out of control.

The girls were screaming at the top of their lungs as the country boys put the beat down of a lifetime on Markee's crew. When shit got too bloody, Shannon and her friends quickly exited the apartment, afraid that someone would start shooting and they would be caught up in the crossfire.

"Y'all breaking my shit!" Markee yelled, watching his table and chairs smash to the floor like wet paper. "Not my entertainment center! Please!"

Still having respect for his cousin, Slade grabbed his opponent into the hallway by his coat, so he wouldn't fuck up his entire crib. Following suit, Major, Killa, Audio, and the others also moved into the hallway. All you could hear was screaming and yelling as the Baker Boys beat Markee's men to an infantile state.

# Chapter 30

**"Don't worry. I got an idea." —Chloe**

Chloe and Mia were sitting on the couch in the living room eating all of Lesa's Oreo cookies and drinking her milk. Having smoked two blunts back to back, their minds were calm, and they were contemplating what to stuff between their jaws next. "Did you notice how clear Farah's face is now?" Chloe asked. "When Dr. Martin called earlier, he said she not seeing him, but doing something else. I wonder what that is?"

"She snapped on me when I called him the last time she got sick," Mia started. "She must be doing something right though, because she look good."

"Well, I need to find out what it is because I'm tired of having to be careful everywhere I go. We can't go out if it's too sunny, we can't be around certain odors . . . I'm just sick of it!"

"What's funny is Grandma got the same shit and she look fine," Mia said.

"Yeah . . . but she don't use soap, and she ain't got no friends either because of her body odor.

Mamma likes to look pretty and wear perfumes and lotions. I guess that's why it's hitting her bad now. Me and you only use the basics, but after a while, we might have to cut everything off too."

"We gonna be all right and so is Mamma. You just keep taking your medicine before—"

Loud screams rang out in the hallway and Chloe, still wearing Lesa's dress, which was covered in weed holes, threw the apartment door open to see what was going on. When she looked outside she couldn't believe her eyes. "Either I've died and gone to heaven, or I see three half-naked niggas fighting in the hallway." Chloe smiled, looking at the Baker Boys. Slade was the only one dressed and the rest had on boxers and T-shirts, and it was fine with her.

"We both must be two dead bitches," Mia said with her mouth hung open. "'Cause I see the same damn thing!"

The Baker Boys had beaten Markee's crew so badly that all he could do was lean up against the wall and shake his head. Instead of begging his cousins to stop, he was now saying, "Please don't kill 'em, y'all. Don't kill 'em. They some good dudes. This going too far now."

Slade and his brothers didn't hear his pleas. Things had been taken to another level and it was entirely his fault. Two goons were able to get away after Audio, Killa, and Major let them go, after hearing cop sirens in the background. Slade, on the other hand, had snapped a long time ago. This was one of the things the brothers feared. There was nothing anybody could do to stop him.

Slade's mind was elsewhere as he held Tornado up by his shirt, and repeatedly hit him in the center of the face with a closed fist. Tornado's eyes rolled to the back of his head and his teeth cut into the flesh of his fingers, but he felt no pain. Slade thought about Knox, and the fact that he hadn't heard from him in days. He thought about his cousin Devon, and how he died over a beef that had nothing to do with him. The beat down was now so brutal that the Baker Boys, Markee, Chloe, and Mia stood in the hallway in shock. Slade was mad at the world and unfortunately Markee's goon was taking the brunt of his frustration.

"The cops coming!" the pudgy kid said.

"Slade," Killa said, putting his hand on his shoulder. "Let him go, man."

He didn't hear him, or any other sound around him. "Slade, we gotta go, man," Audio said, walking up to him. "The cops are outside."

He could not be stopped until Major said, "What about Mamma? And Knox? You gonna get locked up and get her stressed out even more? Let him go, man. It's over."

Hearing their names brought him back to reality and he looked at the man who was no longer moving, and released his shirt. His body dropped and his head bounced on the floor like a ball. He wiped the blood off of his hand, and onto his jeans, before looking at everyone. In his right state of mind, he could finally hear the commotion outside of the building. "Let's go back in the house."

"You can't come in here," Markee said. "They gonna look here first. I can throw him off."

"Then let's run," Audio said.

"It's one way in and out," Markee informed him.

"Y'all can come in," Chloe offered. "They won't know y'all are here."

Mia looked at her sister and said, "What you talking about? This not even our place!"

"Right, so what do we care?" Before Mia could dispute, the Baker Boys piled into Farah's apartment and Chloe locked the door. The moment she turned around and faced them, Audio was eyeing her. This was the first time she was in the presence of a man who she felt was her equal, and considering her violent nature, that wasn't necessarily a good thing.

Slade ran up to the window, moved the blinds slightly, and looked outside. The red, white, and blue lights were flashing in so many directions it was blinding. "There gotta be, like, ten cop cars out there!" he reported. "Shit! Why Markee make me do that?"

"Fuck! What we gonna do now?" Major asked. "We came out here to wait for Knox; now we 'bout to get locked the fuck up! That white mothafucka from Mississippi definitely gonna find us."

"Now who went too far, Slade?" Audio said. "I fought a few niggas in a gas station . . . but you beat a nigga to the pulp in front of witnesses. And you talking about me."

"Why you speaking all wild in front of company?" Slade asked, looking at the women.

"Sorry, man," Audio said. "I lost it for a minute. I just feel like breaking Markee's jaw. Why he put us out there like that? All he had to do was let them bitches get dressed."

"We gonna be good," Slade said. "You just gotta give me a second to think." Chloe and Mia sat on the sofa and looked up at the men. Their bodies, their faces, their presence had them feeling some kind of way. "I'm sorry about this," Slade said, looking at them. He stepped away from the window. "We gonna leave the moment the cops bounce. Just give us a second for this to blow over."

"It's not a problem. We weren't doing shit anyway but getting high," Chloe offered. "Y'all want anything to eat or drink?"

"Water would be good," Audio said. Chloe jumped up and swaggered to the kitchen, so he could witness the way her body wiggled and her ass bounced. He was paying close attention, and could certainly go another sex round, despite fucking two bitches earlier and fighting in the hallway.

"Y'all wouldn't happen to have any men clothes in here for my brothers, would you?" Slade asked Mia. "I'm tired of looking at them like that."

From the kitchen Chloe yelled, "I got some! Give me one second." She handed Audio a cup of water. "I put extra ice in your cup, since I know you like it so much," she said, referring to the meeting they had earlier at the ice machine. He winked and drank his water, his eyes on her the entire time.

"What's going on now?" Killa asked Slade as he paced the living room. "Outside." He pointed. "The cops still there?"

Slade looked out the window. "Yeah; them mothafuckas coming into the building now. I wonder who called them."

"Bro, you was outside crushing, dude. The nigga was crying for his life. Anybody coulda made the call," Killa said.

Chloe returned to the living room with a pile of Zone's old clothes, which included a few pairs of sweatpants and some jeans. "Here y'all go . . . this all I could find. Hope you can fit 'em." Major and Killa made their selections, while Audio unknowingly frowned. Chloe immediately picked up on the reason for his dismay and said, "These were my sister's exboyfriend's clothes. It ain't even like that."

He nodded and took a pair of grey sweatpants from the pile.

"What are your names?" Slade said, trying to make nice so the girls wouldn't be so nervous around them. After all, four country niggas at one time in anybody's house could cause anybody slight disturbance.

"I'm Chloe, and this is my oldest sister, Mia." Chloe moved to shake his hand, but Slade avoided her, and walked closer to the window.

"Okay . . ." she said, feeling that was weird.

The other brothers shook their hands as Slade took another look outside. More cops were coming, and he could hear the sound of walkie-talkies going off in the hallway. Although he was older than the men she usually went for, Mia, still being attracted to Slade, stood up and walked next to him. "You seem like you got a lot on your mind."

He looked at her, made a half smile, and refocused outside. "I do."

"I don't know what happened in that hallway, but whatever it was, that nigga must've deserved it. For you to beat him that way." Slade didn't look at her as she stood so close to him he could feel her body heat. Mia softly touched his arm and said, "You want anything to eat?"

Slade jumped back and moved toward the wall. After seeing how he was in the hall, for the moment she feared for her life. "Look . . . I'm sorry. I . . . I . . ." He swallowed and said, "I just don't like people touching me."

Mia frowned. "You act like I punched you or something."

"It's not like that." He shook his head. "Don't take it the wrong way, please. It's a long story. Can I use your bathroom?"

"Yeah . . ." she said, still stunned at his actions. "The guest bathroom is back there." She pointed, and he walked away. Mia looked at the brothers, hoping they could tell her why he reacted that way.

Audio chose to speak up first. "He don't like to be touched. By women anyway."

Her eyebrows rose. "So what . . . he gay or something?"

Audio's forehead creased and yelled, "Fuck you just say about my brother?"

Just as wild as him in the bark department, she said, "Nigga, who the fuck is you talking to?" Mia continued moving into him. "You in my house." Audio didn't give a fuck and was about to charge her when Major and Killa held him back.

"Stop it!" Chloe said, not wanting her sister to ruin her situation. "Now, Mia, you know that man ain't hardly gay. If he don't want you touching him, leave him alone."

"I never heard of a man not being gay who don't want a bitch to touch him." She sat on the couch. "That shit don't hardly sound natural to me."

"Look at who's touching him," Audio said. "Maybe that's the problem right there."

"Nigga, I will fuck you up in this apartment!"

They were about to square off again when there was a knock at the door. Slade, who was now back in the living room, wondered if the police knew he was involved and was inside.

"Don't worry. I got an idea," Chloe whispered, taking off her dress before flipping off the lights. Then she wiggled to the door and opened it half-way. She peeked out and in a sleepy voice said, "Yes?" She rubbed her eyes. "Can I help you?"

Two white male officers were outside. One of them said, "I'm sorry, ma'am. Did we wake you?" They tried not to gawk as one of her titties revealed itself. "We just have a few questions about a matter that happened in the hallway not too long ago. We were wondering if you saw anything . . . or heard anything at all out of the ordinary?"

"No. I was asleep." She rubbed her eyes again. "But is everything all right?"

"Ma'am . . . do you mind putting some clothes on? So we can come in and talk?"

"I don't mean to be rude, but this is my house and I was asleep." She rubbed her eyes harder for effect. "You can't come in. Now if there is nothing else, I really wanna get back to bed."

One of the officers grabbed a tiny white pad from his shirt pocket, along with a pen. "Actually there is something else. Like I said, there was an altercation earlier tonight. Do you remember hearing anything at all?"

"No. The only thing I heard was you banging on my door and waking me out of my sleep." She paused, and looked into the hallway at an officer questioning Markee. "Was anybody hurt?"

One of the officers cleared his throat. "Ma'am, a man was killed tonight. That's why we would appreciate a little cooperation . . . on your part."

"A man was killed? How?"

"He was beaten to death. Now did you hear or see anything that could be useful in this investigation?"

"No. But if I do, I'll let you know."

"That's all we can ask for now." He handed her a card. "Enjoy the rest of your night and be careful in there. You never know what kind of crazy you have lurking around."

When she closed the door, she put the lights on and slid back into the dress.

"What happened?" Mia asked, walking up to her.

Chloe looked at the Baker Boys and said, "They said a man was killed."

# Chapter 31

**"You do it anyway; might as well
do it to survive." —Farah**

Farah's headache was rocking when she stepped out of her Benz to enter her building. Randy had somebody fix her car temporarily, but warned it would need serious work soon. Last night was long and hard, because Randy came back into the house drunk and wanting sex. There was nothing appealing about him when he was buzzed, but since he almost caught her in a lie at the club, she did what she had to do. The only good thing that came about last night was that she was able to bury the hatchet with Rhonda, when Rhonda called to apologize. She felt like it was only because she wanted her to throw her shower, but after how Lesa treated her the night before, having her friendship was better than nothing.

When she activated her alarm at five o'clock in the morning, she was surprised to see Lesa getting out of DeWayne's white Lexus. Lesa blew him a kiss and he winked before speeding off. At first Farah was going to ignore Lesa because of the fight she had with Courtney, but when they looked at each other, Lesa smiled. "I'm sorry about that shit last night, Farah. My friends be tripping sometimes. That's why we had a falling out a while back. I don't know why Courtney don't like you . . . she's never acted like that before."

Farah stopped walking and said, "I ain't gonna lie, I was mad because I hate when bitches think I'm soft just because I bite my tongue. I'm through being a punk. People messed with me too much when I was a kid. I'm telling you, if she really knew me she would not have carried shit like that. I could snap on her ass."

"Normally I'd go to war for her, for both of my friends, but last night she was wrong as shit."

"I don't see why you hang with her anyway." Farah opened the building's door. They both slogged inside and approached the elevator. "She don't do nothing but hear herself talk. I hate bitches like that."

Lesa laughed. "Courtney kinda cool, but when she's drunk, she trips. Trust me when I say you gave her a taste of her own medicine last night. Sometimes people are afraid of her because she knows a lot of people."

When they got on the elevator Farah said, "So how was your night? It looks like you had fun with one of Juice's friends."

Lesa blushed. "Girl, me and DeWayne, aka Chews, got an understanding just like me and Diamond D. Shit ain't even like that."

"Chews?" Farah giggled as they stepped off of the elevator and on to their floor. "How on earth did he get a name like that?"

"A long-ass story." Lesa reached for her key to open the door. "I just like hanging out with him because he's not heavy. It's nothing for Chews to take me out to eat and bring me back home without trying to fuck. He don't be pressing me out like most niggas just because you smile in they face. Chews is the last of a dying breed."

"I feel you." When Farah opened the apartment and stepped inside, they couldn't believe their eyes. Major and Killa were on the floor asleep, wearing her ex-boyfriend's clothes, while Mia was on the sofa with the one man who made her heart skip a beat. "What the fuck is going on?" she whispered to herself.

Lesa looked around and said, "Farah, can you explain this shit to me?"

"I don't know what the fuck all this is about." She shrugged. "You saw me walk in here just like you did."

Lesa tramped into the living room and said, "Can somebody tell me what's going on?" Everybody shuffled but Slade was the first to rise.

The moment he looked at Farah she said, "I'm gonna check on our rooms." She looked at him again before walking by.

When Farah was alone, she paced the floor. Her puppies jumped around her ankles and she picked them up and placed them in the bathroom. She was just about to go back into the living room, when she heard Lesa's scream from the hallway. "Ahh!" Lesa yelled out. "What the fuck is going on in here? On my new sheets!"

Farah rushed to her room to see Chloe buck naked in the bed with Audio. Lesa's new Gucci dress was lying on the floor, destroyed, and her closet was wide open. The Baker Boys and Mia stood outside of Lesa's door, waiting to see what would happen next. Lesa walked inside, picked up her dress, and said, "Farah, what the fuck is up with your sisters?" She raised the dress in the air as if it were Simba from *The Lion King*. "When I moved in I said I needed my privacy, and I didn't want anybody going through my shit."

"Lesa, you can't be blaming me for this shit. I walked in here with you."

"But this is your family and they in my room." Tears rolled down her face. "I was gonna wear this to the show. I ain't sign up for none of this shit! I feel violated."

"Lesa, I'm sorry," Farah said softly. "I would've never allowed her in here to wear your clothes if I was home." She addressed her sister. "Chloe, what are you doing here anyway?" Farah was enraged. "Before I left out last night, I told you not to go into her shit."

Chloe got up and said, "What it look like I'm doing?" She grabbed Lesa's expensive sheet and wrapped it around her body as if she owned it. "I *was* fucking until y'all came in here with all this bullshit and interrupted us. Oh, before I forget"— she walked to the dresser and handed Farah the note from Dr. Martin—"this message is for you."

Lesa looked at the stationary, and her jaw dropped. "You went in my drawers, too?"

"Chloe, get your shit and get out of this girl's room," Mia interrupted. "I should've known I couldn't go to sleep with you in this house with that boy. You been eye fucking him from the gate."

Chloe was embarrassed. "What . . . you mad 'cause you wanted to fuck him or something?" She was entertaining her audience. "After all," she said, looking at Audio, "he does meet your age prefer- ence now, doesn't he?"

"Little girl, don't make me fuck you up! Come on . . . let's go."

She rolled her eyes, knowing Mia could stomp her into the future if she bucked.

"Audio, let's bounce," Slade said. "We got shit to do back at Markee's anyway."

With everything happening at once, Farah almost forgot he was there until his voice reminded her. She wanted him more than anybody she'd ever wanted in her life. When she looked in his direction, he was staring and her stomach fluttered. He was for her and she knew it.

Audio got dressed and Lesa rushed around her room, examining the damage. "Farah, we gotta have a house meeting. If this type of shit gonna go on, I'm not gonna be able to stay here. For real. I'm not gonna let nobody disrespect me. She went in my closet, ruined my dress, slept in my bed, and wrote on my stationary. What kind of shit is this anyway?"

"So what you want my sister to do, throw us out or something?" Mia yelled, stepping up to Lesa. "Because it seems like you hinting around to it."

"Call it what you want, bitch!" Lesa said, stepping closer to Mia. "Because I think I made myself clear."

"Bitch?" Mia repeated, preparing to pull a few patches out of her hair. "Whore, I would murder you!" Killa and Major held her back before she leaped on her.

"Farah, either they leave, or I will!" Lesa continued. "I'm not about to put up with nobody jumping in my face and shit. My own mamma don't get in my face, and I'm damn sure not gonna take it from nobody else. Fuck that."

"Can everybody just calm down please!" Farah yelled. "We still got people in the house."

There was a lot of shrieking and fussing, until there was a knock at the door. Since the Baker Boys were able to keep Mia from scratching Lesa's eyes out, Farah decided to see who was there. When she opened it, she saw her neighbor from down the hall. "Hey . . . you used to fuck with Zone, right?" Markee asked, pointing at her.

"Yeah. So?" she said with her hands on her hips.

"No reason." He shrugged. "Me and Zone were good peoples."

"Well, how come I don't remember him talking about you?"

"We weren't that close. But I was fucked up when I heard what happened." He looked deeper into the apartment and saw his cousins. "I'm here to get my peoples." He pointed at them. "My cousins."

Slade looked at Farah before walking out the door and his brothers followed him. Farah was just about to close the door when Markee said, "You better be careful; shit been happening in this building. A lot of people are coming up missing, even that fat kid across the hallway."

When Lesa left to go over to Courtney's the house was at peace. Mia and Chloe were in the living room watching the movie *Friday* for the hundredth time, while Farah felt the desire to get what she needed to survive, before remembering she had some in her room.

Farah grabbed the cooler and set it on the bed before going into the bathroom to throw cold water on her face. When she came out, Chloe was sitting on the bed holding an empty vial of her medicine. She'd just finished swallowing it all.

"Oh, my God, Farah! What is that?" She pointed at the tube. "What are you drinking?"

"The question is, why you swallowing my shit? You been here less than two days and already you in everybody shit. That's your problem, you don't respect people's privacy!" Farah put the vial back in the cooler and stood over her.

"What the fuck is that stuff you drinking?" Chloe screamed, wiping her lips. "What is that? It taste like . . ."

"Shut up!" Farah screamed, looking at her with evil eyes. She knew what it was but didn't want to say it out loud. All she knew was that it worked and that was all she cared about.

"Look at me, Chloe! Look at my skin!" She stood up and walked over to her sister. "This shit has done more for me in a month than Dr. Martin could do in years! I'm getting better, Chloe. I know you see it." She smeared makeup off of her face so that she could see her tone clearly. "You see . . . I don't even have to wear makeup anymore. I found the answer to our problems."

"But you can't drink that!" Chloe yelled, as tears rolled down her eyes. "It can't be good for you."

Farah felt like smacking her. She knew people wouldn't understand, and that's why, before her grandmother, she never told a soul. Even Cosmo was unaware of her plan of action. "I'ma tell Mamma!" Chloe acted as if she were still a kid.

"I don't give a fuck what you tell that woman."

"Then I'ma tell everybody else. And then people gonna think you a freak."

Farah couldn't take it anymore. It was bad enough she fucked her man; now she was in her bedroom making her feel like shit. She pushed her back on the bed and crawled over her body before she smacked her again and again. It wasn't until Farah realized that she wasn't fighting back, that she stopped. Chloe had shit with her, but at the end of the day they were still sisters. When Farah saw her body curl up on the bed she sat next to her and touched her back.

"I'm sorry, Chloe. You my baby sister, and I didn't want to hurt you like that."

"Farah," she said, wiping tears off her face, "why are you drinking that shit? I don't understand."

"I have to do this for me, Chloe. And you can't tell nobody because I'm gonna get locked up if people find out. They not gonna understand. Now y'all hurt people all the time and nobody said anything." Chloe was silent.

"But what if it makes you worse?" she said softly. "I don't want nothing to happen to you."

"It won't." A crooked smile spread across her face. "I wish you could see how I feel inside. I haven't felt this good in years. The shit Dr. Martin gave me work for you and Mia, but it never helped me. I would never do this if anything else worked. I wanna live, Chloe."

"Dr. Martin called last night. That was the number on the paper."

"For what?" She frowned.

"He said you were doing something that's not good for you . . . now I know what. He said Grandma called him."

Farah walked away and looked into her mirror. "She called him for real?" It angered her that Elise violated her trust. *I mean, what was the purpose of a confession?* "Did he say what she said?"

"No. Just that you doing something to make you better that's not good."

"Dr. Martin doesn't know what he's talking about." She walked over to the cooler, reached into it, and gave her a vial. "Here . . . drink it again, Chloe." Her arm remained outstretched. "You don't have to die." She smiled and sat next to her. "There's no better feeling than conquering and drinking blood. You do it anyway; might as well do it to survive. I saw the way you looked when you had them rats in that box, when we were kids. Now you got a reason to kill . . . to stay alive."

She examined how great Farah looked and took the container from her sister's hands and drank it all. "Can't believe I did that again." She wiped her mouth with the back of her hand.

Farah put the empty vial away and said, "Now it tastes even better, right?"

# Chapter 32

### "You're right, it's not Farrah Fawcett. It's Farah Cotton." —Farah

Farah had to piss as she drove down the street on her way to the Lucky 7 convenience store. She could hear something knocking around under her hood, and prayed it wouldn't break down on her before she made it home. *That's all I need is for something to go wrong with my fucking car!* Getting money from Randy, and trying to hide where she lived, was more trouble than it was worth.

The moment she stepped out of the car, her body trembled when she saw Juice pull up in a new black Range Rover. His music wasn't too loud, but she could hear the old-school classic "Tender Love" spilling from the speakers. Before she walked in the store, he rolled the window down and said, "I know that's not Ms. Farrah Fawcett over there. A nigga like me don't have that kind of luck."

Juice was right on point because when Farah was born, she was so red that Ashur, who was a fan of Farrah Fawcett on *Charlie's Angels,* gave her a version of the actress's name. It didn't matter that the show had been off for years when she came into the world. "You're right, it's not Farrah Fawcett. It's Farah Cotton." She smiled, walking up to his truck. "What Randy do, send you to check up on me?"

"Naw . . . I'm just coming to buy a pack of blunts." He looked at her through his expensive shades and wiped his goatee. His diamond watch flashed and he saw the twinkle in her eyes. "But you did say Cotton, right? Because that sounds familiar. Your father name Ashur?" He pointed.

She glared. "Yes. How you know him?"

He chuckled. "Your last name rings bells. My father used to run with him but we weren't real close. I remember all the stories he use to tell me about Ashur being a hothead. He murdered that family at the bus stop."

"You disrespecting my daddy now?"

"Never that. Just giving you a little history on your people. So . . . where you going, Farah? And can I take you there?"

She was preparing to answer, when a girl came from behind and bumped her so hard she knocked her into Juice's truck. He quickly got out to examine the damage. "Damn, shawty. You moving a little too quick, don't you think?" The black paint on his new ride was chipped. "Now you fucked my shit up."

"I'm sorry," she said.

Farah stood up straight and looked at who hit her. The moment she turned around, Nova slapped her so hard in the face she hit the ground. "That's for Coconut, bitch! And for telling lies on Shannon, too!"

Farah snapped and was all over her in a second flat. She managed to get Nova on the ground as she continually banged her head into the concrete. Tears fell out of her eyes and her temples begin to thump as she went back to that day on the bleachers. But when her skin started itching, she knew a breakout was coming and it was this bitch's fault. Why did she even step to her? For all Farah knew, she and Coconut weren't even that close.

"Please stop!" Nova screamed, trying to kick Farah off. It didn't work because Farah was on her body like a tick.

"That's the point, bitch! You gonna remember this shit the next time you look in the mirror! You can tell Coconut I'm coming for her next! And Shannon, too!"

When the girl looked as if she were delirious, Farah stood up and popped open her trunk. When Juice saw this, he thought things were about to escalate to murder. "What you about to do now, ma? You know everybody watching this shit, right?"

Farah was zoned out and flipped out and angry at the world. She was tired of people trying her, and she was tired of Randy, her roommate, and her siblings. When Juice saw cops coming, he approached Farah. "You better go," he said as police sirens sounded in the background. She didn't move right away, and instead she felt a warm sensation on her legs. "Them peoples coming . . . You better get the hell out of here."

Farah slowly backed away from Nova, closed her trunk, and hopped into her car. It wasn't until she sat in the seat that she realized she'd pissed on herself. There was nothing she could do about it at the moment, so she left the scene.

Farah's skin was inflamed as she parked at her building, and she could tell she was on the verge of an outbreak. For the moment all she wanted to do was go upstairs, take off her pissy clothes, and do something to make herself better. The moment she got off the elevator and walked toward her apartment someone said, "Can I talk to you for a minute?" Slowly she turned around and saw Slade, but she reeked of dried urine, and she was afraid that he saw her murder. *He knows. Now he's gonna fucking blackmail me or something.* He walked closer and she looked at him before taking a few steps back. All her life she wanted a man of her own, and now that he was standing before her, she couldn't open her mouth.

"I never got a chance to apologize for what happened at your place." He frowned and she couldn't figure out if he liked her. "It was fucked up how my kid brother disrespected your peoples. We from down South and we normally don't get down like that." He rubbed his bald head. "I just wanted to tell you that." Farah nodded but remained silent.

"Okay, I'm not gonna keep you. I guess I'll see you later." Although she felt better because he didn't say anything about seeing the murder, she wished she could tell him how she felt about him, but in her current condition, now was not the time. She stank and needed to change. So she didn't move. "Later."

Since she didn't say shit, he turned around and walked away, leaving her standing in the hallway. Slowly she walked toward her apartment, and tried to gain the courage to talk to him from afar. Maybe say something cute like Lesa or Coconut would.

"Can I have your name?" she heard him ask. She kept walking. If he got up on her and smelled her pissy clothing, she probably would faint. "My name is Slade," he offered. "In case you wanted to go grab something to eat." She kept walking. "You know what? Forget I ever said shit to you." His tone was heavy with annoyance. "Every time I try to talk to you, you act like I'm bothering you or something."

*No! You're not bothering me.* She quickly turned around but he was gone. "I'm so fucking stupid!" she said to herself. "Why didn't I open my fucking mouth?"

Needing her medicine even more, she quickly entered her apartment and nobody was home. Once in her room, she rushed to the place she kept her cooler. When she opened the closet, she knew immediately something was off. Her skin started itching again, and before she knew it she felt nauseated. Rushing to the bathroom, she threw up the egg and cheese burrito that she ate earlier from McDonald's that day. Chloe had been in her room and had taken all her shit.

It was settled. Tonight, she wanted her gone.

# Chapter 33

**"I just need to get some more stuff for my sister. That's all." —Chloe**

Chloe and Audio were sitting on the sofa in Markee's house. He just got the news that a body fitting Knox's description was found in the woods in DC, not too far from where they were.

"She gonna be so mad at me!" she said, trying not to get too upset. Although she wasn't as bad as Farah, any surge of emotion could cause an outbreak, and push the disease into the acute stage. "She gonna kill me, Audio. I just know it!" She cried in his arms as he rubbed her back. Ever since they got together they were hard to separate.

"What you do?" Her vulnerability turned him on. "She ain't gonna put her hands on you again, I know that much. I don't care what y'all beefing about." Together for only days, he had already assumed the protector role.

"It's not even like that, baby. I took something that didn't belong to me. Something she feels like she really needs. I didn't want her to have it, because my grandmother told me to throw it away. Now I'm thinking it was a bad idea."

"I take shit from my brothers all the time. So the fuck what?"

"But this is different." Chloe knew she was wrong for telling him how Farah hit her the other day, but she needed somebody in her corner, and Audio was there.

"You gotta tell me more than that, Chloe. It's like you talking around in circles and shit."

"You wouldn't understand."

"Then what you want me to do?" he yelled. "You over here crying and shit and I'm trying to talk to you. I wanna help, but if I don't know what the fuck is up, then what you want me to do? I'm already dealing with my brother being gone, now you over here adding to my load. I'm 'bout ready to say fuck all this shit and murder a nigga!" He got up off the couch and walked toward the door. Wherever he went, he knew he couldn't stay long, since it was his turn to wait for Knox's call, and somebody needed to be at Markee's crib at all times.

"Where you going, Audio?" She sobbed. "Please don't leave. I'm sorry!" Young and dumb, their emotions were on ten, and she feared if he left, he'd never come back. Audio was the first man she ever felt love for even though things moved so quickly. She walked behind him, placed her arms around his waist, and rested her head on his back. "I just need to get some more stuff for my sister. That's all. If I do that we'll be good."

He turned around and looked at her beautiful face. "Okay . . . so how we gonna do that?"

"I gotta contact the dude who helped her before. That's it."

"Okay, how much is it gonna cost?" He didn't have any cash, and hoped she didn't try to hit him up either.

"We don't need no money for my plan. I just need you to help me bring him to my place. When he's there, you can leave the rest to me."

# Chapter 34

**"When you first moved in, you told
me you could handle the rent." —Farah**

"Girl, can you talk?" Lesa asked over the phone.

As she drove, Farah looked at the phone like it
was a science project because she hadn't spoken to
her in days. When she came home at night, Lesa
was in her room, asleep. And when she got up in
the mornings, Lesa was at work. It was obvious
that she was avoiding her. "Yeah . . . I got a few
minutes," she said, knowing that when she was
done, she was gonna ask her about her rent money.

"I ain't talking to Courtney and Lady no more. I
mean it this time."

Farah rolled her eyes as she continued down the
highway. She couldn't care less. "What they do this
time?"

"How 'bout they told the people on my job that
when I was on medical leave this past summer, I
was actually on vacation. If they investigate me I
can lose my job, girl, and they know that shit."

Farah had heard enough. She knew she was trying to prep her for the "I don't have your money today either" gig and she was over it already. "Lesa, I thought you were giving me the money you owe today. I really need it for rent because Vivian came by earlier asking for it. And since her son died, she been really mean. She gonna put me out if we don't come up with it."

"He died? I thought he was missing."

She bit her tongue. "I meant missing."

"Oh . . . well . . . I'ma give it to you, but I'm not going to lie, I don't have it right now."

"Well, when you gonna have it? When you first moved in, you told me you could handle the rent. So what changed?"

"I can handle it," Lesa said. "But I'm not gonna lie, I don't think the price is fair anymore. I mean, when are your sisters moving?" Then she paused. "Hold up . . . I can't hear you! Farah . . . I can't hear you! Farah, are you there?"

Farah looked at her phone and saw the call was over. "Bitch!" she yelled, throwing the phone in her purse. She hit her with the "my call dropped" shit! If she didn't have her money in the next few days she was putting her ass out. Suddenly, having friends was no longer important.

She was driving down the road and the knocking under her hood got so loud that she could barely hear herself think. Her skin was inflamed and she decided to pull over and to do whatever she had to do. But when her phone rang, she hoped it was Randy so she could get some cash from him to fix her car. Lately she only reached out when she needed something and she knew he was growing tired. When she answered the phone, instead of it being Randy she heard, "You have a collect call from Ashur Cotton, from the federal penitentiary . . ."

She hadn't spoken to her father since she passed out in the gym, because she felt she was on the verge of telling him her mother's secret. Lately Ashur's name reminded her that she wasn't who she thought she was. Farah wondered if reaching out to her real father was a good idea after all. She was having a serious identity crisis, and didn't know which way to turn. She sighed, and knew the time had come for her to stop avoiding him, besides all he did was love her. So she pressed five and accepted and said, "Hi, Daddy."

"Farah, where have you been? I been worried sick about you." Ashur sounded different these days and she wondered why.

"I been around, Daddy. Sorry I haven't spoken to you in a while. Are they treating you okay in there?"

"The best they can, considering." He chuckled. "But how are you managing your illness? When they told me you were in the hospital again, I almost lost it in here. The worst part about being in fucking jail is not being there for your family. Never get caught up in no stupid shit. Do what's right."

"I'm fine, Daddy, and I want you to stop worrying about me. I'm all grown up, and practically taking care of Mia and Chloe."

"Your grandmother told me you're doing something dangerous to get better. And that your mind is wrapped up and confused."

*Damn, did my funky-ass grandmother put an ad in the paper?* "Daddy, I gotta go."

"Farah, please. I never got a chance to tell you this, but I'm sorry for what me and your mother put you kids through. We were young and inexperienced, and had no business raising children. It was our biggest mistake."

"So you wish I wasn't born?"

"Never said that. I said I love you dearly. But if I could've had you when I was ready, I doubt Shadow would've done time in jail. And that you would be so confused, that you think you have to hurt people to survive. You're older now and I'm afraid you might be stuck in your ways. Brownie was wrong for what she made you kids do and now you're actually drinking people's—"

*"Daddy, not over the phone!"*

# Chapter 35

### "You don't have to talk my head off, baby boy." —Chloe

Chloe was in her room alone with Amico Glasser, who she met in the game room at the movie theater earlier that night. When she pulled up on Amico earlier, while he was playing video games as he waited for the movie to start, she knew that he was the one. Amico was so entranced by her small waist and thick ass that he ended his game and fell under her spell. Amico was bored with his sister and wasn't interested in a chick flick anyway. So when Chloe put her sex appeal on blast, he rolled out with her in the hopes of getting some pussy.

"This shit fly!" Amico said, looking around Farah's apartment as they walked through the front door. Audio was with them, and she told Amico that he was her brother. As planned, nobody was home so it would be easier to see her plan through. "Y'all live here with your peoples?"

"Yeah," Audio snapped, angry he wanted to fuck. "Who you think we live with?"

Amico looked at him and shook his head. On the way over Audio seemed down to earth, but now that the three of them were alone, he was acting differently. "Well, I love this joint." He rubbed his hands together. "This shit is like that!"

"Come with me," Chloe said, grabbing his hand and leading him to the room she shared with her sister Mia. Audio followed. "My room back here." When Amico looked around the room and smiled, Chloe gave Audio a menacing grin. They had him alone.

He walked over to the large window and moved the curtains so he could look out of it. "You can see the entire city."

"It ain't like the view is like that," Audio said. "We still in the projects."

He walked away from the window and said, "Wait . . . did I do something to you? 'Cause on the way over we were cool, but now you acting like I slapped your mamma. What the fuck?"

Audio was about to steal him when Chloe jumped in between them. "You got the smoke?" Chloe asked.

Amico sat down on the edge of the bed and said, "I thought you said you had it. Remember when I gave y'all a ride, you said you didn't have gas, but you got the weed."

She'd forgotten her lie already. "Oh . . . yeah . . . give me a sec." Chloe went to Lesa's room, stole another bag of weed, and brought it back. As she rolled up a blunt, Audio stood over her as he looked at Amico with piercing eyes. "Here you go."

"Thanks, Lesa," Amico said, repeating the name she told him.

Amico took the wet blunt and lit his fire under it while Audio patrolled. "Look, you got the dope or not?" he asked. "We ain't got time for all this other shit." Chloe jumped up to silence him. To get Audio to help her, she told him Farah was on heroin, and would get sick if she didn't get what she needed. He didn't know her well, but he had family members on the drug, so he bought everything she said.

"Got what?" Amico said, looking between them. Then he looked at Chloe. "What he talking about, Lesa?"

"Baby, let me handle it from here," Chloe begged, walking Audio to the door. Then she kissed him on the lips and Amico's eyes widened. *Did she just kiss her brother?* "I won't be long, baby, I promise."

"So what you want . . . me to leave you alone with this nigga?" He pointed. "You don't even know this dude like that."

"Please, Audio. This is for my sister."

"Fuck this shit!" he yelled. "If this nigga kills you, don't come crying to me!" He stormed out without saying goodbye.

She didn't move until she heard the front door slam shut. When Audio was gone, Chloe turned around to look at Amico, who seemed scared and confused. She sat on the bed next to him, and rubbed his leg to put him at ease. "What's up with your brother? He's a little too overprotective. It's almost like y'all fucking or something. I mean, he just kissed you on the lips."

"We close like that." she said, hoping he wouldn't press the issue. "What I wanna do now though is have fun with you. You up for it or what?"

"After we light this up." He smiled, raising the blunt. He put fire to it, took a pull, and felt a calm rush immediately.

"Damn!" He coughed and beat his chest twice. "This some good-ass shit right here." He handed it to her. "So what you wanna do? I can't stay long because I gotta get my peoples from the movies later. I'm the ride."

"You don't have to talk my head off, baby boy." She smashed the blunt out in the ashtray. "The sooner we stop talking, the sooner we can fuck."

He stood up, and eased out of his pants, boxers, and shirt before she had a chance to change her mind. Then he slid into the bed. "What you waiting on? Get undressed."

Chloe jumped out of her clothes and cut the lights. The room was so dark they could not see each other. When she was asshole naked, she eased under the covers and rolled on top of his body. "You got a condom?" he asked. She could smell the weed coming off his breath. "I ain't trying to have no baby by nobody I don't know."

Fucking wasn't part of the game; she was just being freaked out. "Me either. That's why I'm on the pill." She moved to kiss him when he turned his head. "What's wrong?"

"I need you to get the rubber now."

Chloe rolled off of him, reached in the darkness for a condom, and handed it to him with an attitude. "Put this shit on so we can get this over with. You acting real ungrateful."

He quickly tore the packaging off and slipped his medium-sized dick into the condom. Then he reached for Chloe in the darkness, but she wasn't next to him. "Where are you?" he said into the blackness. "Stop playing. I'm ready."

"I'm right here," she said on the other side of him.

"Wait . . . how you get over there? What the fuck are you doing?" That was the last thing he said before she grabbed his wrist and stuck him with a syringe.

He jumped out of the bed and knocked her to the floor. His naked body fell on top of hers as he tried his best to get whatever she used to stick him out of her hand. Chloe hadn't banked on him being so strong or on him fighting so hard for his life.

Murder was trivial to her because she'd seen so many die that she'd grown careless. She forgot one thing: when she killed in the past, her family was always present. But now she was alone, battling with a man twice her size with a strong desire to live. Now she wished Audio hadn't left after all.

Somewhere in the midst of her thoughts, Amico managed to get his hands around her throat. "Please don't kill me," she begged softly. "I don't wanna die like this. I was doing this for my sister! I didn't want to hurt you!"

The more he squeezed, the lighter she felt. Chloe Cotton was dying and she was resigned to that fact until someone appeared in the doorway. She couldn't see who it was, but she reached out for help.

# Chapter 36

**"You might not want this no more, but somebody else sure do!" —The Clapper**

The Clapper walked toward the only bedroom in her tiny apartment. She stood in the doorway and watched D.B. sleep peacefully in her bed. Even though their relationship was built on an understanding, and not love, she couldn't help but fall for him. She wondered, if she were thirty years younger, would he be interested? Eleanor's dream quickly came crashing down when she sat on the floor, spread her legs, and stuck the needle in her clit to get the best high of her life.

An hour later, when she saw him toss and turn, she walked inside the room and said, "Hungry?"

D.B. opened his eyes, stretched his muscular arms, and smiled. He wasn't wearing a shirt, so the dog tags around his neck seemed to glisten against his dark skin. Her kindness came to him when he needed it the most, and he would forever be grateful. She didn't know for sure if D.B. was his name when she found him on the side of the road, alone, injured, and cold. The name stuck because of the tattoo on his left bicep with the letters. His leg was broken, his shoulder was dislocated, and he could barely move for weeks without her assistance. But thanks to a phone call from Eleanor, she was able to get him the help he needed by sucking the dick of a friend, who was a doctor.

"I'm hungry as hell." He rubbed his stomach. He sat on the edge of the twin bed and his large feet rested on the cold wooden floor. "What you cooking, ma?"

"Anything you want. You know that." From where she stood, she could see his large dick through the leg of his boxers, and she desperately wanted a taste. "D.B." She smiled slyly. "Can I make you feel better? Like I did when you couldn't move?" She licked her lips.

D.B. felt bad for allowing her to blow him off in the past but he was in so much pain back then that the sexual release she provided was better than medicine. But now, with a clear mind and heart, things were different. He saw desperation in her eyes, and he didn't want to use her any more than he already had.

"Eleanor, let's not do that. I respect you and don't want to do it again."

Disappointment washed over her. "Okay." Trying to skip the subject to clear the tension she said,

"Do you remember anything yet? About who you are, and where you're from?"

His head dropped and he said, "I'm getting some memory back . . . not all." He was careful about what he revealed to strangers.

When The Clapper heard a knock at the door she quickly rushed to answer it. When she opened it, Willie Gregory, the man who stole her heart and never gave it back, was looking at her. Instead of saying hello, the first thing he asked was, "How's he doing?"

She sighed and said, "He's fine, Willie." She wished he stopped expressing an interest in her new friend. "I'm about to cook him something to eat now. So what you want?"

He walked in and she closed the door. "When you gonna tell me where you found that boy from?"

"I told you . . . he was one of my customers." She rested her fists on her hips. "Why do you keep asking about him anyway? I never saw you this much before."

"Eleanor, that boy ain't hardly pay you no money to see your old-ass butt cheeks flap together."

She frowned and said, "Well, it's true! You might not want this no more, but somebody else sure do!" She paused. "Like I said, he was my customer, until he hurt himself and ended up at my house." The more he didn't believe her, the harder she pressed the issue. Originally her lie was born to make him jealous, but now she continued it to save face.

From the living room he looked at the man who didn't know he was watching. "I don't know about all that, but I do know one thing, Eleanor." He smiled slyly. "That young man is going to come in handy. I'm sure of it."

# Chapter 37

**"If you don't want nobody else
to get hurt, you better leave
me out of this shit." —Slade**

Slade sat in Markee's living room with his brothers. A stone look rested on all of their faces as they waited for their mother to tell them on the speakerphone if Knox was dead or alive. Hours passed since a body showed up in DC, and still there was no word from Knox. It was becoming clearer to them that Sheriff Kramer had delivered him the same fate as their cousin Devon.

"This ain't making no sense, Ma," Slade said. "If the body wasn't Knox's, why he ain't call us yet to give word? We checked and the body they found fits Knox's description. They just haven't released his name yet." Slade stood, as his brothers occupied the couch space and the floor.

"I know that ain't my oldest sounding like he's giving up," Della said. The brothers looked at Slade with hopeful eyes. If he fell apart, who else could they lean on? "So let me ask again, is that my oldest child losin' it?"

"Ma, I'm not losin' it. I just gotta know where my brother is."

"And so do I! How you think I feel that none of my children are here with me? Boy, I know you been up North for some time now, but please don't forget where you came from. The South! You're stronger than that shit up there. Besides, nameless dead black boys show up all the time there.

It could be anybody. Stand strong! And that goes for all of you! I don't want y'all faltering now. This Kramer bastard done stole enough of my life as it is, and it's time that I get the rest back. Wherever Knox is, he can handle himself and he'll be in contact soon. You hear what I'm saying, sons?"

"Yeah, Ma. We got you," Slade said.

"Good. Now keep me posted on anything that goes down. Because until they bring me my baby . . . dead or alive, then that means he is out there trying to get to us."

"We love you, Ma," the Baker Boys said one by one before ending the call.

Slade put his face in his hands and paced a few steps before looking at his younger siblings. They were waiting for him to say something, anything, to bring them through this, even though things looked grave. "Y'all heard Ma. We gotta toughen up and stay out of shit. We also gotta make sure that somebody is always here to take Knox's call. No more running to the store and leaving the phone unattended." He looked at Audio. "Shit is serious. It's been serious."

They nodded in agreement and after Slade's speech, Markee walked over to him and said, "I know this a bad time, but can I talk to you for a second?"

Slade hadn't said much to his cousin since he killed Tornado. Had Markee not tested his own family, none of the shit would have happened. Slade walked into the kitchen, grabbed a beer from the fridge, and leaned up against it. It rocked a little because of his weight. "What you want, Markee?"

"People are asking questions about what happened to Tornado and I don't know what to tell them."

Slade took the spout from his lips and looked at his cousin. "What that got to do with me?"

"A lot, man," he said in a low voice. "I mean . . . you killed him in the hallway. In front of them girls down the hall and everything."

"I fought the nigga straight up and he lost. What you want me to do now, raise him from the dead? None of that shit would have happened if you didn't lose it!"

Markee sighed. "That's not fair, Slade. You ain't the one his family coming to every night, asking if you heard from him! I am!"

"Naw . . . what ain't fair is you bringing this shit up when you know I'm looking for my brother." Slade pointed at him.

"I know, man . . . you're right." He lowered his head. "But I'm out here by myself now. I ain't got the family to back me, and the dude you killed was valuable to a lot of people! And people talking about raising money for the first person who finds out what happened." He started crying. "I'm not trying to die, Slade. I wanna live. I still ain't even got no kids yet."

"What about the niggas he was with?" Slade inquired. "What they saying?"

"Well, they saying they don't know what happened after they left. Trying to get my back. Tornado was beefing with some other niggas from around the way, so they said he could be anywhere. But my boss don't believe it, and now he's pressing them to press me. They told him the last time they saw him was when they were with me and you."

Slade leaned his head back against the fridge. "Fuck! If you would've let them girls get dressed, we wouldn't be going through this shit. This your fault, Markee." Slade felt like knocking him out, but knew he couldn't take his blows. "I came out here to get away from bullshit, and you put me in some shit in DC." Slade's voice rose, and his brothers walked toward the kitchen, preparing to break Markee off if he was starting shit again. When

Slade saw them he said, "Everything cool, fellas."
They turned around and headed back to the living
room. Speaking in a lower voice he said, "I don't
need this shit right now. I'm letting you know in
advance. If you don't want nobody else to get hurt,
you better leave me out of this shit."

"I need help." Markee pleaded with his eyes. "I
can't leave you out of it! This dude is gonna kill me
if you don't help me out! Please, man! I'm your
cousin!"

Slade was angry but he couldn't let him go to
war alone. Markee, whether he liked it or not, was
blood. "What's the nigga name you afraid of?"

"Randy George."

# Chapter 38

**"I'm glad you laughing, bitch. I doubt very seriously that you'll last two weeks." —Farah**

Farah was in Chloe's bedroom looking at the dead man on the floor. Standing around her were Mia and Shadow. Chloe was on the bed with her face in her hands as she cried her eyes out. "Shadow, make sure that door is locked," Farah said, eyes still glued on the man, his red blood running into her carpet. "We don't need that bitch coming home and coming into this room."

Shadow locked the door and the sound of his sister crying fucked his mind up. It wasn't like he didn't save her life by coming in at the right time. And it wasn't like she hadn't killed before. "Chloe, stop that shit! You making me mad . . . The nigga dead so get over it."

Farah said, "Chloe, what were you thinking?" Chloe was crying so hard she wasn't audible. "Stop fucking crying and answer the question!"

She took her face out of her hands and looked up at her. "I wanted to help you." She wiped the tears from her face. "Since I poured out your shit, and you got mad at me. I thought you were gonna throw me out." Shadow and Mia looked at each other, wondering what she was talking about.

"This was the wrong way, Chloe! We can't have drama around here like this. You brought a nigga in my house and Shadow had to kill him! With a knife at that."

"Yeah, but . . . he tried to hurt me," Chloe yelled. "What you want me to do, lie down and die?"

"You not going to turn this around on me, bitch!" Farah said, hitting her fist into her hand. "I'm not playing your games anymore!" She paced the floor. "Y'all killed too many people, and truthfully, Chloe, I think you love this shit too much." She looked dead into her eyes. "I think you always have."

Chloe stood up and wiped the fake tears off her face. "So what if I do like it?" She looked at them. "Because if I'm a monster, you're a vampire."

That word made her skin crawl. "I didn't tell you what I did for you to help me," Farah continued. "You brought him in my house, and what if somebody saw him?"

"You not answering the question, big sister!" Chloe persisted. "So what if I do like to kill? Are you gonna stand over there and act like you don't like it either?" She giggled. "So what, you're so much better than me?"

"We gonna pay for this body," Farah said, pointing at it. "You didn't do it the right way. Somebody gonna come looking for him, I know it!" Farah walked away and leaned up against the wall.

"Bitch, don't act innocent. I'm tired of you faking!" Chloe continued. "Tell Mia and Shadow how you killed Zone and how you loved every minute of it. It was all over your face when you watched him fall out the window! She was smiling."

Farah looked at her sister with penetrating eyes. "You going too far."

"Am I?" She put her hands on her hips and walked toward her. "'Cause it seems to me that I'm saying what everybody already knows. That we're killers, and we love what we do. So why fake anymore?"

"Wait, Zone's murder was an accident, right?" Mia asked, looking at them.

"Yeah, Farah," Shadow added. "That's what I heard when I was in the joint."

Farah looked at her siblings, and her heart sped up as she remembered how beautiful Zone looked spread out on the ground. No, she didn't like it, she *loved* it. Chloe did have one thing wrong, though: Zone's death was an accident. But she realized at that moment that she loved murder. "Zone had it coming," Farah said, looking at her siblings. "And I was able to cover my tracks so nobody ever found out." Mia and Shadow looked at each other and grinned. She was finally playing on their side of the team. "But you fucked up by bringing this dude here and somebody saw it! This is totally different! Someone will come looking for him! I promise."

"That may be true, but he was going to kill me. It was me or him!" Chloe looked down at the body. "So I guess it was him."

"She's right," Shadow added. "I saw this nigga try to kill her myself. Had I not walked in she would've been dead. I know it's fucked up how it happened, but I'm glad he's not breathing."

Chloe looked into her sister's eyes. "Tell them what you do to prevent your breakouts. Let's put everything out there on the table."

Right before she responded, Lesa banged heavily on the door. "Farah, you gotta come out here right now!" *Bang bang bang!* "Open this fucking door!"

"What the fuck is wrong with that bitch now?" Mia said.

"Fuck her." She looked at the door. "I'm busy right now, Lesa! Go away!"

"I don't give a fuck about you being busy! Come out here right now! I'm sick of this shit! Somebody paying for my stuff today!"

Farah walked to the closed door. "Go away, Lesa. If I come out there you not gonna like me." She looked at the body on the floor. There was no way she could come in that room.

"I ain't going no fucking where! I'm sick of this shit, Farah!" Lesa continued, sounding intoxicated. "You gotta come out here right now or I'm knocking down your door!"

"Pull him in Chloe's closet," Farah whispered. Mia and Shadow dragged him there and closed the door, while Chloe placed the sheet over the bloodstain. Angry, Farah walked out of the room and her siblings followed, closing the door behind them. When she walked into the living room she was angered to see Courtney and Lady in her house.

In the middle of the floor Farah and her clan faced off against Lesa and her posse. "Farah, which one of y'all went under my bed and stole my weed this time?"

Farah rolled her eyes, because she didn't feel like the drama. Living on her own forced her to grow up quick. There was a situation in her bedroom that needed her undivided attention, yet she was out there talking about a bag of weed. "Lesa, I know you didn't knock on the door for this shit." She stepped so close to Lesa that she could feel the warmth from her body. "Especially since you ain't run me my rent yet, bitch!"

Lesa leaned in and said, "Did you just call me a bitch? Especially when I didn't disrespect you?"

"Then what the fuck you call it?" Shadow asked. "You banging on the door about fucking weed is disrespectful. When she could've handled this shit later."

"Who is this?" Courtney pointed. "The brother from Harvard?"

"Harvard?" Shadow asked.

"Don't worry where he from." Farah didn't want her truth exposed to give her something else to laugh at. "You didn't have no reason asking me about no weed, because I didn't touch your shit."

"Somebody did."

"If you must know, I took it, and it was good, too." Chloe grinned. "Thank you!"

"You need to stay the fuck outta my room! I'm tired of telling you!"

"Lesa, you shouldn't have to pay shit since they smoked up all your weed. That had to be good for at least nine hundred bucks, right?"

"Not only that, if you divide it five ways you would only owe her a few dollars," Lady added. "Look at all these mothafuckas who live here."

"Naw, you got that wrong, baby girl," Mia said. "This chick has yet to pay shit, so technically she just visiting, and as far as I'm concerned, her visit is up." She looked at her sister. "What you think, Farah?"

"I think this bitch betta run me my cash or get the fuck outta my house tonight."

Lesa laughed and looked back at her friends. "You want me gone . . . not a problem. I'll leave in two weeks, *after* my surgery." She wanted to be there, instead of recovering around her mother, who didn't want her to have it.

"I don't give a fuck about no plastic surgery," Farah said. "You haven't even signed my lease yet." She looked at Lady and Courtney. "Why can't you stay with them? Since they always in the business anyway."

"You heard what I said, Farah, I'll be out in two weeks." Lesa sat on the sofa.

Farah knew she and her sisters could take them out but she also remembered the dead body in her room. If she wanted to get at her, she needed another plan. When she thought about how Chloe irritated her the first day she moved in, she had an idea. "Either get the fuck out, or I'm burning all of your clothes . . . shoes included."

"I wish you would touch my shit!" She jumped up.

Farah looked at her brother and said, "Shadow, go in Chloe's room and lock the door. Chloe and Mia, follow me."

A stampede ensued toward Lesa's bedroom. Farah, Chloe, Mia, Lesa, Courtney, and Lady fell into the doorway as everyone tried to get to her clothes first. Fists were being thrown, and faces were scratched, and it was obvious that things were terribly out of hand. When Farah, Mia, and Chloe beat Lesa and her friends to the closet, they began ripping her clothes to shreds. Farah seemed to be enjoying herself because of everything she put her through since she'd been there. They looked like a pack of niggas.

"Get off my shit!" Lesa cried, trying to push them out of the way. This was exactly what Elise feared would happen if Farah didn't get herself together.

"This is so fucking immature!" Courtney yelled, trying to help Lesa out while Lady disappeared. "I can't believe y'all doing this shit."

"Well, come over here and do something about it!" Mia said, egging her on. "I been waiting to kick your ass ever since my sister told me about you." Courtney ignored her, not trying to go one on one.

"I want you out of here!" Farah screamed, as she punished a red La Perla bra before grabbing her vintage Gucci bag. "You gonna leave, or do you want us to start on your purses next?"

Lesa was just about to respond when there was a heavy knock at the door. Everyone rushed into the living room to see what was up. When Chloe opened the door, she was angered to see the same cops who questioned her the day Slade murdered Tornado in the hallway. "We received a call about a fight," one of the officers said. "Can somebody tell us what's going on?"

"Who the fuck called the police?" Farah asked as if they weren't there. Lady walked toward the couch and sat down, making herself look guilty.

This was exactly what Farah didn't want so she decided to give it to them straight. "Sir, this girl won't leave my apartment." She was huffing and puffing. "And I been trying to get her to, but she won't go. Can you take her with you, please?"

"Is she correct?" he asked Lesa.

"No, she's not, sir." She smiled. "I live here."

"I'm confused. What is going on . . . Either you live here or you don't."

"Give me one second." Farah ran into her room to get the lease. When she returned, she handed it to the officer. "This the lease right here and nowhere on it does it say Lesa Carmine. I let her stay for a few days and now she won't go. I want her escorted out."

"Can we come in?" He looked at the ladies, who looked like they'd been in a wrestling match. "We don't want to disturb the rest of your neighbors."

Farah wanted to say, "fuck no," but realized she couldn't, so she backed up and allowed them into her apartment. The officers moved to the living room and examined the lease carefully in silence. She was positive that once he saw her papers all this foolery would come to an end.

"Look, this is quite simple," he said, looking at all of them. "Either you live here or you don't. There isn't a whole lot to it."

"And she don't," Mia said. "That's what we trying to tell you."

"Do you live here?"

"Yes, she does," Farah said. "And so does she." She pointed to Chloe. "And him." She pointed at her brother who reentered the living room to see what was going on. "This is my place. I don't know what else to say."

The officer turned to Lesa. "Let's go, ma'am."

"I can show you my room!" Lesa said. "My pictures and everything are up." Then she looked at Farah. "My clothes that she destroyed are in there, too."

"That's not answering the question. Are you on the lease or not?"

Lesa appeared very confident and said, "No. My name is not on the lease." Farah smiled at her sisters. "But I have been here for *over* thirty days. So I have the right to be here."

*What the fuck does that mean?* Farah thought. Lesa went into the kitchen to retrieve her mail. "See." She handed a jewelry bill to the officers. "That has my name on it with this address. So unlike what she told you, I do live here."

"So what, the bitch got mail coming here?" Shadow said. "That don't mean shit if you ask me."

"Good thing no one is asking you," one of the officers said.

He walked away. "By law, she can't throw her out, because rent or not, she's an official tenant," the officer clarified. "So she has every right to be here." It was obvious that Lesa's sheisty ass had done this before.

"There you go, Mr. Harvard."

"Wait . . . what you saying?" Farah asked, leaning in. "She not on my lease."

"I'm saying whether she pays you rent or not, if she's been here for thirty days, she has a right to be here."

Farah's mouth dropped. "So what . . . people get to fuck up your house? Not pay bills and everything is still sweet? That's not fucking right! Where's the justice?" She ranted as if a dead boy weren't lying in the closet in one of her rooms.

"Ma'am, calm down."

"She has been in my house for over thirty days, running up bills, fussing at my family, and not helping out! It's not fair!"

"Ma'am, you have to go to court and have her evicted properly. In most cases you'll have to give her thirty days to find another place." He handed her back the lease. "But until then she lives here and I don't want to be called down here again for any other issues. Understood?" Farah didn't nod but the officers accepted her silence as an understanding.

"This is our second time here in less than thirty days. We don't wanna come back again."

"You weren't here for us the last time," Chloe interjected. "So don't put that other shit on us!"

"But we were here nonetheless," he said. "You ladies better make sure it's the last. If not, the next time we come back, we locking everybody up!"

When they left the apartment Lesa and her friends sat on the sofa and smirked. "I'm glad you laughing, bitch," Farah said. "I doubt very seriously that you'll last two weeks."

# Chapter 39

**"Sorry, man, but we don't
work for nobody." —Major**

Slade walked into E.A.T. with Markee and his
three brothers. It took every creative excuse Markee had in the book, coupled with a call from his
aunt in Mississippi, to get Slade to meet Randy
to discuss Tornado's death. Markee realized that
Randy was not stupid, so he ended up coming clean
about what happened to Tornado the day he died.
Randy decided to meet with Slade after remembering Farah saying his name.

When the men made it inside E.A.T., Randy had
a scowl on his face. "Which one?" he asked Markee,
who pointed to Slade. "He doesn't look so tough."
Slade was unmoved by his comment.

"Randy, these are my cousins: Slade, Major,
Killa, and Audio. He really is sorry about what
happened to Tornado." Markee looked at Slade and
didn't see any remorse. "Aren't you?" Slade didn't
say a mumbling word.

Randy motioned for them to sit down, but the Baker Boys didn't budge. Markee, feeling like it was just a matter of time before shit kicked off, tried to diffuse the matter. "Sit down, y'all." He looked at his cousins. "*Please.*" One by one, they reluctantly took a seat on the lounge chairs. Slade sat directly across from Randy, who busied himself with a jar of peanuts on the table. Slade didn't like Randy's arrogance one bit and was about to bounce, especially since nobody was available to take Knox's call at the apartment. Markee looked at all the armed men in the hopes that Slade would follow his gaze, see they were outnumbered, and realize now was a bad time to make a country move.

"Explain to me how four of my men walk into your apartment alive, and at the end of the night, one walks out dead." The Baker Boys laughed and Randy smirked. "What's so fucking funny, niggas?"

Killa stopped laughing for the moment and said, "Dead men don't walk."

"Sure they do," Randy advised him, cracking peanut shells. "You're walking now, and technically you're all dead."

Slade's jaw flexed. He was trying his best to keep his cool. "What do you want with me and my brothers?"

"I thought I answered the question already. I wanna know what happened the other night." He popped a few peanuts in his mouth. "Let's start there first. You need to say something to convince me to let you live."

"Your man was murdered. With my bare hands." Slade grinned. "And my brothers didn't have shit to do with it." He nodded. "That's what happened."

Randy looked at Markee. "It was an accident, man. Honestly. They got into a fight and shit got out of hand. Tell him, Slade."

Randy cracked seven more peanuts and chewed them fully before swallowing. If they were back in Mississippi, Slade would've already brought Randy to his knees by stuffing the jar into his mouth. But for the sake of his cousin, for the moment anyway, he would bite his tongue. "Was it an accident or not?" Randy asked.

"If you're asking me if I meant to defend myself the answer is yes. Now, did I think he would break so easily? No." He grinned.

Randy didn't like Slade but he loved his fire. If he could tame him, he would certainly make a come up. "You killed one of my men, so now you work for me." Randy wiped his hands on a napkin before dotting the corners of his mouth. "All of you."

"Sorry, man, but we don't work for nobody," Major said. "We in town on business and when that's done, we on the first thing home."

"You not listening to me." Randy's men aimed their weapons at the Baker Boys, and Markee wanted to faint. "Tornado's life for yours. Don't look at it like a punishment. I'm giving you a chance to right a wrong. And if you knew me, you'd consider yourself lucky."

"He's right, Slade," Markee interjected. He was on him so hard, it was only mere seconds before he had Randy's balls and dick in his mouth. "Normally he wouldn't be so nice. Y'all should go ahead and take his offer."

"You a punk-ass nigga," Killa said. "Sometimes I can't believe you're even my cousin."

"Like my brother said, we not gonna be in town long," Slade interjected. "We just here to take care of a few things, and then we out. So we not gonna be able to work for you."

"I think you're under the impression you have a choice." Randy laughed. "If you are under that notion, let me assure you that you're greatly mistaken." He took off his shades and looked into their eyes. "You took one of my best, and this is how you make it right." Slade laughed. "What's so fucking funny now?"

"That man crushed within ten minutes of me putting my hands on him. And you call that your best?"

Randy couldn't tolerate Slade anymore, so he decided to have the man closest to his head pull the trigger. "Get rid of this nigga!" The Baker Boys jumped up, ready for war, until Randy's phone rang. He raised his hand and said, "Wait." When he picked up his iPhone, Farah's picture came across the screen. "Luckily for you it's my fiancée . . . Farah." He flashed it to him, knowing he was familiar with her name.

"What's up, baby? I'm busy right now." He looked at Slade and could see he finally got to him. He was feeling Farah and it showed all over his face.

Slade's jaw flexed, and his fists clenched, as he watched him talk to Farah on the phone. As if it were even possible, he hated him even more, and was five seconds from breaking his jaw. Killa, seeing his glare, nudged him and woke Slade out of his thoughts. Farah was not his, and he had to realize it or they all would die.

When Randy got off the phone, he was in a better mood. "I'm gonna give you country boys two days to reconsider my offer. After that, your fare back home will be on me, because you'll be going back in coffins."

# Chapter 40

### "If I did do something, I'm sorry." —Farah

Farah sat nervously in the passenger seat as Randy drove speedily down the road. Her puppies, Diamond and Pearl, who she'd grown to love dearly, were barking in the back seat at the top of their lungs. She'd shush them every so often, but it was obvious that they could feel Randy meant her harm. "Have you ever had a man who would ruin a whole city for you? A man who would kill you, so nobody else could have you?"

Farah grabbed Pearl, who found his way in the front seat. She placed him in her lap and began rubbing his head to calm him down. She was growing tired of Randy's threats and she just wanted him to do something, or shut the fuck up. "No, but did I do something to you?" She could feel sweat dripping from under her arms and pouring down the sides of her body under her coat. "If I did do something, I'm sorry."

"You know I'm tired of hearing that shit." He looked over at her. "So don't tell me that anymore." Randy drove in silence for five more minutes before pulling up at an abandoned warehouse. She knew where she was, because she'd been there with him before, but she never went inside. He parked his car and said, "Come on . . . I want you to go with me this time."

Farah grabbed her puppies, and followed him into the drab building and up the dirty stairs. The place didn't have as many bugs as Grand Mike's building, but it was still nasty. They stopped climbing the steps when they reached a blue door. "You know why I brought you here?" She shook her head. "I want you to see who I really am."

Not knowing what he meant, Farah stood behind him as he knocked on the door using a certain rhythm. A few seconds later, Juice came out and smiled at her before even noticing Randy. He hadn't seen her since she got into the fight at the store.

"You know that's got to be the fifth time you eyed my bitch," Randy said. "Make that your last."

"It's not even like that," he lied.

"Good . . . Now how's business?"

"Everything is smooth. Busier than ever."

Farah saw a box full of Independence Cards, which were used for food stamps, on a table by the door. Randy saw where she was looking and said,

"We take them if customers can't pay up. Sometimes for a few months, and then we let them come
back to get them. But it depends on how much they
owe. That's why they're right here by the door."

He stepped inside with Farah on his heels, while
Juice locked the door. In the middle of the large,
open space were eight tables with bags of cocaine
on top of them, in various packaging. Workers
stood around the stations naked, with masks over
their mouths and noses. In between doing their
jobs, a few would sneak looks at Randy, and it
was obvious they were frightened. The grey floor
beneath the table was covered in powder, and
Farah saw it get sprinkled with sweat, which came
from an older woman's body. She was so nervous,
she was perspiring heavily and it was obvious that
everyone feared him.

"Nobody should be looking at me! Get back to
fucking work!" When Farah saw Randy slip a small
package of coke into his pocket from one of the tables,
she wondered why he was stealing from himself.
"Come in the back room with me, Farah."

She followed him into a room that resembled a
coat locker. Her puppies licked her knuckles as she
held on to them tightly. There were fifty hooks on
the walls, and they all held the workers' clothing.
Randy walked up to one of the hooks, took the
small coke bag out of his pocket, and stuffed it into
a woman's royal blue coat. When he was done,

Randy walked back into the distribution area, wearing a scowl on his face, as Farah followed.

"I need everybody to stop what the fuck they are doing," he said. Everyone ceased all actions, as they froze in place. "It's been brought to my attention that somebody in this room has been stealing from me."

A few women whimpered, and Farah even saw one of the male workers shed a tear. It was obvious that he'd done this type of devious behavior before. Now she saw how badly lying could hurt people, although she doubted she could stop. "Before I murder everybody in this room, I'm giving you a chance to come clean." He looked at everyone. "Now . . . who was it?"

Silence.

Juice hung in the corner with a disgusted look on his face. Randy wasn't suited for power and, although Randy didn't know it, he had plans to take him down.

"Okay, since nobody wants to 'fess up we gonna do this a different way." He looked at his partner. "Juice, go back there and check every coat in the room. If you find something, bring the dope and the coat to me."

"Man, what's this shit about? I been here all day, and I didn't even see anybody leaving the table, let alone going back there."

"So you gonna go against your partner? In front of all these people? Now I said somebody was stealing . . . Go check."

Juice glanced at him, then at Farah, and walked slowly into the room. He didn't care if he caught him looking at her this time or not. He was back there for fifteen minutes before returning empty-handed. "I . . . I didn't find anything, Randy." Everyone exhaled but Farah's heart thumped wildly in her chest. She knew for a fact that one of the coats held the drugs, because she'd seen Randy stash it. "I looked a few times."

"Fuck you mean you looked a few times? Either it's there or it's not. If you checked it right, there's no reason to double up. Fuck it, I'll do it myself." He went into the room and returned less than a minute later, holding the royal blue coat. He held it in the air and it dangled under his grasp. "Who does this belong to?"

Everyone looked at an older woman with grey hair, the same one who sweated heavily when he first entered the room. "I had a dream I would die today."

"So you're admitting your guilt?"

"No . . . I didn't do it." She sobbed, shaking her head from left to right. "I promise. Somebody framed me."

He dropped the coat and walked up to her. "You know the consequences of stealing from me, yet you do it anyway."

"Please don't kill me." She cried harder, backing into the wall. "I have six grandkids and their father and mother were murdered a year ago. I'm all they got, and I have been loyal to you for many years."

"Randy, she's our best worker, man," Juice interrupted. "She wouldn't do no shit like this. It ain't her MO."

"Is that why you lied to me when I asked you to go check? Because you think she's not capable?"

"If you wanna pull this stupid-ass shit, you do it on your own. I'm out," Juice roared.

"Fuck that nigga," he said after he slammed the door.

Turning back to the woman, he removed his gun from his waist, and shot her in the throat. When she dropped, he hit her again in the forehead. Farah's puppies barked wildly, before she softly rocked them silent. "Clean this mess up and get back to work," he said to one of his men. Looking back at Farah he said, "Let's go."

She followed him up some stairs and to a doorway. Randy pushed it open and the brightness from the roof hit her in the face. She couldn't be in the sun long, so for a moment, she hesitated. "Come out the door, we not gonna be here too long."

She looked up at the sky. "Randy, I don't want to."

"Don't make me tell you again. I'm getting real tired of repeating myself." Farah slowly walked out onto the roof, and stood in the middle, away from the edge. "I own everything you see, Farah. *Everything*." He walked to the edge. "Come closer . . . I want you to share this with me."

She walked over to him and he said, "I sacrificed the woman in that house for you. There's no greater love than someone who murders in your honor. But if you do me wrong again, I won't be so nice." Then he took her puppies from her hand, and flung them off the roof. Farah screamed out as she watched her animals splatter on the ground.

"Why did you do that?" she screamed. "You gave them to me!"

"I want you to know how far I'll go to get to you. Stay away from Slade. I saw how he looked at me when I mentioned your name. Let this be your final warning."

# Chapter 41

**"Fuck all that . . . let's talk about how we gonna get this bitch back." —Farah**

Farah and Rhonda just finished shopping for the war of the red bones that was going on at her apartment. Farah bought everything she needed to make Lesa's life miserable, and she couldn't wait for the games to begin. Although things hadn't been the same between Farah and Rhonda, she was hoping that their beef would completely blow over, especially since Lesa didn't turn out to be the friend she thought she wanted. Although Rhonda was cool, it was Coconut who she missed the most. After shopping, they decided to get something to eat at Mamma's Kitchen.

"Girl, I'm tired as shit!" Rhonda said, rubbing her belly. "Plus my feet hurt."

"I be glad when you pop that baby out that black-ass pussy. You complain too much now."

"My pussy pinker than yours. Trust me," she said. "Look, I wanted to tell you that I'm so happy you still throwing my shower. It means a lot to me and a lot of people are coming."

Farah was sure she was only befriending her because she wanted her to do something. But since she was friendless, for the moment she'd have to do.

"I still can't believe all that shit popping off at your crib. Lesa seemed so cool."

"Believe it." Farah picked up the menu and immediately knew what she wanted. Every now and again she'd think of Amico and how they disposed of his body. Most times she'd think about the other people she hurt, and how she didn't seem to get enough. Her world had certainly changed for the eerie. "Lesa gonna leave my apartment whether she wants to or not."

Across the way she saw two darker females with their boyfriends. The men kept eyeing her and Farah smiled. "You see that shit, girl?"

"What shit?" Rhonda asked without even looking up from her menu. She had a taste for their lemon cake but the sweet potato pie was good, too. "You always talking about something."

"Look at them niggas over there." She pointed.

Rhonda looked up and smiled. "Damn, they fine as shit."

"Them niggas on red bones hard! I know it."

Rhonda rolled her eyes and dropped the menu. "You sure they not just on pussy?" She sipped her ice water with lemon. "They are with dark-skinned chicks, so your theory seems to be flawed."

Farah knew Rhonda needed her, so she decided to test the limits. "Please don't tell me you really believe that." Farah laughed. "Think about it, how many rappers talk about red bones in their songs versus dark girls?" She stole another look at the dudes. "We run the world."

Rhonda was trying desperately to bite her tongue. Invitations had gone out and she wanted as much stuff as she could get for her baby. "If you say so, Farah."

"I do."

"On some other shit, that video somebody took at the party of you slapping Coconut been going around. It's kind of fucked up that people think you got out on her."

"So what." She shrugged. "Tell 'em it was a game."

"I'm just saying it's messed up, that's all," Rhonda continued. "That girl was drunk and every time somebody shows it, she gets angrier."

"What you want us to do, play again or something? What about her having Nova come smack me?" Farah said, looking back over at the table. "I ain't crying to nobody about that shit, am I?"

"I talked to Coconut, and she didn't have anything to do with that shit."

"Well, who was it, Shannon?" she said, rolling her neck. "Because the bitch said Coconut's name first when she stepped to me."

"I'm just telling you what she said. I don't think she had nothing to do with it. I don't think Shannon did either. Everybody knows that Nova don't like you, so she probably made that move on her own."

"You shouldn't even care what she thinks, Coconut would fuck your nigga if you let her. I'm trying to tell you the truth so you can be careful."

Before Rhonda could respond, the girl across from them looked over at Farah and said, "Bitch, you must got a problem with your eyeballs!" She stood up and approached Farah's table. The cute dark-skinned girl with a black jacket hated light-skinned people believing that they were better. So Farah had met her hate-crime match. "You looking at my nigga like you wanna suck his dick or something!"

"Actually I *was* wondering how good it would taste. Maybe I should go see." She looked at her man and licked her lips.

Rhonda didn't want to fight, due to being pregnant, but she took off her earrings and put them in her purse. She'd been out with Farah before, and lost $500 worth of jewelry when they got into fights in the past. She wasn't taking any chances.

The dude wearing a Red Hat, who was at the table, walked up to the girl with the black jacket and said, "Don't pay them bitches no mind. We was having a good time! Why you gonna let them ruin it?"

Black Jacket shook him off. "I wanna know what this bitch's problem is. I mean, damn, she don't even know you." She turned around to look at him. "Or do she?"

"Listen, bitch. If I want him he'd be gone," Farah said. "Trust me."

They were about to fight when Shadow, Mia, and Chloe walked through the restaurant's doors. They decided to meet up with Farah and Rhonda after everybody got what was on their list to get Lesa out of the house. "Hold up," the girl with the black jacket said to no one in particular, "is that Mia Cotton?"

Mia and Chloe, seeing the look on Farah's face, stepped up, ready to snatch some weaves out. "Everything cool?" Mia asked. Black Jacket got silent and took her seat.

Farah grinned. "Everything fine now."

Mia, Chloe, and Shadow piled into the booth and grabbed the menus. But Shadow eyed Red Hat, who was still looking in their direction. He hadn't been in a fight since he'd been home, and welcomed the battle. "You good, man?" Shadow asked. Red Hat raised his glass and proceeded to entertain his girlfriend. He looked at Farah and said, "That bitch put a lock on her door. Just wanted you to know before I forgot."

"Who said she could do all of that? She gonna be leaving in two weeks anyway. If not sooner."

"I know you didn't know. That's why I wanted to give you a heads-up."

"What was that shit over there about?" Mia asked after making her meal selection. She was going with the smothered chicken and rice. "Them bitches seemed mad as shit at you before I walked in."

"Them jealous bitches mad because I'm light skinned—"

"Oh, my God!" Chloe yelled, throwing her hands in the air. "I wish you stop that dumb shit! Don't nobody give a fuck about all that bullshit but you! You talking about me . . . Maybe you should grow up."

"Whatever, Chloe. You just mad because I'm telling the truth."

"You know what . . . I wanna put this shit to the test right now!" Chloe said. "Order me the fried chicken salad, Shadow."

He put the menu down and said, "Why you can't do it yourself?"

"'Cause for one, I got the money and for two, I'm about to make my sister eat her words."

Farah frowned. "And how do you intend on doing that?"

Chloe scanned the restaurant and saw three dudes at the bar. "Over there . . . you see them guys?"

"Yeah . . . so what?"

"Let's both walk over there and sit on separate ends of the bar. Like we don't know each other."

"What's that gonna prove?" Farah was nervous because she hated to be wrong. "I don't have to do no dumb shit just because you don't believe what is true."

"Whoever they try to holla at, that's what it is." Chloe smirked. "If it's all about red bones, they shouldn't pay me any attention. So you with it or not?"

Farah looked at everyone and decided to take her up on her offer. "Let's go. But after I win this shit I don't wanna hear nobody's mouth when I talk about red bones being better for future reference. You all gotta say we better and that's it."

Farah and Chloe walked to the bar and sat down. After telling the waitress that she wanted water, Farah decided to get on a fake phone call to make noise, in the hopes of getting their attention, while Chloe gave the men eye contact.

The men spotted the women and not even a minute passed before Chloe got first catch. Not only was the dude into her, he offered to buy her dinner. She was feeling Audio so she decided to pass, and just took his number instead. Besides, there was nothing else to say; her point was proven. Realizing Chloe won, Farah slogged back to the table where everybody, including Rhonda, was laughing hysterically.

"The only reason that dude hollered at her instead of me was because I was on the phone." Everybody rolled their eyes, including Rhonda.

"You such a sore fucking loser, sis. Damn!" Chloe said.

"Right . . . The rules were whoever lost couldn't say shit else about the topic," Mia said. "So that mean you, Farah."

"Some niggas like red bones and that may be their preference, but the average dude like a sexy bitch. And that's me. I don't care how black my skin is, my pussy's still pink and they love it." Chloe pointed in her face. "Point proven."

Embarrassed and irritated, she said, "Fuck all that . . . Let's talk about how we gonna get this bitch back."

"Now you talking a language we all love," Mia said. "Revenge!"

# Chapter 42

**"Randy, I can do some things
too, if you get me wrong.
I need you to know that." —Farah**

Farah was thirsty because of the white sock
stuffed in her mouth. She was lying on her stomach
with her wrists and ankles bound together, as Randy
circled the bed like a lunatic. She wasn't scared
because, for Randy, this was all normal; she just
wanted it to be over quickly. Besides, war had been
called in Platinum Lofts and she could only imagine
what was happening now, since she wasn't home.

"Don't look so sad," Randy said. "You came out
of the house half dressed, with your ass hanging
out of your clothes, so you must've wanted me to
fuck you. Didn't you?" Randy would make up these
ambitious stories to get himself into the mood,
and Farah always did a horrible job of playing
the victim. Since she couldn't talk because of the
obstruction in her mouth, she nodded.

"Well, I'm going to do all kinds of things to you,
because you deserve it."

*Then do it, mothafucka, and let's get this over with. My mouth is dry as shit!*

"I'm gonna give it to you nice and hard, Farah." He was dragging things out, when all of a sudden her cell phone rang. Randy, knee-deep into her business, picked it up and answered. "Who's this?" Farah was heated as he held her phone to his ear. She didn't have a lot of people calling, but it really could be anybody. "Oh . . . hold on." He handed the phone to Farah. "It's Chloe."

Farah looked at him oddly. How could she answer when he had her limbs bound, and her mouth stuffed? Realizing his mistake, he laughed, untied her, and removed the sock. She rubbed her sore wrists, wet her tongue with spit, and placed the phone to her ear. "What's up, Chloe?" She looked up at Randy from the bed. "Everything cool?"

"Can I have some of your apple juice? Your roommate is being a bitch as usual. If I touch her shit I'ma have to kill her."

Farah sighed. She hated to be called for bullshit, and Chloe was famous for it. "Yes, girl."

"Ugh . . . Why you sounding all like that? You shouldn't even be with Randy anyway. And why you let him answer your phone? Don't you got a restraining order out on him or something?"

"Chloe, I gotta go."

She laughed. "All right . . . Oh, before I forget, I wanted to tell you that Slade got locked up tonight."

Farah's eyes widened. "What? Why?"

"He got into a fight at some club . . . and they holding him in jail. Just thought you wanted to know since whether you know it or not, he belongs to you."

"Is he okay?" She looked at Randy. He wondered who the "he" was she was talking about. If he found out she was even talking about Slade, he would kill her. "I mean, is she okay?"

"She?" Chloe repeated.

"Bitch, is she okay or not?"

"If the 'she' you talking about is Slade's fine ass, I'd say no. He has a bail and his brothers can't help him out right now. Markee ain't been at home all day, so they can't go to him either. I don't know if you know, but Markee works for Randy. You better be careful." Farah could hear juice being poured in the background. "Well . . . I gotta go. I'll see you when you get back."

Farah got off the phone, slid off the bed, and put the cell in her purse. "Randy, I gotta leave early."

She walked over to Randy, who was sitting at his desk. "How come?" He didn't look at her.

"My sisters are fighting my roommate again."

Randy spun around to face her in the chair. He was irritated and it showed all over his face. "Well, what your mother saying? It ain't like it's your house. Let her handle that shit."

"I told you my mother is sick," she said in a low voice. "She can't stop them from ripping her apartment up if they in there fighting. If you want, I can come back later. I just gotta go now to see about things."

Randy wanted to complain but he had shit to do also, so he said, "Okay . . . What time you coming back?"

"The moment I'm done." Farah put on her clothes, and Randy kept his eyes glued on her.

"You sure you being real with me? Because you know if you're not, I will find out. Remember what I did to your animals, and that old bitch? Well, that will seem innocent compared to what I have in store for you if you fuck me over."

"Randy, please don't threaten me."

"I haven't threatened anybody since I was in grade school. Besides, you seen what I can do." He put his grey sweatpants on. "So why would you think I'm anything but serious?"

"Randy, I'm being straight up with you. But sometimes I think you want me to lie so you can start a fight with me or something."

"You sound stupid." He slid into his slippers. "I just wanna take care of you and I'm ready for the games to stop." Randy kissed her lips. "You still young, and you don't know what it means to be with a real man. So I gotta show you."

When Farah was dressed, she stopped short at the door. She still needed money for rent because the landlord had already begun eviction proceedings, and she spent up all her money on weed, smoke, and food. "Randy . . . can you . . ."

"I know . . . you need money." He reached in his drawer and handed her $2,500. "That should be enough, right?"

She hadn't expected him to give her so much. "Yes . . . this is perfect!"

"Good . . .Now let me take a shower." He walked toward the bathroom. "Take your key, because I expect you back later." Farah was almost out of the room when he said, "If I ever find out you were lying to me, about anything, I don't know what I would do."

"Randy, I can do some things too, if you get me wrong. I need you to know that." Her threat was deadly serious, but instead of heeding her warning, he was turned on.

# Chapter 43

**"He's still family." —Slade**


Slade was just about to wrap his hands around the neck of one of his cellmates when an officer walked up to the cell and said, "Slade Baker, you made bail." At first Slade thought it was a mistake because Markee was not home, and his brothers were dead broke. If they did bail him out, he hoped they didn't do anything that would land them in jail right next to him. "You wanna leave or not, Big Country?" the officer taunted as he unlocked the bars. "You moving slower than a bitch in a miniskirt."

"If my bail paid, what difference do it make how slow I move?" Slade slid out of the cell at his own speed. He went through processing for longer than an hour, courtesy of the hating-ass CO, and was eventually released. He was surprised to find out that they didn't have him listed as a wanted man. Sheriff Kramer really was trying to do shit underground.

The moment he walked outside of the jail, he heard a car knocking loudly. When he looked in the direction of the noise, he recognized the driver immediately. Because his truck was impounded, he walked up to the car, hoping she'd give him a ride. "You bailed me out?" he asked, already knowing the answer. She nodded. "Thanks, and I'll pay you back when I get the money."

He waited for her to open her mouth, because with everything going on, he wasn't in the mood for her mute games. He'd rather walk home than subject himself to constant rejection. Besides, he remembered seeing her picture on Randy's phone, and figured she belonged to him anyway. It wasn't like he had anything to offer except hopes and a few dreams.

Slade was about to walk away when Farah said, "You need a ride? I'm going back to the building. It's not a problem."

He stopped in his steps. "Uh . . . yeah."

"Well, get in." She smiled.

Slade walked around to the passenger side, and she reached over to unlock the door. Once he got into the car he said, "How did you know I was here?"

"My sister told me." She pulled into traffic. "I guess your brother told her." She paused. "Oh . . . and you can give me the money whenever you can." Farah used the entire $2,500 on him, and now she didn't have money to get her car fixed, or pay her bills.

Slade was quiet for a minute as he observed her from the corner of his eyes. She was beautiful, wore stylish clothes, and her quietness made her mystical. In a lot of ways, she reminded him of himself. He wanted her badly, but how was he gonna step to her? The nigga Randy put her in the Benz, and was probably paying her bills, too. Although he wouldn't be down long, he couldn't say for sure when he'd be able to take care of a bitch like her. He wanted to say something that could make her see that although he was strapped for cash now, with the right woman behind him, he could go places. He could be somebody. He just needed a reason to fight.

"You been living there long?" Slade asked, looking at her.

"Where?" Her voice was low and she tried to avoid eye contact. He seduced her.

"In Platinum Lofts."

"Yeah . . . I been there for some years." She moved out of the way to prevent hitting a black cat that dodged across the street. "It's nice, just expensive."

"You live there with your sisters and roommate?" He looked at her, and then back out the window. A man was pissing in a trashcan, and he shook his head in abhorrence. "It seems like everybody I run into wanna move over there for some reason."

"Yeah, I live with them." She shrugged. "For now." She was being short and he didn't know how to take it. Was she interested or not was his only question. If she wasn't, he wouldn't be bothered and they could go their separate ways. It wasn't how he wanted it, but he wasn't gonna press the issue either. Fucking with her would do nothing but put him into a tougher war with Randy.

"Look, do you want me to leave you alone?" He was used to girls falling all over him and Farah was too weird to know what she was doing. Maybe they were the same. "You been fucking with my head for a minute now, and I'm tired of the shit."

She looked at him and decreased her speed. "How am I fucking with your head?" She focused back on the road. "I answered all your questions. Just keep it light, okay?"

Not understanding what she meant he said, "When I approached you in the hallway that day, and you acted like you didn't have the time, I made a decision to leave you alone." That hurt and her stomach flopped. "Then I get arrested and you bail me out. What the fuck you want from me? Did you bail me out for your nigga, Randy?"

She looked at him. "You know about Randy?"

*Yeah. It's that nigga.* "I know of him. So where he want you to take me? Because I still don't have his answer yet."

"I don't know anything about what you're talking about. And I'd appreciate if you didn't tell him I picked you up, or paid your bail either."

"You must not fuck with him for real, if you got to lie to him."

"I do what I have to, to keep him happy. Let's leave it at that."

Slade never wanted to talk to this chick again. He couldn't believe he let her into his mind without even knowing where her head was first. All he wanted to do now was find his brother Knox, and get the fuck out of the city he hated. "Can I use your phone?" He pulled his out his pocket. "My battery dead."

"It's on the charger." She pointed at her console.

He pulled the charger out of the cigarette lighter, and it broke in his hands. "Fuck!"

Farah looked at her broken charger and got slightly angry. With everything going on at her house, and the way her sisters blew her up every five minutes, she needed a charged phone. "What happened?" She frowned. "How did you break it?"

"I'm sorry. I . . . I fucking . . . pulled it too hard." He held it in his hand.

"How?" She looked at him and then back at the road. "It's brand new."

"Look, I said it was an accident. I'll buy you another one." He looked at her and then at the phone. "Just put it with the other money I owe you. Can I still use your shit?"

"I guess." She shrugged. She wasn't trying to act like a bitch, but she was dead broke.

He held her phone carefully. If she was crying over a broken charger, he certainly didn't need her whining over a phone. Farah saw the anguish in his face. "It's okay. For real," she reassured him. "I'll buy another charger. You don't have to be extra careful with my phone. It's built to last."

After dialing the number, he put the phone to his ear and turned away from her. He didn't want to tell her that no appliance or human was safe around him. The phone rang three times before Markee finally answered. "What's up? I thought you weren't in the house."

"I just heard, man. I was gonna come bail you out."

"Sure you were; put Killa on the phone."

"You out of jail?" Markee sounded excited.

"I wouldn't be calling if I wasn't."

Thirty seconds later, Killa picked up. "You a'ight, bro?" He was excited and he could tell it in his voice. "What happened?"

"Some nigga got mad because his girl was trying to talk to me." He looked at Farah, wishing he didn't start the conversation in her car. "One thing led to another and I ended up in jail." He looked at Farah again and then out his window. "Any word from our brother?"

"Yeah."

Slade's heart raced. "What? When?"

"He tried to call the house, but Markee was on the other line and didn't click over." Slade felt rage wash over him. Markee knew how important it was that the family talked to Knox. It was life or death. Killa reduced his voice to a whisper. "I swear I think this mothafucka is a stone-cold hater. We gotta watch this boy."

"Stop, man. He's still family," Slade said, although the words tasted like shit in his mouth.

"Why else would he not click over? We been screaming Knox's name since the day we got here."

"I don't know, but at least we know he's alive." Slade shook his head at his cousin's carelessness. "How we know he called if he didn't click over?"

"When he finally got off the phone with some bitch, he told us there was a message. It was from Knox."

"What it say?"

"It said he'd been hurt, but he'd get back up with us as soon as possible, and not to worry. He said he'll connect with us in a few more days."

# Chapter 44

**"Well, whoever it is, they better
not try me." —Farah**

Farah woke up to complete silence, and she knew
something was wrong. Ever since her sisters moved
in, her apartment was anything but peaceful. Farah
tossed and turned a little as she thought of Slade
Baker. Now it made sense why Randy brought him
up the day they were on the roof; he'd personally
met him already. She threw the covers off of her
body and looked down at her neutral toenails. She
didn't like not being able to wear polish, but that
was her life. She wiggled her toes before sitting
up straight, and looked out the window. Life was
boring, and she needed a change soon. She was up
all night, watching the maintenance man pull up the
carpet in Chloe's room, courtesy of Amico's blood.
Life was getting crazy for sure.

When she felt a slippery sensation between her
legs, she pulled the waistband of her pajamas and
saw a puddle of blood. She'd gotten her period,

which explained why she was moody. Rushing to the bathroom, she was angry when she opened the cabinet drawer under the sink and saw that all her tampons were gone. Lesa was always screaming about them not going into her room, yet she'd come in hers freely and take her tampons without asking.

*How heavy do that bitch bleed anyway? Used up all my fucking shit.*

Farah stepped into the cold tub, turned the faucet on instead of the showerhead, and squatted. She positioned the water's direction so that it smacked against her vagina. Her blood ran down her legs and into the drain before running clear. After cleaning up, she grabbed a pad and eased into her white panties. Then she threw on her pink velour sweat suit and brown Ugg boots. When she walked into the kitchen she saw that the refrigerator was open and a half-empty jug of water was sitting on the counter.

"Why can't people clean up behind themselves?" She placed the jug in the fridge and closed the door.

When she opened the cabinet to grab a bowl, she heard a noise coming out of Lesa's room. Looking at her white ceramic ToyWatch, she noticed that she was due at work. So she tiptoed in the direction of her room to see what was up with the rent. From the doorway, she could see Shadow holding his dick. He was wetting Lesa's carpet, shoes, and her bathroom toilet with his urine.

Farah fell out laughing, holding her stomach. "What the fuck are you doing, boy? You starting the party already."

Shadow turned to the side to stuff his penis back into his pants. She couldn't lie; she was happy to have him home for reasons like that. "I want this bitch out of here like yesterday." When he was no longer indecent, he turned around to face her. "She got up this morning and threw my beer away that I had in the fridge. Talking about it was flat and been in there too long. Who the fuck is she to throw my shit away? And what she do, take a sip?"

"I'm so sick of her too!" Farah said, thinking about the first day she met her. She seemed so nice back then, and now she realized it was all an act. "I thought she got locks put on her door."

Shadow walked toward her and closed the door. "She did, but she went downstairs to wash clothes and forgot to lock it back."

"Oh . . . she still here? She supposed to be at work." "Yeah . . . she must know something's up. I heard her call out when I first got up this morning. She scared we gonna kick the door down, locks and all."

Farah shook her head. "That bitch is so fucking dumb." She went to the kitchen and poured herself a cup of water. "Why you leave the water jug out on the counter anyway?"

"Because I drank half of it so I could use the bathroom. I wanted to be on full so I could piss on her shit."

She shook her head. "Where everybody else at?"

"Chloe with the nigga Audio, and Mia at work." He grabbed some bread and mayonnaise to make a sandwich. "What you getting into today?"

"I got an appointment, and I gotta go buy some tampons." He looked at her, and she looked away.

"An appointment, huh? You sure you not going to get your murder fill?"

"Don't start with me, Shadow. Stay out of my business."

"Sis, I'm not gonna give you a hard time. You gotta do what's best for you. I just want to make sure if what Chloe said is true that you're operating safely." He looked her over. "You my baby sis, so I'ma be like that."

"She just had to give you the details." She took a sip and swallowed. "Chloe couldn't hold water if it was in a cup."

"You know, as fucked up as it is, she looks up to you. She wants to be like you."

Farah pointed to herself. "Like me?" She dropped her hand. "I thought she was Mia's cheerleader."

Shadow laughed. "Yeah, right. That girl has been a Farah fan since the day she was born. I'm surprised you couldn't notice that shit. That's why she was always hanging around and stuff."

*And taking my men.*

Farah couldn't lie, hearing that Chloe looked up to her instead of Mia made her smile. "A'ight, baby boy," Farah said, washing her cup. "Let me go see this dude. I left some money for you in your room."

"I thought you were broke."

"I am. I'm still richer than you are though." Shadow smiled. "Don't be too excited though . . . it's only fifty bucks. I'ma see what I can do later." She went to get her purse from her room. "Don't kick nothing off with that girl until I get home later tonight!" She called out from the back of the apartment. She walked back into the living room. "She gonna lose it when she see what you did in there." She grabbed her coat out of the closet. "I don't need this bitch calling the police, trying to get you locked up."

"I would break that bitch's neck."

"No!" she yelled, pointing in his face. He was a killer, and that was real talk, but Farah wasn't afraid of him. "We gonna handle her together. But not the Cotton way. You got me?"

"Yeah, whatever." He followed her to the door. "Farah, why you tell them peoples I went to Harvard? You ashamed of me going to jail?"

Farah knew this was going to come up sooner or later. "I'm not ashamed of you. I'm ashamed of how people think about you. Jail or not, you still my brother, and I want people to respect that. We cool?"

Shadow nodded and Farah walked out the door.

Farah was sitting at Rhonda's kitchen table with her, going over the plans for her baby shower. With everything going on with Lesa, she almost forgot she was having it at her place.

"So that's everything," Rhonda said with a smile on her face. "And Coconut said she'd help you with anything else you needed. She not gonna reach out to you first though."

Farah gathered the papers on the table and said, "I can't believe you're talking to her, after all the shit she did to me.

You don't give a fuck that Nova smacked me in the face and said it was from her? None of that shit matters to you?"

"Farah, Coconut said she didn't do that and I believe her. I told you that already. We are grown-ass women," she said, "and can't be responsible for another bitch. You should take that up with Nova."

Farah rolled her eyes and said, "If you so cool with her, why don't you tell her to have your shower at her house?"

"I'm not going to even start with you." She laughed. "You made a promise, and you gotta keep it. We friends, right? So friends look out for each other." Farah smiled weakly. "Anyway, you saw the video of you and her on YouTube. She got a right to be mad."

"I'm not gonna keep talking about that shit," she said. "What's done is done."

Farah stuffed the papers in her purse for the shower. "Oh . . . before you go I forgot to tell you that a group of girls been coming around here asking for you."

Farah frowned. "A group of girls?"

"Yeah . . . I don't know what it's about but it don't look too good. Who you beefing with now?"

"Nobody." She couldn't pick out one bitch from another. She was hated by many. "Who they ask about me?"

"My mother. Coconut said they asked her about you too, when she was at the movies with her boyfriend." Rhonda got up from the table and rubbed her belly. "Just be careful."

Farah didn't understand who could be asking about her but she wasn't going to give it any more time. "Well, whoever it is, they better not try me."

"Farah . . . before you leave, you ever hear anything about that man? That we hit?"

"No. And I don't want to. Why?" Her forehead wrinkled between the eyes. "You think that's related to the girls or something? Nobody saw us."

"I don't think it's about that, but you just can never be sure."

# Chapter 45

**"Oh, my God! She can't be . . ." —Lesa**

Lesa brought up her last load of clothes and decided to use the bathroom. When she opened the door and sat on the toilet, it was completely wet. "Ugh!" she screamed, jumping up. She placed her hand on the yellow liquid and put it to her nose. "It's fucking piss! Them mothafuckas!"

She was mad at herself for leaving her bedroom door open, but even madder that Farah would stoop so low. She washed her hands and said, "You wanna take it there . . . then let's go!"

At that time she decided she didn't know enough about her little roommate. Since she was out of the house, and no one else was home, she decided to go through her shit. She flung open dresser drawers, closet doors, and everything else. Outside of a box of empty cylinders, like the ones used in chemistry class, she didn't find anything out of the ordinary. She was about to leave and reach out to Coconut, knowing she could dig up some dirt, but she was stopped in her tracks when Farah's personal phone line rang.

She walked over to the bed, answered the phone, and snooped through her jewelry. "Hello," she said, rustling around in Farah's jewelry box. "Who is this?"

"Is this Farah?" she heard a white man ask.

His voice intrigued her. So she sat on the edge of the bed and thought of Farah's voice. To her she sounded breathy, so she did her best to imitate it. "Yes. This is Farah. Who is this?"

"Where have you been?" He sounded worried. "I've been calling you nonstop, especially after Elise called me and told me what you were doing. Did Chloe tell you I called?"

"Uh . . ."

"Farah, you shouldn't be out there dealing with this illness on your own," he interrupted. "You really do need to be under a doctor's care. And there's nobody more concerned about you and your family than me. Now I know things didn't work out in the past, but I have some new medicines that I'm sure will do the trick."

"I'm going through a lot." She looked at the caller ID on the phone, and saw Doctor Martin's name. "Dr. Martin . . . A whole lot. That's why I haven't been able to see you. I'm doing better though . . . really."

"But, Farah, you're going to get worse if you don't let me care for you. I know this illness is rare, but I'm one of the top doctors in this field."

Lesa didn't know Farah was that sick, and she certainly didn't know it was so serious. She remembered the day she fell out in gym, but thought it was an isolated event. "Well, if you can help me, how come it hasn't worked?"

"Because porphyria is uncommon and it impacts people in different ways. Some can't be in the sun, like you, or be around fumes, like you also. The thing that makes your disease so unique is that it seems to be triggered by stressful events. If we can get your stress under control, we can get this disease under control."

*Porphyria?* "Uh . . . I . . ."

"Listen, Farah, Elise told me about what you're doing. What you're drinking. Please don't be mad at her; she's really concerned about your health. But I must tell you that you're going about this the wrong way. The way you're treating yourself is an urban legend. It's not real, and it can go horribly wrong. If you continue, you can get all kinds of diseases, like HIV and hepatitis."

Lesa was curious about what he knew. "Dr. Martin, what did Elise tell you I was doing? To self-medicate?"

Silence.

"Dr. Martin?" She was getting anxious. It seemed like he had something juicy to say, yet he was holding back. "What did Elise tell you?"

"This isn't Farah, is it? You're calling your grandmother Elise. Why would you do that?" Silence.

"I've already said enough," he said. "I have to go now. Please give Farah my message."

She hung up the phone and her curiosity was killing her. Dr. Martin did more snitching than Rayful Edmonds. She needed to know what illness Farah had that would cause her doctor to worry so much. So she went to her room, pulled up a chair at her desk, and got on the computer. Then she typed "P-O-R-I-A" and information about a fungus appeared. She read through a couple of articles, but nothing seemed interesting. So she typed the letters "P-O-R-I-P-H-I-A." Finally, looking at the Google header, she saw "Did you mean Porphyria?" She selected the link. Still not getting what she wanted she combined the words "urban legend" with "porphyria." The first word she saw caused her heart to drop.

"Vampire? Oh, my God! She can't be . . ."

# Chapter 46

### "Don't worry, girl!
### I made plenty!" —Farah

Farah had a few things up her sleeve as she walked around the house in her red Victoria's Secret pajama pants and white wifebeater. Once again, the house was eerily peaceful, and everybody seemed to be staying out of each other's way. But why? For instance, Lesa was sitting on the couch with Courtney and Lady, and they barely looked at her.

*What the fuck are you bitches up to? I know something's up.*

Farah was washing chicken breasts in the sink when Chloe came out of her bedroom. Audio was still inside her room watching TV. "Came up for air?" Farah asked, stealing another look at Lesa and her friends.

"Bitch, please. What I'm gonna do with Mia's fat ass in there cock blocking and shit?" Chloe smacked her tongue. "Why can't she share a room with Shadow? Or you? Why I got to be the one to sleep with her fat ass?"

"Why you got to be the one who ain't giving me no fucking rent?" Farah asked, putting seasoning on the chicken. She looked into the living room again, and Lesa looked back at her and grinned. She whispered, "You see that shit? I thought something was up before, but now I'm sure."

Chloe grabbed a beer from the refrigerator and took a sip. "See what shit?"

"That shit." Farah nodded in their direction. "Something ain't right. They been acting awfully nice to me. It's almost like they are scared of me or something."

"Maybe they checked our resume." She shrugged. "Shit . . . I don't know."

"Naw . . . watch this." Farah looked into the living room. "Hey, Courtney, are you and Lady staying for dinner?"

"If you make enough, girl. I don't want to put you out though." She turned back around and looked at the TV. Lesa and Lady didn't bother to trade sly faces at each other, like they normally did whenever she opened her mouth.

Chloe flapped her eyes. "Oh, hold up, something is definitely up! That bitch can't stand your ass! You better watch your food, sis. They could've made a move on you before you."

"Bitch, I don't eat shit in here I don't bring in the same day and prepare myself. They won't catch me slipping." She put the chicken into the oven. "Did you do everything I asked?"

Chloe grinned. "Sure did." She leaned in and whispered. "Right before I came in. Audio helped me even though he didn't know why."

"You are so in love."

"It's nice too. If you stopped faking on Slade, you could see what I'm saying. He asks about you all the time."

"Well, how come he don't come over here and ask about me?"

"Maybe you should go over there and ask about him." She shrugged. "Anyway, everything for my part of the plan is in order."

Farah tried not to think about Slade, because she hadn't spoken to him since she gave him a ride home. She was sure he was done with her for good, especially after knowing she was with Randy. She doubted she'd even get her cash back.

Farah reached under the sink and grabbed the blender. "Get the ice out the fridge." Chloe grabbed the bag of ice and Farah piled it into the blender. Then she added the ingredients to make frozen martinis. But to get the visceral reaction she wanted, she added one more item to the mix so it would be just right. Pulling a bottle of ipecac syrup out of her purse, which sat on the counter, she poured it generously into the drink. Ipecac was used to induce vomiting for those who ingested poison. Farah poured the entire bottle into the mixture.

"What is that?" Chloe murmured.

"I call it 'Set It Off' syrup."

"What it's gonna do?"

"Stand back and watch." Farah looked into the living room. "Who's thirsty?" She held up one of her martini glasses and wiggled it. "I'm making my prize-winning drink."

"I'm with it," Lady said, standing up and moving toward the kitchen.

Courtney followed and said, "I can use a drink too. Thanks, girl."

"What about you, Lesa? You down?"

Lesa seemed scared of Farah, and she couldn't understand why. A few days ago she couldn't wait to jump in her face and give her a piece of her mind. So what changed? That bitch had a plan; she just didn't know what it was about. "I'll take a drink." She smiled weakly. "If you got any left."

"Don't worry, girl! I made plenty!"

# Chapter 47

**"Bitch, if you wanna play,
now it's really on!" —Lesa**

Lesa was on her knees, praying to the porcelain god in her bathroom. If she wasn't throwing up, she was shitting. She couldn't move, or she'd be running back to the toilet. She was furious that Farah fooled her into thinking that for the time anyway, things were cool. She had plans to lay low and move out of the apartment after her little discovery. But now, Farah had declared war and she was going to see the battle through. Sitting on the toilet, Lesa tried to piss out whatever poison Farah exacted upon her, when there was heavy knocking at the door. "Lesa . . . you finish yet? I gotta go too!" Courtney yelled.

"I'm not done! You gotta wait!" she yelled, rubbing her sore stomach. She wished they could get in their cars and go the fuck home. Suddenly she wasn't in the mood for company. "Use the other bathroom."

"They got the door locked!" Courtney sobbed. "And I gotta go bad, too! I can't believe they did this shit to us!"

Lesa felt bad for her friends, but at the moment she wasn't good to anyone. After all, she drank the poisoned martini too. "What you gotta do?" she yelled, spinning the toilet paper roll to get a ball of tissue. "Number one or two?"

"I gotta throw up!" she said. "And Lady do too."

"Well, use a trash can!"

Lesa could hear her friends calling Earl in her bedroom, and hoped vomit didn't get on her carpet or clothes. Courtney was regurgitating so badly that she was gagging and crying at the same time. Feeling sorry for them, she tried to man up and push her illness to the side, so that they could use the bathroom too. After all, it was her fault that they fell victim to Farah's plan. Had she not called them over to sit with her after learning Farah was crazy, they would not be in this position. And had she left like Farah suggested, none of this would be happening, but even now she was too stubborn to call a truce. After the last drip of piss left her body, she rose up off the toilet, and dabbed herself with the tissue.

When a burning sensation hit her ass, her jaw dropped and she froze in place. "Aww!" she screamed. "What the fuck is that?"

Without knowing, she was now experiencing the second part of Farah's plan. It was executed when Farah instructed Chloe to unravel an entire roll of toilet paper, spray it with mace, and roll it back. This action wasn't easy, and took her a long time. It had to be done in the open, and it had to be on the floor. Chloe and Audio had to wear masks as they soaked the tissue with the spray, just to get the effect they were getting now.

"Bitch, if you wanna play, now it's really on!" Lesa yelled.

# Chapter 48

**"What if I tell you that I'm ready to let him go? Would he even matter?" —Farah**

Farah was lying face up on her bed as she listened to the soothing sounds of Lesa and her friends regurgitate like it was going out of style. When someone knocked on her door, she grabbed her robe and walked toward it. "Who is it?" she asked before opening.

"Your oldest brother," Shadow said.

"You mean my only brother," she corrected him, opening the door. When she saw who was standing next to him, she felt light. "Oh . . . I didn't know you had company. I would've put something else on."

"I don't have company. You do. Who the fuck is this nigga?" Shadow pointed to Slade.

"Should I come back later?" Slade asked.

"No!" Farah said quickly. There was no way on earth she was letting him get away from her this time. And he looked so good . . . standing in her doorway. "Come in. I'm not doing anything."

"Who is this, sis?" he persisted.

"Damn, Shadow! You act like you fucking me or something." He glared at the vile idea. "If you must know, this is my friend, and his name is Slade. So I got it from here, thank you."

"Slade, huh." Shadow looked him up and down. "Well, whoever you are, you betta treat my sister right."

Slade didn't respond because he was overprotective of his siblings too. "It's not even like that, man." He looked at Farah. "I'm just here to settle a debt and after that I'm out."

Shadow looked at Slade and then at his sister. "Let me know if you need me." He walked away.

She nervously smoothed her hair and said, "Come in. I was just watching TV. If you got a few minutes anyway you can sit with me." When he walked inside, she locked the door.

Slade stood in the middle of her room, and was about to walk to a chair when he heard Lesa and her friends. It would be guts and butts all night and she knew it. "What's that? Somebody had a hangover or something?"

Farah tried to act as if she didn't hear all the commotion outside her door. She didn't want him thinking she was a troublemaker, or somebody capable of hurting another. In his eyes, she wanted to be innocent and pure. "I don't hear anything," she lied. "Whatever it is, you don't need to worry

about it. My roommate could be doing anything."
She cleared a place on her bed. "Sit down right
there. The chair is broke." He took a seat. "You
want something to drink? I can whip you up a
mixed drink right quick."

When she said that, Courtney yelled, "Bitch, I'm
not drinking nothing else in this mothafucka! I can't
believe you tried to kill us!"

Slade grinned and looked at the closed door.
"Naw, I'll pass." He reached in his pocket and
handed her some cash. "That's all the money I
owe you. For bailing me out and for breaking your
charger. I appreciate you looking out, because you
didn't have to."

When she looked down at the green money,
it was tinged with blood. She figured he took it
from some unsuspecting victim, or victims. She
slowly tucked the cash in her pocket, and hoped
this wasn't the last time she'd have a reason to be
around him. "You didn't have to give it to me right
away. I mean . . . I could've waited a few more days.
I know how tough shit be."

"Naw . . . I pay what I owe. Always." He looked
up at her. "I said I was going to hit you back and so
I did."

She couldn't lie, she needed the money because
the landlord had already begun eviction proceedings. With her son missing, she was impatient and
heartless. Even the tenant down the hall, who was

pregnant and alone, got the cold shoulder when she asked for a few days after going into labor. Farah didn't feel like dealing with her so Slade was just on time. "Thank you. I needed it." She sat next to him. "Can I tell you something?" She looked down into her hands. "I think about you. A lot. I think we got off to a bad start, and I don't want it to be that way. If we get to know each other, maybe we can be good friends."

Slade was caught off guard. "Why you say that?"

Farah felt stupid for opening up to him so quickly. Instead of being shy around him, she decided to do the opposite, and now felt as if it were an epic failure. "No reason. Just drop it."

"A'ight, well, let me go." He stood up and walked into the living room, with Farah on his heels.

"You sure I can't get you something to drink before you leave?"

At that exact moment, Lady crawled out of Lesa's room and into the hallway on all fours. "I hate you, Farah Cotton, and you gonna get everything you deserve, too!" Lady stood herself up using the counter, grabbed a bowl, and put some ice cubes into it. Then she looked at Slade and said, "If I were you, I'd stay the fuck away from her."

When she ambled back to Lesa's bedroom and closed the door, he said, "Naw, I'm good. I don't need nothing to drink."

"No, really, it's water." Slade didn't feel comforted. "Bottled water." She didn't want him to leave, and was trying her hardest to get him to stay. She couldn't fix her lips to say the words, so she used every other trick in the book. "It's not open."

"Bottled water will be cool."

Farah rushed into the kitchen and handed him the water. But when her finger brushed over his, the bottle dropped out of his hands, and bounced to the floor. She quickly picked it up and said, "I'm sorry, Slade. I must be clumsy today." She wiped off the bottle and handed it to him. "It was me not you." She swallowed. "Look . . . you sure you don't wanna go back into my room? So we can have some privacy? And maybe talk?"

When Chloe and Audio came out, she was blown. "Chloe, what do you want now?" Audio was right behind her.

"I wanted to see how everything was rolling. With our plan?"

She rolled her eyes and said, "Good, now go back in your room."

"Audio, you not over here getting into shit, are you?" Slade asked.

Audio rolled his eyes. "I told you we should've stayed in the room," he said to Chloe. "I knew I heard my brother's rough-ass voice out here. Now he trying to treat me like I'm a fucking kid again." He looked at Chloe and said, "Can we go back now?

Even though I can't get no pussy, because your sister won't take her ass to sleep."

When they were gone, Slade stepped closer to Farah. She loved his scent. It was natural, and not intrusive. Everything about him made her pussy water. "Like I was saying, you wanna go in my room and chill?"

"I got a few minutes. Somebody in the house waiting on my brother's call, so for now I'll be fine."

"One of the brothers I met the other day?"

"No. It's a long story."

She could tell he didn't want to talk about it, so she wouldn't press the issue. On the way to her room, they bypassed several evil stares from Lesa, Courtney, and Lady, as they sat on her floor and bed. When they made it to her room she closed and locked the door. "You sure everything cool here? Your roommate friends don't look so good."

"They're not my friends and it's a long story." She sat on her bed and tried to think of something witty to say; it was no haps. "Thank you for keeping your promise . . . with my money. I love when somebody says they're gonna do something, and do it." She looked into his eyes. "That shit's real attractive to me."

"It wasn't easy. I'm fucked up out here now, but I'm working on changing my game. You can't do too much of nothing without cash in your pockets. You know?"

"Yes, and if I can do anything to help, let me know." She smiled. "Maybe I can help you look for a job or something."

He laughed. "Naw, sweetheart, I'm never working for anybody." Then he sat next to her. "So I finally did something you were attracted to?" He searched her eyes. "Because you had me feeling all I could do was wrong when it came to you."

"Well, you not good with reading women." She sat closer to him and he moved away. "What is it with you? Every time I go to touch you, you pull away. Yet you get mad at me when I'm quiet."

"I know . . . it's not you."

"Don't lie." She looked at his eyes but he looked away. "I'm not pretty to you? Is that it? What kind of girls you like? Maybe I can learn to be better."

"You got to be fucking kidding me. There ain't shit about you I don't like."

"Then what is it?" She moved to touch his leg and he jumped up again. "What am I doing wrong? Am I too rough? Too ugly? Too dumb? Talk to me!"

"No! Why you acting all weird?"

"Then why won't you connect with me?"

"Look, I came to bring you your money. I gotta go now."

"Please don't go, Slade. Don't leave me. I don't want you to." He stopped. His back faced her. "Please don't leave without telling me what I can do. To make you like me. Or to make you mine."

"You got a man." He turned around. "What you want with me? I don't have shit to offer." He looked around her room. "Everything in here probably cost more than I made all month."

"That's why I want you. You're not like the rest. You a real nigga. Who gonna do what he gotta to take care of his woman." She was so close, if he moved an inch she'd be touching him and she wanted it so badly. "What if I'm the right one, and you're pushing me away?"

"Listen, you don't know the kind of nigga I am. If you really care about that dude, you would leave me alone. I can seriously hurt him, Farah, if I even thought you were still dealing with him and me at the same time."

"What if I tell you that I'm ready to let him go? Would he even matter?"

# Chapter 49

**"That ain't enough for me.
Not anymore." —Farah**

Farah pulled the warm covers over her head. She wasn't feeling well and realized she needed to get some medicine. She needed to kill. Her only problem was that her body was so weak, she could barely move out of bed. When Slade left last night, she was disappointed that they still didn't make a connection. Because of it, she was suffering from a broken heart of the worst kind.

Realizing sleep would not come anytime soon, she decided to jump into the shower. Before getting inside, she allowed the water to run for a while, so the bathroom could be steamy. Normally steam would cause havoc on her hair, but since she was going to wash it anyway, it didn't matter. Dropping the robe to the floor, she wiped the mirror with her hand, and examined her yellow skin in its reflection. She was both beautiful and sexy, and yet she couldn't see it. When she felt a heat rush come over her, she moved toward the toilet, and threw up an empty stomach.

When she was done, she stepped into the shower, grabbed her soap and washcloth and formed a thick lather. Wiping the vomit off of her mouth, she scrubbed her neck and upper body. She washed her body several times before realizing her back needed some love too, so she grabbed the long wooden back brush hanging off the showerhead. She lathered the bristles and cleaned her back thoroughly. For some reason she was horny and decided to pleasure herself. Easing down onto the shower floor, she allowed the warm water to spray against her face. She spread her legs, and used the opposite end of the brush to push it into her pussy. Thinking about Slade caused her to feel hornier than she ever did in her entire life.

"Slade," she moaned. The sloppy sound of the handle entering and exiting her pussy got louder. Her body was shivering and she felt she was about to cum. "Slade." She continued saying his name again. "Fuck me, Slade. Please."

"Bitch, Slade not in here!" Chloe moaned.

Farah hopped up and threw the brush down. From behind the blue curtain she said, "Chloe, what the fuck you doing in here?" She remained hidden and waited for her response. She was tired of her morphing abilities.

"Shitting." Farah could hear large plops hitting the toilet water. "I had to go bad."

"Bitch, how come you not in your own room?" She wiped soap out of her eyes. "I'm tired of not having no fucking privacy around here!"

"I can't go in my room because Mia shitting in there."

"Why you ain't use the guest room?"

"Because Shadow shitting in there."

Farah felt like screaming on everybody. She wanted privacy, but now she had anything but. To make matters worse, her first orgasm on Slade was thwarted thanks to her baby sister.

"What were you doing playing with your pussy? That's what I want to know." She giggled.

Farah was overcome with embarrassment, as she thought about all the people she would probably tell. "You don't know what the fuck you talking about." She could smell shit in the air, and was five seconds from slapping Chloe in the face with her wet foot. "Just hurry the fuck up and get out. Damn!"

The toilet flushed and for a moment the water turned cold. "Girl, you so ridiculous. Instead of playing with your old-ass pussy, you need to go see about that nigga." She washed her hands. "Because if his fuck game anything like Audio's, you're in for a treat."

When Chloe walked out, Farah hopped out of the shower with the water still running. The cold air smacked her body and she closed the door. Easing back into the shower she decided to wash her hair and forget about busting a nut. Turning the top off of her shampoo, she shut her eyes and poured it over her head. For some reason, she felt things crawling over her face. At first they felt like leaves, but they seemed to have feet. Whatever was on her, she was sure it wasn't shampoo. When she put the bottle down, and opened her eyes, she saw that her body was covered in roaches. One of her greatest fears was taking place, and there was nothing she could do. Although they were just bugs, she couldn't shake the feeling of impending doom. Her chest hardened and despite the water being hot, she felt chills all over her body.

"What the fuck is that?" she screamed, hopping around. "Oh, my God! Help me!" They were on her arms, lips, hair, and feet. A few of them were even moving rapidly toward her vagina, in an attempt to get away. Unable to fight a phobia that plagued her all her life, she fell into the shower curtain, and it smacked against the floor.

When Farah opened her eyes, she was on the bed. She looked at the white ceilings before looking down. She blinked several times when she saw Chloe, Mia, Shadow, and Audio staring in her direction. She smiled at first, thinking it was all a dream. But when she looked at the bathroom floor, the curtain was still down. Remembering everything, she hopped wildly out of the bed. Everyone moved out of her way to prevent getting hit. Farah shook her head and arms, thinking the bugs were still on her body. She continued to flail like a madwoman, until she got so tired she could only sit down. With her hair all over her head, she breathed heavily and looked at everyone.

"Where is that bitch?" Farah asked, huffing and puffing. She clenched her fists. "I want her now."

"She not here." Chloe sat in between Audio's legs on the floor. "She rolled out after you fell down. Mia was trying to beat the brakes off of that ass, and she got scared. Maybe she won't come back now."

"That ain't enough for me. Not anymore. I gotta do something else to that bitch now. She took shit to another level." Farah stood up and paced the floor.

"You might not be able to get your chance, sis," Shadow said, popping pizza-flavored Combos into his mouth. "Earlier, before she left, I saw boxes in her room. I think she really may be leaving this time."

Farah was thinking of more ways to seek revenge, whether she lived there or not, when all of a sudden she felt a piercing pain inside her stomach. "Ahh!" she yelled, falling to the floor. "Oh, my God! Help me!"

Her siblings jumped up, and surrounded her as worry dressed their faces. "What's wrong?" Chloe said on the verge of tears.

"Talk to me, Farah!" Shadow yelled.

"Call 911!" she cried. "Call 911!"

# Chapter 50

**"That bitch is gonna really get it now!" —Lesa**

Lesa was over at Courtney's house, and they were in the kitchen eating Oreos and milk. Lady stepped out to get some ice cream and was on her way back. Placing roaches in Farah's shampoo bottle, when she knew she had entomophobia, made her feel guilty at first. Part of her wanted Farah to pay for the martini poison, but the other part didn't know if she did more damage, considering Farah had porphyria. After all that time, Lesa still hadn't told her friends about Farah's condition, because she wasn't sure if they'd even believe her. She even thought about the night of their party, when the officers took Kirk out yelling that she bit him. It all seemed so weird now. The night they were poisoned, she only told them that she was very dangerous and to be careful. Her warning worked, because the three of them avoided her the entire night. But now, she wondered if the truth wouldn't be better.

"I still can't believe that bitch did that shit to us," Courtney said. "My stomach and ass are still sore to this day."

"I feel you. My throat sore, too." Lesa rubbed it. "She went too hard."

"I don't know why you don't just leave, girl. They probably fucking with your shit right now."

"Naw . . . I got locks on the door." Lesa popped off one side of the cookie, and licked the icing. "Plus I'm leaving, just not right now. I told you I packed."

"You and I both know they can break that lock if they want to." She laughed. "Why don't you move back with your mother? At least until you get your own place."

"Like I said, I'm not leaving right now, because I'm not gonna give her what she wants." She sipped some milk. "Plus you know I'm not fucking with my mother right now. What I look like moving with her? She hates me and the feeling is mutual."

"You know she loves you, Lesa. It ain't like she gonna be mad at you forever." Courtney pushed the cookies away, and grabbed a half-cut lemon cake from the refrigerator that she bought from Cakes Plus in Maryland. "Maybe you shouldn't alter your body anymore. Since that's what she's mad about anyway."

"So you taking her side now?" Lesa threw the naked cookie on her plate. "Because when I first told you why she was mad, you acted like you were on my side. So what changed?"

"Lesa, don't try to put this shit on me! You the one who left your mother's house in the middle of the night without letting her know where you were. When she called me what was I supposed to do? Lie? The next thing I know, you living with some chick in Platinum Lofts apartments. You just don't do people like that you love!"

"She was trying to control me! That's why I left."

"Lesa, you almost died from that last plastic surgery you had. She got every right to be angry and, if nothing else, concerned."

Lesa frowned. "I wish people just do them, and stay the fuck out of my business. Damn!"

Courtney put her hands on her hips and said, "Who the fuck you talking to?"

Lesa stood up and got in her face. "Who answered?"

They were five seconds from getting into a fist-fight when Lady came back with the ice cream. She put it on the kitchen counter, and looked at their face-off. "Everything cool?" She took the ice cream out of the brown paper bag, and placed it on the counter. "Because I know y'all not about to fight in here. Please tell me this bitch ain't cause us to start beefing again. Because if she did, this time I'm not talking to both of y'all bitches for a whole year!"

Lesa looked at Lady and then Courtney. She sat down and said, "Can you give me some ice cream please?" Courtney took a seat, even though her face was still distorted in anger.

"Instead of us fighting each other, we need to find a way to get her ass back," Lady offered. "And we should do it before you leave, Lesa. That shit she pulled could've killed us."

Courtney seemed to be deep in thought before she said, "I got an idea!" She went to the black phone on the wall, and dialed a number. Lesa and Lady waited for whatever she was about to do. "Hey, Juice! This Courtney. You got a second?" She paused. "I'ma need Randy's number from you. It's very important."

Lesa snuck home to pack a bag so she could stay over at Courtney's for the night. When Markee saw them, he told her that Farah was taken away in the ambulance, and that her family followed. Now things were taken too far, and guilt plagued her even more. The only benefit to her revenge scheme was that the house was empty, and she'd be able to grab a few things without confrontation. When she got to her room door, she saw it was open, and a heavy odor permeated the walls.

"Oh, my God, what is that?" Courtney said, holding her nose. "What is that smell?"

Lesa turned the knob and couldn't believe what she saw inside. Human feces were smeared all over the walls, dresser, and her bed. "That bitch is gonna really get it now!"

# Chapter 51

**"You need to know that I plan on doing anything I can to make my sister get better." —Chloe**

Chloe stood in the hospital room with her sister and brother, wondering if Farah was going to make it. She was worried sick, and for the first few hours was virtually inconsolable. "Y'all don't think we gonna lose her, do you?" Chloe asked. "Because I'ma die if I lose my sister."

Mia wiped the tears from her own face before she smacked her so hard, her lip cracked and bled. "Bitch, you betta never say no dumb shit like that again." She pointed in her face. "I'm sick of you talking about people dying around me and shit!"

Chloe accepted that smack like a gangster, and licked the blood from her lips. "I'm sorry. I'm just fucked up by all of this."

"Why do you think it always hit Farah the hardest?" Shadow asked softly. "It's like all our lives, she had it rougher than us."

"I don't know," Mia responded. "Maybe it's because she wants it to be gone badder than we do. Whenever you want something so hard, you never get it."

They watched over her for a half an hour before Dr. Martin stepped inside the room. Chloe called him, even though she knew Farah would never approve. He placed his hand on Shadow's shoulder, and looked solemnly at the rest of the family. Over the years, he'd grown into a respectable doctor and surgeon with an impressive patient list. Through all of his accomplishments and accolades, he could never help the Cottons with their ailment. He was so obsessed with making things right, that although they never knew it, he practically worked for free.

"Has she opened her eyes yet?" Dr. Martin asked.

"No," Shadow said. "I wish she would though."

"So what can we do, Dr. Martin?" Chloe asked. "You should've seen her in the room. She was in so much pain that she couldn't move. I haven't seen her like that in so long. She was doing so much better."

"We can continue to medicate but her liver is taking a beating right now. So anything we do will be after we monitor her for a while. So it's kind of hard to say what else will need to be done, until we get more tests. That's why it's so important that she sees me, regularly."

"Dr. Martin . . . when Farah was self-medicating, she was fine," Chloe said. "But now . . ."

"Listen to me," he said, looking at all of them. "Because I already know what you are going to say. That is an urban legend! It's not true." He scanned over their faces for confirmation. "It is virtually impossible for her to get better that way."

Chloe looked at her and then back at him. "I don't understand . . . I mean . . . with the illness we have, our bodies aren't making heme properly, correct?"

Reluctantly he said, "That's right, Chloe."

"Okay, you also prescribe us hematin which is blood related, right?"

He swallowed and said, "Yes, Chloe, that is correct also."

"So doesn't it make sense that drinking blood could help her?"

"No, Chloe, it doesn't make sense!" He looked at all of them. "That's what I'm trying to tell you."

"But I've been reading up on it. And it says back in the day, when the medicines were unavailable, some people with this illness drank blood and felt better. So how do we know it won't work now?"

"Because it's been tested." He was adamant. "That's why! We can't have people roaming the earth, drinking each other's blood. Your sister was raised in a violent home. *Very* violent." He looked at all of them. "I spoke to your grandmother extensively and she told me a lot about you and your family." Someone was going to have to talk to Grandma about her lip game. "Farah doesn't feel better because she drinks blood, she feels better because she craves violence. There's a difference." He could tell Chloe was not buying anything he said. "Chloe, please believe me. I want the best for you. For all of you. But if I find out you're doing anything illegal, I'll be forced to tell the police."

"Dr. Martin, I respect you." Chloe looked at her brother and sister. "We all do. But you need to know that I plan on doing anything I can to make my sister get better. And I do mean anything. So if you have a problem with anything I said, I suggest you step out of my way or get run over."

# Chapter 52

**This is so stupid.**
**You not gonna hurt**
**her if you touch her. —Slade**

After learning from Audio that Farah was sick, and confined to bed, Slade decided to pay her a visit. He didn't know if he could do anything to help, but at least he wanted to be in her presence. When he got to her apartment Chloe opened the door. "Hey, Slade." Chloe smiled, although it was obvious she was very upset. "Farah isn't up yet. She's still feels pretty bad. The doctor gave her some sleeping pills." She opened the door wider. "Did you still want to come in?"

"Yeah. If you don't mind." He stepped inside, and waved at his brother who was sitting on the sofa. "Where is she? In bed?"

She closed and locked the door. "Yes, you can go back there if you want to." Before he walked away she said, "She really likes you, Slade. Sometimes my sister finds it hard to open up, but I really do hope you hang in there with her. Please."

Slade nodded, and moved down the hallway and toward her room. When he opened the door, the room was mostly dark with the exception of a white rose-shaped nightlight plugged in the socket. Once inside, he removed his Nike boots and walked to her bed. For a second he looked down at her while she was asleep. She was beautiful and vulnerable all at once. He didn't know what made her so sick, but he sincerely wished she'd get better so they could start their lives together. What was he saying? Being around her made him think about the future.

"Farah," he said softly. "You 'sleep?"

When she didn't answer, he removed his jacket and threw it over the broken chair. Then he slowly eased on top of her comforter, so he wouldn't wake her. She was wheezing heavily, and although her eyes were closed, she seemed to be distressed. Slade wondered who she was and where she came from because their meetings, although brief, left a lasting impression.

When she moved slightly, her hair fell in her face and he wanted to wipe it away. But what if he hurt her in the process? He would never be able to live with himself. Still, after all those years, she was the first person who ever made him sincerely consider breaking his vow. After five minutes of struggling with whether to touch her, he slowly moved the hair away from her face without touching her skin. Now he wondered what her skin would feel like under his fingertips and thought about touching her. Anxiety overcame him and he could feel himself holding back.

*Fuck! This is so stupid. You not gonna hurt her if you touch her. Just do it!*

Remembering all those he hurt in the past, he decided to keep his hands to himself. And then she started whimpering, like she was having a nightmare. Her head moved quickly from right to left, and she was crying with her eyes closed. "No . . . Mamma, no. Please don't do it." Her head shook rapidly. "I love you," she cried. "Don't make me! Please!"

Slade couldn't take it anymore. So he carefully placed his hand on her arm, and the whimpering ceased before she exhaled. It was as if he had pulled the nightmare out of her mind with one touch of his hand. Loving the texture of her smooth skin, he rubbed her slowly and she fell into a deeper sleep. For the rest of the night he remained in her bed, watching over her. But she would never know, because in the morning he'd be gone.

# Chapter 53

**"Hmm, that felt so good." —Chloe**


Chloe's hips swerved slowly from left to right in a wavelike motion. Her arms were raised in the air sensuously, as sweat glistened over her chocolate skin. The red top she wore exposed her flat belly, and the black skirt squeezed her curves. Chloe had the attention of every man in the club, but she only needed one. Finally after watching her seduce every man present for most of the song, a dude name Dio decided to try his hand. He was a well-known drug dealer from New York, who was in town on some quick business. He hadn't planned on staying as long as he did, but when he spotted Chloe, he made an excuse. Stepping up behind her, he put his arms around her waist as if she belonged to him. Out of his eyesight, she grinned because her mission was accomplished.

"What's your name, ma?" His voice was heavy with bass and his lips were inches away from her ear. He wore cologne, which normally exacerbated her illness, but the scent was light and rich. "I been trying to get at you all night."

"That depends," she cooed, grinding harder into his stiff dick as he stood in position.

His warm breath tickled her ear. "On what?"

"On who you want me to be."

He laughed, looked over her shoulder, and down at her breasts. "On who I want you to be? You sure about that? Because a man like me could take that many ways."

"I don't say things I'm not sure about." She wiggled her ass into the center of his jeans until she felt him grow. "The only question now is do you have a fantasy? That you want fulfilled?"

"I don't do a lot of dreaming," he said, massaging her warm shoulders, "I got too much money to make. I can sleep when I'm dead."

"Come on, baby. Everybody has a fantasy. Or a wish."

He grinned. "Put it like this: after watching you dance all night, I could think of a few things I'd like to do to you. But first I have to get you out of here, to see if you fuck as good as you dance."

She laughed. "If you come with me, you gonna love my work. Trust me."

"Where you live, sexy? Since you not gonna tell me your name."

"I live in DC, and my name is Lesa Carmine."

"Okay, Lesa. Can I take you where you wanna go?"

She twinkled. "I wouldn't have it any other way."

Chloe was dancing in her room as Dio sat on a chair in the middle of the floor. "A Woman's Work" played on the small radio, and she wasn't wearing anything but a pink lace underwear set with the crotch out of the middle. She had the stink of dancing all night on her skin, but Dio loved her musty odor. Chloe watched as he opened his jeans, released his dick, and rubbed himself to a thickness. She looked at the time on the clock, and wondered when the plan would go into action. The anticipation was killing her.

"Lesa, get over here," Dio demanded. "I'm tired of looking at you from afar. I wanna feel you." She moved toward him. "Get rid of the panties . . . you won't need them."

Chloe grinned and eased out of her bottoms. Her pussy was neatly shaven, and she licked her lips before putting her finger in her mouth and sucking softly. The way he looked at her made her horny, and she wanted tonight to be about more than what was intended. "You like something you see over here?" She moved slowly to him. "Because once I get started, there's no stopping me. You do understand that, don't you?"

She stood directly in front of him and he grabbed her hand, while stroking his dick with the other hand. "I ain't worried about you stopping . . . just make sure you can keep up." He placed his finger between her pussy lips and took it out. It was covered in her cream, and he rubbed it under his nose so he could smell it all night. Her scent in his opinion was perfect. "You a bad bitch . . . I wonder if you do this kind of shit all the time."

"Don't worry about all of that," she told him. "Whatever I did in the past won't have anything to do with me and you tonight." Chloe grinned and pulled two pills out of her bra. She popped one into her mouth before crawling on top of his lap and gyrating on him.

"Why you gotta be so fucking sexy?" he asked, gripping her hips to keep her in place. "You trying to make a nigga kidnap you and take you to New York."

"You don't have to steal." She kissed him and eased the other pill into his mouth. "I'll go wherever you want me to. Just as long as you treat me right."

Dio got down with ecstasy from time to time, so he swallowed the pill without any water and said, "You really trying to have a lot of fun tonight."

"More fun than a roller coaster." She smiled. "Welcome to the party, baby."

After kissing him passionately again, she ran her tongue along the sides of his neck. She could taste the salt from his skin, and heard his breaths increasing. She had him exactly where she wanted him, and the poor man hadn't a chance, or a clue of what she had planned for the evening.

"Hold up, ma." He felt like his neck was heavier than usual. "What you just give me?"

"Something to take some of the pain away." She eased off of him, grabbed her robe, and unlocked her bedroom door. Five seconds later, Shadow and Mia helped Farah into the bedroom.

"What's going on?" Dio asked, although his words were hardly audible. "I . . . thought we were . . . I thought you lived here alone."

"Just stay calm, baby. We gonna make this as painless as possible. The more you fight, the harder it will be, so just go with the flow." She looked down at his stiff dick and her mouth watered. She knew it was wrong to desire him considering the circumstances, because she was feeling Audio, but the freak in her couldn't resist. "Mia, let me have him first." She was off the ecstasy and wanted to satisfy her craving. "He look so sexy sitting over there." Dio's neck dropped backward and his arms fell by his sides, but his dick had yet to soften.

"Well, we ain't got time for all of that." Farah leaned on Shadow as Mia placed a chair next to Dio so Farah could sit down.

"What's going on?" Farah asked. "Who is he?"

"We got him for you," Chloe said. "Isn't he perfect?" Focusing back on Mia she said, "Please let me fuck him before you kill him. It ain't like he going no place," Chloe begged. "It'll only take me a second."

Mia ignored her and said, "Where's the blade, Chloe? We don't have time for all that other shit. Damn, you too horny for words! You need to be a rabbit."

Chloe reached in her pocket, and handed it to her. "I don't understand what the problem is. I found him! I should be able to do whatever I want to him."

"Fuck it! Do what you gotta do," Mia said once she situated Farah in the seat next to him.

"Thank you!" Chloe cheered, clapping her hands. Her mood was totally out of place, considering the moment, but she was too crazy to care. A man was about to be murdered to fill Farah's insatiable desire to kill, drink, and live, and all she could think about was sex.

"This some wild-ass shit," Shadow said as he pulled his cap down so he couldn't see his sister's body when she dropped her robe. He was cool with Chloe getting her rocks off, knowing that if this was going to be their regular thing, he had all intentions of placing a bid for a bad bitch for the next kill. And he didn't want to hear a word about it, either.

Grinning from ear to ear, Chloe climbed on top of Dio and rode his stiff dick. Dio was so delirious and out of his mind that he no longer cared that originally he walked into the room with one person, and now there were three present. Chloe's slippery pussy sucked up his thickness with one pull. With full control of her hips, she wound her body on top of his stiffness and pushed down into him. His head rolled from left to right, and he was in a world of his own. So when he felt a sharp pain on his wrist, at first he didn't notice. Mia slowly sliced into his vein, and placed it against Farah's lips.

Her pink tongue slickly glided against his brown skin, as his red blood flowed into her mouth. At first she wasn't sucking, because she was emotionally beat down and weak, but when she realized what was happening, she gripped his wrist and suckled harder. The pain mixed with pleasure was overwhelming to Dio, because he'd never experienced anything like it in all his life. Farah's warm mouth on his wrist, coupled with Chloe's hot pussy on his dick, had him both confused and aroused at the same time. If this was how he was about to die, what a hell of a way to go.

"I'm cumming," Chloe moaned, jumping up and down. "I'm cumming." Using the little strength he had left, he released his nut into her pussy. "Hmm, that felt so good."

She placed her hands on both sides of his face, snaked her tongue into his mouth, and suckled his bottom lip. It was his last ounce of pleasure before life escaped his body.

It was the first murder the Cottons committed where a unified excuse loomed in the air, even though it certainly wouldn't be their last.

# Chapter 54

**"Tell me that *after* you hear
what I have to say." —Lesa**

Lesa sat in the car with Courtney and Lady, wondering who the guy was who entered the apartment with Chloe. After speaking with Randy, and finding out Farah lied a lot, she decided to snoop around before going into the house. She couldn't believe it when she learned that Farah was possibly responsible for Zone's death, and that Tank was still after her for getting him into trouble with the police. She also found out through Diamond D that the two men trying to kill her in the hallway the night of the party were friends of Tank. Farah had a hit on her head, and they were on a mission to earn the bounty and Lesa almost got in the way.

Digging a little deeper, she also learned that a group of girls led by somebody named Boo was trying to find her, so they could jump her because of what she did to Tank. Randy said he would no longer protect Farah, and that she was officially on her own. Even though Lesa could hear in his voice that he was distraught that Farah lied about where she lived, she could also tell he would in one way or another seek revenge. She knew if she didn't get away from the apartment, she could be in danger.

"I wonder why he ain't come down yet? It's been four hours, it's almost daylight and everything." Courtney yawned. "I mean . . . don't Chloe fuck with some dude in the building?"

"Yeah . . . but I think Coconut's friend fucks his brother, Slade. The girl's name is Shannon or something like that. He was at the house the day she put that shit in our drinks," Lesa said, peering out the window.

"Oh, yeah! That nigga was fine as shit!" Lady recollected.

As Lesa thought about everything Farah was into, she decided that now was the time to tell them the truth about her. "I got to tell y'all something about Farah." She swallowed. "But I don't think y'all gonna believe me."

"Girl, after meeting that crazy bitch and her family," Courtney said, "I'd believe anything."

"Tell me that *after* you hear what I have to say."

# Chapter 55

**"When I was younger, I used
to pray for you." —Farah**

Farah was finally on her feet and feeling better. She was in the kitchen preparing breakfast for her sisters and brother, because of the limits they went to, to make her healthy. As the days went by, and she would kill without regard for another person, she was beginning to feel invincible. From this day forward, she was on a mission to do whatever she could to survive, even if it meant drinking blood.

It was a good thing, because she had a big week ahead of her. For one, Rhonda's shower was Saturday, and she still had to move on her plans to get Lesa fully out of her apartment. They'd already paid a service to clean the shit from Lesa's walls, and Farah went hard, by throwing most of her stuff in a storage area in the building. She wanted to move things along because she had taken too much of her time. Nice went out the window, and she would step to anybody who got in her way. The only things she allowed to stay inside of Lesa's room were her computer and purses. And that was only because they were valuable, and could be sold if she didn't run her the back rent she owed.

After finishing the pancakes, she removed them from the stove, buttered them, and placed them on the counter. She was about to fry some eggs when there was a knock at the door. Wiping her hand on the towel, she looked through the peephole and saw Randy on the other side. Gas escaped her body as she quietly paced around in place. She couldn't believe he came over to her house, and she couldn't believe she was home. That meant he knew she didn't live with Brownie. If Lesa came in, or her sisters or brother, she'd be caught red-handed.

"Fuck!" she said in a low voice. "How did he know I was here?"

"Farah, either open this mothafuckin' door or I'm breaking this bitch down! I know you in there! Don't fuck with me!"

She backed away from the door, and sat on the couch.

Placing the tips of her fingers in her mouth, she chewed on her nails to settle her nerves. There was no getting out of her situation now.

"Bitch, I know you in there! Your roommate told me everything." He banged on the door like he was the police. "I put out no less than fifty thousand on your ass in less than six months, and you carry me like this?" Bang! Bang! "You never lived with your fucking mother! So why the fuck you lie?"

Silence.

"You want to play it like this?" He was breathing so heavily that she could hear him from the other side of the door. "You better wear a bulletproof vest, bitch, whenever you step outside. I got fifty thousand to whoever murders you. I ain't got to do shit but sit back and watch them work." He laughed. "I'll get up with you later. Believe that."

When he left, she tried to pull herself together. She thought about the way Dio's face looked as she sucked the life from his body. He was so sweet that she drained him, so he could last her for the rest of the month. What good would it do her to worry about Randy right now? If he was gonna make his move, he was gonna make his move, and there would be nothing she could do to stop him. Suddenly she thought about getting a new victim, so she could feel even more powerful. There was something about the act that drove her more than the taste.

From the moment Farah discovered she had porphyria, which started the legend of the vampire, she was obsessed with making it go away. Unfortunately wishing didn't work, until the day she met Grand Mike. So what the doctor told her that drinking blood was an urban legend, she felt better when she killed, and would continue to do so, until she was arrested or murdered.

After frying the eggs, there were a few quick raps on the door. She doubted Randy would come back, but that didn't stop her heart from pounding outrageously in her chest. Like a cat, she quietly moved toward the sound, increased her height by standing on the tips of her toes, and looked out the peephole. A smile covered her face when she saw Slade; what a great morning treat. She examined her clothes, dusted herself off, and opened the door.

"Hi, Slade. Were you here for Audio? Because I think he walked to the store with my sister."

"I'm not here for him, I see his ass all the time. I came to see if you're doing better." He smiled. "You had me worried about you. You gotta take care of yourself."

She looked into the hallway to be sure Randy wasn't coming. For a brief moment she forgot that she had a hit on her head. "Was anybody in the hallway when you knocked?"

"Naw . . . why?" He looked around. "You look scared about something. I mean, is everything okay?"

"No." She pulled him by his wrist into the house, and locked up. When she realized she touched him she dropped her hand and said, "Oh . . . I'm sorry . . . I know you don't like that shit. I forget sometimes."

"It's cool." He shrugged. "I don't want you to think I'm crazy or nothing. There's a reason I'm like that. Maybe I'll tell you later if I start fucking with you hard."

"If you fuck with me hard?" She giggled. "Well, I'm not worried about none of that. Once you spend time with me, you'll be wanting to tell me everything."

"Is that right?"

"All the way." She dropped her head, and tried to conceal the happiness that spread across her face. "Hungry?" She pointed to the food on the counter. "I made enough for everybody."

"If you can burn." He grinned, rubbing his stomach. "I can eat."

After fixing his plate, they ate in silence in her bedroom. The TV was on but the sound was muted. Every now and again she would look over at him. Where did he come from? What was his story? There were so many questions, and she hoped this time that he'd hang around long enough to give some answers.

"I see you can burn. I ain't gonna lie, I didn't pick you for the cooking type," he said. "I can't give you too much, but this food almost as good as my mamma's. And if you knew Moms, you'd know that's a huge compliment."

"Thank you. I can't cook a lot of stuff, just the meals I eat a lot. Chicken . . . rice, and things like that. Oh . . . and breakfast food." She looked down at the floor. "I'm real good at morning food." She placed her plate on the floor, and picked up the remote. "You wanna watch a movie? I have a few DVDs."

"I'm not trying to watch TV; we played games long enough." He paused. "I want to talk to you. I want to know who you are, and where you come from."

"Okay, ask me anything."

"A'ight." He set his plate down. "Where you from?"

"I grew up around here . . ." Before she could finish her statement, Slade moved in for a kiss. Her breaths were heavy, and she was aroused by the wetness in the seat of her panties. When the kiss was over she said, "Uh . . . I grew up around here . . ."

He kissed her again and broke away a minute later. "I been wanting to do that forever. It was better than I thought."

"Can you do it again?" He grinned and their lips connected like magnets. They fell on her bed, and she eased on top of his body. Slade hadn't kissed a woman in years, so to him, this moment spoke volumes. "That felt so good."

He wrapped his arms around her waist and said, "It was better than that." Farah crawled off of him, and stood before him. Then she gave him a strip tease by dropping her pajamas, and then her shirt. Naked, her nipples hardened and small chill bumps rose on her skin as he looked at her.

Slade rose and looked over her body. His dick was so hard, he knew there was no way he wasn't gonna hit that pussy today. Appreciating the fact that he broke his vow, he moved his rough hands over her soft breasts, arms, and thighs. Now that he touched a woman again, he knew there was no way he was ever going back. How could he be so stupid to give up God's gift to man?

"When you touch me, for some reason, I feel like it's the first time," she said. "Like you never touched a woman before. I never had that feeling before."

"If a nigga never appreciated your body, you don't need him." That was a jab at Randy and she knew it.

She grinned. "I feel safe around you."

"You don't know it, but I was here the first night you were sick. You were having a nightmare or something. When I put my hands on you, you went back to sleep."

"I don't remember." She pulled him to her, and leaned against his chest. "I have nightmares most of the time, especially when I was a kid." She hugged him tighter. "When I was younger, I used to pray for you. I'd pray somebody strong would enter my life and protect me. You believe in stuff like that?"

"Yeah . . . you don't have no reason to lie to me. So until you prove me wrong, I'm gonna trust everything you say."

Keeping her eyes on him, she unbuttoned his pants. His blue boxers peeked through the top of his True Religion jeans, and she ushered them to the floor. He stepped out of them one foot at a time, and tossed them into the corner. Wanting to see all of him, she removed his jacket and T-shirt. It was as if she were unwrapping a gift with too much paper. Standing in the middle of the floor, they held each other closely, slowly rocking in place. With her head on his heart, she wondered how good he would taste. She thought about how the red blood pouring out of his body would look against his chocolate tone. When she realized the vile thoughts in her mind, she pushed away from him, and put her clothes on.

"Okay, what just happened here?" he asked. "Did I do something wrong? Did I squeeze you too tightly?"

"No . . . uh . . . I just got some stuff on my mind." She rubbed her arms. "I'm sorry, I shouldn't have teased you."

They were caught up in the moment when Chloe yelled, "Ahh'n, ahh'n, mothafucka, you can't come up in here!" She paused and then said, "Farah, lock your door! Randy is in the house acting crazy!" Upon hearing his name, Farah rushed toward her door at top speed. Randy was just about to twist her doorknob, when she slammed it shut, leaned up against it, and activated the lock.

Slade quickly got dressed, and was about to move her out of the way to deal with Randy man to bitch when she whispered, "Please . . . please don't go out there." She shook her head and tears rolled down her face. "He's gonna kill me . . . and you."

In the lowest voice possible he said, "I don't care about that shit. Look at how scared you are. I can't have this nigga come up in here, and carry shit like that."

"Please . . . I'm begging you."

As she looked into his eyes, Randy continually kicked the door. Her body would move forward with each thump, and it was obvious that his mission was to break it down. "Come out here and talk to me, Farah! I gotta know why you been lying to me!" he yelled. "You fucked with the wrong nigga. You might as well kill yourself. You better not have no nigga in there."

"Let me go out there," Slade whispered. "This nigga's a fucking punk. I can handle him, Farah. Trust me."

"Please, don't," she sobbed. "Don't go out there. I'm falling in love with you, and I don't want you hurt." Slade bit down on his bottom lip, and tried to hold it together. Hiding from a human being was not his thing.

Randy continued to kick and bang on the door, when they heard Shadow say, "Nigga, what the fuck you doing in my crib?" The last thing she wanted was Shadow and Randy to go at it. He was in jail most of the time Farah was with him, but he still heard the stories.

"Shadow, I ain't got no beef with you," Randy said. "This shit is between me and your sister."

"If you think beefing with my sister means you don't got a problem with me, you don't know shit about me," Shadow said calmly. "She ain't trying to be with you no more. Just leave it at that. Cool?"

Farah listened intently for Randy's response. "You tell your sister to remember what I said earlier."

"I ain't telling her a mothafuckin' thing."

Randy laughed, as she heard his footsteps walk away.

Focusing back on Slade she said, "I'm sorry about that. I don't know why he doesn't just leave me alone."

"You must be leading him on," he said, taking his frustration out on her for not being able to push off on Randy. "Why else would he come over here like that?"

"Slade, it's a long story. Just keep it light, baby."

"Stop saying that shit to me! I hate it!"

"I'm sorry." She swallowed. "I won't ever say it again. Can't we just start all over?"

"We'll rewind when you keep shit straight with me." He moved her out of the way of the door. "Until then, I'm out."

# Chapter 56

**"There's gonna come a time
when you have to choose a side.
Be sure to choose right." —Slade**

The weather was nicer than it had been all winter, as the Baker Boys put traffic on a momentary pause. Every female in view, and a few men too, couldn't believe their eyes. In the dead of winter, four men jogged down the street shirtless, and in jeans. Although it was cold outside, sweat poured off of their bodies as they performed their daily routine. This workout was particularly important, because Slade needed to get Farah off of his mind. She invaded his thoughts, and forced him to forget about what was important . . . bringing his family back together.

When Major seemed to be slowing down, Slade turned around and yelled, "Major, push it! Go harder, faster, and longer!"

When he seemed to be disconnected, Slade slowed down his pace, so he could jog by his side.

"I miss him too, Major. We all do. That's why we gotta stay strong and keep shit together." Major avoided eye contact. "Do it for Knox." He placed his hand on his shoulder, and Major looked at him. "Now push!"

With the mention of their brother's name, all four brothers ran faster. They already jogged four miles, and only had one more to go. "Move!" Slade yelled as he pointed forward. "We almost there!"

They were so motivated that in the last few minutes they were able to beat their record. When they finally made it back to Markee's apartment, they sat wherever they could to catch their breath. Markee was in the living room watching TV, but cut it off when Slade walked inside and into the kitchen.

"What, man?" Slade threw each of his brothers a water bottle from the fridge before twisting off the cap on his own. "Did my brother call or something?"

The brothers walked in the kitchen and waited for Markee's response. "No, not yet."

"So what the fuck is up?" Major asked, breathing heavily. "Why you looking all crazy and shit?"

"Randy wants to meet with y'all tonight. He has a job he says can't wait."

Slade wasn't feeling the shit one bit. After the situation at Farah's apartment, he hated him even more. But to prevent Randy from killing his cousin, he reluctantly agreed. "What he want us to do?"

"He says he's meeting with someone he don't trust. It's the first of the month, so he got his other men out on the streets making collections. He says he needs y'all, and he's not taking no for an answer."

"How this mothafucka know we won't put the gun to his head and pull the trigger ourselves?" Killa laughed.

"Yeah. He bet' not give me no gun," Audio added, rubbing his hands together and grinning slyly. "Because I'm liable to do that shit too."

"You not going," Slade said. "I need you here safe. I ain't got time to be worrying about where you are."

Audio looked confused. "But I wanna help my brothers out." He looked at all of them. "Y'all can't keep treating me like I'm some bitch . . . I'm tired of this shit."

"Audio, shut the fuck up," Slade barked, still breathing heavily from his workout. "I said you staying here and that's the end of it."

"Actually Randy wants all four of y'all," Markee said. "He said it specifically." He paused. "Sorry, Slade, but it's all or nothing."

Audio smiled until Slade gave him a stare that knocked the grin off of his face, like a jab to his jaw. "Where does this nigga live?" Slade asked.

"Huh?"

"I ain't stutter, mothafucka!" Slade yelled. "I said where does he live? If you in contact with him like you are, I know you up on where he rests his head."

"In Maryland."

"You know where exactly?" Major asked.

Markee seemed uncomfortable. "Yeah, I know . . . but why?"

"What difference does it make, nigga?" Killa ranted. "You act like we not family. If we ask you where he stay and you know, then you best be telling us."

"I know y'all family but I'm just asking because—"

"Because what?" Slade interrupted.

"I'm only asking because y'all seem upset." They looked like they were five seconds from deboing his ass to the floor. "Randy ain't the kind of nigga you can step to like that. I know y'all used to that kind of shit in Mississippi, but out here things run differently."

"There's gonna come a time when you have to choose a side." Slade said. "Be sure to choose right."

The parking lot was dark and desolate as Randy waited for a man he hadn't seen in five months. The silver six-passenger Ford van Randy rode in was so quiet on the inside that you could hear butt cheeks clap together. "I think that's him right there," Randy said from the passenger seat. Major was driving and the others were in the back. "When we get out don't say shit to him. Thinking ain't your job, country niggas." He turned around to look at all of them. "Looking pretty and protecting me is."

He was reckless with the mouth and Slade was getting tired of it.

"Who is he?" Slade asked. "The nigga you meeting."

Randy looked back at him as if he had no business questioning him. "My pops."

Slade looked at his brothers and said, "All this for your father?"

Randy smirked. "If you knew him, you wouldn't say that shit."

Willie Gregory, Randy's father, was very cunning and conniving. In fact, Randy learned every hateful and deceitful characteristic he possessed from him. Although it was true that they shared the same bloodline, the two couldn't stand each other. There was so much hate between them that when they were in each other's company, people assumed they were enemies instead of father and son.

Randy always wanted love from his father, and when he was younger he'd do everything in his power to get it. From wearing his crocodile shoes to taking his father's side when his mother was angry with him, he went over and beyond to prove he wanted his acceptance. And after all this time, despite many tries, nothing seemed to work. Randy didn't realize that there was nothing he could do to win him over until later. Willie hated everything about him, including the dead woman whose pussy he slid out of.

Although the love wasn't there, Randy did a great job of fashioning himself in his likeness. So much so that Willie could never trust him. Willie was sure that the moment Randy had a chance, he would stab him in the back, and he was correct. Willie had worked for years to build his DC-based drug operation from the ground up. When he was arrested for a drug-related offense, he reluctantly turned over power to Randy. Five years later, when he was released from prison, he fully expected to regain his position in the business, but Randy thought otherwise. Randy traded the need for affection for the desire of power, by giving Willie a small piece of real estate before overthrowing him completely. He remembered when Willie told him he could be nothing but an errand boy. So this meeting was just to confirm that he was in power, and would never give it up.

When the black Lincoln Town Car pulled closer, Randy looked at the Baker Boys. He wasn't sure if he could trust them if something popped off, but for now he didn't have a choice. But since they were muscular and tall, he felt he could use them for intimidation purposes, if nothing else. "Remember what I said," Randy advised, pointing at them. "Don't say shit unless I ask you to open your mouths. The only thing you need to be saying is yes, and that's when I address you."

*I should kill this mothafucka right now,* Killa thought, placing his hand on his heat.

Slade placed his large hand over his and said, "Not right now."

With the situation under control, the Baker Boys filed out of the van, and Audio walked around to the passenger side to open Randy's door. When Randy stepped out, he adjusted his black leather coat and dark shades. Whether it be day or night, Randy never stepped anywhere without them. Some said it was to conceal the hate in his eyes.

A few seconds later, one of Willie's men opened his car door. Willie floated out of his seat as smoothly as a '70s pimp, and approached his only child. Three men covered Willie and at first Slade thought he was losing his mind. He was so sure that he blinked several times, just to be sure his eyes weren't playing tricks on him. When he looked at his brothers and he saw their eyes were wide open too, he knew what he saw was confirmed. Standing behind Willie, holding a shotgun, was their brother Knox. They were about to rush to him when he shook his head, and placed a finger over his lips. Using his eyes, he begged them not to approach. And it took everything in Slade's power to honor his request.

# Chapter 57

**"If you think I had anything to do what that shit, call the police." —Farah**

Farah pressed her warm body against Slade's, and ran her foot lovingly down the side of his leg. She couldn't bear to be near him without feeling him in some kind of way. Every part of her body craved him like water to a dry garden. Although the drama in her apartment, and her late-night missions to sooth the urge of violence, prevented them from making love, the bond they were building would last a lifetime. She wasn't interested in having sex right now anyway, not wanting to turn him off because of her inexperience in the bedroom.

Pulling the covers over their bodies, she rolled on top of him, and looked into his eyes. After everything Randy attempted to do to thwart Farah's actions to go on with the rest of her life, she was still able to get through to Slade. The night Randy came over and threatened her life, she spent an hour outside of Markee's door, on her knees, trying to get him to let her in. It took some time, but eventually her plan worked.

"Slade, when you gonna let me in on a little bit of your life? I told you a lot about me," she embellished, "but I don't know a whole lot about you."

"Yes, you do. You know what I like to eat, drink, and what ticks me off, and makes me want to kill."

"I'm serious. I don't know where you're from and things like that."

"Farah, I got a lot of things going on right now. I'll start letting you in my life when I clear some things up with my family, *and* you start letting me in on yours." He pulled her closer and kissed her lips.

"So you going tit for tat now?"

"I don't even know what the fuck that means," he lied.

"Seriously, Slade." She rolled off of him, eased out of the bed, and walked across the room wearing a pearl-colored short camise. Slade's dick rose immediately. "I can tell something's bothering you."

"What you talking about?"

"Whenever you're with me, you seem to be somewhere else mentally. It makes me feel like you gonna leave me at anytime. And I been abandoned a lot as a kid. I don't want to be alone anymore." She walked to a table, which held snacks and her coffee machine. Then she opened the refrigerator and grabbed a bottle of water, and poured it into the pot. Farah made every movement seductive to keep his attention.

"What you doing with all this food in your room? And the fridge?"

"I can't keep my food out there, they eat it all." She smiled before opening a packet of coffee and slowly pouring it into the pot. The real reason her room looked like a kitchen was because she was afraid of what Lesa might do to get her back. It was obvious that she was playing dirty by telling Randy her business, so she couldn't be trusted. Mia and the rest just went for the "I wish the bitch would" method. It didn't matter that most of her things were in storage, Lesa would find all kinds of reasons to enter the premises, and when she was refused, she'd threaten to call the police. Farah had plans to deal with her on a deadly note the moment she could make her move, but now was not the time.

When she tripped over one of Rhonda's baby shower baskets, she put both of them by the window.

"You want something to drink?"

He raised his hand like he was waiting for a football and said, "Yeah."

She threw it, and when he caught it she said, "Don't try to skip the subject, Slade. What is going on with you?"

Slade looked into her eyes, and felt he could reveal more to her than he could to any other person unrelated to him. Twisting the cap off of the water bottle, he took a sip, swallowed, and said, "I been looking for my brother, for months. We finally found him the other night, but for whatever reason, he couldn't talk to us."

"Why not?" The smell of fresh coffee filled the room. "Is he mad at you or something?"

"Naw . . . it's deeper than that. For real I'm not sure what's going on with him. When I saw him, he acted like he couldn't speak to me." He placed the bottle on the dresser next to the bed. "Now I gotta talk to my mother, and I know she gonna be fucked up with me. The only reason I'm in DC is to find him. I don't know what I'm gonna say to her. I never loved a woman stronger than I love my mother, and I hate seeing her hurt."

Farah didn't like knowing that another person was out there holding an extra key to his heart. "Just tell her the truth." She shrugged. "That's what my grandmother always says anyway." She opened a pack of white coffee cups and set it on top of the fridge. "What's the worst that can happen?"

"If I tell my mother I had my eyes on my brother and let him get away, she'd probably beat my ass. If there's one person you don't try to get over on, Della Baker is it."

Farah laughed and said, "Wait, your mother still whipping your ass?" She focused back on the brewing coffee. "All that man over there on my bed? I'd pay a ticket to see that shit."

He grinned. "I'm being straight up. My mother not gonna understand how I let him go. And truthfully I don't understand either."

Farah poured a cup of coffee, walked back to the bed, and climbed under the sheets without spilling anything. "I'm sure he gonna get back in contact with you." She took a few sips, and the bitter taste caused her to squint. "He got your number, right?"

"Yeah. But I don't have access to that number when I'm out. If I'm not at Markee's, one of my brothers gotta be there so we can catch his call." He grabbed the bottle and sipped some more before setting it back down. "He got a cell phone, but he can't use it for a lot of reasons. So he mostly uses pay phones and shit like that. That's why I wanted to talk to him, to at least give him my new cell number. I think I fucked up."

She set her coffee down on the table and rubbed his shoulder. "Things gonna work out." She smiled, hoping he'd believe her, even though she didn't know his situation. She didn't want his attention anywhere but on her. This thing with his brother was pushing them apart and she needed that to stop. "But when you with me, we have to enjoy our time together. I'm sure your brother would want you to be happy. I mean, that's how I feel about my sisters and brother anyway."

Slade felt her comment was a tad bit on the selfish side, but he understood her point of view.

"Why were you with that nigga? It's obvious you're scared of him."

She shrugged, and picked her cup up from the table. Slade could smell the scent of her morning breath mixed with the sweet, pungent odor of black coffee, but he was feeling her so he didn't care. "Randy is different. I was never really feeling him, but when I was a kid, he always took care of me." She laughed to herself when she recollected a thought. "I remember when these girls were about to jump me, I hid in his car to get away from them. He took me in his house, fed me, and his mother told me I was gonna be his wife. I was a kid back then." Slade frowned. "But I kind of believed her."

She put the cup down, slid off the bed, got on her knees, and pulled out a brown box. Then she rustled through old and new journals before pulling out a black leather book. She sat on the edge of the bed, dusted off the cover, and looked at him. "This is what I wrote, when I was a kid." She turned to the appropriate page:

Farah was on the roof baking in the sun. She was so excited when she saw her skin turning the color of her mother's. When it got late, she went home and all her family could talk about was how beautiful her chocolate skin was. Later, she went outside to play with the prettiest girl in her school, who was also her best friend, Coconut Elway. Coconut talked about her boyfriend and Farah talked about hers. She said his name was Sam, and his skin was dark as her mother's, and that he was as handsome as her father. The coolest thing about Sam was that he was as strong as Superman.

Slade's jaw dropped. He couldn't believe she wanted to look different, because she was stunning. And then there was the Superman thing, which really tripped him out. He didn't know anybody stronger than him, and definitely not Randy's butter-soft ass . . . and that made him smile. For so long he hated his condition, and now he was in the company of a woman who appreciated the thing he loathed most about himself. It was almost too weird to be true. "You don't have that shit in there for real. Do you?"

She slowly handed him the book and said, "Look."

Slade sat up in the bed and leaned against the headboard. Then he examined the words she just read, and looked over at her. "That's some crazy shit."

"You think I'm weird?"

"Fuck no! You willed this shit into existence. My only question is, who the fuck is Sam?"

She punched him on the arm. "Shut up, boy!"

Slade looked at it again and said, "I never saw nothing like this in my life. It's kind of fucking my head up a little." When he glanced at the page again, he saw another entry:

And then somebody killed and raped Farah and everybody in the family felt guilty because they didn't come see her!

"What's this about?" He pointed. "Why you write this?"

She looked at the passage and was embarrassed at what he saw. Farah snatched the book and tucked it back under the bed. "Please don't read my shit without asking. I don't like that," she said as a little bit of crazy eased out.

He raised his hands and said, "I'm sorry, babes. It wasn't like that." He sipped his water again to allow the awkward moment to pass, and to quench his thirst. "So did you think Sam was Randy at first?"

"I wanted him to be. I thought he was, but he isn't."

He rubbed her leg, and goose bumps floated on her skin.

"He's obsessed with you. How come?"

"Because I'm light skinned." She smiled. "He's into red bones and I fit the bill." She kissed him. "I had this conversation with my friend Rhonda and my sisters the other day. They don't believe that most niggas prefer lighter females."

Slade shrugged, because it didn't make him a difference either which way. "Yeah . . . some dudes be on that shit."

"Tell the truth, you liked me because I'm red too, right?"

"Ma, you red and it looks good on you, but I'd love you if you were as white as Demi Moore, or as black as my dick."

Farah didn't like his response. All her life she was made to feel unworthy because she wasn't like the rest of her family. It took a long time to embrace the trait that made her different, but she took it to an unhealthy level. She constantly searched the media for reaffirmations that she was better than the darker girls of her race. Violence and feeling superior was how she survived. What Farah really needed was psychological help, but she didn't know it. "You said love? Is that how you feel about me?"

"I meant . . . like." He swallowed. "Anyway . . . I don't believe in that light skin versus dark skin shit. It's all a part of the Willie Lynch syndrome."

"What's the Willie Lynch syndrome?"

He pulled her toward him, and she placed her head on his chest. "Back in the day, down South, Willie Lynch, a British slave owner in the West Indies, delivered a message to other slave owners in Virginia. He coined the term 'lynching,' after his last name."

"What was the message about?"

"Basically he said his method, which included pitting black people against each other, would last for at least three hundred years, and he was right. He took differences in the slaves, and made them bigger than they were. He said at the top of his list was age, but that it was only because age started with the letter A. He said the second difference he blew up was color."

"I don't understand."

"He suggested they pit the old against the young, the dark-skinned slaves versus the light-skinned slaves. Female against male and male against female. It was done with the intentions of making the slaves depend solely on their masters, and it worked. Years later we free, and people still buy into that shit to this day. It's dumb. He got into some other shit too, you got to read it to understand it though."

That was the first time Farah heard of Willie Lynch, and it resonated with her, so she knew it was true. She stopped rubbing his chest, and looked at her light hand on his dark skin. The combination was beautiful, but did it make her better? Farah was confused because her mother made her feel like shit for most of her life. Didn't she know about this syndrome too? And what about her grandmother, who acted older than Harriet Tubman.

Deciding to skip the subject she said, "So when you find your brother, then what happens?" She sat up in the bed, leaned against the headboard, and grabbed her coffee. "Are you gonna stay with Markee? Because I don't think he has enough room over there." She took a few sips, trying to gain the courage to ask him to live with her.

"When I find him, I gotta go back home."

She looked up at him. "Go home? Why?"

"You know we don't live here." He rubbed her leg but she moved it away.

"But . . . I thought . . ."

"What you thought?"

"I mean, you been here so long that I thought you were staying."

"Naw." Slade laughed. "I can't stand these DC niggas out here. Plus I'm not getting paper. I gotta be where I know how to survive. If I wanted to take you out, I couldn't even do that shit right now. How you think that makes a nigga feel?"

"I know somebody you can get money from. What if we rob my boyfriend Randy?"

Although he appreciated her go-hardness, it also showed another characteristic he wasn't sure he liked. "I wouldn't get you involved in no shit like that."

"Trust me, I'm involved in more shit than you know."

"Not sure what that means, but I do know this . . . if I step to him the way I want, he'd be dead." He looked into her eyes. "I gotta go home and work on getting shit in order. A lot of people are depending on me."

Farah was so angry that he was leaving that she bypassed everything he said of importance and picked up on the shit she wanted to fight about. "Oh, so you don't like DC niggas, but you wanna fuck their bitches?"

He frowned. "First off I didn't fuck you. Second of all, what the fuck are you talking about?"

"I mean, it's all good to fuck me, but I'm not good enough to stay with." She was growing angrier, and the blood rushing to her skin caused her to look flushed. "Is that how you move?"

"What you want me to do? Abandon my family in Mississippi?"

It was the first time she heard where he came from. "Well . . . what about me?" She touched his arm. "I need you too."

This shit was blowing Slade. "Let's take it one step at a time. We might find out we don't even like each other like that."

She sat on the edge of the bed and placed her feet flat on the floor. "You played me." She stood up, grabbed her baby blue robe off the chair, and put it on, pulling the belt tightly around her waist. "I should've known something was up with you."

He laughed. "Fuck you mean, something is up with me?"

"You probably gay, like my sister Mia said." She giggled. "I'm glad I'm finding out now." Rejection was eating her up, and reminded her of when she was a sickly girl, confined to bed with no friends. She walked over to the dresser, grabbed her brush, and tamed her wild hair. Slade eased out of bed, and dawdled in her direction. She looked at the reflection of his muscular body in the mirror, and she caught a glimpse of the aggravation on his face. If this man walked out on her she would be fucked up in the head and she knew it.

"I'm gonna ask you to take that back. But if you don't, I'm not fucking with you no more." He rubbed her shoulders unknowingly a little too hard, and she was in pain. She was too afraid to tell him to ease up, fearing he might not care. "Now I know you're mad, and that's why you just said some shit you didn't mean. I get that. From reading your journal, I can tell you never had a man like me in your life, who really cares about you. You're scared but you don't have to be. But I'm a man, Farah. Straight up, with no chaser, and you not gonna talk to me like that." He paused. "So what you gonna do?"

She knew she had to apologize. Not only was she dead wrong, but everything he just said was right. She had taken things to another level by disrespecting his manhood, and she was out of order. But the other part of Farah, the side that was too afraid to show emotion, didn't like having her card pulled by a man who invaded her thoughts. Who was he to bring up her journal, and use it against her, to display her innermost fears?

"Are you gonna take back what you said to me, Farah? Or do you want me to walk out of your life forever?"

Farah looked in the mirror at him and said, "Maybe you should go find your little boyfriend in Mississippi. Since it's obvious you like dudes anyway."

Slade removed his hands, threw on his clothes, and walked toward her again. As she looked into the mirror, he crashed his fist into their reflection, shattering it into a million pieces, before leaving the room. The moment she heard the apartment door slam, she flopped on the bed, looked at the broken mirror, and sobbed uncontrollably. When she heard someone moving around in the living room, she wiped the tears off of her face, pulled her robe tighter, and walked toward the sound.

Vivian James was standing in her apartment with a distraught look over her face. Farah rolled her eyes and walked up to her. She wiped her face and said, "What are you doing in my house? I paid you the rent for this month already."

"Yes, you did, but I'm here to discuss another clause of the lease."

"You better stop harassing me," she said. "Because I don't like being threatened, nor am I in the mood."

"I've heard, Farah Cotton. But trust me, I'm a long way from threatening you." She threw her a serious stare. "The lease says that a tenant is not to permit, or suffer, any act or omission constituting a nuisance to other residences." She recited the lease as if it were the United States Constitution. "Including, without limitation to, excessive noise, excessive traffic into and out of the premises, like the man who just stormed out of here and broke the door in the process." She pointed at the knob which was hanging on loosely. "It also states that violence, or threats of violence, are not permitted." She stepped closer.

Farah rolled her neck and said, "What does that have to do with me?"

"Oh, I think you know, Farah Cotton. This letter was slid underneath my door last night." She raised a folded pink piece of stationary with green flowers, which Farah knew belonged to Lesa. "And although it was anonymous, I believe everything it says."

Farah walked away, took a seat on the recliner, and Vivian followed. "Vivian, I don't know what you think I'm involved in, but you have the wrong person."

"I think otherwise." She fanned the letter. "This letter says that the sixteen people who died in this building over the course of a month may all be attributed to you." Tears streamed down her face. "That count includes my son." She wiped her face with the palm of her hand.

Farah rose and said, "I didn't kill that man in the hallway!" Chloe told her the whole story, about how Slade punished him with his bare hands, resulting in his death.

"So what about the other fifteen? You had a hand in that?"

She was caught. "Look, Vivian, you can believe what you want. If you think I had anything to do with that shit, call the police. Otherwise, you can get the fuck out of here, and leave me alone!"

# Chapter 58

**"Do what you gotta do." —Slade**

Markee's house was peaceful as Slade sat on the couch with Shannon, the first woman who properly welcomed him to DC. It was Slade's turn to wait for Knox's call, and since he was beefing with Farah, he didn't mind it one bit. Their fight fucked his head up, and he had all intentions of staying true to his word, and cutting her off for good. It wasn't like they fucked, so why was he tripping anyway? After she popped off at the mouth, he knew she couldn't be the woman in his life. He'd be liable to kill her.

"What's on your mind?" Shannon said as she leaned on him, while they sat on the sofa and watched TV. Since his "no touch" vow was broken, courtesy of Farah, he rubbed her arm. It wasn't as loving as when he touched Farah; instead, it was as if he were trying to start a fire with two pieces of wood. "It don't seem like I have your undivided attention. And after all the things I did to you earlier"—she grinned, groping his dick through his jeans—"I think I at least deserve a smile."

He stopped rubbing her and said, "How come you always bring up what you do for me?" He looked down at her cute face. "I hate that shit. If we gonna do what we do, that's got to stop. Just keep it light, okay?"

When she heard the phrase Farah used at Mamma's Kitchen, she was enraged. For him to quote the phrase so easily meant they spent a lot of time together. "Is it because of Farah?" She looked into his eyes. "Because from what I hear, she's two kinds of crazy."

"I didn't know you knew her."

"I do. We not friends or nothing like that, though. Somebody who knows both of us reached out to me through my friend Coconut. They used to be cool too, but Coco don't fuck with her no more either. Everybody cutting that bitch off." She giggled to herself. "Anyway, they said Farah thinks she's a vampire, or some shit like that." She put her head on his chest, and she could feel that he was as stiff as a board. She sat back up and said, "If I were you, I'd stay away from her, but that's just me."

Slade shook his head. He couldn't stand catty-ass females. "What the fuck you talking about? How the fuck does she think she's a vampire?"

"They say she have something called porphyria." Shannon leaned in, relishing in the opportunity to bash red-bone Farah. "I looked it up when I was in my house, to see what I could find on the Internet.

She can't stand chemicals, perfumes and things like that, so if she's around it she'll run. It said she can break out into hives, get sick, and all other kind of shit like that. She was real sick in school too, when we were younger, but I didn't know what it was about. Apparently it's a blood-deficiency illness, and she's playing it up as something else, probably to get attention from you."

"How could she? She never told me nothing like that."

"I don't know why she thinks she's a vampire then. Anyway, everything I found on the Internet said people don't crave blood, they crave violence. So it ain't like she needs blood for real, she just thinks she does." She looked up at him. "I know you like her, Slade, but you should really be careful. I'm just saying." She rubbed his chest.

He knocked her hand away. "Who told you some dumbass shit like that?"

She backed away a little. "I can't tell you."

"Well, when you can give me facts, we can talk. Until then, worry about what we got going on right here before it's over." He looked back at the TV.

"I didn't mean to make you mad, I'm just worried about you, Slade. That's all."

He knew how much she liked him, but they could never be anything more than "good time" friends. His reason had more to do with their first connection than it did with anything else. A girl that loose in the pussy he couldn't take seriously, plus he wasn't gonna be in DC long anyway. What she said about Farah being a vampire had him vexed, because he couldn't imagine anything like that being halfway true. He was still crawling around in his head when Shannon said, "Still mad?"

"Naw."

"Can I do something to put a smile on your face?" She dropped to her knees, and crawled between his legs. "It won't take me no time to make shit right."

He grinned. "Do what you gotta do."

# Chapter 59

**"Let's go, Rhonda! Now!" —Farah**

Farah was on her second green apple martini. The red dress she wore hugged her curves, and she was pulled seven different times by various men. Rhonda was just as sexy in the tight-fitting jeans she chose to wear, and stylish leather jacket to cover her large belly. From the back that ass was fat, so she was also pulling them left and right. "You hear about Gary from around the way?" Rhonda asked. Farah remained silent. "Anyway, they said they found him in an alley, with the vein on his dick slit. He's been there for weeks, and they just found him today. That's some crazy-ass shit, right?"

She knew who he was, and most importantly what happened, so she wasn't going to say anything either which way. "Don't know him and don't care."

"Anyway, I didn't know this spot was gonna be this live," Rhonda said. "I would've worn some other shit. I ain't been in a club in eight months!"

"Girl, please," she said, looking at her outfit, "you killing them and you pregnant."

Rhonda didn't want to go out, but her shower was tomorrow, so tonight she was at Farah's beck and call. "You right, these bitches in here a mess, and half of them showing all they ass. It's too cold outside for all of that."

"Right, it ain't a bitch in here who can fuck with us." Farah placed her empty glass on the bar and scanned the club. She was worried Randy wasn't where she thought he should be. "I know I gotta find another sponsor, since I'm beefing with Slade, and Randy wants to kill me."

"Slade wasn't sponsoring shit anyway," Rhonda clarified. "I hear he running around with Shannon. I don't know what he looks like, but people keep saying he's fine as shit!"

Her heart dropped. "Shannon? For real?"

"Yep. So don't worry about him. If anything he need to be sucking the juice out of your dirty panties." She looked around and spotted a cute chocolate brother, who was staring in her direction. "Now Randy is another question. You should not have even been dealing with him. You know that dude is sick in the head."

"He sick but rich." Farah motioned for the waiter to get her another of the same. "And losing him fucked up my game play. I swear I feel like going off on Lesa and them for jumping in my business. Every time I try to put her out, she bitch up, and threaten to call the police. I got something planned for her, though."

Rhonda danced a little in place. "I can't believe you even came out tonight. I figured I'd have to celebrate me getting a new house in Maryland with somebody else."

Farah looked at her and rolled her eyes. "You talking about Coconut and the rest of them dry-ass bitches ain't you?" She laughed. "You did the right thing by calling me. We both know right now the only people Coconut cares about is Shannon and herself. Plus since Randy out of town, I had to help you celebrate the move. I don't blame you for leaving! Get out of DC while you still can." She accepted her drink from the bartender.

"Let's put on a show," Rhonda said, grabbing Farah's hand.

Farah and Rhonda did the "Calling All Dicks" dance, by rotating their hips and rubbing on each other like a couple of Rick James freaks. They were acting loose and ready to fuck, as they ground against one another like it was going out of style. It was foolery at its finest, and in no way appealing. When Farah tried to wiggle her ass in front of Rhonda, she told her to stop for many reasons. First, her belly was in the way, and secondly, Farah couldn't move her body to save her life. Her fuck game was off, and it was being exposed on the dance floor.

"You stand over there against the bar, and I'll dance." Rhonda laughed.

It was fine with Farah, because she loved being a spectator anyway. Leaning on the bar, sipping her drink, she watched Rhonda work the floor as if she were a stripper on a pole. How could she be so sexy, and pregnant at the same time? When a few men waved, trying to get Farah's attention, she blushed and enjoyed the moment. The liquor had Farah feeling seductive and beautiful. They were having a good time, until four guys strolled into the club looking like new money. They were wearing expensive jeans, and designer shirts, and they resembled movie stars. When she saw who was leading the quartet, she wanted to rush up to him and beg him back. Wearing a brown button-down shirt, blue jeans, and a pair of Louis Vuitton shoes, she knew her man when she saw him. Now she felt foolish for speaking to him in a foul way. It was time to apologize, until she saw who was on his arm.

"Rhonda, come over here," she said, pulling her off the floor.

"Stop, I'm feeling good." She snatched her hand away.

"You gonna fuck around and have that baby early. Now get over here, and look over there." She pointed at him. "That's Slade."

"You lying! That nigga so fucking sexy!"

Farah couldn't move her mouth to respond. Sure she disrespected him, but as far as she was concerned, he should be home waiting for her call. She took for granted that he was trying to find his brother, and never imagined him being in the club with someone else. Slade didn't see her as he bent down and whispered into Shannon's ear. But Shannon spotted Farah. She grinned and planted a kiss directly on his lips.

"Shannon going hard now," Rhonda said, shaking her head. "See girl, you should go on 'head and leave him alone. Any nigga that fine gonna be trouble anyway." Farah felt tears forming, but she refused to let him see her cry. If they wanted to be together, they could go stuff shit in each other's asses for all she gave a fuck.

Farah was just about to suggest they leave the club when Juice walked up to her, and blocked her view of Slade. "Farrah Fawcett," he said, smiling. He was so sexy that for a second she forgot all about the man she loved. "You got away from me last time, but I'm not gonna let that happen again." Farah looked to her left and saw Rhonda was already keeping time with his friend, DeWayne. "What you sipping on?"

Afraid Randy sent him she said, "Are you here because of Randy?"

Juice frowned. "After what that nigga did back at the shop," he said, "I don't say more to that nigga than I have to. So stop asking if I'm coming for him when I pull up on you. I represent myself." He smiled. "Now . . . what you drinking?"

She grinned, loving his style. If she was going to use somebody to make Slade jealous, Juice was the perfect candidate. "An apple martini."

He ordered her another, along with a double shot of Patrón for himself. "So what's up? You gonna make me go through hell to get your number this time? I'm sick of seeing you only when you're around that dude."

"You gonna use it?" Farah looked around him to see if Slade was watching . . . he wasn't. Instead he pulled Shannon into his body and kicked it with his brothers, who also had dates, and she was devastated. She wondered if he was trying to make her jealous. *Who brings bitches to the club? They ain't nothing but some country-ass niggas.*

"Listen, I been trying to get at you for a minute." Juice interrupted her thoughts. "If I get your number, I'm damn sure gonna use it." He handed her his phone. "So put it in there."

When she finished programming her digits, she saw Slade and his crew walking to the bar. Focusing on Juice she started laughing in his face for no reason, as if he were Kevin Hart. She was trying her best to appear enthralled by Juice's presence, so that she wouldn't have to suffer the agony of Slade being with another woman. Once at the bar, Slade put his hand on the small of Shannon's back and said, "What you want?"

"An apple martini," she said, looking at Farah's drink.

Slade followed her eye contact and saw Farah for the first time, "What's up, Farah?" Then he nodded at Juice as if they were homies. And like he didn't care, he focused back on Shannon, and didn't speak to her anymore.

"You coming to my shower, right?" Rhonda asked Shannon.

She looked at Farah and grinned slyly. "I'm still invited?"

Rhonda looked at Farah and said, "Girl, she don't care nothing about what you do." Rhonda looked at Slade and back at her. She was being greedy as shit for baby gifts. She knew Farah didn't want that bitch anywhere near her house. "Farah got her own business over there."

Farah knew if she opened her mouth, her words would be broken so she nodded. "Well . . . I guess I'll see you there." When their drinks came, they walked away and Slade never looked back.


Farah knew Juice wanted to fuck, because he suggested they leave early, when all she wanted to do was cry. As he maneuvered down the streets of DC, the vision of Slade acting like she wasn't in the building trapped her mind. She mentally bashed herself with the realization that had she taken back her comment, he would be in her room, and in her bed.

Rhonda was laughing it up in the back seat with Juice's friend, who happened to have a fetish for pregnant pussy. "Y'all wanna grab something to eat?" Juice asked, placing his hand on her knee. His eyes alternated from her to the road. "Farrah Fawcett . . . you heard me?"

She looked at him and with an attitude said, "Please stop calling me that shit! I already told you that's not my name!"

Juice's friend and Rhonda wondered what caused her to be so snappy all of a sudden. Fifteen minutes ago you would've thought Juice was on stage at the Apollo, the way she was laughing it up in his face. "My bad. I won't call you that shit again. So . . . you hungry?" Juice asked, removing his hand to focus on the road.

"Yeah. I guess." She shrugged.

"What you in the mood for?"

When Farah faced him, from the driver's side window she saw somebody jump out of the passenger seat of another car, and aim a gun in their direction. The bullet shattered the glass and hit Juice in the neck.

Rhonda screamed to the top of her lungs, and bent over to protect her belly. "Don't hurt my baby! Don't hurt my baby!"

"Oh, my God!" Farah screamed.

Juice's man grabbed his weapon from his waist, rolled his window down, and started busting at the shooter. Gunfire flew from every direction, and she had no doubt that she was going to get hit. Juice, barely alive, pressed his hand on his neck as blood oozed through his fingers. He pressed the gas, and did his best to drive wildly away from the scene. When his eyes closed, and his hands dropped, the truck rolled into an active construction site a few feet ahead. Some of the workers tried to move out of the way but unfortunately one of them didn't make it. Pinned underneath Juice's truck Farah could hear the man beg for his life.

Thinking the shooter was coming back to finish her off, Farah hopped out of the truck and opened Rhonda's car door. She was in the backseat, stuck and motionless. Bloodstains were splattered on her face, and her eyes were wild and bugged out. Randy wasn't playing, and she knew it was just a matter of time before he finished what he started.

"Let's go, Rhonda! Now!"

# Chapter 60

**"Tonight you just saved a whole
lot of lives."** —Beverly Glasser

Beverly Glasser walked into the police department with hate gripping her heart. Her coat was
open, revealing her light blue housekeeping uniform, with a gold name badge that protruded from
her right breast as if it were being seen in 3D. She
had a gun in her brown leather purse, and was
fully prepared to shoot at least twenty cops in the
name of love. She was devastated that her only son,
Amico, had not been found, and that the police department seemed uninterested with her case. She
slogged up to the white officer behind the counter.

"Good evening, ma'am, how may I help you?"
He smiled.

Beverly was trembling so hard she could barely
speak. Sweat poured off her forehead and into her
eyes, making it difficult to see. She never committed
the smallest crime, yet she was fully prepared to
commit the ultimate offense known to man. She

wiped the sweat from her face, reached into her purse, and placed her hand on her weapon.

"Ma'am . . . are you okay?" the officer asked sincerely. He came from around the counter, and it was apparent that he was one of the good guys. Unfortunately for him, the uniform he wore put him on the wrong side. "You don't look so well. Do you need a doctor or something?"

She was just about to shoot him when Nadia Gibson approached the two. "Mrs. Glasser?"

Beverly turned around with her hand still on the gun inside her purse, and faced the officer. "Yes."

Nadia smiled, but it dissipated when she noticed the way her hand seemed to be stuffed inside her purse with a purpose. "This is so uncanny." She looked at her hand again. "My name is Nadia Gibson, and I was just about to call you." She looked at the officer. "I got it from here, Daniels." He smiled, touched Beverly on the back, and walked away.

When they were alone she said, "You were gonna call me for what?"

"Because I've just been assigned to your case. I'm so sorry to hear about your son, Amico, but you need to know that he's my number one priority. Not to mention, I think I may know who is involved with his disappearance. They gave one name, but I'm pretty sure it's another person." Beverly's hand remained firm inside her bag. "It may be hard to prove at first, but I'm gonna give this everything

I have." She smiled. "The funny thing is, I met the person I believe is responsible some time back." She was being presumptuous and unprofessional, but she didn't care. She was sure Farah was involved, and all she had to do was prove it.

"How? They told me they didn't have any information on his case. I'm not even sure how you knew it was me."

"I came to talk to you at work today, but they said you quit." Beverly's head fell in shame because she'd been at that job for fifteen years. "They also said that you indicated that you would be going away for a long time." She looked at her hand in her purse again. "Your picture was on the wall for outstanding customer service, for every month this year." She smiled. "Your supervisor said he was going to offer you a promotion next month and everything. So I hope you reconsider leaving."

"This whole thing has been killing me. I love my daughter, I truly do, but there's something about a mother's love for her son that just goes deeper."

"I understand, but I think we can solve this case. I interviewed a few people and, I'm sad to say, I almost rented a room from the person I believe is the culprit, in Platinum Loft apartments. If I had taken the room, I might not be talking to you right now. Who knows how crazy this chick is."

Beverly looked her over, and made a quick assessment of her character. She was trying to determine if she could trust her, or if she should pull her weapon and finish what she came to do. After a few seconds, Nadia's eyes told her she had a motive, but she was willing to accept her help even if she did. In her opinion, motivation was the best way to win a war.

Removing her hand from her weapon, and from her purse, she pulled the zipper to close it and smiled. "You're an angel, Nadia Gibson. Because tonight you just saved a whole lot of lives."

# Chapter 61

**"Whenever we talk, I need to make sure it's in person, especially now." —Knox**

Knox was looking at the Platinum Loft apartments from across the street. He'd just stepped out of a cab, but couldn't enter the building right away. Getting out of a Benz was the girl who haunted his dreams for the longest time. Trotting across the street, he made it into the building and into the elevator to be with her before the doors shut. The left side of her body was covered in blood spots, and she appeared distraught. He wondered what held her mind and what she just went through. It took everything in his power not to harm her, but he mastered the art of self-control a long time ago. Everything had to be done in the right time.

"Thanks for holding the elevator for me," Knox said, trying to get a complete look at her face. He knew it was her, he just had a need to be sure. "It's cold as shit out there."

Her eyes remained on her feet when she said, "Huh?" She was still thinking about the murder she just witnessed, knowing full well that the hit was in her name.

"Never mind, you look like you in deep thought right now."

"I am." Farah continued to look at the dirty floor, as if it could explain to her why Randy wanted her dead so bad. The last thing she needed was to hold a conversation with a complete stranger. "Sorry, I'm having a bad day."

When the elevator doors opened, they both stepped off on the same floor. Knox wanted to see her face more than he did his own mother's. Hoping she'd turn around, he didn't knock on Markee's door right away. Instead he watched her slog down the hallway and toward her apartment. When she reached her destination, she placed the key in the door, looked at him, and smiled. "Good night." She waved.

*It's her.*

Knox focused on Markee's door, and pounded heavily. When he opened up, his mouth dropped when he saw who was standing there. "Oh, my God!" Markee said, covering his mouth like the bitch-ass nigga he was. "Are you fucking serious? Do you realize how many mothafuckas are looking for you?"

Knox, remembering why he was so secretive in the first place, checked his surroundings and said, "Are you gonna let me in or what?" He took one last look at Farah's door. "It's too hot to be out here."

Markee backed up and said, "Oh, yeah . . . I'm sorry, man. Come in. It's just that I can't believe you're actually here." Markee closed and locked the door. "You want a beer?" He walked toward the kitchen.

"I don't drink."

"You want something to eat?"

Knox examined Markee's robust body and declined. "Where are my brothers?"

He turned back around to the living room. "They went to a club." He could tell from his attitude that he didn't fuck with him. "I gave them some cash so they could have a nice time." He embellished the fact. The true story was that Randy gave him a little money to give to Slade and his brothers for being on the scene when he met his father. He was also trying to seduce them with cash, so he didn't have to result to violence. Lately he couldn't trust anybody around him, and although he was sure Slade hated his guts, unlike some of his crew, at least he knew where he was coming from. "Since you been gone they ain't been right, Knox. Y'all never been without each other, so they been taking it hard. You want me to call Slade on his cell?"

"No . . . don't use the phone to call him about me." Knox looked at him seriously. "Never use the phone to call a cell phone about me." He sat on the sofa. "Whenever we talk, I need to make sure it's in person, especially now. That's why I'm here." His mind was still on the girl in the elevator. "Do you know everybody on this floor?"

"Most of them. Why?"

"The girl who lives on the far end of the hall. You know her too?"

"The cute red bone? In 1316?"

Knox wasn't impressed. "I guess."

"Yeah . . . Slade fucks with her. Why you ask?"

Knox stood up and said, "What you mean he fucks with her? That bitch been around my brother?"

"Yeah. Why? Is something up?"

"Nah . . . but, look, I gotta go take care of something. I can't stay right now."

"Where you going?" If he left and got lost again in the world, Slade would kill him. So he moved for the phone. "Maybe I should call Slade, man. Just to let him know he needs to come home. And that it's important." He picked up the handset. "That nigga hates my guts, and he'd kill me if I don't say something."

"I said don't worry. I'm gonna be back. Now put down the phone." Markee slowly placed it on the hook. "Don't say nothing to my brothers . . . any of them. I'll talk to them when I get back. If they get back before I do, and I'm not here, tell them to go see The Clapper. I'll probably be with her."

"Wait . . . you talking about the white bitch who be on heroin?"

"If you wanna fuck with me, never disrespect her like that again," he said seriously. "That white bitch you talking about saved my life."

# Chapter 62

**"I'm confessing my sins because I want you to give God my message." —Farah**

Farah was preparing water for a bath when there was a knock at the front door. When she came home, and the apartment was empty, she was excited about having a night to herself. Hoping Slade was stopping by to make up, she looked over herself, stood on her toes, and looked out the peephole. It was the man she met in the elevator, so she thought about her next move, and slowly opened the door. "Farah?" Knox said, standing before her. "Don't think I'm crazy; my cousin just told me your name."

Her throat felt like it was about to close, so she swallowed and said, "What do you want with me?"

"You don't remember me, do you?"

Her jaw flexed. "Should I?"

"Maybe you should or maybe you shouldn't." He grinned, and Farah didn't seem amused. "Let me stop fucking with you. I'm Slade's Brother."

A short, uneasy feeling pierced her stomach. "Really?" Her face appeared to brighten with understanding. "The brother he's been looking for?" Knox nodded. "I heard so much about you, it's like I know you already."

He raised his arms. "You got me. I'm the one and only Knox Baker." He looked her over. "Can I come in?"

"I'm not sure if it's a good idea." If he came in, she didn't know what would happen. She couldn't judge her actions as they changed from moment to moment.

"Aw, come on. We almost family now."

She stepped back and said, "Enter at your own risk."

Knox stepped inside and observed her apartment. "Flyass crib." He looked into her eyes. "You live here alone?"

"No, I have a roommate I can't stand. My sisters and brother live with me too." She closed and locked the door. "They aren't here now though, so we're alone. So you don't have to worry about your privacy."

"Why would I worry?"

"Because your brother made it sound like you're hiding. Anyway, I was running my bath; give me a second to turn the water off. Okay?" He nodded and she walked into her room before coming back a few minutes later. When she got back she asked,

"Can I get you something to drink? Beer? Water?"

"No." He walked into her space and she felt violated.

"So how can I help you?" She stepped back. "I know Slade is happy to have you home. Your mother too."

"He told you why I couldn't connect with them?"

"No." She shook her head. "Slade doesn't say much of anything."

He grinned. "My brothers don't know I'm back yet." He moved in closer, almost as if he had a strong desire to be sexual with her. "In fact, you're the first person I came to see. And if I knew you were here, I would've been here sooner."

"You don't seem too happy to see me now." She stepped away from him again.

"You *really* don't remember me, do you? How many people have you killed? Where you can't even remember my face?" Farah was motionless.

"You're not Slade's brother, are you?"

"Sure, I am, but I'm also the person you hit and left to die under your Benz. Had it not been for Eleanor, I wouldn't be alive today. Then again, you don't give a fuck, do you?"

"You have the wrong person."

"I'm gonna tell my brother who you are," he threatened. "I'm gonna make sure that he never bothers himself with you again." Losing Slade forever made her feel doomed. When he noticed her dismal expression he said, "You love him, don't you?" He laughed, and pointed in her face. "Too bad, because I want you to know how it feels to be alone, and broken. Only to have someone step up to you, and place their dirty hand over your mouth and nose, so you couldn't breathe. You are a killer, and a manipulative one at that, and you're going to stay the fuck away from my brother and the rest of my family." Farah's husky laugh caught him off guard. She went from exhibiting fear to humor in a second flat. "Glad you're not playing games anymore."

He walked up to her, grabbed her jaw and applied extreme pressure. Her mouth flew open and he said, "If I catch you around Slade, I will kill you. If you think I'm a joke—"

The blade entering his stomach, and piercing his liver, halted the rest of his words. When he released her face, she turned the knife clockwise, followed by a quick counterclockwise motion. He tried to squeeze her neck, but she pushed it in deeper before he dropped to the floor. Not wanting blood on her favorite robe, she tossed it to the clean part of the kitchen floor, and crawled on top of him in her white panties and bra set.

With her hand on the handle, she took her fist and hit the top of the knife again. His feet flew up in the air before slamming back to the floor. She bent down, looked into his eyes, and in a soft voice said,

"I knew who you were the moment you stepped into the elevator. But I figured you didn't know me, but I was severely wrong, wasn't I? I thought you were dead." She pushed the knife in deeper. "You should've never come here, Knox. You should've gone on with your life." She removed the blade, licked the blood, and smiled. "Your blood is sweet; you must be a diabetic." She placed the knife on the floor and said, "You know, I've killed over fifteen people since I've been here. I killed the man who tried to rape me, I killed a kid across the hallway from Markee, but this was the first time I ever tried to hold myself back. I warned you about coming in here. Even said enter at your own risk. Yet you came inside anyway."

"Please . . . I need help."

"I know you do, Knox." She grinned. "But right now, I'm confessing my sins because I want you to give God my message. My heart was in the right place at one point in my life." She ran her hand along the side of his face. "My mother made me this way, and that's why she's sitting in front of a TV right now alone . . . with her throat slit. She was asleep when I walked in, and was wearing this black Muslim shit. She even had a veil over her face. After I stabbed her, I took it off so everybody would see how ugly she really is." She was tearing up, and quickly wiped them away. "When I took off the veil, her face was so destroyed I didn't recognize her. This disease . . . this awful, fucking disease ate up her skin. And it was then that I knew even more that I'm not gonna look like that. Nobody goes to see her, so I'm sure she'll be there for days." She exhaled and her face produced a deranged smile. "I gotta tell you, though, that I've never been better. I feel so much more alive, now that I told you all of this. Thank you so much."

When he tried to speak, she placed her ear next to his mouth to catch his words, "Please . . . get . . . get me some help." Red blood started to cover his pink tongue. She placed her lips against his, and sucked some of the blood from his mouth.

"So fucking good!"

Knox couldn't believe this was happening, but he couldn't waste his last breaths on asking why. "If . . . you say you love my brother . . . you have to let me help him. I have evidence . . . to keep them out of jail." He tried to reach into his pocket, but he didn't have the energy. "I . . . promise not to . . . say anything."

Farah rose, dug into his pocket, and pulled out a black phone in a silver case. "So this will save your brother? A cell phone?" She laughed. "Well, unless Slade does me right, he won't be needing this anyway."

When someone knocked at the door, she stuffed a dirty dishrag in his mouth and reached under the sink to grab a roll of duct tape. She placed a long strip over his mouth from ear to ear to silence him. When someone began to bang harder, she washed her hands, grabbed her robe, and walked to the door. When she saw a woman she didn't recognize, she looked behind her to be sure Knox didn't crawl into view. Finally she reluctantly opened the door.

And older black lady was standing there with a smirk on her face. "Who are you?"

"Is Lesa Carmine here?"

"Not right now, but can I help you with something?"

"Yes. Tell her I know that she killed my son. The day he went missing, he sent a text message with her name. Today, with a little help, I was able to get this address."

"Well what is your message?"

She looked into her eyes. "Please tell her that I intend on burying her alive."

# Chapter 63

**"Plenty of niggas wanted to be with me
and I wasted my time on you!" —Chloe**

Chloe was sitting in Farah's broken-down car,
trying to stay warm. She was waiting for Audio to
pull up from the club, knowing he'd be home any
minute. When one of her friends told her he was
with another girl, she made it her business to find
out for herself. Audio was her world, and she didn't
want anything or anybody coming in the way of
that.

When Slade pulled up, she jumped out of the car
and approached the truck. Her hands were folded
over her chest, and her eyes were bloody red.
"Where the fuck were you, Audio?"

Slade and his brothers looked at her after they
closed the doors. "Fuck you mean where was I?"
Audio shot back, embarrassed how she was carrying
it in front of his family. "You must've lost your
mind if you think you can talk to me like that." His
brothers nodded in approval for checking the bitch.

"I heard you were with some girl." She placed her hands on her hips. "Is that true?"

"Y'all go upstairs," he told his brothers. "I'ma be up in a minute. I gotta holla at Chloe."

"You sure?" Slade asked, looking at them both. "Because y'all don't need to be doing all this out here."

Chloe rolled her eyes. "I'm sure. I got this," Audio replied.

When they walked into the building Chloe said, "Why you cheat on me, Audio?" Warm tears ran down her face, and she wiped them away before they froze onto her skin. "I thought you said you love me."

"What you talking about, babes? I do love you. All I did was hang out at the club with my brothers. That's it . . . You gotta stop tripping."

"I saw you with my own eyes, Audio. You weren't just in the club. You went with another bitch! I know that she is one of Shannon's friends. Her name is Wendy. That bitch old as shit!"

"She two years older than me. So stop tripping." Realizing he said too much he said, "I was just dancing, babes. That bitch don't mean nothing to me. I don't ever have to see her again."

"You know what? I gave up a lot in this relationship! Plenty of niggas wanted to be with me and I wasted my time on you! You don't even have no fucking money! It's over!" She stormed toward the building.

Although his ego was bruised, he grabbed her arm to prevent her from walking out of his life. "Okay . . . I let the girl Wendy suck my dick in the bathroom. Is that what you wanna hear? But you know I'm not fucking with that slut no more, babes. I got with her before I even met you. Her and her friend Nova fucked me at the same time. But I'm done; bitches like that can't stand next to you." Then he took his fist and softly hit her chin. "Did you have to call a nigga broke though?"

She rocked in place, folded her arms over her chest, and said, "I'm sorry." Chloe's temples began to throb, and she wondered how quickly he would die if she shot or stabbed him. Nobody fucked over a Cotton and lived too long to talk about it. "You can't do that kind of shit to me."

"You forgive me, right?"

She looked into his eyes and said, "If you love me, it won't be so easy."

"Okay . . . what I got to do?"

"When my daddy did my mother wrong, he committed murder." Audio's eyes widened. "And that's what I want you to do."

He looked at her and she was fully expecting him to back out. Instead he said, "Would you kill for me too?"

# Chapter 64

**"What exactly did my brother say?
And don't leave anything out." —Slade**

Slade woke up with a throbbing headache, due to the TV being on too loud. The couch he slept on every night at Markee's was starting to wreak havoc on his bones. Easing off the sofa, partially bent over, with his hand in the small of his back, he walked a few feet before stretching the pain away. Then he stepped over his brothers who were asleep on the floor. Hungry as a stray dog, he walked into the kitchen to get something to eat. When who did he see . . . fat-ass Markee, scrambling eggs.

"How come whenever I'm in the kitchen, you are too?" Slade asked.

"From the movie *Friday?*"

"From the movie *you need to pull the fuck back from the table*." Walking to the cupboard, he grabbed a blue plastic cup and poured some orange juice. "Where were you last night, Markee? I thought you were gonna be here in case my brother called. You been dropping the ball lately, and I'm getting tired of your shit."

Markee turned the stove off, turned around, and said, "What you talking about, man? Knox was here last night."

The cup dropped out of his hands and slammed to the floor before rolling to Markee's feet. Slade rushed over to him, gripped his shirt, and raised him in the air. Since Markee was far from a petite man, this move only exemplified Slade's strength. His socks were soaked with juice. "My brother was here, and you ain't tell me?"

"He told me not to call you." He started shaking when he looked down and saw that his feet were nowhere near the floor. "He said never to use the house phone to call the cell phone or some shit like that. I tried to call you, man. But he got mad and said he was coming back later. So I gave him a key and rolled out."

"Where were you last night?" he asked, the veins in his arm popping through his skin like worms.

"I had to bounce because Randy wanted me to check on something since he was out of town. Another one of his friends got killed last night." Looking at the TV he said, "That was him right there."

Slade released him and he plummeted to the floor. He slowly walked into the living room to get a clear look at his face. This was the nigga he was halfway from killing last night, when he saw him with Farah. The news was reporting that two men were found dead in a black Range Rover by the names of Todd Melon, also known as Juice, and DeWayne Harvey. A third man name Todd Ferguson was also found at the scene, pinned under the truck. He was confirmed dead this morning. He was relieved that Farah was okay because he knew she was with him and they didn't mention her name.

"I'm sorry, Slade," he said, walking behind him, breaking his concentration on the news. "I thought you knew he was here."

"What exactly did my brother say? And don't leave anything out."

He coughed a few times and said, "He knocked on the door, asking where y'all were. He said not to use the phone, because he didn't know if anybody was watching him. Then he said that Eleanor saved him, and to tell you to look for him there."

Slade frowned. "Who the fuck is Eleanor?"

"This old white bitch up the street. She's a dopehead who can do this ass clapping trick better than the baddest stripper." He laughed, rubbing his hands together. When Slade didn't share in his humor, he cleared his throat and said, "Sorry, man."

"Did my brother say anything else?"

"No. That was it." He paused. "Maybe he's coming back later today."

Slade was tired of looking at his cousin. He was about to walk away until he said, "Oh . . . I almost forgot, he also asked about your girl Farah. I don't know what that's about."

# Chapter 65

**"This is your fault, not mine,
so you can put this on YouTube
if you want to." —Farah**

Farah was a nervous wreck as she stirred the meatballs in a pot. She was up all night watching a movie about vampires, and wondered if she was a real one come to life. She couldn't be like them in her mind. Unlike the fictitious movies, she had a need to survive or be killed. And although people wouldn't understand, she wouldn't share their problems anymore. Some people ate meat, she drank blood, so what was the difference?

She had a lot on her plate today. For starters, she was throwing Rhonda's baby shower, she killed her lover's brother, and she was certain that Juice died because somebody was trying to get to her. To make matters worse, Amico's mother stopped by to threaten Lesa about a murder Chloe committed. Before it was all said and done, Farah had no doubt that things were going to end badly and whenever she had that thought, she was right.

"I know you not still thinking about that shit," Mia said, walking up behind her. "They'll never find his brother, or anybody else we dumped for that matter. You may be new to getting rid of evidence, but we kill all the time," she continued, as if they were talking about dumping bags of trash.

"You sure?" Farah asked, turning off the stove. "I feel like I'm about to go down."

"Stop worrying. And as far as that bitch who came here yesterday, maybe it's a good thing they think Lesa was involved instead of Chloe. But if she keeps snooping around, that old hag can get the business too. Now help me move this table in the living room. That girl's shower is in four hours, and we not hardly ready."

Farah moved slowly, and she was wearing an expression of desperation on her face. "I killed his brother, Mia. If he finds out, he'll never talk to me again."

"He's not talking to you now."

"I'm serious! He's the first person I've ever loved." Mia sighed. For the first time, she could tell Farah was serious. "Listen, Farah, you got to act right today and not think about Slade or his brother. If the police investigate, they gonna question everybody you've been around before and after the murder. You want them to say that you were acting normal, not the other way around. Now let's move this table."

Farah pulled herself together, and helped Mia organize the apartment so that everything was beautiful for the celebration. The details were strongly cared for, and they knew Rhonda would appreciate everything. Blue and pink was the theme, and the living room was flooded with baby party favors and balloons. Because Farah was out of it even Shadow pitched in to help out by going to the store and grabbing a few last-minute items on her list.

When he came back with five big bags he said, "Where you want this stuff?"

"Put it on the table."

When he walked away Mia said, "He's lonely, Farah. We got to find him somebody."

"How do you know he's lonely?" she asked, helping Mia put streamers on the wall. "He seems okay to me."

"Well, if you weren't self-consumed, you'd know he got shit on his mind too." Farah looked over at him. "You not the only one with troubles."

"Well, I'm dealing with shit too," she said selfishly. "I can't deal with Shadow now."

Mia shook her head. "Still the same old selfish Farah."

"Take it how you want," she said. They were almost finished decorating when Farah remembered she didn't have the cake. "Hold up . . . where is Chloe?" She looked at her watch. "She was supposed to bring the cake."

"I'll call her cell, but she probably with the nigga Audio," Shadow replied from the kitchen. "If you want, I can get one from the grocery store."

"Thanks, I appreciate that." She tossed him the keys to her half-broken car. "I don't know why she fucking with him anyway. I saw him with some bitch at the club last night. And Slade too."

"And we also saw Chloe ride a nigga's dick she knew for less than a hour, while you drank his blood," Shadow said, putting on his brown leather jacket. "Bitches kill me pointing fingers and shit. Cheating is cheating no matter who does it."

"That bitch you talking about is your sister." Mia frowned. "Act like it."

"I'm out." He left the apartment.

When there was another knock at the door ten minutes later, Mia said, "I'll get it. Blow some more balloons up, Farah, and put them in the kitchen. It looks kind of boring over there." Mia opened the door, and saw a light-skinned woman standing before her. "The baby shower doesn't start for another three hours. You're a little too early."

"I'm not here for a shower. I'm here to talk to Lesa Carmine. I have some questions for her regarding a missing person's case."

Mia swallowed and said, "Well, she ain't here. But what's your name? I'll give her your message."

"I'm Detective Nadia Gibson." She flashed her badge. "Is Farah Cotton home?"

"No," Mia said with an attitude.

"Yes, I am." Farah walked up behind her. Mia rolled her eyes at them both, and sashayed away. "What do you want with me, Nadia?"

"That's Detective Gibson to you." She nodded. "Say, Farah . . . you wouldn't happen to have a room available for rent now, would you?" She joked.

Farah grinned, and put her hand on her hip. "I told you already . . . the room is taken."

Nadia laughed. "Always the smart ass."

"And always the hating-ass cop." She smiled back. "Now what do you want with me? I'm busy."

"I want you to know that I'm going to be the thorn in your ass I promised. So get used to seeing my face, because in the upcoming weeks, we'll have lots to talk about. It'll be just like we're roommates after all."

Farah watched Rhonda frolic around her apartment as if she didn't have a care in the world. The murder she witnessed last night didn't seem to be on her mind in the least. Jealousy consumed Farah when people would rub her belly and congratulate her on the future. She wondered what she had to look forward to in her own life. She didn't even have Slade. Remembering what Mia said about acting normal, she decided to drink a martini to relax her mind. After awhile, she left out the martini juice and rocked with the liquor. Five drinks later, she was floating around the shower as if she were a star. Since this wasn't normal behavior, some something was off.

Mia made sure the food trays stayed stocked, while eating in the process, and Shadow ran errands for things the women continued to forget. But when someone knocked at the door, Mia opened it, because Farah was playing a baby name game with Rhonda and her friends.

When she opened the door, Coconut, Shannon, and the rest of the crew piled inside . . . including Nova and Wendy. "Hey, Coconut," Mia said with a slight attitude. She blocked their path and said, "One second." She looked for Farah and yelled, "Farah, can they come in?"

Farah saw the troublemakers waiting to destroy her day and said, "Everybody can come in except Nova."

"You still tripping off of that shit?"

"Bitch, you can't come into my house after you tried to smack me in the face."

Nova rolled her eyes and said, "I'll see y'all later. Fuck this cunt."

The girls glided inside, but Coconut stopped when she saw Shadow. "Damn, I didn't know you were home from jail." She looked him over. "I didn't know you looked this good either."

Shadow was just as taken with her as she was with him. "Lifting weights and eating pussy does a body good." He licked his lips and her pussy jumped.

"Is that right?"

"No need to repeat myself." He winked.

Coconut smiled at him again, and followed Shannon and her friends into the living room. Everybody there stopped playing the game and rushed toward the hood stars. Farah was immediately blown. She didn't have a chance to step to her about fucking with Slade at the club, and now the bitch was in her house. "Shannon, I know Rhonda said you could come, but why are you here, really? Because you not gonna start no shit in my house."

"Come on, Farah, I know this ain't about last night. We didn't even know you were alive. Trust me, me and Slade weren't hardly thinking about you." Coconut leered at the sound of her words. "Besides, I'm here to support Rhonda and her baby. Like you say all the time, keep it light." The crowd erupted in laughter.

Coconut ignored her all together and that hurt Farah the most. The entire time they were at the party, Coconut seemed to have an attitude whenever she'd catch Farah in a corner, staring her way. When she'd walk over to talk to her, she'd respond in one-word sentences, and act like she didn't exist. After a while, Coconut, Rhonda, Shannon, and the rest of the crew seemed to abandon the shower to hold conversations in private.

Feeling like an outsider caused her to grow angrier by the minute. Before long, Coconut emerged from the crowd and approached Farah. At first Farah was relieved, hoping they could finally move past the drama, until she saw the malicious look in her eyes. "So, Farah, you wanna play the smack down game again?"

"Now?" Coconut smirked. "You scared?"

"Naw . . . it's cool with me. But after this, we got to talk in private, okay?" she said softly. "I don't want to fight with you anymore. I miss my friend." She reached for her hand, and Coconut pulled it back and wiped it on her jeans as if it were dirty.

"Sure . . . whatever you want." She shrugged. "Anyway, you not playing with me." Shannon stood up. "You're playing with her."

Farah knew playing with Shannon would end up in a fight, but this was a great opportunity to seek revenge for last night. But remembering Knox, Amico, and the fact that Nadia wanted her blood, she felt it would be best to pass. "Naw . . . If I hit this girl, it won't end nice."

Farah walked away when Mia blocked her path. "Bitch, if you don't go back over there and lay that whore on her back, I'ma fuck you up in here myself."

Farah looked into her sister's eyes, and saw she was deathly serious. Turning back around, she stepped up to Shannon, and smacked the dog shit out of her like it was nothing. She hit the floor so hard, the heel of her cheap boot broke and hung to the right. "I told you I ain't wanna play." Farah pointed down at Shannon before looking at Coconut. "This is your fault, not mine, so you can put this on YouTube if you want to . . . I don't give a fuck."

"Damn, Shannon, I ain't know you bought cheap shoes," one of the girls said.

Shannon was enraged, and took her anger out on Farah. "Bitch, that's why I got something you want, and his name is Slade Baker!" She continued ranting from the floor like a mad woman. "He chose wisely because you could never be better than me." She was so mad spit was popping out of her mouth like a sprinkler. "Plus, you're too fucking weird." She looked at everybody. "Watch out for her, she's claiming to be a vampire."

Mia marched toward Shannon, preparing to knock her out, when Farah stopped her and said, "I got it, Mia." Then she looked down at Shannon. "What you just say to me?"

Shannon stood up and tried to balance herself on uneven shoes, although her heel had given out. "You heard me."

Farah was about to hit her again when Shannon reached into her jacket and pulled out a bottle of perfume to spray in her face. Farah immediately felt burning sensations throughout her skin, and it felt like she was on fire. Her eyes were inflamed, and her face itched so badly she was about to cry.

Enraged, she started swinging wildly in Shannon's direction, but she hit Rhonda instead. Rhonda was punched so hard that she fell to the floor, and her head flung back and hit the edge of the living room table. Farah couldn't see what she'd done, or who she hit, but she heard everyone's reaction. Before she could ask any questions, Mia rushed behind her and led her toward the front door.

"I'ma handle this, Farah!"

"What happened?" she yelled, trying to see. "What did I do?" Farah could hear the angry voices geared toward her.

Just as she expected, the day didn't end well and she was sure it would get worse.

"You need to get out of here!" Mia continued. "That's the only thing you need to be worried about right now."

"What about my coat? It's in my room!"

"You want your coat or do you want to go to jail?" Mia opened the door, and pushed her out without a response, before slamming it shut.

# Chapter 66

**"I ain't one of them niggas you
can talk to any kind of way." —Slade**

Slade was about to pull off to handle some business when he saw Farah stumble out of the building without a coat, as she repeatedly rubbed her eyes. He hopped out of his truck, took his jacket off, and wrapped it around her body. At first she fought with him, not knowing who he was, but when she heard his voice she relaxed and gave in. "It's me, Farah. It's Slade." No longer fighting, she allowed him to usher her inside of his truck. "What the fuck happened to you?" he asked, looking at her red face.

"I need to wash my eyes out," she cried, rubbing her face. "I can barely see. You got some water or something in here?"

Slade reached in the back and grabbed from the holder the cup that Major was drinking out of yesterday. He walked around to her side of the truck and opened her door before carefully helping her out. "Okay, I'ma throw this water in your face, okay?"

"Yes . . . do it now! Please!" She kept moving in place. "Please . . . my eyes are killing me!"

Slade took the lid off the cup and threw the water in her face. A few ice cubes bounced off of the edge of her nose, and crashed to the ground. "Ow!" she yelled. "What the fuck was that?"

"Oh, shit!" He laughed. "I didn't know ice was still in the cup. My truck must've been cold as shit all night." He helped her back inside and pulled off. "You okay over there?"

Although her face was still inflamed, Farah slowly began to open her eyes. "I'm okay . . ." She started laughing hysterically. "Even though you threw a block of ice in my face." She was grateful she didn't suffer an outbreak.

He grabbed a napkin from his console and handed it to her. "Sorry, babes. Use this to dry off." She patted the water off her face. "I don't know what happened, but you smell good." He smelled the fragrance that Shannon sprayed on her.

"Don't get used to it. I'm not a perfume type of girl."

Slade drove down the street and said, "What happened?"

She rubbed her eyes a few more times and said, "Your girlfriend sprayed perfume in my face. That's what happened, Slade. I wish you told me you fucked with her like that. I would not have wasted my time."

He felt Shannon's move was ugly and had plans to check her later. "What girl?"

"Slade, cut the shit. I'm talking about the bitch I saw with you at the club last night. She came to my friend's shower, and sprayed some shit in my face because she knows I'm allergic to it."

Slade remembered Shannon talking about the disease, so he decided to ask her about it. "What is porphyria?"

Farah felt her head spinning and she wondered how he knew. She opened her eyes and although her vision was blurry, she could see him better. "It's an illness. That I was born with. It's a blood disorder." He decided to spare her the vampire details, because of everything she was going through. Skipping the subject she said, "I can't believe you would even associate yourself with that bitch. She ain't nothing but a whore."

Slade felt bad about Farah seeing him in the club, and he was fucked up by it all night. He felt so guilty that he dropped Shannon off at home, even though they had plans to get a room. At the same time had Farah never disrespected him, he would have never seen her again. "I'm sorry about what you saw in the club, but I didn't know you were there. But you were wrong for disrespecting me,

Farah, and I told you I meant what I said. I ain't one of them niggas you can talk to any kind of way. And until you apologize, me and you could never be like that."

Farah was silent. "I'm sorry." She looked at him. "I just got mad that you weren't willing to stay with me once you found Knox. I guess I took shit the wrong way. Slade, I don't want you to be with her; you belong to me."

"How did you know my brother's name?"

She made a great mistake that she was just realizing. "You told me."

"No . . . I didn't. I would never have said his name. We got too much shit going on."

"Well, you did. How else would I know?" She looked at him, and blinked a few times because the perfume was drying her eyes out.

"I saw on the news that dude you were with last night was murdered. What happened?"

She was grateful they were past the Knox situation. "I think Randy tried to kill me, and he got them instead." She adjusted her seat so she could sit back more. "I know he not gonna stop until he kills me though." Slade didn't like that she was going through so many struggles, but if she acted right, he had intentions of giving her a serious role in his life. "Where we going?"

"I gotta see this lady about my brother Knox. Her name is Eleanor. You know her?"

# Chapter 67

**"When I was younger, I used
to take care of people better
than I did myself." —Eleanor**

Eleanor was sitting down in her favorite corner in
her house. The drugs rushed through her veins, giving her the sensation of a constant orgasm. She was
in dope bitch heaven. The brown tourniquet used
to enlarge her broken veins remained tightly on her
arm, as the needle dangled from her skin. She was
just about to nod off and deal with the world later
when there was a knock on her door. Wiping the spit
strings from the sides of her mouth, she removed
the syringe, hopped up, and answered it. When she
saw Slade and Farah, she tried to slam it shut. But
Slade was able to block this move by wedging his
foot in the door.

When she tried to run, he pushed her to the
floor. "Farah, go lock the door."

Farah did as she was told, and stood at his side.
When he saw the dog tags belonging to his brother

hanging around Eleanor's neck, he prowled toward her. "Where is my brother?" he asked through clenched teeth. "Don't fucking lie to me."

"I don't know who you talking about."

"Eleanor, where . . . the . . . fuck . . . is . . . my . . . brother?" He gripped the tags hanging around her neck. "If you knew how much he means to me, you wouldn't fuck with my head. Start talking."

"I know him as D.B. I got it from the tattoo on his arm."

"It stands for Della Baker. My mother."

Wiping the sweat off her head she said, "He left here last night." In the middle of talking, the drug gods called her name, and she nodded off until he said, "Farah, slap her."

Without hesitation she went in, and slapped her awake. "I'm sorry . . . I dozed off."

"I'm growing impatient with you, and I don't wanna do that," Slade said. "Now where is he?"

"Okay . . . He said he was going to see his brothers. He said he remembered who he was and had to find his family. That's all I know."

"What do you mean, remember who he was? Why would he forget?"

Eleanor looked at Farah. "He was involved in a car accident. A hit and run. But he said the person who hit him tried to kill him by covering his nose and mouth."

"Slade, this bitch is a dopehead," Farah said, trying to shake them off her trail. She could tell Eleanor knew more than she was letting on. That explained why she looked at her funny the day she was sitting in her car outside of this building. "You can't listen to shit she say."

"She's right. Don't listen to me," she responded. She didn't want to die behind what she said while high. "I've been shooting dope in my veins most of my life. I'm half out of my mind most times."

"My brother said you saved his life. So for now I trust you. So please, tell me what happened. How did he end up here?"

She swallowed and said, "When he was left for dead, on the side of the road, I saw him lying in the street. He was bleeding everywhere, and had a few broken bones in his body. I bought him back here and nursed him to health. When I was younger, I used to take care of people better than I did myself . . . I guess I still do today." She smiled. "If you can believe it, I was a nurse before I married heroin."

"Did he say if he was coming back?"

"No . . . but I got the impression he wasn't, because he gave me this chain and told me thanks for everything."

Slade couldn't believe he missed Knox again, and he was starting to fear the worst. "Thank you, and I'm sorry if I scared you." Eleanor looked at Farah once more, who was staring her down. "I gotta get my family back together." Spotting a late notice on the table, he grabbed a pen and jotted down his number. "I want you to have him call me there."

She took the letter and placed it in her lap. The high was wearing off, and she needed another hit. "I can do a dance for you. You got any money?" she asked. "I really need some money."

Slade handed her fifty bucks, and ignored everything else. "I don't care what you have to do, Eleanor. If my brother comes back here you make him call me. If you do, there's a little something more where that came from."

# Chapter 68

**"You no more better than me.
You just got more money to
hide your shit." —Farah**

Farah was sitting in Slade's truck, mentally shaken. At some point she was going to have to pay Eleanor a visit, because something told her she knew more than she was letting on. How could she be so careless? She should've finished Knox off the moment she ran into him with her Benz, and none of this would be happening. Her fuckup meant she had a lot of loose ends to clear up. While driving down the road Slade said, "When Knox was home last night, he asked Markee about you." He looked over at her. "Do you know why?"

She was trying to think of the best way to weasel out of the situation. "How would I know him? If you haven't been able to find him, how would I?"

Slade seemed disappointed. "I never asked you this before, about what happened that night. When you were with that dude in the basement. The one who was about to hit you the day we first met."

She looked out the window. "Talking about Kirk?"

"I guess." He shrugged. "I don't know the nigga's name."

She avoided his eyes. "Why you wanna know? Because for one thing, he tried to rape me," she snapped. "If that's what you talking about."

"I'm not judging you, babes. I just want to know what happened, that's all." He touched her leg. "Because even though his body was partially hidden on the side of the washing machine, because he was lying on the floor I noticed that blood-stained boot. And I saw you crouched over him. What were you doing?"

Farah turned away from him. She was so sure that after all this time, he didn't know, even though at first she swore he saw her. Now she realized she was wrong. "I don't know what happened to him, Slade. Maybe we should just leave it at that."

Standing outside of Randy's house, she knocked on his door. A minute later, he opened it up and it was obvious that he wasn't happy to see her. "What do you want, Farah? I'm surprised you're still alive. I must have to give niggas more money."

"I want to talk to you, Randy. Can I come in?"

He frowned. "I got company." When he opened the door wider, she saw Lesa, Courtney, and Lady sitting on the couch. "So now ain't the best time."

"She can come in," Lesa said. "We were just leaving. Plus I have to meet somebody later tonight." Looking at Farah she said, "I'll be over tomorrow to get the last of my things." Farah watched them laugh all the way to Courtney's car before pulling out of sight.

"What were they doing here, Randy?"

He trudged away from the door and sat on the couch. "You coming in or out?" Farah walked inside, and closed the door behind her. "The real question is, what the fuck are you doing here? I was on my way out, and don't have time to talk to you about shit."

"So you fucking one of them now?"

"Again . . . none of your business."

She walked over to him. "I wanted to say I'm sorry, Randy. I was mad at you for killing my puppies, so I just started tripping and shit. You gave them to me, and I loved them dogs so much." She remembered how they always seemed to be happy when she came home, and was consumed with sadness. "So, after you dropped them, I been trying to get back at you ever since. I wanted to hurt your feelings, like you did mine."

"I don't believe shit you say to me anymore, especially after speaking to your friends."

"They're not my fucking friends. Stop believing everything you hear from random bitches." It was obvious that she wasn't as frightened as she should've been of him, and this bothered him. "And what did they say about me anyway?"

He laughed. "For starters, you don't live with your mother anymore, which I know about already. And secondly, that you're fucking with Slade, a nigga I was about to put on." Thinking about her being with him enraged him even more. "Now why are you here?"

"Because I miss you."

He laughed and shook his head. He wanted to believe her so badly, but he hated being played for a fool. "You must be here for money. Because you and me both know that's the only time you call my name. The worst part about all of this is, you put Slade in a deadly situation, and you don't even know it. How you gonna smile in my face and take my bitch?"

"Slade was smiling in your face?"

His forehead crinkled a bit and he screamed, "You know what the fuck I mean!" He paused. "But out of everything they told me, there's one thing that I really can't believe. Are you really drinking blood?"

She knew in a few days, everybody would take her for a sick, crazy bitch now. "All you gonna do is laugh and not believe me if I tell you anyway."

"Try me." He crossed his legs and clasped his hands together. "Tell me you're not the crazy-ass broad they made you out to be."

Farah grew angry. "What if I do drink blood?" she said flatly. "What difference does it make to you?"

He looked up at her. "You serious?"

"What if I am? What if I love the feeling of holding someone's life in my hands? Ain't that the same thing you do? I watched you kill an old lady after you stashed some shit in her coat pocket. You no more better than me. You just got more money to hide your shit."

For the first time, he realized he didn't know her like he thought he did. When his phone rang, he looked at her once more before getting up to answer the call. "Hello?" He paused. "What you mean they got us?" Randy was covered in a veil of fury as he paced the floor. "Tell everybody to meet me at my house in twenty minutes. Don't be late!" He scowled. "And I want you to find my father, too. I got fifty grand on anybody who brings him to me, because I know he was involved." Randy hung up and looked at Farah. "Before you came over here, I was going to have you killed tonight. Lucky for you something else came up that requires my full attention. I'll be over to get my ring tomorrow."

"Did you have Juice killed?" she interrupted.

"What you think? The nigga DeWayne put a call in to me, and told me you were in the club with Juice."

Her jaw dropped. "DeWayne? But he was killed too!"

"He was a casualty of war. My only complaint is that he didn't finish the job, because you're here." He pointed at her. "You got three days to disappear. If you don't I'm gonna murder everyone in your family, starting with your father. And when it's all said and done, I'm gonna murder you."

Farah's heart dropped. "My father? What the fuck you talking about?"

"So you don't know." He crossed his arms over his chest. "They found Tank a few weeks back in Virginia. He's in prison, in the same cell as your Ashur."

# Chapter 69

**"This your first time, so consider yourself a virgin tonight." —Slade**

Slade was lying face to face with Farah in a hotel room on the bed. After the long day, they needed to be alone. When he looked into her eyes something whispered, *leave her alone,* but she was so alluring that he couldn't walk away. "You know you remind me of my girlfriend back home."

She raised her head off the pillow. "You got a girlfriend?"

"No . . . she died." She placed her head back down. "She was a fighter like you. Real bullheaded, too." He chuckled. "Never listened to shit I said. I'd tell her to go left, and she'd go right. But later . . . when I wasn't looking, I would find out that she always took my advice, and followed my lead."

"And you liked that about her? Because you got out on me when I talked back to you."

"You called me gay," he corrected her. "That's questioning my manhood and I don't play that shit." He paused. "Anyway, I loved that about her. A woman with her own mind is attractive. Just like me, she always seemed like something was on her mind, and I could never tell where she was coming from. It kept me on my feet, and made the relationship interesting. Anyway, we got into a fight after I found out she lied to me. Keeping secrets and speaking your mind are two different things. You understand what I'm saying?" She nodded but remained silent. "When I found out she wasn't who I thought she was, I ended the situation." He turned on his back and looked up at the ceiling.

She put her head on his chest. "What happened?"

"I found out she was snorting coke and I couldn't get past it. I was asleep and woke up to find her in the living room with a mirror on the table, sniffing shit into her nose." He shook his head. "I walked over to her and crashed my fist into the wall, inches from her face." Farah seemed nervous. "Don't worry. I would never hit a female, because I know I would kill her instantly." He looked into her eyes. "You know I didn't even say shit to her. With my eyes, she knew how I felt. She was so hurt that she stormed out of my house, and drove away in the rain. We'd been together since we were kids, and I didn't stop her. If I had, she would still be alive today." He exhaled. "Anyway, the next morning I found out her car had been wrapped around a tree. And her head was severed from her body. That same feeling of loss came over me when I saw Juice's picture on the news, because I knew you were with him. I realized then that I can't let you go." He got up to get another beer from the table across the room, and she followed like a shadow. "I should've gotten her help to get off the drugs, but I didn't." He pulled the tab off of his beer, and took a man-sized gulp.

"It wasn't your fault, Slade."

He placed the half-full beer down, and pulled her into his body. "I know, babes. It took me years to understand that, but I finally get it. It doesn't stop me from feeling fucked up about it, even to this day. I was supposed to protect her, but I didn't." He looked into her eyes. "I told myself if I ever fell in love again, that I would never abandon her when she needed me the most. And, on my mother, that's a vow I won't break." He raised her chin, snaked his tongue into her mouth, and kissed her passionately. "Let's get ready for bed. I gotta brush my teeth first."

"Ugh, why you ain't brush your teeth before kissing me!" She giggled, hitting his arm.

"Because I love you, girl." They walked into the bathroom, and Slade took the toothbrushes out of the bag they bought from CVS earlier that evening. Farah grabbed the blue one and wet it before putting paste on the tip. "That's mine, babes. You got the red one."

She cut the cold water on. "I know who it belongs to." She smiled. "But when you're with me, I don't want you to do anything I can't do for you. And that includes brushing your teeth. Now open up."

Slade opened his mouth, and looked down at Farah as she happily scrubbed his teeth. She was doing her best to make it known that she wanted to be his everything. In awe, he looked down at her and silently thanked God for bringing her into his life. "What you looking at, boy?" She looked up at him.

He put his hand under the faucet and rinsed his mouth. "You're different now."

She cleaned his toothbrush up and rinsed her own. "I'm the bitch who's gonna take care of you for the rest of your life. Get used to seeing me."

"I got to keep shit real with you. I met Willie, Randy's father, the same night I saw he was with my brother. I was looking for Knox, but he wasn't there. I must've missed him because later, I found out he went to Markee's." She appeared uneasy and he wondered why. "Anyway, Willie ended up being cool, and we planned to make moves together. Juice was in that meeting too. So later that night, when I saw you in the club, I wondered what was up. I knew we had plans to rob his stash house, because we had inside help with Juice." He paused. "Randy was supposed to be out of town, but he wasn't. It fucked me up to get you involved, by keeping him busy."

She brushed her teeth and said, "It didn't bother me." She rinsed her mouth, and stroked his face once. "Your brother Major was outside, strapped and ready, and I was sick of Randy anyway. The nigga tried to kill me the night before! But I also knew if he really wanted me gone, I'd be dead already. So I knew our plan would work. I would do anything for you." She rinsed her mouth again, to get rid of the paste taste. "Did I keep him busy long enough?"

"Yeah . . . we hit his shop heavy and hard. It's just fucked up that Juice is gone. We gave a little something to his peoples, though."

"Do you think you can trust Willie? I mean, he is stealing from his own son."

"Apparently it was his operation first." He reached into his pocket, and handed her some cash. "That's for you and your part in everything tonight." The money made her beam. "That's just the beginning."

"Wait . . . does this mean you're staying in DC now?"

"Yes . . . at least until I find Knox. I'm trying to prevent my mother from coming up here because if she does, it's gonna be hell come to life."

Farah wasn't concerned with some old woman. "That's the only reason you staying?"

"No. Because I can't leave you."

Farah's warm, naked body covered the top of Slade's. Staring into each other's eyes, it was apparent that love had found them, and they didn't want to let go. "I'm ready to make love to you."

"You sure? Because you seemed real hesitant at first."

"I need this. For me."

Inspired by her desire, Slade placed his hands on her waist, and pushed his thickness into her pussy. It was difficult to enter at first, because she was dry and tense. Thinking she'd warm up soon, he pumped in and out of her slowly. Farah began to wildly move her head and shoulders, and Slade tried to guide her motions. When she started yelling sounds you'd hear in a cheap porno, as if she were possessed by the devil, he knew something was off. "Baby," Slade said softly, as she continued to twist her neck as if it could pop off. "Farah, open your eyes and look at me."

She finally heard his voice, and looked at him. "What's wrong?" Tears started to form in the wells of her eyes. "You hate me, don't you?" His dick was still in her body, but he was no longer fucking. "I'm gonna die! This is so embarrassing!"

"Calm down, Farah. Nothing is wrong." He rubbed her hair. "Why you upset?" His voice was easy, patient, and loving. "This is supposed to be right. It's our first time, babes, so I need you to look at me. Cool?"

"Okay," she said, totally mortified. "I'm gonna look, I just don't want you to dump me."

He slapped her ass lightly, and because of his strength, it stung a little more than usual. Smiling he said, "Stop saying that shit. I'm not going anywhere. You're not fucking me, we're fucking each other. So don't be sad. Just look into my eyes and work that body." Slade placed his hands on her hips and slowly pumped into her. Scared to do the wrong thing, Farah remained as stiff as a board. Fear of not being able to satisfy him forced her still.

"Farah, do you feel how much I care about you?" He continued to fuck her. "Can you see how fucking sexy I think you are? Look at me . . . Can you see how much my body responds to yours? Can you remember the first day I saw you, and how I wanted to kill that mothafucka for scaring you?" Her pussy was warming up like an iron recently turned on, and it was starting to feel good. "Yeah . . . you feel me. I see that pussy heating up."

"I feel you, baby." She kissed his lips and felt a trembling sensation throughout her body. If only she could trust her body and move, it would be so much better. "You feel so good."

"Then move that pussy the way you feel about me." Farah started crying. "Don't be sad, Farah. This is the first time you made love."

"But I've had sex . . ."

"I don't give a fuck about them other niggas. If any of them cared about you, you'd know how to fuck." His seriousness caused her to shiver. "Now move your body like you love me." Focusing on the man under her body, she started to slowly wind her hips. "That's it, baby." He bit his lip. "That's my bitch right there." Slade moved in and out of her until he could feel her slickness on his dick. "Damn, baby, you wet as shit now. That's how I like it."

Normally she would have to add spit, or Vaseline, while having sex so she said, "Am I? I never got wet before."

"What I tell you? This your first time, so consider yourself a virgin tonight." Slade kissed her passionately, and increased the speed one notch. As if Farah were a pro, she started fucking him back slower at first, before going a little faster. It wasn't just about a man this time, the sex was about her too. Their bodies danced as they explored one another for the first time.

"Oh, my God!" Farah cried. "Baby . . . I'm . . . I'm about to . . ." She stopped moving.

"What's wrong?" He felt himself about to bust inside of her. He wanted them to reach at the same time.

"What is this feeling?" She got her rocks off with Coconut a few times, but never while having sex. She was starting to believe it wasn't even possible. The feeling was so grand that she wanted to taste him. She imagined a stream of blood lying on his skin, and her tongue slowly licking it off. This caused her to get even more into the motion, as she bucked him with all her might.

"You're about to cum. Me too! Keep it right there! Just like that, baby," he ordered, as he released himself into her body. "Aww . . . that was so fucking good!"

Her cum was being pulled as if it had a force of its own.

Her toes spread, and she bit into his shoulder, hard at first, before she went lighter. Slade didn't seem to be fazed one bit by the pain. Resting her head on his shoulder, Farah's body let go as she clawed at his arms.

"I love you so much, Slade Baker." Tears rolled out of her eyes, and ran down his arm.

"Then why you crying?"

"Because I hope when you find out about me, that you'll love me the same."

"Babes, there ain't shit nobody can tell me about you that I won't crack them in their fucking mouth for. Now get some sleep, we got a lot going on tomorrow."

The next morning when Slade woke up, his phone was ringing. When he went to answer it, he realized the top of his finger was cut. He was so drunk the night before that he didn't remember how it happened. Reaching for the phone, he was rattled by the sound of his brother's voice. "What's wrong, Major?"

"Audio ain't come home last night, man!" he yelled. "Some niggas called and said they got him! And we got to come up with some bread or else he's dead!"

# Chapter 70

**"No! This can't be happening!" —Farah**

When Farah got to Markee's house with Slade, she was surprised to see her sister and brother in attendance. "What's going on?" She alternated her eyes between Mia and Shadow. She was immediately frightened. "What y'all doing here?" The door closed behind them, and Slade locked it.

"Somebody snatched Audio last night," Major interjected.

"And your sister was with him," Markee added.

"What?" she screamed, covering her mouth. "No! This can't be happening!"

"Where the fuck were you, Farah?" Mia yelled. "I called you twenty times last night! So much shit happened, and you were nowhere to be found! It wasn't until I went into your room and found your phone"—she raised Knox's BlackBerry in the air—"That I realized you left it."

Seeing Knox's spiritual attempt to get her caught from the dead, Farah rushed over to Mia and snatched the phone out of her hand. The case made the phone unique, so she hoped the Baker Boys didn't notice that it belonged to their brother. When she looked at them, they appeared unwise. "Why you do that shit?" Mia asked. She had no idea what she'd just done.

"I'm sorry. I just can't believe somebody got Chloe. My baby sister is gone!"

Slade stood in the middle of the floor in a shock of his own. He couldn't imagine all the drama circling his family at this time in his life. Maybe God was saying they had to grow up, and with two brothers missing, he heard Him loud and clear. When his mother found out, she was going to lose it, he was sure of it. Slade rubbed his bald head, trying to think of what to tell Della. "Markee, what do we know about this shit?"

"What happened to your finger?" Markee asked, because of the Band-Aid he was wearing.

"What difference do it make, bitch-ass nigga? I asked you a mothafuckin' question."

When there was a knock at the door, Slade ignored him and opened it. Willie Gregory walked inside, and looked at the solemn look on the Baker boys' faces. "I'm so sorry about this shit, young bloods. I knew my son could be a cruddy mothafucka, but I didn't think he would stoop this low," he said as Slade closed and locked the door.

"You think Randy know we ran up in his house?" Major asked. "I mean, why else would they want my brother?"

Willie looked at Markee and then Slade. "You sure we can speak around him?"

Slade looked at his cousin and said, "He good."

He sighed. "Okay . . . I don't know how Randy would know that shit." He rubbed his head. "Half of his men couldn't wait for me to get out his jail, that's why we didn't have a problem recruiting Juice, God rest his soul. And I know everybody else involved would not have said shit. Randy just added things up and got me. The boy smart enough to know I was coming back for what's rightfully mine. I'm not sure how he figured you fellas were involved, though. But I swear on my life, I'm gonna get your brother back."

"What about my sister?" Mia asked from the couch.

When his eyes moved in the direction of the voice, he saw Farah sitting by her side. "Wait, what is she doing here?" he asked, pointing at her. "I met her when she was no more than thirteen years old. Randy was obsessed with this girl!" He pointed. "This is probably how he knew right here!"

"You use to fuck with Randy?" Killa asked, gripping the .45 in his waist. "I knew he liked you, but I didn't think it was that deep."

On cue, the rest of the Baker Boys moved in like vultures, and Mia and Shadow stood on guard to protect Farah. "I know y'all betta back the fuck up away from my sister." Shadow pointed. "That nigga been chasing her for years, and she didn't want nothing to do with him."

Slade walked over to the altercation in motion, and said, "Back up, fellas." When they didn't do it he roared, "Now!" They dispersed like fog and Slade addressed Willie. "I don't know about all that, but she with me now."

"I don't trust her. She use to fuck my son, I'm trying to tell you."

"Maybe I should make myself clearer. This is my wife, and she's also the one who kept Randy busy while we ran up in his spot. She deserves a little more credit than that."

Willie gave Farah and her siblings another look, and she wondered if Eleanor told him anything about the accident with Knox. "Whatever, son. I'm not gonna argue with you about what you want. It's clear your mind is made up. Just know that I'm going to be combing the city looking for Audio." He heard Shadow grunt. "I mean both of them." He cleared his throat. "And that's on my last name. I don't know where Knox is either, but I'm sure Randy had something to do with this too." Farah looked at Mia, and Killa caught the glance. "I knew the young man a short time, but he meant a lot to me."

"And what if we can't find them?" Major said.

"We'll give them the half a mil they asking for," Willie continued. "When I said we would do business, I meant good business. I could tell by being around your brother that he came from a solid breed. I need that type of man on my team, and it's a shame it couldn't be my son. But I'm gonna make him pay for everything if he harms one hair on their heads. Blood relative or not."

# Chapter 71

**"I got this for my godson.
I think he's gonna love it." —Farah**

Farah walked into the hospital to visit her friend and her new baby. She was beside herself when she heard about the horrible news. Walking into the room, holding a glass vase full of yellow roses and a bag, she set them on the table. Rhonda was lying on the bed, looking out of a window. She was in a hazy world all her own.

"Rhonda . . . are you up?" Farah asked softly.

She turned around to look at her. There was a blank expression on her face, and she appeared neither happy nor sad. "Yeah . . . I'm up."

"I'm sorry about everything. I didn't mean to hit you. That bitch sprayed some shit in my face, and I was trying to defend myself. I hope you know I would never do something like that on purpose. I'm sorry you went into labor early." Rhonda rolled her eyes. "I didn't know about any of this until this morning."

"How could you know? You left the baby shower, remember?"

"The only reason I left was because I couldn't see. You saw me, Rhonda. I was fucked up! And I'm gonna pay Shannon back for it too. Technically all this shit is her fault," she threatened. "Look, I don't want to argue with my friend, and I didn't come here for all of that." She reached in the bag and pulled out a fluffy yellow teddy bear. "I got this for my godson." She smiled, waving the toy. "I think he's gonna love it. I bought it from Build-A-Bear."

Rhonda took the stuffed animal out of her hand, and held it to her chest. She squeezed it so tightly the neck bent backward. "I'm sure he would . . ." Tears ran down her face. "I'm sure he would have loved it, if he was alive." She looked back out of the window at the clear blue sky. "Please leave, Farah. I'll see you later. Believe that."

# Chapter 72

### "I don't think the devil himself would want to fuck with me now." —Della

Della rode silently in the cab on her way to Markee's apartment in Platinum Lofts. She was heavy with grief, and hadn't felt this emotionally broken since she lost her mother, the great Renita Scott. Since her children had been in the nation's capital, two of her sons were missing and nobody had answers. Growing up in the country a few years shy of the slavery days, she knew if you wanted anything done, you had better do it yourself.

"Here's the place," the black male cab driver said, parking the car. He turned around to look at the old woman, who had so many frown lines on her face it resembled a road map. Her expression was hard, but she was heavy with love, *if* you were on her good side. "This building hasn't been up long at all. I heard the apartments inside are real nice and spacious though." He chuckled to himself. "I'm more of a three hots and a cot man myself, if you know what I mean." Della kept her silence. "Don't need all this fancy stuff at all, no siree!" he lied, knowing if his coins were in order, he'd move with the quickness.

"Thank you for the ride," she said in a heavy country accent, thicker than her sons'. "You have a card? I got money to spend on a driver who can be there for me whenever I need him." She handed him a one hundred dollar bill for a forty-five dollar fare. "You think you can handle that?"

The driver greedily tucked the money in his shirt pocket and said, "Ma'am, for this kind of cash"—he tapped his shirt twice—"I'll sleep on your doorstep," he joked.

With a stern expression, she said, "That won't be necessary. I do have one request though. I don't mind a little talking here and there, but when I ride, I prefer my silence. Can you work with that?"

He turned around and faced the road, figuring she was referring to the way his mouth yapped nonstop all the way over from the airport. "Look no further. I'm your man." Della had a feeling he wouldn't be able to help himself, but at least he was on notice. Because if she snapped, he'd know why.

She opened the door, and eased out of the back of the cab, holding nothing but a big black purse and a wooden cane. She didn't bring luggage because as long as she had a few dollars in her pocket and a beating heart, she had everything she needed.

Clothes and the like she could get once she got situated.

Before pulling off the driver leaned over to the window and said, "Be careful in there. I don't believe what I'm hearing but—"

"If you don't believe it, why would you tell me?" she asked, interrupting him.

Slightly embarrassed he said, "I'm just giving you this so I can sleep better at night." Della shook her head in annoyance. In her opinion, there was nothing worse than a gossiping-ass man. "I just wanted you to know that they saying some crazy bitch lives there, who likes to drink blood and stuff. I know of at least three people who moved out already because of that."

Della smirked. "Sir, as angry as I am, I don't think the devil himself would want to fuck with me now, and certainly not a vampire."

# Chapter 73

**"I can't deal with her right now. I got to use all of my energy on Chloe." —Farah**

After leaving the hospital from visiting Rhonda, Farah trudged into the house with a heavy heart. Everybody she loved was turning against her, and she wondered if she really needed to change. When she went into her room, Mia and Shadow were sitting on her bed in silence. The window was open, and the daylight absent of the sun lit up everything. "Why are y'all in here?" She sat next to them, and kicked her shoes off one by one. Then she flung her purse to the floor. "Any news on Chloe yet?"

"No . . . I can't believe this shit!" Mia said. "Our world is coming down hard!"

"Why is all of this happening? I can't deal with this bullshit right now!" Shadow yelled. "Fuck!" Then he looked at Mia, and it was obvious they knew something. "We should tell her."

"What's wrong?" she asked. "Stop playing games and tell me what's up! Please . . . I don't think I can take any more bad news."

"Mamma's dead," Mia cried, while Farah was relieved that this was the reason for their dismay. "We went to tell her that Chloe was missing. She changed the locks so we couldn't get inside, so we called the police. I smelled something foul, but I didn't know what it was. When the police came, before they even got to her apartment, from the outside they knew what was up. She was dead. Sitting in front of a TV. Somebody slit her throat, and shot her in the chest."

"Wait . . . shot her in the chest?" She was confused. "Why . . . why they do both?"

"They didn't know she was shot at first. But when they took her to the hospital, and lifted the black gown she wore, they saw the bullet hole over her heart." Mia was breathing so heavily she had to fan herself to prevent from passing out. Shadow popped up and marched toward the window. He leaned up against the wall, and looked out through the pane to prevent from crying. "You should've seen her face, Farah. Oh, my God! She didn't look anything like herself. The porphyria ate her up terribly! Our beautiful mother is gone."

Farah didn't feel the same as her siblings about the loss, and it was evident by her expression. In her opinion Brownie got everything she deserved, but she didn't understand who shot her, and attempted to hide it. "I can't deal with her right now," Farah said. "I got to use all of my energy on Chloe."

Mia wiped her face, and touched Farah's knee. "I understand you don't feel the same as we do." She looked at Shadow and back at her. "After everything she put you through, it's wrong for us to expect you to." She gave her a hug and Farah gladly accepted. She loved her family, Ashur included, but Brownie she couldn't care less about. "Grandma said she's coming over here in about an hour. You know she never comes out, but she wants to be there for us." That's all she needed was to see Elise's face right now. She was growing increasingly uncomfortable. "I almost forgot, Slade and them were over here earlier. They wanted to talk here instead of at Markee's. They said they can't be sure if they can trust him yet."

"I never liked dude," Shadow said, looking at them. "He got a lot of shit with him if you ask me." He looked back out the window.

"Something happened while they were here though. I gave Slade my key to get back in, because we were going to the morgue to identify Ma's body."

As Farah replayed the tapes of what Mia just said in her mind, a frightful expression covered her face. Immediately she hopped off the bed, and dropped to her knees. Shadow stood up straight and looked at his frantic sister in motion. Removing the box from under the bed with her stories, she was desperately seeking two things: her journal for the month, and Knox's phone.

When Mia saw her fling the books out of the box, she finally understood her horror. "Please tell me you didn't. Tell me you didn't write about what you did to Knox in your book." Farah looked at her without a response and Mia had her answer. "How could you be so fucking stupid?"

"I been writing in these books all my life! What am I supposed to do? Just stop?"

Shadow walked over to them. "Farah, after all these fucking years? What the fuck is in them books anyway?"

She held her head down. "Everything."

He leaned in. "*Everything?* Including the stuff we did that you knew about?"

"Yes."

He put his hands over his face and paced in place. "Get the fuck out of here! Who does that kind of shit anyway? Just call the police and make a fucking recording!"

The moment he said that, the front door slammed. Farah hopped off the floor, and they all walked into the living room to see who was there. Standing side by side in the middle of the living room were Slade, Killa, and Major. Della Baker was sitting on the recliner.

When Farah walked out she said, "So this is Farah Cotton? The girl who stole my son's heart." She looked at her oldest son and using her cane, she pulled herself up.

"Yeah . . . that's her." It was obvious that he was avoiding eye contact with his lover. She tried to search his eyes to see how he felt about her, but at the moment they were empty.

Mia and Shadow stood next to Farah as they waited for what would happen next. "Earlier today, Farah, my son found something on the way to the bathroom. In your house."

Mia looked at Killa and rolled her eyes. When she was home earlier, he kept saying how he had to go to the bathroom; now it all made sense. He made no fewer than ten trips within an hour, but she didn't think anything of it because her sister was missing. "So you were snooping around?" she asked him. "In my house?"

Killa remained silent.

"I think we're asking the wrong questions, young lady," Della said. "How about we start by telling me how you got this?" She raised Knox's phone in the air. "Let's start there."

# Chapter 74

## Present Day Mooney's House

Mooney sat in her brown recliner and looked at Cutie Tudy, whose mouth hung open. She knew the story would intrigue her, so she was certainly amused. "Close your mouth before something fly in it, child."

Tudy slammed her jaws shut and said, "Well, what else happened?" She chewed the last of the cheese part of the pizza in her hand. This was the most interesting shit she heard in her entire life. "You can't end it like this."

"That's all I'm telling you for now." She rubbed her left elbow again. "I'll tell you the rest when I see you later."

"Well, it don't make no sense!" she said, charged with her usual attitude. "The least you can do is tell me what happened when Della got there! Dang! That's why I hate you sometimes! Always playing with people heads and shit!" She pouted, slinging the pizza crust to her white plate. Mooney laughed until she said, "You probably lying about the whole thing anyway!"

Aggravation took over, and for the moment, she lost her cool. Mooney leaped up, faster than Tudy knew she could move, and hung over the child like a lioness. "I don't lie, child! And if I was going to start today"—she pointed her right finger in her face—"it damn sure wouldn't be about this."

"Okay . . . I'm sorry." She trembled so hard the crust on the plate was vibrating.

Mooney backpeddled toward her chair, and sat down without looking. "That story is all true, and you don't even know the rest. Before you start judging people, know what the fuck you talking about first." She turned to her left and rustled through a few newspapers on a nightstand. When she found the one she wanted, she said, "So I take it you can read right? Fighting with your foster sister ain't the only thing you know how to do, is it?"

"No. I can read," she said, still shocked at Mooney's reaction.

"Good, take a look at this newspaper." Tudy stood up, and toddled in her direction. When she didn't take the paper Mooney said, "It's too late to be scared of me now. If I wanted you dead, you'd be gone already." Tudy didn't feel any more comfortable, but she did as she was told. "Look at the headline." Tudy eyed the bold black print and her jaw dropped again. "You better get that thing fixed before somebody put something in it." Tudy giggled and Mooney was grateful they were able to move past the bad moment. Teenagers could be a little disrespectful at times, so she never had a problem putting them in place. "Read what is says out loud."

"Farah Cotton . . . woman or vampire?" Up until that moment, she thought the crazy woman was pulling her legs, but now it was revealed that she was telling the truth. Still stunned, she handed the paper back. "Hold up, you're not . . . you're not Farah Cotton, are you?"

"Not at all."

"Well, who are you then?"

"In the beginning, I told you about the screaming girl who came to the door when Farah was borrowing sugar."

She nodded quickly. "Her boyfriend's name was Kirk. The one who died?"

"Exactly." She nodded. "I see you're paying attention . . . Well, that girl was me." She grinned. "Back then I didn't have a lot of worries." For a second, she took a trip to the good old days. Coming back to reality she said, "That was then, but this is now."

"But how did you know all of these things? Were you friends?"

Mooney removed her robe, and showed Tudy her amputated left arm. The child never knew she was armless, because she never really looked at her baggy left sleeve, which was always tucked in the robe's pocket. "No . . . but I did run into her again, and when I did, she gave me this to show for it."

## ORDER FORM
## URBAN BOOKS, LLC
### 97 N18th Street
### Wyandanch, NY 11798

Name (please print):_____

Address:_____

City/State:_____

Zip:_____

| QTY | TITLES | PRICE |
|-----|--------|-------|
|     |        |       |
|     |        |       |
|     |        |       |
|     |        |       |
|     |        |       |
|     |        |       |
|     |        |       |

Shipping and handling: add $3.50 for 1$^{st}$ book, then $1.75 for each additional book.

Please send a check payable to:

**Urban Books, LLC**

Please allow 4-6 weeks for delivery